SHADOW & FLAME

SHADOW & FLAME

SHADOWS OF GRAYMOURNE BOOK TWO

SYLVIE HELSTAFF

First Edition

Helstaff Books
Please visit us on the web at
https://linktr.ee/sylviehelstaff

ISBN: 979-8-9911841-1-3

DEDICATION

If you've ever wished you could just open a grimoire and summon your perfect partner, then this book is for you. You might get a little more darkness than charming with your prince, but the joke's on him, because you're into that, right?

And especially for Rose, who wanted to get spicy in shadowspace.

ACKNOWLEDGEMENTS

Subject matter depicted in this book may be sensitive for some readers. Content includes: brief animal death, violence, death, blood/gore, discussion of homophobia, and sexual situations.

Table of Contents

Prologue 1

Chapter 1 14

Chapter 2 23

Chapter 3 38

Chapter 4 51

Chapter 5 60

Chapter 6 70

Chapter 7 81

Chapter 8 99

Chapter 9 115

Chapter 10 136

Chapter 11 148

Chapter 12 163

Chapter 13 182

Chapter 14 201

Chapter 15 218

Chapter 16 237

Chapter 17 256

Chapter 18 266

Chapter 19 280

Chapter 20 292

Chapter 21 301

Chapter 22 318

Chapter 23 330

Chapter 24 347

Chapter 25 357

Chapter 26 369

Chapter 27 385

Chapter 28 396

Epilogue 416

About the Author 425

Prologue

Stumbling over the uneven terrain, Kelsey Cresswell followed the raucous sound of laughter ahead of her. The weak moonlight that managed to weave its way through the tightly knit canopy of branches above did little to guide her. She sighed, wondering why she had allowed her boyfriend to drag her into this.

"Hurry up, Kelsey," Harrison shouted.

The chattering voices paused for a second before breaking out into unintelligible whispers and snickering. She rolled her eyes, stepping through the open gate and into the yard where the jagged silhouette of a once grand manor rose up in the darkness.

"Stop yelling, I'm coming, you asshats," she hissed, hustling across the open front lawn towards the structure. Short beams of light flitted behind what was left of the western wall, revealing where her friends had gone ahead of her. She traced their path around the ruins to the back of the house where the group had congregated.

Harrison was crouched down in the clearing already trying to get a fire going in a hastily made fire pit. He looked up when she ground to a halt a few steps away, the mischievous look on his face dappled with a gentle glow from the few licks of flame.

"Finally," he grinned, "I almost thought you ditched us. What's the matter, Kels, you scared the ghost is gonna get us?"

The other three laughed and she felt a heady mix of embarrassment and anger flash over her. He could be such a dick when he was around his friends, which was part of the reason she didn't want to come tonight. Anna was actually pretty nice, but Travis and Brittany's idea of a good time usually consisted of dragging them all somewhere they weren't supposed to be and doing something borderline illegal. Which was how Kelsey now found herself standing behind the burned out ruins of the old Graydon Manor, one of the most notoriously dangerous places in town. That was the second reason she had been reluctant to come along; not only was the crumbling manor a structural hazard, it was also widely known to be haunted.

"No, I'm scared my mom is gonna turn me into a ghost if we get caught here," she shot back, irritably. "You guys are so loud."

"Chill out, Kelsey," Brittany interrupted, handing her a cheap hard seltzer. "No one's gonna hear us, it's just forest for, like, miles." The brunette fixed Kelsey with a shit-eating grin as she plopped herself into Travis's lap next to the fire. "So, if the ghost does get you… nobody will hear you scream."

Kelsey gave her an unamused look and then pointedly ignored her when the other girl burst into a fit of laughter. There was something obnoxious and a little bit mean about the sound of her laugh; it always reminded her of a hyena. Instead, she moved to sit on the other side of Harrison between him and Anna, who gave her an apologetic smile.

"Cheers, I guess," she said, knocking her seltzer can against the one in Anna's hand before taking a swig. Harrison slung an arm around her shoulder, and she leaned into his warmth, attempting to relax. She was already here, she figured she may as well try to enjoy the night. Kelsey leaned her head on his shoulder and stared into the fire while she sipped her drink, tuning out the banter between the other teenagers.

This wasn't how she had pictured spending Thanksgiving break, but at least there was no snow. The ground was dry, the fire was warm, and it was actually a really nice night out.

She wasn't sure how long she had spaced out, but it must have been a while because suddenly her drink was empty and everyone was looking at her expectantly.

"What?" she asked, defensively, eyeing the four of them who were all staring at her at once. She had no idea what they'd been talking about while she was daydreaming. Judging by Travis's snickering and the pleased look on Brittany's face though, she could guess they had been making fun of her.

"You wanna explore with us or stay by the fire?" Harrison asked, whispering quietly in her ear so the rest of the group couldn't hear.

"Explore where?" Kelsey asked, hesitantly. She was pretty sure she already knew the answer and that was only confirmed when he raised his eyebrows at her and nodded towards the ruins. "In there? Umm…"

Neither option seemed appealing to her. Stay outside in the forest by herself, or go into some structurally unsound (and probably haunted) ruins with her friends. Either way felt like the beginning of a horror film. Begrudgingly, she decided that staying with people seemed like the wiser option, as splitting up never ends well in scary movies, and she stood up to follow the rest into the manor.

Brittany went first, choosing the nearest entrance and skipping down some stone steps into the cellar. Whatever door had originally covered the entryway had rotted away ages ago. With a glance towards the fire behind her, Kelsey stepped into the dark space and followed the sound of Travis's voice as it echoed off the low ceiling and stone walls. She could just barely make out the blurry silhouettes of a couple of her friends standing near the center of the space, and she paused a few feet from the stairs to look around for her boyfriend.

"Did you know that this spot is supposed to be where they burned the witch?" Travis asked the group, animatedly. "That's the only recorded witch burning in

Graymourne's history. And it happened right here." His excitement was palpable.

Kelsey knew coming here was probably his idea; Travis was a total horror buff. He knew every local ghost story and legend by heart. As she listened to him recount the story of the Graydon witch trial, she felt a warm presence step up behind her and the familiar sensation of an arm slipping around her shoulder. She leaned into it, surprised that Harrison was being so considerate, hanging out with her instead of traipsing all around the ruins with his friends.

"Can we get out of here after this, Harrison," she asked quietly, not wanting the others to hear her and give her shit for leaving early. They could hang out all night in creepy ruins if they wanted, Kelsey would much rather go make out with her boyfriend in a nice warm car.

"What was that, babe? I can't hear you," Harrison replied.

She froze, hearing the sound of his voice float towards her from the middle of the cellar where the other teenagers stood. The hand on her shoulder squeezed once and then slowly receded, leaving her cold and shaken. Kelsey felt her stomach drop.

"Um, where are you?" she questioned, her voice quaking with fear. "Are all of you over there?"

Silently, she tried convincing herself that one of them had to be fucking with her.

"Yeah," her boyfriend confirmed.

"Yup," Travis replied.

"Over here," Anna said.

"Uh huh," Brittany sounded off.

With a panicked gasp, Kelsey ran blindly towards the voices of her friends, shoving herself into the center of their small circle. She was nearly hyperventilating and shaking like a leaf when Harrison grabbed her, confused but quickly trying to calm down his utterly terrified girlfriend.

"What the fuck, Kels?" he asked. "You good?"

"No!" she squealed, trembling violently. "I am not good. Someone… something touched me. There was a fucking hand on my shoulder and all of you idiots were over here, so who the fuck was it?"

Her grip on Harrison's forearms was desperate, her fingers digging painfully into his skin even through the thick fabric of his jacket. Murmurs of confusion and disbelief sounded as she shook in his arms.

"You're messing with us, right?" Anna ventured, her normally calm demeanor cracking with doubt. She knew Kelsey well enough to know that she wasn't the type to play practical jokes, that was much more Brittany's forte.

"I don't think she is," Harrison answered for her, earnestly. "She's fucking terrified. Maybe we should go."

He started to herd the group back towards the stairway despite two of his friends' annoyed protests. They only made it a few feet before a vicious growl erupted behind them in the darkness. Five discordant screams rang out as the kids panicked, running for the exit. But before they could flee the way they came in, a massive silhouette coalesced before them, its humanoid outline taking up the entire doorway and blocking off their escape.

Utter chaos broke out as the teenagers skidded to a halt, kicking up dust on the dirt floor, and pivoted to run in three different directions. Kelsey reached out and grabbed the first hand she could, dragging Anna to the left towards the dim light where a section of the ceiling was open to the floor above. Brittany veered right, tripping over a pile of stones in the dark and tumbling face-first into the hard packed ground. Travis and Harrison, meanwhile, turned straight around and ran back into the black depths of the cellar. With every single one of them shouting a stream of nonsense and profanity, a cacophony of noise filled the stone-enclosed space, reverberating loudly.

The dim moonlight filtering in through the open floor above seemed to snap Anna back to her senses. She clambered up a pile of fallen rubble near the wall and motioned Kelsey to follow her up.

"Give me a boost, I'll pull you up after," she suggested quickly. Kelsey swiftly bent down on one knee to help the taller girl up. Anna was on the basketball team, a good several inches taller and by far the stronger of the two of them. She managed to pull herself up to the ground floor and immediately laid down on her stomach to reach back down for her friend. Kelsey stood on her toes, reaching as high as she could to grab onto Anna's outstretched hand. She kicked her feet against the wall, trying to gain purchase and climb up as the other girl pulled with all her might. Finally, Anna was able to heave her out of the dark cellar and onto the ruined floor of what was once a parlor.

Most of the floor was gone, only the skeleton of the walls remained and a stone fireplace whose chimney teetered precariously above the ruins. The girls barely paused to catch their breath before calling out to their friends who were still trapped in the cavernous space.

"Shit, shit, shit," Brittany cursed to herself in the suddenly quiet cellar, kneeling while she fumbled through her jacket pockets for her phone. She had dropped her flashlight when she fell and now she was alone in the pitch black.

With shaking hands, she managed to turn the phone's light on and shine it into the space to get her bearings. A stone wall sat a few feet in front of her. Slowly and hesitantly, she panned to the side, looking for the way out. The wavering light moved over foot after foot of empty, dust-covered space until the edges illuminated something solid and dark; there was a set of pitch black claw-tipped limbs crouched several feet away. Brittany shrieked and lost her grip on her phone, darkness falling over the brief glimpse of whatever was here with her.

Gulping in panicked breaths, she felt around the ground for her phone, praying that whatever that thing was wouldn't eat her. A huge hand clamped around her wrist, prompting a strangled scream from the girl, which cut off in a confused gasp when the thing thrust her phone into her hand and then let go.

It laughed.

It was not a friendly sound. No, this was the laugh of a predator playing with its food. Fear overtook shock and Brittany leapt to her feet, running in what she hoped was the direction of the exit.

It wasn't.

In her panic, she miscalculated and headed deeper into the cellar. She didn't get very far before something took a firm hold on the hood of her jacket and yanked her backwards. She screamed as it dragged her across the floor, kicking her legs frantically at the dirt and trying unsuccessfully to shrug out of her coat. She was now certain that she was about to die.

But, then it suddenly and unceremoniously dropped her in the open doorway.

"GET OUT," an inhumanly low voice growled.

She couldn't tell exactly where it was coming from, only that it was very, very close. She scrambled to her feet and fled back up the stairs to the relative safety of the open yard. She was still alone out here, but alone in the woods was better than in there with that thing.

Brittany waffled; Travis and Harrison were still in there, maybe Anna and Kelsey too. There was no way in hell that she was going back in that cellar, though, so she decided to head back towards the car and hope that her friends made it out in one piece on their own.

Meanwhile, Harrison felt his way along the stone wall while Travis followed close behind him, keeping a death grip on the other boy's jacket. They had both unwisely left their flashlights outside with their drinks, next to the fire. And after hearing the sounds of Brittany screaming as she was dragged away somewhere in the dark, they were too afraid to use the lights on their phones, fearful that the light would draw attention to them next. So, as quietly as possible, they picked their way along the wall in one direction, hoping it would bring them to an exit eventually.

A few tense and silent moments later, Harrison came to the edge of a partial wall that divided the space. Sparse light streamed in through the broken ceiling on the other side, where Anna and Kelsey had made their escape a few minutes earlier. He breathed a sigh of relief and headed for the opening with Travis in tow. Harrison jumped, grabbing onto the edge of the ruined floor above. Ignoring the splinters he got in the process, he pulled himself up and rolled onto the floor next to a large fireplace.

"Come on, man, give me a hand," Travis hissed from below, trying to convince himself that he was not, in fact, feeling something breathing down the back of his neck.

He reached up, grasping his friend's hand and flailed as the two of them struggled to get him out of the cellar. Travis let out a high-pitched shriek when something seized the waistband of his jeans and hoisted him up as if the six-foot-tall varsity linebacker weighed nothing.

It released its hold at the same time that Harrison yanked hard, and the pair fell into a heap on the narrow patch of mouldering floor. The two of them stared wide eyed at each other for a second before the sound of stones falling drew their attention towards the fireplace.

They watched, petrified, as a trickle of small stones cascaded down from inside the chimney. There was a silent, dread-filled pause before the motion was followed by one enormous, smoking black hand and then another. The sharp and spindly fingers curled around the edges of the firebox, leaving grooves in the stone where their talons scraped noisily along its surface. A rumbling growl sounded from inside the chimney.

Neither boy wanted to wait around to see what was going to come crawling out of the stonework. They nearly fell over each other, scrambling to run along the precarious edge of the destroyed floor before diving out the front of the overgrown ruins. Tumbling into a heap in the front yard, they spotted the three girls huddled together near the low stone wall that enclosed the property.

"Come on guys, we need to go!" Kelsey urged, frantically motioning for the befuddled teenagers to get moving.

Harrison dragged Travis to his feet and made a beeline for the girls.

She was right - they never should have come here.

Tenebrae leaned against the framework of what used to be the front door, chuckling to himself as he watched the five human children flee into the night. He could hear them yelling accusations at each other all the way down the hiking trail back to their cars.

"Enjoying yourself, my love?" Lazarus asked, smirking as he sidled up next to the amused shadow demon.

He slid a semi-transparent hand over the corded muscles of Tenebrae's arm and slotted himself against the demon's side.

"Mmm," Tenebrae rumbled in assent. "Humans are so easy to frighten… pathetic. Still, it offers some entertainment."

Turning away from the now empty woods, he moved to face the shorter man, wrapping an inky limb around his waist. It was impossible not to notice the slight insubstantiality of the figure pressed against him, and Tenebrae felt a brief pang of longing for the warmth and solidity that his husband's form once had.

"Not all of us are such easy prey," Lazarus teased, catching a glimpse of his lover's melancholy and attempting to distract him. "I recall, Miss Quinn, for one, would have none of your menacing."

"Foolishly brave," Tenebrae agreed with a slight admiration to his tone.

When she had come to the manor seeking help a few months before, the woman had surprised him, standing her ground and even daring to challenge him verbally. She hadn't hesitated at all to go deep into the forest with him alone to retrieve Lazarus's grimoire. That was what finally convinced him that her intentions to free the shadow demon in her house were true; why else would she put herself in such obvious peril?

"Nearly as vexing as you were when we first met," he declared.

"Oh, come now, you hated me far more," Lazarus laughed, heartily, sliding his arms around the demon's waist and regarding him affectionately. "You tried to kill me at least twice. And you would have succeeded had we not already been bound."

"In hindsight, that would have been unfortunate," the demon intoned regretfully, grimacing at the violence of the memories. As passionately as he had initially abhorred the man in question, he now could not fathom parting from him with equal measure.

It was difficult enough to bear that Lazarus had been reduced to this half-existence as a Shade for the past two centuries. The demon was grateful that his husband still lived at all, but the pain of knowing that his human body was dust beneath their feet never left him completely. The shadows in Lazarus's blood kept his spirit semi-corporeal, enough that he could be seen and touched but neither as solidly as when he was properly alive. The remnants of his physical form that were still embedded in the soil here served as an anchor, preventing Lazarus from leaving the manor ruins and its immediate surroundings.

Tenebrae felt the ghosted warmth of a hand at his cheek, realizing he must have been wearing his longing on his face. Lazarus pressed a breeze of a kiss against his lips and let out a burdened sigh.

"Soon, my love," he reassured the demon, sensing the restlessness overtaking both of them.

They had waited this long, and it would only be a few months more now. The stars would align for them once again, and neither would allow anything to stop it.

Chapter 1

Dry leaves blew across the clearing in front of the manor ruins. Crisp winds whistled through the skeletal branches of the trees that surrounded it. Even in the bright morning light, the overgrown property held a crypt-like aura, unnaturally still and bereft of the forest's usual fauna. It was not only the local villagers that tended to avoid this place.

The crunching of approaching footsteps broke the silence first, followed by the murmur of soft voices, one impossibly deep and rumbling and the other bright and melodic. Tenebrae roused in the shadows, uncoiling his incorporeal form from around the Shade of his husband. Lazarus looked at him quizzically, his ears not yet able to pick up the distant sound.

"Someone is coming," the shadow demon explained, melting through the dark of the cellar and re-emerging on the floor above.

In between the trees to the west of the house, he could see a large dark shape next to a much smaller, obviously human one. A stray beam of sunlight glinted off familiar long, blonde locks and he knew at once who it was.

"Who is it?" Lazarus asked, curiously, sidling up next to where Tenebrae looked out of a broken window frame.

"The human you gave your grimoire to," Tenebrae replied, sourly, "and she is not alone."

"Wonderful!" Lazarus exclaimed, clapping his hands enthusiastically. "The unbinding spell must have worked. I was beginning to wonder when they would visit us." His transparent form was positively glowing with excitement.

In contrast, Tenebrae's dark countenance stiffened with apprehension. He still did not entirely trust the woman and he'd been wary of giving a relatively unknown human such a powerful tool of magic. It was only his husband's insistence that had swayed him to help her retrieve it from Devil's Circle. In addition to dealing with the human's presence, however, it appeared that he was also about to meet one of his own kind for the first time. He wasn't sure which one was more disconcerting.

Before Tenebrae could stop him, Lazarus nimbly escaped through a crumbling opening in the wall and began crossing the side yard to greet them. His footfalls made no sound against the underbrush as he crossed the space.

"Good day, Miss Quinn!" he called, grinning affably at the pair as they stepped out of the tree line. "What a joy it is to see you again. Please, do introduce your companion."

Tenebrae quickly caught up to him, sliding an arm around his waist, and the shadow demon pressed closely at his side.

"Hi, guys!" the woman replied, brightly, giving them both an awkward little wave with her free hand. Her other hand was clasped tightly in the grip of the demon at her side. "This is Myrkrið. Myrkrið, meet Lazarus and Tenebrae. And please, call me Zori."

"Well met, sir," Lazarus said with a nod to the shadow, who acknowledged him with a slight incline of his head in return.

The two shadow demons eyed each other warily, silently assessing each other with unabashed distrust.

Myrkrið was taller than the already towering Tenebrae by six or eight inches. Both sported muscular builds; but while the former had a bulkier physique with softer edges, the latter was slim and sharp, like a panther compared with a cheetah. Myrkrið's comparatively more mellow demeanor was reflected in his languid posture, while the fiery Tenebrae stood rigidly, poised to strike.

Neither seemed to be willing to break eye contact nor to be the first one to speak. The uneasy silence stretched on for a bit too long.

"Wow, and I thought I was awkward at meeting people," Zori said, cutting through the tense atmosphere with a lighthearted laugh. She caught Lazarus's eye, and amused understanding passed between them. Her demon's attention returned to her, and his expression softened immediately.

"It is good to meet you both," Myrkrið said, looking first to the witch and then to the other shadow. "Thank you for assisting Zori. Without your help, I would still be trapped."

Tenebrae watched as Zori clutched the other demon's arm tightly, hugging it against her body while she beamed up at him with adoration. Next to the relatively giant shadow demon, she looked tiny and breakable. The top of her head barely came up to his chest, even though she was taller than many of the human women Tenebrae had observed. As he had the first time they met, he found her fearlessness both admirable and a bit foolish. But her obvious devotion to Myrkrið began to make him reconsider his initial hostility.

"You are welcome," Tenebrae rumbled, genuinely relieved to see that the human had made good on her promise to free his fellow shadow. Though he had little personal connection to the rest of his kind, the idea that one of them was imprisoned was still an affront to him.

"Come inside," Lazarus invited, taking his husband's hand from around his waist and squeezing it in approval. He beckoned their guests towards what was left of the house. "We have few amenities to offer guests these days, I am afraid, so please do accept my apologies for any deficiencies in hospitality. We are quite pleased to have you, though."

"No worries," Zori chuckled, following the shade inside with her shadow demon close behind. "We're not exactly dressed for tea or anything, anyway."

She was bundled up in a black thigh-length wool coat with an oversized hood lined with black faux fur, thick fleece leggings, and matching black hiking boots, while her companion wore the standard shadow demon wardrobe of nothing at all. There was little point; the elements had a negligible effect on their kind and the clothing would only fall away whenever they shifted between forms anyway.

The four of them gathered in what used to be the kitchen at the back of the house. It was the least damaged part of the ruined manor. Zori was surprised to find a set of garden chairs arranged in a cozy circle at the center of the space.

"After your last visit, I expected we might be entertaining guests again at some point," Lazarus explained, chuckling at her raised eyebrows as he took a seat in one of the chairs, "so Tenebrae rounded up some seating for us."

Zori sat down across from him and the two hulking shadow demons folded themselves into the too small seats next to their partners. She shook her head and laughed.

"My neighbor up the street was wondering where her garden furniture disappeared to," she explained. Graymourne being a small town, even the relatively introverted Zori had heard all about the mystery of Frances Donovan's stolen garden set. "I only live three houses down from her, you were right in my neighborhood."

Myrkrið made a noise of disapproval, grumbling when she casually gave away the location of her home.

"You should not tell strangers where you live," he admonished, not bothering to lower his voice.

"They're not strangers," she argued, rolling her eyes at the protective demon. "They helped us free you, they're friends."

She smiled apologetically at their hosts.

Friends? Tenebrae scoffed, surprised to be referred to so warmly by someone other than Lazarus. All he had done was threaten her and then reluctantly take her to retrieve the grimoire. His actions could hardly be considered friendly.

"We are honored to be counted amongst your friends," Lazarus interjected, "and if it puts you at ease, I cannot leave the bounds of this property, and Tenebrae would never harm Miss Quinn. Would you, husband?"

The expectant look he aimed at his shadow demon made it glaringly obvious that there was a correct answer to this question.

"No," Tenebrae said, flatly, pausing long enough that Lazarus turned back to their company with a pleased smile. "So long as she makes no attempt to harm you."

Close enough, I suppose, the witch sighed internally.

Surprisingly, this seemed to sufficiently appease Myrkrið's misgivings and he sat back, relaxing as much as was possible in the undersized chair. A tentative truce appeared to have been struck between the two demons, and some of the tension eased from Tenebrae's posture as well.

"Okay, well now that we've established that we're all friends and no one is going to try to murder each other," Zori said, fishing a hand into one of the large pockets of her coat. She pulled a black leather-bound book out of its depths. "I wanted to give this back to you, Lazarus. You mentioned something about a resurrection when I was here before and I figured you might need it."

Lazarus took the book when she held it out to him, turning it over in his hands. This was the first time in two-hundred and fifty years that he had held the grimoire. Its cover was more worn and the edges of the pages frayed, but it was in remarkably good condition, especially considering the book had been in his family already for generations when he had acquired it.

"Thank you, Zori," he said, his voice wavering with the emotions that washed over him upon holding this piece of his history. The old pang of longing for his twin, Levi, flared brighter, along with memories of the many times they had cast spells from this book and its counterpart together. Dark tendrils wrapped tightly around his waist, anchoring him back to the present.

"If there's anything we can do to help, please let us know," she said, sincerely.

"She will attempt to help whether you ask or not," Myrkrið drawled, looking at her fondly despite the reproachful tone. Zori shrugged in mild embarrassment; he wasn't wrong. "And I will give whatever assistance I can."

Tenebrae frowned; he hadn't expected the other shadow to be so forthcoming. Granted, his only experience with other demons were a couple of chance encounters during his travels. The friendliest of these had been a fire demon who was bathing in an active volcano when Tenebrae came upon them. They had been curious and pleasant enough, but their opposing elements had made it difficult for the two to interact for very long.

"Have you met others of our kind?" Tenebrae asked abruptly, interested to know the answer, but also to test the waters, conversationally. All three pairs of eyes turned to look at him at once, obviously surprised to see him initiate an exchange.

"Yes," Myrkrið answered, a strand of his shadows lazily curling around Zori's wrist as he spoke. "There have been a few over the years that I became familiar with and more in passing that I did not. It has been a very long time though."

Tenebrae saw Lazarus raise an inquisitive brow out of the corner of his eye and knew that his husband was pondering the same question he was. Just how old was this shadow demon? The way he said 'a very long time' held too much gravity to simply refer to the forty years he had languished in the Dew Lane house.

"We are not noted for our social graces, as a whole," Myrkrið continued with a dry chuckle, "but I will tell you about them sometime, if you wish."

"I would like that."

Tenebrae threw a side-eyed glare at his husband, who was grinning proudly at him, not bothering to hide his pleased expression at his attempts to socialize with the other demon. He was certain to hear about this later.

"Had you been summoned before?" Myrkrið asked, with a nod to the smiling witch.

"Once," Tenebrae grumbled, rolling his eyes, "but only this human was foolish enough to bind me." His eyes narrowed as he turned towards Lazarus, but his glare held none of the venom it once did. "And you?"

"Several times," Myrkrið commiserated with a weary sigh. "Perhaps once every hundred years until the humans began persecuting magic users more frequently. And then not again until Jonas Graydon summoned me here. Although, it is fortunate that he botched the binding spell when he did." Zori slipped her hand into his and laced their fingers together, his claws almost completely swallowing her smaller hand.

"It seems to have turned out well for you," Tenebrae agreed, distractedly, jealous of their easy interactions. He averted his gaze, trying not to allow his impossible yearning for his partner's physical form to translate into a resentment towards their guests.

"That reminds me," Zori interjected excitedly, "I'm dying to know how you two met."

Lazarus looked briefly to Tenebrae, who merely shrugged, content to let the witch take the reins in telling this story. It would be a good distraction from his pining, at least.

"Summer was just coming to an end in Graymourne, and the year was 1767," Lazarus began, setting the scene for his rapt audience.

Chapter 2

AUGUST 1767

A warm breeze shifted the humid late summer air, loosening its heavy grip on the sun-baked town. The sound of birds chirping and insects humming was once again overtaken by a sedate murmur of voices as villagers filed out of the timber-frame meeting house near the center of Graymourne. The crowd dispersed efficiently as folks returned to their homes and places of work, especially mindful after the Reverend Poole's diatribe on idle hands.

Exiting at a calculatedly middle point in the throng, Lazarus Graydon gave the Reverend a polite greeting as he passed, making sure the man noted his dutiful attendance. With the clergyman's perfunctory nod, he quickly moved on, unwilling to linger lest he be drawn into conversation with the Reverend and his odious brother. As one of the church elders and a founding member of the village, Elbert Poole considered himself to be the leader of their community, second only to the Reverend himself.

Where the tall and dour Hezekiah was quietly stern, delivering sermons with the unwavering severity of a cold Northern wind; the younger Poole was bombastic and loud with a permanently sour expression on his rounded, sagging features. Elbert Poole had never liked Lazarus and the feeling was enthusiastically mutual.

Once safely out of earshot of the brothers, he paused just outside the building to wait for the rest of his family. Lazarus's twin Levi was still inside with his wife Sarah and their young son. While he awaited them, Lazarus exchanged pleasantries with a few of his neighbors. Some of the local farmers were going to the nearby tavern, but he graciously declined Enoch Dodson's invitation to join them this time. His brother emerged, soon enough, shepherding his wife and young child before him.

Lazarus looked up, inadvertently catching the eye of a young woman who passed in front of their group, and she quickly averted her own eyes with a blush. He would prefer to think that the warm sun could be blamed for the color in her cheeks, but as the more handsome and, importantly, single of the Graydon brothers, he knew it was not.

If only you were my type, dear Anne, how much simpler things would be.

He sighed, shifting on his feet, eager to get back to the shady haven that awaited them. Even in his relatively lightweight dove gray linen coat and waistcoat, Lazarus was already sweating as the sweltering heat of the day settled in.

Levi fell into step at his right side and the four of them trod down the path towards the covered bridge that would take them home. They moved slowly, matching four-year-old Elijah's short stride as he toddled along with his hand in Sarah's gentle grasp. He was a curious child, prone to wandering off to investigate whatever caught his fancy. A little agent of chaos who was a bit too like his Uncle Lazarus for his parents' liking.

"You should consider it," Levi said to his brother when they were out of earshot of any other villagers. He rested a protective hand at the small of Sarah's back, gently guiding her around some rough terrain.

"Consider what, dear brother?" Lazarus inquired, knowing full well what his twin meant by the comment. His shrewd eyes flashed with mischief and a little bit of annoyance in anticipation of the coming conversation. It was one they had rehashed many times over the last year and a half.

"Taking a wife, Laz," he sighed, exasperated by his refusal to see reason. "They are already suspicious of us as it is. That you refuse to marry only compounds the issue. Anne Barnet would be a fine match, you should at least hear her father out."

Despite the uncharitable gossip that they were more and more frequently the subject of, Thomas Barnet had offered his eldest daughter's hand in marriage to the unattached Graydon twin. It was the reason he hadn't wanted to go to the tavern today, loath to be cornered again. Barnet had sprung the proposition on him mid-conversation, with an enthusiasm that made it clear he was willing to overlook the rumors in order for her to live in the richest house in town. The Graydons' wealth and success had become a double-edged sword of late, affording the family a comfortable life but at the cost of their reputation.

Luck seemed to cling to them; their crops were the most bountiful, their health always excellent, and their hardships few and far between. It was not an easy life in the New England village, and their charmed existence had soon engendered envy and resentment in their neighbors. Such sentiments were frowned upon by the rather strictly moral community, so these swiftly turned to blame and thus the rumors began.

There must be something unnatural about the Graydon brothers, it was said, only whispered at first but lately those hushed voices seemed to be getting louder.

"You know I have no interest in a wife," Lazarus reminded him, equally frustrated that his brother would not drop the subject. "Especially a pious little thing like Anne Barnet. As you say, they are suspicious already; marrying one of them can hardly be the remedy. I will take my chances."

He would rather be alone than trapped in a sham marriage with someone he could never love, just to appease the status quo. At least on his own, there was the possibility that someday he might find the man of his dreams, however dim the flame of that hope might be.

It had been perplexing, as a young man, to realize that he didn't share the same attraction towards the opposite sex as his brother and their peers. Instead, his heart raced and his cheeks warmed whenever the minister's handsome son looked at him. It took a long time and many late night conversations with his twin for him to come to terms with his sexuality, finally having his first relationship when he turned twenty.

It had been terrifying trying to hide his affair from their parents, but Levi aided him at every turn, never wavering in his support. Lazarus knew their mother would accept him unconditionally, while their father was more likely to grumble something about it being the result of "occulty nonsense" from his mother's side of the family. It wasn't their judgement he feared so much, but the more people who knew, the more danger there was of his secret coming out. When Levi married a year later, he offered Lazarus to come live with him and his new bride, as much for the twins to stay together as to allow Lazarus to live in a home where he didn't feel he had to hide.

Levi had not begrudged his twin's taste in partners then, and he didn't now, save for the fact that it served to draw a spotlight on the man. Shielded by his status as a respectable husband and father, the more incisive village gossip was always focused on the charming and carefree Lazarus. Never mind that the whispers of witchcraft were true, that wasn't the point. They needed to blend in for safety's sake.

"You needn't love her, brother," Levi appealed, torn between his opposing desires to see his twin happy and to ensure that he was safe. Sarah squeezed his hand in silent reassurance, encouraging him to continue. She had heard this exchange before and preferred to stay out of their squabbling. "It would merely be a means of protection. You are not invincible."

Lazarus was silent as they crossed the echoing expanse of the covered bridge, a deep frown of contemplation etched across his graceful features. It was a look that Levi recognized easily, one that told him he would not be winning this fight today. He could see the stubborn determination that turned the wheels of his twin's mind as they passed into the shaded stone walkway leading to their home.

The silence continued until they reached the front door, which Levi held open for Sarah and Elijah to enter first. Lazarus paused in the doorway, his bright hazel eyes resolute as he returned his attention to his brother and finally broke his silence.

"Perhaps not, but I will be."

Lazarus tucked the knife carefully into his satchel, nestled between a small canvas bag of salt and a bundle of herbs. He consulted the list for the last time to be sure that he had everything that he would need. A gentle knock sounded behind him and he snapped the book shut, turning to face his brother. Levi stood in the doorway, his arms crossed at his chest with a resigned look on his face.

"I cannot dissuade you from this, can I?" he asked, defeatedly. It had been a week since that fateful walk back from the meetinghouse when the idea had stuck in

Lazarus's mind. When he told his twin what he intended to do, Levi immediately tried to talk him out of it, concerned that his brother's solution to alleviate their problems was too ambitious and too dangerous.

But Lazarus wouldn't be swayed.

"No brother, you cannot," the determined man assured him, crossing the dark room to clasp him on the shoulder. "You wish me to be protected, and there is no protection greater than this."

Neither was a stranger to the casting of magic; its liberal yet careful application was responsible for much of the success they enjoyed in life. They had performed many rituals and castings both together and on their own. This one, though, would be different.

"This is not like our simple charms, Laz," Levi reminded him, ever the voice of reason between the two. With a sigh of resignation, he relented. "Please, just be careful."

"I will," he promised, honestly. "Now go, your wife must be wondering why you are out of bed at such a late hour."

Lazarus smirked as his brother shook his head and turned to leave. The whole village would be asleep at this time of night and his destination was far enough outside of town that it was certain to be deserted. During the several days he had to wait for the moon to reach its fullest, there had been plenty of time to scout for a location where he could complete his task without risk of being discovered.

Invincible.

When Levi had said the word, it was like an arrow shot through his mind and landed on a frequently overlooked page in his grimoire. Most of the summoning spells in the book offered too little in the way of reward to be worth the risk of conjuring an entity anywhere near the judgmental eyes of their community. Only one bestowed the caster with virtual invincibility.

With this particular spell, one could summon a living shadow and bind their life to the demon's. So long as the demon lived, so would the human. The spell caster became virtually indestructible and in return, the shadow gained 'corporeal powers immune to light' whatever that meant. It seemed like a fair trade to Lazarus.

Slinging the satchel onto his back, he made his way out of the manor quietly and slipped down the stone steps to the walking path. Instead of left towards town, he turned right, heading farther into Whitmack Forest. Beyond their home in this direction, there was only wilderness and the trail was mostly unused except for the occasional hunter or trapper. Trees and shrubs hugged in close on both sides, and the ground was rocky and uneven.

It took the better part of an hour to cover the distance, even at the brisk pace he set, driven by nervous energy. The last twenty minutes or so, Lazarus veered off the beaten path, sparse as it was, and treaded through the thick forest.

Finally, he emerged into a wide pool of moonlight cast over a natural clearing. Few from the village even knew of this place, and those that did would not speak of it, let alone set foot inside. A ring of standing stones took up most of the space, their varying heights and shapes like a crude crown upon the ground. He had no idea who had constructed the circle, but it thrummed with power.

This place was very old.

Wasting no time, Lazarus set to work. First, he consulted the grimoire, raking his eyes over the page to study the complex symbol in detail. Grabbing a fallen branch from a nearby tree, he traced the intricate image carefully into the earth. It took some time to inscribe the line work and all of the arcane lettering into the dry dirt. Eventually, he stepped back to check his work, glancing back and forth between the sigil in the book and its likeness scrawled in the center of the clearing. Avoiding the lines with care, he gingerly stepped toward the top of the circle to correct one of the characters. He stood back and compared the images again.

Now it was perfect.

Gathering up the beeswax candles, he distributed them around the carefully drawn sigil, matching one to each of the stones. Once the herbs and candles were lit, he moved to the center of the space, knife in hand. Lazarus took a deep breath, staring down into the palms of his hands.

This moment was the point of no return; once he began the ritual there was no going back. If, for some reason, the spell failed, he would most likely bleed out and only the wildlife would find him. His fist clenched around the smooth wooden handle of the knife; this had to work.

Before he could change his mind, he sliced deep into the palm of his right hand, hissing as the first few dark droplets hit the dirt. Lazarus recovered quickly, knowing he had one more cut to make. The text advised that the ritual would leave a mark, something he needed to be sure would remain hidden to avoid suspicion. He closed his eyes and drew the blade across his inner thigh, letting out a sharp gasp as the metal easily cut through the left leg of his trousers and into the tender flesh. The knife fell at his feet and Lazarus blinked to clear his head of the pain. He had to begin the incantation, time was ticking with every pump of his veins.

"Ex vacuo te obtestor
Spiritus tenebrosus ut nox
Sanguis diei super terram
Vocationem eius audi et veni

Sanguinem Noctis trahere sentiunt
Nigra aestus tenaci tam firma est
Negari non potest

Apparere spiritum, umbra facta
Ostende mihi

Veni
Tenebrae"

As he spoke, the light of the moon seemed to dim and the flames of the candles shrank under the pressure that gathered in the air. It felt as though the atmosphere itself held its breath in anticipation.

Dark mist began to swirl inside the summoning circle, drawn to a point just in front of Lazarus where it was slowly gathering into a mass. It pulsed as he uttered the final word of the summoning.

Encouraged, he thrust his bleeding hand into the cloud of darkness, and with renewed energy, began to recite the binding portion of the ritual.

"Tenebris lux tenebris
Bargain percussit, Libra est
Et sanguis noctem Si obvium habueris
sanguinem diei
Una fluxus et misce sicut unum
Et commutatio spirituum ligatum et in viribus

Et simul iam fuerit tenetur
Sicut vincula extraxerunt firm, sicut funem coiled
stricta
Et conversus est ad portam clausa est key
Futures joined in sempiternum"

A stream of shadow shot out from the mass and wormed its way into the gash on his thigh. Cold spread through his veins as he felt the darkness wind its way through the labyrinthine passages. More tendrils branched off from the source and began constricting tightly around the leg.

His hand, obscured inside the steadily growing cloud, felt as if it was being drained, a deep tidal pull seizing hold of his blood. He could faintly see threads of light weaving around the limb, as if tying the darkness to it. Both bindings wove tighter as he spoke, becoming more and more painful with every breath.

"Tenebris lux tenebris
Quisque in altera vigemusque
Clara in umbra, Tenebrosus in lucem
Vel in terra Vitare
unitum nunc
Sic fieri"

With great relief, Lazarus felt the tight threads sink into his body, settling into a warm buzz as the pain dissipated. The wound in his palm was already gone. He looked down to check on his bloodied leg, but stopped still when a loud growl rang out before him. The dark cloud stretched and converged, beginning to take on a more human-shaped form. Lazarus nearly leapt out of the summoning circle, somehow having the presence of mind not to disturb the markings.

"Human…" a booming voice rumbled, reproachfully.

It sounded to Lazarus how he imagined a crack of thunder would sound if it were angry and a little disappointed in you. It occurred to him then that since the grimoire claimed the binding was beneficial for both parties, he hadn't entirely considered what he would do if the demon was not on board with the situation.

This one certainly sounded less than pleased.

"Good evening, I- ," he attempted to introduce himself, feeling it was only the polite thing to do, but cut off as the angry fog arranged itself into a solid body.

The book had not provided much physical description for the type of demon it would summon, and it certainly hadn't prepared him for the seven-foot-tall creature that stood before him wearing not a stitch of clothing on its lean, muscular, and very masculine body. Lazarus felt his mouth go dry and a hot blush crept up his neck.

The shadow demon was unsettlingly attractive and very naked.

The moonlight shone faintly through the dark fog of the demon's skin, just barely highlighting black bones beneath the surface. Smoke-like tendrils arose from his skin like dark flames licking the air around him. Everything about him was a bit sharp, from the claws that tipped each finger to the almost elfin features of his face. Obsidian eyes glared out above angular cheekbones and the demon's sensual lips were set in a grim, displeased line. The front of his neck was adorned with what looked like a shining, light gold tattoo in the shape of a circle with a cascade of rays flaring down over his collarbones. He had a terrifying sort of beauty, but fear did nothing to dissuade the ferocious desire that Lazarus felt upon looking at the being he had summoned.

Surprise and distraction kept him rooted in place while the demon slunk his way closer to the edge of the circle. Lazarus happened to glance down as he reached the outermost markings, only to see a twisted smirk on the demon's face when he looked back up.

Pointedly holding the man's gaze, he took a deliberate step out of the summoning circle.

Lazarus stumbled backwards instinctively, eyes wide as the demon took two long strides and seized the front of his coat in one huge hand. His claws ripped through the linen fabric effortlessly as he yanked the man to him, putting the pair face to face. The creature narrowed his eyes at Lazarus and then tilted his head ever so slightly, as if confused by whatever he saw in the man's expression.

The witch's heart pounded in his ears and his breaths quickened, now confronted with the shadow's appearance up close. His head clouded with the demon's scent; cold and earthy yet edged with something sharply floral, like snowy cypress spiced with night-blooming wisteria.

Lazarus wrestled his mind into focus with difficulty, but the moment he opened his mouth to speak, the demon gave an irritated growl and struck the claws of his free hand across his throat, slicing through it from ear to ear.

All that Lazarus could do was gurgle helplessly and clutch his bleeding neck in shock as the demon released him and disappeared into the night, barely giving him a second look.

He fell to his knees, panic setting in. Blood poured from the wound, soaking the ground around him and cascading down the front of his gray coat. He began to feel a strange prickling sensation somewhere beneath the blinding pain, though it was hard to focus on as his mind grew foggy and his vision dimmed.

It only lasted a moment before everything went black.

Chapter 3

THE MORNING AFTER

'**B**irds twittered cheerfully and a light breeze ruffled softly through the foliage. Golden light warmed his closed eyes as Lazarus returned to awareness. He lay awkwardly on his side on an expanse of grass surrounded by a ring of tall trees. The blue sky overhead was dotted with fluffy white clouds.

He shot up with a gasp, clutching his throat in horror as the previous night's events came rushing back. Confused relief washed over him as his fingers trailed over smooth, unbroken skin. If the front of him weren't stained and still tacky with fountains of his own blood, he could have dismissed it all as a dream.

Well, it worked, Lazarus thought, climbing to his feet and brushing the dust from his clothes habitually. It was a futile but comforting gesture; his coat and vest were thoroughly ruined. *I suppose I am invincible now… and bound to a very cross demon.*

He began scrubbing the traces of the summoning circle from the ground, brushing dirt and leaves back over the lines to conceal them. It was unlikely that anyone would visit this place, but not worth the risk of leaving it. When that was done, he gathered up the book and remnants of candles while pondering how to win over the shadow demon. His ire was an unexpected complication.

Lazarus chided himself for his stupefied silence last night; if he could just speak to the creature, he was sure that he could reason with him. His charismatic nature, after all, was one reason the Graydons were still in good standing with the village, even with the rumors that followed them. Levi had always been the responsible twin and Lazarus the more gregarious.

The thought of his family stopped him short. The shadow demon wouldn't go after them, would he?

Hurrying to collect his things, Lazarus grabbed his satchel and made haste back towards the manor. He could forge some protective amulets for them, but all of the supplies were at home. He moved along the path as quickly as he could while keeping an eye out for anyone that might see him. It was still early morning; most would be working their land, but he could not afford to be seen in the state he was in.

Fortune smiled on him and the forest was empty of other human souls. As he neared the manor, he left the trail to cut through the dense forest next to the property. This way, he could enter the back of the house and hopefully slip up to his bedroom unseen where he could change out of his blood-stained clothes. He didn't want to frighten Sarah; she was accepting of the brothers' practice but didn't dabble in witchcraft herself. And he would never hear the end of it from Levi, if his twin saw him like this.

Lazarus slipped off his boots just inside the back door, padding in stockinged feet through the kitchen and up the staircase to the second floor. He could hear the faint voices of his brother and sister-in-law from behind the closed door of their bedroom. Sneaking silently into his own room, he shut the door carefully behind him, mindful of making the slightest sound.

Stripping himself of the gore-encrusted garments, he stashed them in the back of the armoire and quickly scrubbed his skin clean, turning the water in his wash basin red in the process. Washing away the dried blood on his leg revealed a small black crescent moon with jagged radiating lines adorning the spot where he had made the incision for the ritual.

The spell had indeed left a mark.

Now clean enough, Lazarus changed into a fresh shirt and matching brown cotton waistcoat and breeches. The other clothes would have to be disposed of later. For now, he was eager to begin crafting the protection amulets for his family.

He dragged the small wooden chest out from beneath the bed and lifted it up onto the drop-front secretary desk by the window. The chest and its contents had served the Graydon witches for generations, an heirloom that had traveled with them through time and now across an ocean. It held an assortment of herbs, various powders, minerals trinkets, stones, and other materials for crafting nearly any magical working imaginable.

The sensation of the demon's claws rending his flesh flashed through his mind suddenly, causing a shiver to run down his spine. Lazarus knew he would need something exceptionally strong as the basis for the talismans. He picked out three lumps of jet, raw gemstones taken from the treacherous cliffs of Whitby by one of his more intrepid ancestors. The material was notoriously difficult to carve, prone to breakage and shattering, but if you could manage the delicate task, its protective properties were impressive.

I'll need to cleanse it first, Lazarus noted, lighting a small cone of incense in a brass dish set atop the desk.

He held each of the raw black gems in the smoke, one after the other, allowing the scented cloud to wash over the surface of the pieces. Rolling out a soft blue cloth on the wood to catch any stray shards, he laid the pieces side by side and retrieved his carving tools from one of the secretary's many small drawers.

Lazarus sat down and threw himself into the work of shaping the jet. It was tedious work, demanding all of his concentration to encourage the stones into the design he wanted without damaging the material. By the time he was able to coax them into three shield-shaped pieces, the late morning sun was streaming in and brightening up the entire bedroom. He had just begun inscribing the front of the first one with a septagram when there was a hesitant knock at his door.

"Laz? Are you in there?" Levi asked quietly, from the other side of the bedroom door. He sounded unusually reluctant, as if he wasn't really expecting an answer.

"Come in, brother," he replied, not bothering to look up from his work.

He could almost feel the relief wash over Levi as he immediately opened the door and hurried inside. Lazarus continued the painstaking inscription while his brother loomed expectantly at his side, shifting anxiously on his feet.

"Well?" Levi prompted when it became clear that his twin was too absorbed in his task to speak first. "Did the ritual work?"

A hum of assent was his only answer from the focused man for a few moments, as he finished the final line on a seven-pointed star. Looking up, Lazarus added darkly, "I would not be here had it not."

"What does that mean?" Levi demanded, unsettled by his unusually serious demeanor. At least satisfied that his twin was unhurt, he finally noticed what Lazarus had been working on. The three half-finished amulets lay in a row on the desk. "And why are you making protection amulets? If the ritual worked, you should have no need of these."

"The amulets are for you," he corrected quickly, with a slight tone of irritation. He wanted to finish the work, but he knew that Levi wouldn't relent until he explained at least enough to pacify the man. "And for Sarah and Elijah. But, it is only a precaution."

This did not seem to assuage whatever fears were brewing in Levi's mind. On the contrary, the concern etched on his face was now overlaid with suspicion. He narrowed his eyes and crossed his arms over his chest.

"A precaution against what, exactly?" Levi pressed, his posture stiffening as he awaited the explanation.

"Alright," Lazarus sighed, "the ritual was successful, however there was a minor complication afterwards. The demon was, well, let us say less than pleased with the arrangement."

Levi simply stared at him for a few moments, ruminating over the implications of this information. On the one hand, he was happy to have his brother home in one piece and apparently magically protected. On the other hand…

"So, you are telling me that you conjured a demon and now it is angry with you?" he clarified. When his twin merely nodded, he took a deep breath, summoning as much patience as he could. "Do you know where it is?"

"No," Lazarus admitted, with a frown.

"And I assume that it threatened you," Levi continued, "otherwise I doubt you would be carving protection talismans before breakfast."

"In a manner of speaking, yes," he replied.

Threatening seemed like a wild understatement for what had happened, but it was preferable to admitting that the shadow demon had immediately tried to murder him. Indeed, he would have succeeded were it not for the incredible healing ability that the binding had bestowed on him. Lazarus caught himself unconsciously rubbing the healed flesh of his throat. His brother didn't need to know that gruesome detail.

"Fucking hell, Laz," Levi cursed, exasperated. The urge to say 'I told you so' was strong, but what was done was done and no amount of gloating or yelling would change the situation. He scrubbed a hand across his face and sat down on the edge of the bed. "What can I do to help?"

"Convince your wife and child to wear these pendants at all times," Lazarus said, gesturing to the stones he needed to finish. "I have no reason to believe that he will come after any of you, but I would rather be safe. I will figure out a way to smooth things over with the shadow demon."

Levi shook his head. If anyone could charm an irate supernatural being, it would be his headstrong and maddeningly persuasive brother.

"Is all of this worth it?" he asked, then. Lazarus grinned impishly at him and gestured for him to come closer.

"Watch this," he instructed, drawing the sharp edge of the carving tool across the back of his right hand. A shallow scratch appeared with small beads of blood rising to the surface. Before it could even begin to bleed, tiny black threads of shadow wove the skin back together, sealing it tightly. Lazarus brushed away the tiny bit of blood that had escaped and his hand looked good as new.

Levi gaped at his twin, awe written all over his face. He didn't know what he'd been expecting the 'invincibility' that the binding ritual afforded to look like, but he could never have imagined this.

It was astonishing.

The shadow demon moved languidly through the formless dusky void, still bristling intensely at the evening's events. He had only been summoned once before, but the presumption of it irked him.

Humans thinking they could conjure and control him.

It was ridiculous.

The first time, he hadn't known what was happening. One moment he was perfectly content being one with the dark expanse of shadowspace and the next he had been abruptly pulled from that serenity into the assault on the senses that was terrestrial space. Everything was too bright, too loud, and too much.

It was not the first time he had been in a human space. Like most shadow demons, few though they were, he traveled seamlessly through the endless nothingness of his natural habitat and the shadowy places where it connected with humanity's domain. In the relatively short time since he came into existence, somewhere between one and two centuries ago, he had enjoyed exploring the earth, in spite of the strange beings that inhabited it.

At first, he'd been curious about the creatures. They were somewhat similar to himself physically, if somewhat smaller and more fragile, with strangely colored flesh. Unlike him, they flitted freely between light and darkness, though they seemed unable to change their shape like the shadow could. The humans' eyesight in the dark was poor, and so they feared what lurked within its inky depths with a surprising amount of violence. The shadow soon learned it was better to avoid them altogether.

Being forcibly called to appear where he had not chosen was galling, to say the least. The first human to attempt it had the nerve not only to conjure him, but they tried to make demands of him as well.

The foolish mortal had first offered him wealth, then sacrifice, and then their own soul, in exchange for his services in battle. The shadow demon had no use for any of these things, least of all their soul. The situation had devolved swiftly from there and when the conjurer tried to trap him and force his hand, they found themselves on the business end of his claws instead.

This time he had understood what was happening almost immediately. A familiar strong tide had gripped him and he felt himself drawn inexorably forth by an unexpectedly pleasant voice. However, there was a strange warmth to the sensation this time that he hadn't experienced before; it was not unpleasant, in fact it felt invigorating.

But when threads of light and shadow had begun to weave around him, he knew something was terribly wrong.

Once the chaos of the ritual had settled, the shadow demon found himself hovering before a neatly dressed human with shoulder length dark hair, who was looking down at his own hands in quiet contemplation. Irritation had rolled through the demon, and a loud growl erupted out of him. The startled human blinked up at him then, his piercing eyes a curious blend of green and brown with little flecks of gold in them. He scrambled back from the demon with surprising grace, stopping several feet outside of the summoning circle.

"Human…" he had growled, menacingly. Whatever this person had in mind, he wanted no part of it. The shadow demon decided to put an end to the situation promptly this time. He shifted into a more solid form, preparing to make quick work of dispatching the witch.

Then the man began to speak what sounded like an incongruously friendly greeting before abruptly falling silent, while his complexion tinged a strange pink color across his face and ears. He seemed mesmerized as the demon made his way towards him, his gaze only faltering when the shadow approached the edge of the circle.

Why do they think these things will contain us? the shadow demon wondered, smirking maliciously at the man as he made a show of stepping out of the circle.

It only took a couple of long strides for the demon to reach the awestruck human, taking hold of his clothing and wrenching him closer. The witch didn't even let out a sound at his rough handling.

What struck the demon as even odder still was that he looked afraid, but not nearly as much as expected, and his eyes held a strangely intense look about them. The pupils were dilated wildly until there was only a sliver of hazel surrounding them. Perplexed, he glared at the man, trying to identify the unfamiliar look on his face. It was fear and something else that he couldn't place.

The witch seemed to take the shadow demon's momentary lack of action as his cue to speak. But the slight movement of his lips shook the demon out of his confusion, and he rumbled with irritation. Remembering the pointlessly lengthy back and forth he'd been drawn into with the previous conjurer, he decided it wasn't worth allowing the man to speak.

Lightning fast, he swiped his claws across the front of the human's neck and promptly dropped his hold. He didn't feel the need to stick around, knowing that the witch would exsanguinate from such a wound in just a few short minutes. The demon stepped back into the shadows, retreating to familiar ground where he sulked in the comfortable silence of the void.

He remained there for some time, allowing his mind to calm once more after the chaos of being dragged so unexpectedly into terrestrial space. After the first incident, he had languished for nearly a week, brooding and unwilling to leave the soothing familiarity of shadowspace. Eventually, both then and now, he had grown restless and the wanderlust had returned.

Now, what was I doing before being so rudely interrupted? the shadow demon wondered, trying to recall his last whereabouts.

There were still so many dark places on earth that he hadn't seen, many of them blessedly inaccessible to humankind. His favorite pastime was picking a direction in shadowspace and seeing where he would end up when he pushed through to the other side. This had led to him visiting some fascinating places both manmade and natural, including a vast network of catacombs, a deep cave lit only by glowing worms, and a forest of evergreens so dense that sunlight could scarcely penetrate it, lending it an atmosphere of perpetual night.

He would not mind visiting there again, and meandering among the verdant sea of trees.

The shadow demon held its image in his mind, and tried to set off in the direction of the dark wood. However, no matter how hard he pushed and searched, he always emerged from shadowspace in the wrong place. There was forest surrounding him, but the types of trees and vegetation were all wrong and it was entirely too bright. The sun was just beginning to set. Unless he was mistaken, this was the same forest where he had just recently been conjured.

With a noise of discontent, he shoved back into the void and took off in a different direction, this time heading for a remote mountain whose craggy summit held a spectacular view of the night sky.

But again, he exited the void to find himself in the same environment. His location had moved slightly, but the terrain was unmistakably similar. Again and again, he tried, attempting to travel in every direction only to find himself restricted to the same area.

Something is wrong, he realized. Thinking back to the peculiar sensation and threads of light, he began to suspect it had something to do with the summoning. That hadn't happened the first time. *I dispensed with the witch, though, the magic should have died with him.*

The shadow demon sighed deeply; there was no other explanation he could think of at the moment. He stepped back into the shadows and reluctantly made his way to the clearing with its circle of stones.

Perhaps revisiting the scene would give him something to go on.

It was fully dark out when he finally returned to the site of the previous night's events. The moon, just past its fullest state, cast a bright glow onto the open expanse. With the demon's excellent night vision, he could see the scene as clear as day and what he saw there was nothing short of baffling.

Aside from some scuff marks where dirt had obviously been kicked over it, the sigil that had been inscribed in the center of the stone circle was wiped away. The candles and herbs were gone.

And most frustratingly, there was no body.

Where the bright-eyed witch had fallen, there was a large patch of darkened earth and stained grass that still smelled of dried blood. However, the human himself was nowhere to be found.

Searching the surrounding area carefully, the shadow demon was able to pick out a single set of faint footprints leading away from the clearing and into the woods southeast. There was still a hint of the man's warm, spicy scent clinging to some trees he must have touched as he passed by.

All of the evidence indicated that the human had walked out of the forest on his own two feet, but that was not possible. His wounds should have been fatal.

How did he survive? the demon wondered, as he followed the trail.

Chapter 4

Supper in the Graydon manor was unusually quiet that evening, save for the oblivious chattering of the youngest member of the household. Elijah prattled on, listing all of the wildlife he had seen that day while he helped his mother with chores in the garden. His uncle gave the boy his full attention, occasionally reminding him to eat his food in between small questions and encouragements.

Lazarus could feel the heat of Sarah's glare from across the table being mildly softened by the way he doted on her son. He was a good uncle, impulsive and brash perhaps, but when it came to Elijah, he was patient and devoted. She often wished he would pour a little more of that attitude into the rest of his life. He turned to meet her eyes finally when the boy had run out of animals to describe.

"The stew is delicious, Sarah," he complimented, genuinely, flashing her a familiar dazzling smile. "I daresay we are the most well-fed men in Graymourne thanks to your talents." Despite the sincerity of his words, she knew it was an attempt to mollify her.

"Yes, Mama, delicious!" Elijah agreed, always eager to emulate his beloved uncle.

She couldn't help the reluctant smile that bloomed then, ever so slightly smoothing the sharp edges of her anger into a state of weary exasperation. As she turned to look at her child, the amulet pressed against her ribcage where it was pinned into her stays. She could feel a warmth emanating from it, a tell-tale sign of just how much energy Lazarus had poured into its making.

"I am pleased that you like it," she said, "someone has to keep you boys fed for all of your adventures. Now, it is time to get ready for bed."

Sarah stood, collecting the dishes as she gave a pointed look to her husband. Understanding her unspoken request, Levi coaxed Elijah up to bed with the promise of reading him a story, giving his wife a moment to speak with his brother.

Lazarus helped her gather the plates and silverware, bringing them to the kitchen where he stood by her side at the wash basin, drying them as she washed. He worked quietly, knowing she had something to say and allowing her time to gather her thoughts.

"You are a good man, Lazarus," she began, keeping her gaze on her task. Her voice was quiet and contemplative, laced with both frustration and understanding. "And you are a better Uncle. What you have done is reckless, and I fear what consequence it will bring for all of us."

She paused, her hands gripping the edge of the basin as she contemplated how to express her mind.

"Sarah, I-," he interjected, setting down a large bowl to reach out to her. She turned to face him then.

"Let me finish," she insisted, waiting until he gave her a nod to continue. "I am angry with you, but I can also feel the love and strength that you put into these amulets. I know your only intentions were to safeguard yourself and us, but you must take more care from now on. For your own sake as well as your family's."

He nodded, acknowledging the truth of her statement, but loath to make a promise he wasn't certain that he could keep. Where his family was concerned, he had no trouble vowing to tread more carefully. When it came to himself though, he could feel the magic of the shadow demon's blood thrumming in his veins. The temptation to test the extent of his new abilities was difficult to ignore despite the looming threat of the angry demon.

"Good," she said, taking his silent demeanor as the contrition it at least partially was. "And if your demon harms my son, do not doubt that I will find a way to make you pay for it, invincibility or no. Understood?"

"I do not doubt it, sister," he replied, almost proudly.

This was the fierce woman that his brother loved so much. Sarah was often quiet and watchful, which could be mistaken for demure by a less observant person. When she did speak her mind though, it was clear how formidable she was.

They bid each other goodnight and Sarah went upstairs to join Levi in giving their son his bedtime story. Feeling pensive and restless, Lazarus headed for the back garden, hoping the night air would ease his agitation. A chorus of crickets welcomed him, chirping rhythmically as he wandered through the rows of plants.

He took a seat on the small wooden cart parked towards the rear of the garden where a copse of trees separated the manor yard from their farmland. The sky above was clear and bright with the waning gibbous moon. It seemed brighter than it should be. As his eyes adjusted, Lazarus realized that he could see much better in the dark than ever before.

Another benefit of the bond, he assumed.

He watched the stars twinkle and a few thin wisps of cloud waft across the sky for several minutes, allowing his mind to wander. It didn't take long for his thoughts to turn to the events of the previous night. He recalled the effervescent rush as the binding took hold, the unexpected heat he felt upon seeing the demon for the first time, and then the grip of terror as his life ebbed away. The hair on the back of his neck stood up, and after a moment he realized it wasn't just from the intensity of the memory.

He was no longer alone.

Quickly, Lazarus turned, casting glances all around in search of the source of his unease. The dark yard was still and he only now noticed that the crickets had ceased their chirping. His eyes panned right again, catching the slightest movement. A large silhouette leaned against a tree trunk, watching him. When his eyes locked onto it, the figure pushed off of the tree and started towards him with a leisurely menace that could only belong to one being.

"How are you alive?"

"Wait, please, allow me to speak."

Both of them began talking at the same time, the human's cordial tenor a stark contrast to the gravelly bass of the shadow demon. Lazarus put both hands up in front of himself reflexively; he knew it wouldn't stop the demon but hoped to placate enough of his aggression to begin a conversation. The shadow stopped just out of arm's reach, for which he was immensely grateful.

"Speak then, witch," he commanded, curtly.

The gruff sound gave rise to an embarrassingly fluttery sensation in the human's chest.

"Lazarus," he corrected, clearing his throat and affecting a calm, amicable tone. "My name is Lazarus Graydon. It is my great pleasure to make your acquaintance. May I know your name?"

"I do not have one," the shadow demon stated flatly, narrowing his eyes suspiciously. He was confused by the man's friendly demeanor; the previous summoner had never asked him for a name nor made any attempt to get to know him.

"Well, I must have something to call you," Lazarus insisted, patiently.

The shadow demon rolled his eyes in annoyance, a gesture that was almost unnoticeable except for the shifting reflections across their black surfaces.

"What was it that you called me in the summoning," he said, dismissively. "Tenebrae? That will do."

Lazarus smiled.

It seemed unlikely that the demon knew how apt a name he had chosen. It was the latin word for "darkness" or "night," but that was perhaps a conversation for another time. In the meantime, he intended to take full advantage of the precarious peace.

"Tenebrae. Yes, it suits you," he agreed honestly, feeling his body warm as he allowed his eyes to roam over the demon's form again. He relaxed a bit as it seemed like the shadow demon was less inclined to immediate violence this time. "As for how I am alive, that is a result of the ritual. It gifted me with some of your impressive regenerative abilities, and you will have acquired some of my corporeal qualities in return."

The shadow demon raised an eyebrow at this. He had not noticed any change in himself aside from the restriction on his ability to move about freely.

"And what would those be?" Tenebrae asked, curiosity forestalling the simmering rage that had driven him here, for the moment.

"You must excuse my lack of certainty on that point, the language of the grimoire is quite archaic," Lazarus explained. "It is difficult to be precise in the translation, you see, but I believe it is something to do with being immune to light."

The translation of the text that described the benefits of the binding was a little vague on the finer points beyond the 'nigh immortality for the human' part. Some of it he had assumed to be metaphorical, but seeing the intrigued look on the shadow demon's face, he began to consider that perhaps it was more literal.

Interesting, Tenebrae mused.

He had not attempted to move about here in the light of day; he was so used to avoiding it that the idea simply did not enter his mind. He decided that he would have to test this claim. If what the witch said was true, it could be quite useful.

Even more useful were I not trapped in this fucking forest.

"What kind of ritual, precisely?" he pressed, now even more convinced that this was no ordinary summoning.

The man paled slightly beneath the warm pink hue his skin had taken on again. Tenebrae had a feeling that he was not going to like the answer that was coming.

"A binding ritual," Lazarus admitted, bracing himself for the shadow demon's reaction. He hurried to expand on the statement, before Tenebrae could cut him off. "One which effects an exchange of power by binding a human's life to a shadow demon, bestowing both parties with benefits."

Lazarus flinched at the indignant growl that rolled through the demon. His eyes squeezed shut for a second before he found himself lifted off the ground by just one of the shadow's hands, which clamped viciously around his neck. His toes were only barely able to graze the ground, and he fought an urge to kick out in panic.

"You bound me?" the shadow snarled, squeezing tighter until he completely cut off the human's ability to breathe.

Lazarus's hands shot up, grabbing onto the demon's forearm. Tenebrae was surprised by how warm the soft skin of his palms was where it smoothed over his own rough and smoky flesh. He shivered slightly at the sensation; he'd never been touched this gently by a human before and it left an unexpected tingle in its wake.

"And now I cannot leave this place," he ground out, with an angry grimace.

What?

A look of confusion darkened Lazarus's face, and he pawed at the demon's hand insistently. He mouthed words but no sound came out, so he resorted to pleading with his eyes for the shadow to release him.

Tenebrae sighed and relented, easing his hold on the witch's throat just enough to allow him to speak.

"I was unaware that would happen," he rasped, sucking in a desperate breath of air between words.

His head spun from the lack of oxygen and the steely grip that was still restricting the flow of blood to his head. The demon's hand flexed against his throat, and Lazarus flushed a deep crimson at the breathy whimper that he was unable to suppress. It seemed to catch the demon off guard, and he racked his imprudently lust-addled mind for a distraction while Tenebrae blinked at him curiously.

"Kill me again if you wish, but I will be fit again tomorrow and you will still be here. We may as well get used to one another," Lazarus said, the hoarse sound making the words come off a bit more flirtatiously than he intended.

"You will release me from this bond," Tenebrae demanded grimly.

Idly, he wondered if he could get him to make that sound again, pressing his claws against the human's neck experimentally. It was intriguing, not quite fearful or pleading; it stirred a strange feeling in him.

"I cannot," Lazarus croaked, shaking his head as far as the demon's tight hold would allow. "I am sorry."

Tenebrae hummed low as he thought.

The man looked genuinely contrite, perhaps he was telling the truth about not having known that the spell would entrap him. But truth or not, it did nothing to change the reality of their situation.

"You will be," he growled, ominously, and then dissipated into a black mist before promptly vanishing.

Chapter 5

THE DEVIL IN THE WOODS

The next few days passed in a state of tense anticipation. Lazarus found himself startling at every small sound, hyper aware that the shadow demon could appear at any moment. He was torn between dreading what Tenebrae might do in retaliation for the binding, and hoping for another opportunity to appeal to his curiosity.

Their recent conversation seemed to be going rather well until the revelation that the shadow demon was now stuck in Graymourne because of the ritual. At least, it had gone far better than their first encounter; a "comparative success" as he described it in his journal.

Luckily, he did not have too much time to dwell on the matter with plenty of work to do around the farm.

It was time to begin harvesting the first of the fall crops. Together with Levi and a couple of hired hands from the village, they worked the barley fields, cutting the grain down by hand with a scythe. The Graydons preferred to work the land themselves as much as possible, both for financial reasons as well as privacy. But as their success and the farm grew, so too did their need for helping hands. With the assistance of the Dodson boys, Emmanuel and Enoch, the barley had been harvested in one day where alone it would have taken them at least two, if not more.

Today, Lazarus focused on catching up on repairs around the property. Damage to the outbuildings and fences had increased the last few days, and judging by the claw marks he found amongst the splintered wood, he knew the cause.

Leaning against the fence post that he had just finished replacing, Lazarus lifted the hem of his linen shirt to wipe the sweat from his face. The late afternoon sun warmed the skin of his chiseled abdomen, which glistened with a sheen of perspiration from the day's hard work.

He paused, suddenly, feeling eyes upon him.

Self-consciously, he tucked his shirt back in place and glanced around the golden lit field. There was no one to be seen. On a hunch, he crossed the open expanse and approached the line of trees where the shade of the forest began. Something rustled to his right and he thought he heard a faint growl.

"Tenebrae?" Lazarus called, tentatively, making his way slowly towards the source of the sounds.

Whatever it was had already gone by the time that he reached a large oak that was adorned with five distinct claw marks that were far too large and deep to be made by any of the local wildlife.

The demon's mischief seemed limited to the destruction of inanimate objects so far, much to Lazarus's relief. It was inconvenient but manageable.

The frequency of the sabotage seemed to be increasing, though, and he hoped that it wouldn't escalate beyond broken farm equipment. They would have to be careful about keeping the farm hands from noticing though. He sighed and started back for the house.

Levi was in the backyard when he arrived, crouched down near the side of their wagon. He looked up at his twin with a grim face and gestured to the spokes which had been sliced clean in half.

"This is getting costly, Laz," he said, standing up and wiping his hands on his breeches. "That's four fences, two barrels, the chicken coop, and now a wagon wheel we've had to repair just this week. We're due to take the next shipment of cheese to town tomorrow, if we miss Sarah's cousin on his way down from Manchester, it won't make it to New York on time. You know how much we rely on the market sales for revenue."

"I will sort the wheel out," Lazarus assured his brother, clasping him on the shoulder and pushing him towards the house. "After dinner. You should eat something. I will take the cart and meet Alden in the morning. Let me fix it, Levi."

His twin nodded, knowing that he meant more than just the wheel.

Voices conversing on the floor below woke Lazarus from a fitful sleep. He lay on his bed listening, unsure if he had been dreaming or if someone was about in the house. It was far too late for anyone to be up at this hour. But there it was again, a high piping voice and a low rumbling one. An icy shiver ran down his spine and he leapt out of bed.

The distant conversation came into focus as he hurried quietly down the stairs.

"Are you a friend of my Uncle Laz'rus?" Elijah asked, brightly, not a hint of fear lacing his curious tone.

"Not exactly," the shadow demon intoned ominously.

"How come you're solid? Mama says spirits are incorp'ral," the little boy insisted with conviction.

Lazarus rounded the corner to see his four-year-old nephew reaching a hand out to the intimidating shadow demon before him. Even crouched down as he was, Tenebrae loomed almost twice as tall as the boy.

"I am not a spirit, child," the demon answered, sounding almost amused by the boy's questioning.

Darting over quickly, Lazarus shoved himself between the two, pushing his nephew farther behind him protectively. The shadow demon tilted his head, amused at the action, and stood up to his full imposing height. Lazarus suspected that Tenebrae could hear the wild thumping of his heart, and tried to take a calming breath before turning to the now grumbling child.

"Back to bed with you, Elijah," he said firmly, voice trembling slightly. "You know your mama will be furious if she finds you awake so late." Lazarus gave the boy a gentle push towards the stairs, to which he pouted slightly but toddled up to his room with a few reluctant glances back towards his new 'friend'. When the sound of little feet pattering ceased, Lazarus turned back to face the demon.

"I don't care what you do to me, but please," he implored, voice filled with quiet desperation, "do not harm my family. They are innocent in all this."

Regardless of his confidence in the amulets they wore, he found himself terrified at the idea of the shadow demon focusing his ire on his loved ones.

"Curious," Tenebrae rumbled, taking a step forward and invading the man's space.

Lazarus reflexively took a step backwards, retreating from the advancing demon until his back hit the wall. The shadow leaned down, his face brushing along the side of the human's neck as he took in a deep whiff; the warm cinnamon and clove of his natural scent was spiced with the bitter tang of fear. Lazarus's breath hitched at the contact when Tenebrae's nose ghosted across his skin. His body tensed, unsure whether to flinch away or lean into the shadow's touch.

"W-what is?" he stuttered, still trying to decide if he was frightened or turned on by the demon's proximity. When Tenebrae shifted to meet his eyes with a beguiling smirk twisting the corner of his dark lips, Lazarus thought, *Oh no, it's both, isn't it.*

"Your fear," Tenebrae said, tapping his claws against the plaster wall at either side of the man, caging him in.

"This is the first time you smell genuinely afraid. Do you not fear for yourself, witch?"

The shadow demon found himself enjoying the way the human squirmed under the intense scrutiny, his full rosy lips trembling slightly as he spoke and his wide hazel eyes never daring to look away from the black depths of the demon's.

Tormenting this human might prove to be more satisfying than I initially anticipated, he thought.

"Not as much as I fear for them," the man admitted, reluctantly.

He knew it was probably unwise to admit to the rather appalling lack of self-preservation he seemed to have around the shadow demon, but for some reason, he couldn't bring himself to lie.

The demon merely hummed in response, raising a claw to touch the side of Lazarus's face. He took a moment to study the human in earnest.

I suppose he is rather pretty, for a human, Tenebrae thought absently, recalling the way the golden afternoon light had highlighted the planes of the witch's toned torso while he watched him work in the fields the other day. The mental image made him feel hungry in an unfamiliar way, and a sudden urge had him dragging the sharp point of his claw across the human's cheek in a shallow reddening line.

Lazarus winced at the pain, but remained still, helplessly enraptured by the shadow demon's piercing gaze. His skin tingled as black wisps of shadow wove the scratch back together almost instantaneously.

Tenebrae pointedly licked the blood from his claw, before taking a step back. Lazarus only had a brief moment to be distracted by the inhumanly pointed length of that black tongue before the demon spoke again.

"Be assured," the shadow demon said, "my quarrel is not with them. Save your fear for yourself, human."

He took his leave then, casually melding into a dark corner of the room.

Lazarus exhaled a stuttering breath, and slid shakily down the wall. His heart was still pounding and he was mortified to realize that the breeches he had hastily pulled on now felt uncomfortably tight.

That went well, he thought, dubiously.

Early the next morning, Lazarus hitched the small one-person cart with its now-repaired wheel to their horse and prepared to set out for town. As the horse's hooves echoed loudly against the wooden planks of the covered bridge, he replayed the previous night's events over again in his mind.

Though he had felt much like a mouse being toyed with by a cat, it had been an almost cordial interaction with the demon, relatively speaking. The promise to keep the rest of the Graydons out of their disagreement was reassuring. His seemingly unshakeable attraction to the shadow demon, however, was becoming a bit of a problem.

It was a distraction at the very least. The dreams he'd had after they spoke last night brought a blush to his face even in vague remembrance; he had awoken that morning panting and painfully hard, with the fleeting impression of a rough tongue against his skin. Against his better judgement, he hadn't been able to resist sliding a hand beneath the hem of his nightshirt to finish what the dream started, biting his lip to keep from moaning the demon's name as he came.

Arriving at the center of town, Lazarus tried to clear his mind and focus on the task at hand. Alden Taylor was already set up, delivering items to a few townsfolk and taking on goods to be conveyed down the road to other villages. Sarah's cousin was a good man and an excellent merchant, reliable and punctual. The Graydons owed part of their good fortune to their continued arrangement with him, in which he delivered their goods to be sold in wealthier markets. Lazarus made his way over to where it seemed that the gregarious blonde merchant was being caught up on the local gossip.

"Folks been hearing all sorts of evil sounds coming out of them woods," Silence Best told the merchant. She was perhaps the most inappropriately named person in town, as the biggest gossip. A short woman with a hawkish face and drab gray hair, she seemed to have little to do other than mire herself in everyone else's business since the death of her equally unpleasant husband. She turned to look over her shoulder as Alden nodded to Lazarus behind her. "Oh, Mr. Graydon, you must have heard it, living over the bridge that way. Devilish growling and whatnot."

"Can't say that I have, Widow Best," he replied in a carefully congenial tone. "You may rely upon me to keep an ear out though. Should I hear any devils afoot, you will be the first to know."

This was an unwelcome development. He knew that the shadow demon's shenanigans might eventually draw attention, but to have the town's tongues wagging so soon did not bode well.

"There's something unnatural in the forest, alright," a man agreed from the other side of Alden's wagon. Amos Dinsmore, a local hunter and trapper, was sorting a pile of furs he must have sold to the merchant. "Seen claw marks the other day, too big and too deep to be made by any animal I've seen. And the growls! Inhuman. If you ask me, the Devil's in the woods 'round this town."

"Surely, it could simply be an unusually large bear, Amos," Lazarus interjected, throwing an appealing look at Alden as he spoke. "This time of year, they'll be fattening up for the winter, will they not?"

The merchant caught on quickly and jumped in to help steer the conversation away from devils and the supernatural.

"Mr. Graydon's right," he offered, "we've had some well sized bears near Manchester this year. That would explain the growls and all." With a pat on the shoulder, he paid Amos Dinsmore for his furs and sent him on his way. "Can I get you anything else, Mistress Best?"

With her business concluded and her audience disbanded, Silence shook her head and ambled away towards her house, no doubt contemplating who to tell first about this interaction.

"What was all that about?" Alden asked, as he began to help Lazarus transfer the shipment of cheese to his cart.

"Who knows? You know how these village folk can be," he deflected with a shrug.

The merchant eyed him dubiously, but nodded and didn't press the issue while they worked.

"Take care, Lazarus," he said, clasping the other man's hand in both of his. "I will come by the manor on my way back through town, it would be good to see cousin Sarah and the boy."

"Our home is always open to you, Alden," Graydon replied, bidding the merchant safe travels and heading back home. There was still much work to do and the day was just getting started.

Chapter 6

My new companion does not take well to idleness, Lazarus wrote in his journal one evening. A bored shadow demon, he had quickly come to learn, is an absolute menace. Sabotaging inanimate objects around the farm only seemed to hold his attention for about a week before the inconvenient mischief escalated to something a bit more threatening.

After a long day of chores and repairs, Lazarus ascended the stairs in the manor, eager to slide into bed for some much needed rest. Upon opening the door to his bedroom, however, he was immediately accosted with an acrid coppery smell.

Hesitantly, he stepped inside and went to light a candle to illuminate the darkened space. He stopped short, realizing that he could see well enough in the dark now not to need one.

In the center of the narrow-planked floor, a crude approximation of the summoning circle had been drawn in blood. Dread gripped him as he noticed a large dark lump lying on the floor against the far wall. He stepped carefully around the still wet symbol and approached the object. It was a sizable deer, a stag with a large rack of antlers. Its throat had been clawed open in a mockingly familiar way, and the resulting fountain of red liquid then used to messily paint the sigil upon the floorboards.

Lazarus sighed deeply, looking into the lifeless glassy eyes of the deer for a long moment before running his hands anxiously through his hair. It looked like the day just got a lot longer.

He trudged down the stairs to retrieve a mop and a pail of water to clean the mess from the floor. Removing the stag from his bedroom would require assistance though, and he was already dreading what Levi would have to say about this development.

Mopping up the gore from his bedroom floor afforded him time to think, and the more he thought, the angrier he became. How could he have known that the shadow demon would be trapped here after the binding? If he had known that would happen, Lazarus thought he might not have gone through with the ritual. Or maybe he would have. The point was, he didn't know at the time and now he was cleaning blood off the floor when he should be sleeping all because the stubborn shadow demon preferred to sow chaos over simply talking about the situation like a reasonable person.

I suppose that is to be expected of demons, he lamented, wringing out another mop full of bloody water. *Next time we meet, I will make him listen to me, no matter what it takes.*

After finally wiping up the last of the mess, he took the pail outside to empty the stained contents and rinsed out the mop with water from the well. Returning to the manor, he found Levi awake and waiting for him in the kitchen.

"Awfully late to be mopping, is it not, brother?" Levi questioned.

"That it is, but needs must," he sighed tiredly, replacing the mop and pail in the closet. "I require your help with something, but I would very much appreciate it if we could forego any discussion about it until the morning."

Sensing his twin was nearly at his wits end, Levi nodded and followed him up the stairs. His raised eyebrows betrayed his alarm at seeing the large dead animal in his brother's bedroom, but he managed to keep from making any comments about it.

"Grab the hind feet and help me get this thing down to the barn would you?" Lazarus asked, hopefully. The two of them were tall, both just about six feet, and fit from the difficult labor on the farm, but the pair still struggled to get the large animal down the stairs and out of the house.

The barn was equipped with basic skinning and butchering tools. They didn't often use them for game, but both brothers were knowledgeable enough to process a deer. Levi moved to begin, but his twin quickly stopped him.

"I will do it," Lazarus insisted, "this is my mess to clean up."

Levi could see the exhaustion and irritation setting in. This business with the demon was clearly taking a toll on him and he hated to see his usually carefree brother so dour.

"Nonsense," Levi chided him, taking the skinning knife from his hand. "It will go faster with two of us. And besides, when was the last time we had venison? This will keep the family fed for weeks."

A tired smile spread over Lazarus's face, his mood instantly bolstered by his brother's optimism. He was right, the meat from such a large deer would provide plenty of meals.

It was a gift, even if it had been intended as a threat.

Fortunately, the dead animal in the bedroom seemed to be a singular occurrence. For a time, Lazarus had worried that there would be more, like a cat periodically leaving its kills for their human to find. But soon, the demon found something else infinitely more amusing to keep him occupied: startling the very life out of Lazarus any time he walked by a shadow.

It began with an inky hand shooting out from beneath his bed frame to latch onto his ankle in the morning, which caused him to shriek and trip, catching himself on the nearby desk. Lazarus kicked out and jerked his foot free from the grasping claws, while the demon's low throaty chuckle resounded from the dark floor. He dressed quickly and escaped to the first floor, only to be snatched by the arm as he passed the slightly ajar door of a linen closet.

That evening the family welcomed Sarah's cousin, Alden, into the home for dinner, and Lazarus silently begged the universe that the demon would let him be until the visitor left. Surreptitiously eyeing the dark corners of the room, he found it difficult to be his usual gregarious self after being on his guard all day.

He excused himself rather quickly after the meal, ascended the stairs, and made a beeline for his bedroom, eager to get some rest after the exhausting day. He hadn't slept more than two hours, before he suddenly was jolted awake by movement. He found himself tangled in the heavy quilt as it was dragged from the bed, nearly taking him with it.

The next morning was suspiciously calm, almost lulling him into a false sense of security until a sharp-clawed swipe from a blackened tree hollow caught his calf, shredding through his stockings as well as his leg.

Any time he strayed from the bright glow of sunlight, he found himself dodging an attack, always followed by the taunting sound of the shadow demon's mirth. Though the intermittent strikes frequently drew blood, they were not especially harmful. Lazarus could tell that Tenebrae was merely toying with him, and apparently having a grand time doing so. The knowledge that his suffering was a source of entertainment for the shadow only further rankled his rapidly-fraying nerves.

He found himself jumping at every small noise and peripheral movement by day three. Two of his shirts and three pairs of stockings had required mending by now and he was slightly delirious from lack of sleep. When he did manage to sleep, his dreams were no refuge, his mind serving up a disconcerting melange of violent and erotic visions.

Thankfully, everyone was out of the house on the third day, when the worst incident occurred.

As soon as Lazarus took the first step onto the stairs, he knew something was awry. Time had seemed to slow, and his skin prickled with awareness. His head swung side to side, searching for the source of danger.

He should have looked down.

His back foot left the floor and caught on a shadow tendril that stretched out from under the hall table and across the landing like a trip wire.

Flailing for balance, he had missed the railing by less than an inch, his fingers glancing off the polished wood as he tipped forwards. Headlong, he had tumbled down the stairs in a way that he was certain would break his neck. It would have healed of course, thanks to the shadows in his blood, but it still would have hurt like hell. By some miracle of happenstance, he only ended up in a crumpled heap at the foot of the staircase, his body sore and his pride bruising even further from the satisfied laughter that echoed from above.

His nerves were raw by the end of the fourth day, wound tightly as a bow string. Lazarus had been unusually irritable all day, choosing to work alone in the back fields rather than risk taking his mood out on Levi or the hired hands. As the afternoon waned, he set out for the manor, stomping diagonally through the trees as he hurried to beat the sunset and get out of the open.

The shadows lengthened as the sun began to edge its way towards the horizon, casting long dark lines from the tree trunks all around him.

Lazarus felt the hair on the back of his neck stand up.

He tensed, anticipating what was about to happen. This time, when the sinewy dark arm snaked out from a cleft in the large oak tree at his side, he was ready for it.

Lazarus grabbed the limb around the wrist with both hands and yanked, twisting his body and throwing all of his weight into the movement. His tired muscles screamed in protest, but surprisingly, he managed to heave the unsuspecting shadow demon out of the darkness. The pair of them tumbled across the leaf strewn ground, both grappling for control.

It was the very last thing that Tenebrae had expected the human to do, which lent Lazarus the element of surprise that he needed to gain the upper hand, however temporarily, against someone of such greater size and strength. Out of curiosity and a tiny bit of budding admiration, the shadow demon graciously allowed the furious human to wrestle his way on top of him.

"Enough!" Lazarus shouted, panting as he straddled the demon's waist. His hands gripped Tenebrae's muscular, bone-plated shoulders tightly, blunt fingertips digging into the smokey flesh.

The shadow demon smirked at him from below.

"Did you not like my gift?" Tenebrae purred, antagonistically.

He grinned then, watching an irate frown spread over the human's face and noticing that the man even let out a little growl.

How cute, he thought, *this should be interesting.*

The man's eyes were flashing with fury, his chestnut hair tangled and wild; the shadow demon decided that he liked seeing Lazarus a bit unraveled.

Wrath looks good on him, he thought, enjoying the fruits of his tormenting.

"No, you bloody menace," Lazarus seethed through gritted teeth, "I do not enjoy having my farm constantly sabotaged or finding an animal carcass bleeding upon the floor of my bedroom. Nor do I enjoy dodging attacks at all hours of the day from some self-important, overgrown storm-cloud."

His chest heaved and rage vibrated through every muscle in his body.

"Your reflexes are improving, though," Tenebrae teased, shifting to prop himself up on his elbows.

The movement caused Lazarus to slide back further into his lap, and the man's fingernails reflexively dug into his shoulders.

"What the fuck do you want from me?" Lazarus demanded, irritably, rolling his eyes in exasperation.

His jaw clenched with anger and his grip tightened, wanting nothing more than to wipe the smug smirk off of the demon's annoyingly handsome face. His question seemed to do the trick, though, and the shadow's expression darkened, all traces of mirth dropping from his face.

"You know what I want from you, witch," Tenebrae growled, fixing the man with an unamused stare.

He sat up fully then, leaning down to glare at him face to face, not seeming to notice the man's borderline painful grip on him.

"I cannot," Lazarus breathed, his exhausted desperation breaking through the wall of his anger. Frustrated, he shook his head, holding back the indignant tears that prickled at his eyes. Swallowing his pride, he began to plead. "There must be something else… Anything."

The shadow demon only cocked his head slightly and continued to stare at him impassively, unmoved by his entreaty. The uncompromising blankness of his expression relit the fuse of the witch's fury and then, sitting atop of Tenebrae's muscular thighs with their faces mere inches from each other, something snapped in Lazarus. One moment he was grinding his teeth, poised to begin shouting a tirade at the infuriatingly attractive shadow demon, and the next moment he launched into motion, his body moving of its own accord before his mind could do anything to stop it.

Lazarus lunged forward with an explosive force, his lips colliding with the demon's like a meteor hitting the earth. His mind was completely blank for a minute, except for the sensation of his lips pressed against the warm rough curvature of the demon's mouth. Instinctively, his tongue swiped along the seam of Tenebrae's lips, prompting a low sound from the shadow. All at once, his sense of self-preservation caught up to him and he realized what he was doing.

He reared back, eyes flying open in alarm as he let go of the demon's shoulders as if he'd been burned. Stalling in panic, his hands hovered in the air between them awkwardly. Try as he might, Lazarus could not for the life of him decipher the look on Tenebrae's face.

Where before he had looked merely unamused, now the shadow's pitch black eyes were sparking with a blistering intensity that Lazarus hadn't seen since the night of the ritual. Bloodthirsty was the closest descriptor the witch could think of, but even that didn't quite seem to cover it.

Shit, I'm about to die again, aren't I? he thought, with a sigh of resignation.

He tensed, bracing for an attack.

Instead of the anticipated slice of claws, though, his world spun and he suddenly found himself flipped onto his back and pinned harshly against the dirt beneath them. He barely had time to register the ferocious growl or the set of claws closing around his throat before the shadow demon's mouth descended on his, muffling the yelp of surprise that he made.

The kiss was aggressive and unskilled. Tenebrae's sharp teeth nicked his lips and a surprisingly prehensile tongue smoothed over the tiny cuts before bullying its way into his mouth at the first opportunity. He tried to meet its clumsy movements with his own as the shadow overwhelmed him.

Mindlessly, Lazarus wrapped his free hand around the demon's waist, gripping onto the bony protrusions along his spine to pull him flush against his chest. He felt Tenebrae's large hand clutch tighter around his other wrist where it was pinned firmly against the earth and a thick thigh wedged itself between his legs. When the heavy weight of Tenebrae's hips ground against the growing erection in his breeches, Lazarus moaned around the intrusion of the shadow demon's tongue.

The sound seemed to startle both of them out of the spell they were under, and the frenzied kiss was suddenly broken.

They stared at each other wide eyed, the normally unflappable shadow demon looking equally as bewildered by what had just happened as Lazarus did. Drawing a sharp breath, the witch opened his mouth to speak and then, suddenly, Tenebrae was gone, leaving him confused and achingly hard on the forest floor.

Oh, fuck. What have I done?

Chapter 7

THE BLIGHT

Five days passed without any sign of the shadow demon after their confusing encounter. It was a welcome change of pace from the previous weeks; nothing was mysteriously broken and Lazarus was no longer constantly looking over his shoulder or eyeing every dark corner with dread after the first couple of peaceful days. Admittedly, the lack of contact weighed on him for other reasons.

What was I thinking? he lamented, drifting back to the moment he'd kissed Tenebrae once again.

He remembered feeling absolutely furious, overtaken by an angry energy that needed an outlet somehow and he'd acted purely on impulse. He tried not to ruminate too long on why that impulse was to kiss the person who'd spent the last few weeks trying to kill, maim, and torment him. Lazarus leaned his chin on his palm and closed his eyes.

I have the most inconvenient taste in men.

"Alright, brother?" Levi asked, startling him with a sturdy clap on the shoulder.

He picked his head up to find his twin standing over him with a concerned look etched on his face.

"I am alright, just thinking," Lazarus replied, debating how much to share of his current troubles. Perhaps it would help to speak to his brother about what had happened. He set his pen down and closed his journal. "It is possible that I may have blundered rather spectacularly."

He looked down at his hands atop the table, stopping himself from anxiously picking at a callous on his thumb. A flash of lightning temporarily illuminated the room, followed a few minutes later by a loud clap of thunder. Outside the manor, an unseasonable thunderstorm continued to rage. It had forestalled their work on the farm for most of the day already.

"Whatever it is, it cannot be that bad," Levi reassured him, taking a seat next to him at the table. "We have had no repairs to make this week. You must have done something to placate the demon."

"That is, perhaps, the problem," Lazarus muttered, hoping his twin could not see the furious blush that crept over his face at the thought of how their current state of peace came about.

Perhaps it wasn't such a mistake, he considered. *He did kiss me as well, rather enthusiastically, at that. But then, why is he avoiding me now?*

Anxiety crept back in, leading his thoughts in a dizzying spiral.

"Laz," his brother called, redirecting his attention to the present. "Tell me what has happened."

"I, well, I lost my temper," he started, breathing a weary sigh and fixing his gaze on the ceiling. He knew he wouldn't be able to get the words out if he looked his brother in the eye right now. "The demon had been tormenting me. Striking out anytime I was near a shadow, more to scare me than harm of course, but nonetheless it took a toll. He managed to find the very end of my patience and so, I struck back. We fought, and he let me win, I am certain of that. And then I, um, I kissed him."

"Oh," Levi said quietly, taking a moment to process the unexpected revelation. Rain pattered loudly against the windows as they sat in a tense silence. Eventually, he asked, "Did he return it?"

"Yes," Lazarus laughed wryly, his voice colored with his own disbelief of the situation. "Yes, he very much did. And then promptly vanished. I have not heard from him since."

Saying it aloud brought some clarity, and he realized that what he was feeling was the sting of rejection.

"Be thankful for the respite in the meantime," Levi suggested gently, reading the dejection in his twin's tone. "Perhaps he simply needs some time to come around. If the minister's son could not resist your charms, I doubt that a demon can."

Lazarus's head snapped up at the teasing tone that his brother's voice took, face bright red at being called out for his previous affair. They didn't speak of it often, but it was one of the reasons they had moved to Graymourne years ago. He had broken things off with Josiah when it seemed they were close to being found out. The budding village to the North had seemed like a perfect haven to escape the rumors and set down roots. With their wealth, they had been welcomed as co-founders with open arms, and Josiah had gone on to marry a nice, reputable girl just like his father wanted.

"I suppose you are right," he acquiesced, an uncertain but hopeful grin blooming as he took in his twin's gentle expression.

The storm had blown through later that night, and the Graydons were able to begin their corn harvest the next day. Emmanuel and Enoch weren't able to pitch in with the labor until the following day, busy helping their father with repairs to their own homestead. From the sounds of things, the properties east of the river had fared much worse in the storm.

Despite the unseasonable storm just before the harvest, the corn yield from the Graydon fields was bountiful. They would likely have enough to sell as well as generate food for the family and the livestock. With the help of Sarah's careful calculations, the brothers divided the crops into stores for their needs and set aside what they could spare to sell. Levi volunteered to take it to town in the morning, concerned that if other farms hadn't been so lucky, some folks might be in need of the extra grain.

He was, unfortunately, more right than he knew. The farms east of Lucent River had been hit hard with hail during the thunderstorm. Each and every one had their corn crop decimated just before harvest time.

Whether it was the shelter of the surrounding forest, the slightly lower elevation on their side of the river, or something else, the Graydon farm had been spared the devastating deluge. A little rain and some bombastic thunder had cost them a day's work, but otherwise their farm was untouched.

It didn't look good.

Combined with the continued talk of disturbances in Whitmack Forest, which they lived on the edge of, a 'miraculous' sparing of their harvest when everyone else had suffered harshly only served to solidify certain townsfolk's suspicions about the brothers.

Levi rolled into town with healthy corn to sell and all hell broke loose.

"How come your crop looks like that when everyone else's was destroyed?" James Cresswell sneered. "What kind of witchcraft is that, huh?"

His father, Bazel, was one of the other two founders of the town and their farm was the second largest in the village. The Cresswells, particularly, had always been envious of the Graydon twins' wealth, even though it was only slightly greater than their own.

"Simple luck is all," Levi countered in a placatingly calm tone. "And a blessing at that, we have enough to share. We would be happy to donate the surplus to any who need it."

Originally, they had hoped to make a small profit from the extra crops, but seeing the dire situation the other farms were in, it didn't feel right.

"Oh, you want us to take your devil corn, is that it?" a familiar loud nasal voice chimed in. Levi immediately recognized Silence Best's accusatory tone. "Grown over in that haunted forest. We'll not be falling for that trick, young man."

Levi took a deep breath and tried to summon as much patience as he could muster. This was going south fast. A crowd was starting to gather, drawn to the commotion and the sight of his cart full of corn.

"Widow Best, we simply wish to help the good people of our community," he offered. "As we know they would help us in our times of need." He kept his tone even, keenly aware of the growing number of ears listening to the exchange.

"And when's that, then? When are the Graydons ever in need?" James Cresswell demanded. "It's hard to call it luck when things always go your way. More like 'charmed' isn't it?"

Murmurs of assent rolled through the crowd; hushed whispers of 'witchcraft', and 'charmed', and 'devildry' flaring here and there.

"Hold on, now," Levi said, trying to regain control of the situation.

"We won't be told what to do by no witch," Silence Best interrupted, poking a gnarled finger in his direction, emboldened by the grumbling spectators. "And twins too. Unnatural!"

The gossipmongers had always danced around the accusation, but this was the first time anyone had spoken it outright. The word seemed to light a fire in the crowd. Shouting broke out and the townsfolk jostled each other as they lurked closer. Levi backed towards his cart, unsure whether to run or try to get on his horse.

"Grab him!"

"Put him in the stocks!"

"Witch!"

"Let's get the other one!"

At the mention of his brother, he turned to run, but a few villagers had already flanked him.

He was surrounded.

By the time the unruly mob had dragged a struggling and protesting Lazarus to the market at the center of town, Levi had his feet securely restrained at the ankles by the wooden stocks. He sat uncomfortably on the stone slab that served as a bench, his legs stretched out straight before him. The Reverend Hezekiah Poole stood a few feet away, arms crossed, conferring with Elbert and another church elder, Bazel Cresswell, presumably about the punishment of the Graydon twins.

"What has come over you all, we are your neighbors!" Lazarus exclaimed, indignantly, as three men manhandled him onto the bench beside his brother.

They wrestled his feet into the restraints and then scampered back to join the crowd.

"It is not we who are in question here, Mr. Graydon," Elbert Poole announced with a sneer, his arrogant tone carrying over the unquiet crowd. His eyes twinkled with cruel glee, relishing the chance to finally air out his simmering hatred for the twins. "What have you to say for yourselves?"

"We have done nothing but offer to share our crop with the townsfolk," he insisted.

Truly, there had been no witchcraft involved in the blighting of the town's corn nor the sparing of their own. Plenty of other things, yes, but on the subject of the harvest, his words were absolutely true. But that didn't make a bit of difference to the gathered mob.

"They will not hear you, brother," Levi admonished him quietly. He had made all the same appeals he knew his twin would make, only for them to fall on deaf ears. Even Lazarus would not be able to talk them out of this situation.

"Admit your sins and repent," Reverend Poole commanded sternly, raising his voice so all could hear. His enjoyment of the spectacle was more subtle than Elbert's, yet it was still plain on his face and the villagers were all too eager to play their part to see it. "You shall remain here for five days, or until you confess."

"We cannot admit that which we have not done," Lazarus contended, levelly. "It would be a sin to lie." The intensity of his glare belied the calm tone of his voice.

Elbert huffed, denied the drama he desired when the twins steadfastly resisted the Reverend's baiting and remained resolute. Hezekiah turned away from the accused men, dismissively.

"God will sort these sinners out," he announced, waving the gathered throng of people away.

They went about their business begrudgingly, reluctant to leave the ripe drama unfolding in their midst. It did not go unnoticed by the Graydon brothers that their offering of corn was swiftly confiscated by the Cresswells. Worries about 'devil corn' notwithstanding, they were certain that if it were shared at all, the Pooles might partake of some, but the rest of town would go without.

The day passed slowly. With nothing to do but wait, the twins spent much of it in silence, watching the town bustle as usual. Occasionally folks would swear at them as they walked by. They had to dodge spittle and the odd vegetable lobbed their way, but fortunately food was too precious to waste on throwing it at the accused for the most part.

Once she had finished her chores, Sarah brought them dinner and some blankets, leaving Elijah with a neighbor so he wouldn't have to see his father and uncle in the stocks. She was steadfast, but there were still faint tear marks beneath her eyes where it was clear she had been crying. When Lazarus began apologizing to her, she shook her head sternly.

"This is not your fault," she said, resolutely. Anger was clear in her tone.

Though she had known, as the brothers did, about the suspicions that the villagers harbored, she never imagined that a simple act of weather could incite such a reaction. Obviously, the situation with the demon that her brother-in-law had summoned did not help, but she couldn't place all the blame on that. This had been brewing a long time.

"Thank you, my love," Levi said, raising her hand to his lips for a gentle kiss. Sarah bid goodbye to her husband and then his brother, and set out to return home.

The first night passed excruciatingly slowly and in discomfort. The cold stone of the bench sapped the warmth from their bones despite the woolen blankets that Sarah had brought for them. A clear sky kept them blessedly dry, but the bright sliver of moon did nothing to help them sleep. The two brothers managed to angle themselves so that they could lean almost back to back, propped upright sturdily enough to doze a bit.

It was going to be an uncomfortable five days.

Tenebrae paced the void restlessly, back and forth across the inky expanse of nothingness.

What the fuck was that? he scoffed for the hundredth time, re-examining the moment again.

The shadow demon wasn't completely naive; he had observed humans engaging in physical affection before, perhaps not in great detail, but certainly enough to know what the gesture was and what it meant. So, he ventured that a better question would be 'why' or 'how?'

Things had been going so well; his diligent tormenting was finally paying off. The human was on edge, fearful, and desperate, just where he wanted him. But when the deceptively soft-looking brunette had actually managed to pull him from the shadows, he was taken by surprise.

It was a bold move, even if, as Tenebrae suspected, the witch had gained a bit of supernatural strength in the process of their binding. He'd been impressed by the ferocity with which Lazarus had confronted him, going easy on the man in their tussle just to see what he would do.

What did he hope to gain by such an action? Tenebrae wondered, certain that it must have been a ploy of some sort. *A distraction, perhaps? It must be a trick of some kind. He couldn't possibly desire a demon, could he?*

However he looked at it, it didn't make any sense. The only thing more confusing to him than what Lazarus had done was his own reaction.

After the initial contact, Lazarus had looked so surprised, lips still parted as if he was about to speak and an enticing dusting of pink across his cheeks. All Tenebrae remembered thinking was that he wanted to devour him. When the sharp edges of his teeth snagged against the witch's plump lips and little droplets of blood arose, they sparked against his tongue, fanning the flames of whatever madness had seized him. He could still taste the inside of his mouth, and feel the way Lazarus had clutched onto him as if he genuinely wanted the shadow demon closer.

And the fucking sound he made, Tenebrae recalled, a small growl rumbling at the memory of it.

The sound of the moan had startled him, almost as surprising as the way that it had caused his cock to stir inside its sheath. He'd broken the kiss then, his mind slamming back into overdrive as he tried to make sense of the situation. The witch had looked just as shocked as he felt, but Tenebrae couldn't be sure if that wasn't all just a ruse. What if this was some kind of magic, a further attempt to control and entrap him?

I will have to be more careful, the shadow demon thought.

Having had a few days to regroup after the bewildering encounter, he felt like it was time to confront the witch. This situation had gone on long enough, he wanted it to be done with one way or another.

Stepping out of shadowspace, Tenebrae found himself in a slightly different part of the forest than he'd grown accustomed to. In addition to tormenting Lazarus, he had spent some time exploring the region and testing the bounds of his cage. Fortunately, much of the area was uninhabited wilderness, which he explored in great detail. The shadow demon could walk the length of this verdant prison, from top to bottom, in about four hours if he moved in a straight line.

The place where he stood now was farther east than the usual boundary. He moved west, testing a hunch, and immediately found resistance. It seemed that the confines of his entrapment had moved somewhat. Not far, but just enough to be noticeable.

Moving quickly through the night, he traversed the now familiar way to the Graydon Manor. The windows were all dark and he could hear only faint sounds of movement within. He shifted into a less corporeal form, seeping into the silent house as a nearly imperceptible fog. Tenebrae made a quick search of the rooms, but found both the witch and his brother missing.

Only the woman and the overly curious young boy were home, both fast asleep.

The men's absence was unusual based on the patterns of behavior he had observed over the last few weeks. Though he was loath to make use of their 'bond,' it was his best chance for finding his quarry. He pushed back into the void, holding the image of Lazarus in his mind until he felt a familiar prickle along one side of his body. It was irritatingly easy to locate the man, which he could only assume was due to the fact that they now each had a not insignificant amount of the other's blood in their veins. He tried not to let that knowledge affect him as he crossed the distance in several long strides.

When Tenebrae stepped back out into terrestrial space, he found himself in the one place he had avoided during his explorations: the center of Graymourne village. He had observed it from afar, watching the village folk bustle about their day from across the river. This particular portion of his confinement could remain unexplored for all he cared. Tenebrae had one too many humans to deal with already. He would have happily continued to shun the town, except for the fact that apparently the witch was currently in it.

He stood in a grassy open area surrounded by dirt lanes and small buildings on all sides. The only structures on the green were a small covered well and a strange wooden contraption, behind which the Graydon brothers sat upon a stone with their legs held fast by wood planks. They appeared to be sleeping, propped awkwardly against each other. Lazarus was uncovered while his brother shivered beside him beneath two thin blankets.

Dropping to a crouch beside Lazarus, the shadow demon took hold of his arm and roughly shook him awake. The man's bloodshot eyes opened blearily and he blinked in confusion. His twin grumbled slightly but remained asleep.

"Why are you here?" Tenebrae demanded, irritably, while the barely awake Lazarus reconciled that he was, in fact, not dreaming.

"Not by choice, I can assure you," he croaked quietly, his voice hoarse from dehydration and exhaustion.

The shadow demon wondered how long they had been out here. Neither of them looked well.

"Someone imprisoned you here?" Tenebrae snarled.

He would have expected the irony of his captor's imprisonment to bring him joy or at least some amusement, but he found only fury instead. The idea of someone else persecuting the man roused an unexpectedly territorial reaction in him.

Lazarus nodded.

"The storm destroyed everyone's crops but our own," he explained, clearing his throat as he shifted uncomfortably on the cold stone. "Townspeople accused us of witchcraft, so here we are. Five days in the stocks."

He gestured tiredly to the wooden contraption, to illustrate his point.

"That is… ridiculous," the shadow demon stated flatly, bewildered by both the supposed crime and its punishment. Humans were so strange sometimes. "They did not know you were a witch before?"

"No. Shhhh," the man shushed him, looking around furtively, though it was the middle of the night and nearly pitch black with the new moon. "Any kind of witchcraft is forbidden by the church. They have long been suspicious of us, but this is the first time we have been accused outright."

"Why did they suspect you? Something more than the weather, I hope," Tenebrae snarked, dryly. The man had summoned a demon and these people punished him for a storm he could not possibly control.

Idiots, he thought, derisively.

"Not much better, to be honest," Lazarus admitted with a wry chuckle. "Our luck and success mostly. And because I will not take a wife."

He frowned deeply, letting out a weary sigh. Tenebrae could tell it was an issue that weighed on him heavily, but even after the witch explained what a 'wife' was, he still didn't understand.

"You do not desire one?" the shadow demon questioned, appraising the man's reluctant demeanor. It seemed to be a fairly standard practice from his somewhat limited understanding of human behavior. In his travels, he had seen plenty of humans paired as the man described.

"Not a wife, no. Perhaps a husband," he answered, shyly, casting his eyes towards the ground as his face warmed. He gathered himself for a moment before meeting Tenebrae's curious eyes again. "I, um, I am only attracted to men. Of course, that too is forbidden by the church. I had a partner where we lived before, but we were nearly discovered and it became too dangerous for me to stay, doubly outlawed by my very existence. So, we moved here."

He gave a defeated shrug and fell silent.

Oh, Tenebrae thought, the memory of their heated encounter coming back to him unbidden.

It had not occurred to him that humans were so particular about gender. He had never considered having a partner, much less what gender they would be.

"Is there nowhere you can live without hiding what you are?" he asked, somewhat incredulously.

"Not safely, no," Lazarus confirmed, a quiet resignation invading his tone.

Tenebrae sat still as a stone as he absorbed this information. He was beginning to understand the precarious position that the witch was in, and perhaps why he had resorted to binding himself to a demon for protection. His anger at what Lazarus had done to him did not abate, but instead the seething pit of his wrath deepened to hold space for the humans who had driven him to such a desperate action in the first place.

He began examining the wooden contraption, looking for a way to open it.

"What are you doing?" the witch asked him, nervously.

"Getting you out of here," he snapped, glaring at the man for the stupidity of the question.

"Wait, no, you can't," Lazarus insisted, frantically. "If we miraculously escape, they will believe we had help and it will only put others in danger. Please."

He gripped the shadow demon's forearm desperately, his cold hands shaking with anxiety.

"Then, I will take care of the accusers," Tenebrae growled. The violence of his intent was loud and clear as he unconsciously flexed his claws, making the muscles of his forearm ripple under the human's palms.

"You cannot kill the whole town," the witch pleaded, fearful that he was, in fact, quite capable and willing to do just that.

"You underestimate me," the demon scoffed.

He shook off the man's hold and stood to his full height, crossing his arms over his chest.

Levi stirred beside his twin, unfocused eyes fluttering open before closing again. He was never this heavy of a sleeper; the lethargy and pallor that hung over him worried his brother. Lazarus waited for him to settle and then turned back to the impatient shadow demon.

"Alright, fine! If you promise not to do anything until I get out of here, then I will set you free," he offered, with a sigh of defeat. "We only have two more days to get through. Please, Tenebrae."

Tenebrae searched his face for any signs of deception. He saw desperation and resignation, but could discern no trickery. He could wait two more days to be free once more.

"It is a deal."

Chapter 8

A HEAVY PRICE

When Sarah returned the next morning with freshly baked bread and boiled eggs for the brothers' breakfast, they both eagerly wolfed down the food, warming their bellies after the chill of the night. She gingerly touched her hand to the cool skin of Levi's forehead, her brows furrowed in concern as she looked him over.

"I am fine, love," he insisted, taking her hand in his own and giving it a firm squeeze. "Do not fret. We will be home tomorrow and all will be well." He took a few sips of water, before handing the canteen off to his twin.

Seeing the imposing figure of the Reverend Poole approaching, she held off on speaking more and simply nodded. Clutching his hand tightly, she said, "I will return later with dinner." Then she turned and wound her way across the green, careful to avoid the attention of nosy townsfolk.

By now, both of the Graydon brothers could recognize the plodding footsteps of the town's religious leader. Each day at the same time, he had come to demand their confession, and each day they had given him the same answer.

Today, it seemed, would be no different.

They listened to his approach with equal parts annoyance and dread, already knowing the script for this interaction by heart.

"Good morrow, my sons," he droned, in a tone dripping with false sympathy, his bushy eyebrows arching in distaste. "Are you yet ready to confess your sins?"

Taking up a superior stance several feet in front of the stocks, he waited, both for their answer and the attention of the townsfolk nearby. The exchange would doubtlessly attract at least a small crowd.

"Reverend Poole," Lazarus greeted, dryly, eyeing the man with practiced detachment. "As we did yesterday, and the day before that, we have nothing to confess. The storm was an act of God. Does it not seem rather blasphemous to insinuate that we mere humans could possess such a power as to rival the Almighty?"

As the days wore on, his patience was wearing thin and his tongue growing sharper.

"Brother," Levi warned gently, placing a hand on his twin's shoulder to forestall him saying anything further. He eyed the Reverend warily, noting the way the his jaw clenched beneath his jowls and the veins at his temples pulsed angrily. "No, Reverend, we have nothing to confess."

"Then I leave you in God's hands," Poole huffed scornfully, turning on his heel and pushing through the few people that had gathered. A few of them hissed curses towards where the brothers still sat in the stocks as they slowly dispersed.

"We should try not to provoke them further, Laz," Levi reminded, sternly.

"I know, I know, I'm sorry," Lazarus sighed, dragging a hand over his face wearily. "It is just so infuriating. Are you sure you are alright, you look pale."

He eyed his twin doubtfully, wanting to trust him but alarmed by the cast of pallor across his usually sun-kissed complexion.

"Merely tired, brother," Levi insisted, waving off his concerns. "I can bear one more night if it means we will sleep in our own beds once again tomorrow."

If the brothers had thought the previous nights unusually cool, they were wholly unprepared for their fourth and final night in the stocks. A cold front had blown in from the North, bringing with it sharp winds and low clouds. By midnight their teeth were chattering as they huddled together to conserve warmth.

Lazarus insisted that Levi take both of the blankets again, knowing that however miserably cold he might feel, the shadows in his blood would at least protect him from permanent harm. His brother did not have that luxury. In the small hours of the night, the situation worsened.

It began to rain.

A slow but insidious drizzle rained down from low-hanging gray clouds, steadily dampening the green and its unprotected occupants. The twins shifted one of the blankets to drape over them like a tarp to protect against the rainfall, but it soon soaked through, rendering the wool heavy and cold. The precipitation lasted perhaps only an hour, but it was enough to leave them both thoroughly drenched and vulnerable to the bite of the winds gusting against their wet clothes.

When sunrise finally crested and the warmth of the day began to ease their suffering, Lazarus nearly wept with joy. That is, until he got a good look at his brother in the morning light. His complexion had taken on a worrying blue tint, particularly in his lips, and his shivering did not cease even as the air began to warm and their clothes began to dry.

"Levi," he called, shaking the man gently to rouse him. When his eyes opened they were confused and unfocused.

"Wh-where are we?" Levi stammered, his speech slow and slurred. He squinted at his twin and then looked around them, nearly tipping himself off balance as he moved his head. Lazarus grabbed him to keep him upright.

"Still in the stocks, brother," he explained, patiently, holding the shivering man tightly. "It is the last day, though, we will be home soon. Hang on for a bit longer."

Lazarus could see the figure of his brother's wife in the distance, hurriedly approaching with a basket under her arm. They locked eyes as she neared and he almost missed the Reverend's arrival. This time he was accompanied by Elbert as well; matching expressions of disdain adorned their pinched faces.

"It would seem God has seen fit to punish you after all, Mr. Graydon," Reverend Poole gloated, taking in the pair's rain-bedraggled appearance. "A storm for a storm. Have you anything to say on your fifth and final day of punishment?"

"We will not confess to that which we did not do, Reverend," Lazarus stated, unwavering from their position. "We have served out your sentence, now release us."

He held Poole's gaze with a steely resolve, refusing to rise to any provocation or discussion. The Reverend was silent for a few moments, and Lazarus began to worry that he would contrive some reason to keep them imprisoned.

"Hmm, that, it appears you have," he eventually relented, begrudgingly.

Nearby, Lazarus could see Sarah sag with relief. She and a few other townsfolk had gathered around to witness the Graydon brothers' release. Reverend Poole gestured to two able-bodied men in the crowd.

"Release the prisoners. But be warned, my sons, God's eyes are upon you," he cautioned.

As soon as the wooden slats of the stocks were opened, Lazarus was on his feet and helping his brother up. Sarah rushed over, putting one of Levi's arms over her shoulder to help support his weight. Ignoring the murmuring of the townsfolk around them, they guided him across the green and together they helped him down the path back to the manor; it seemed far longer than usual with how unsteady on his feet he was.

"We must get him dry and warm," Lazarus said, as they entered the house, guiding the three of them upstairs to the couple's bedroom. Silently, they worked to strip Levi of his still damp clothes and re-dress him in dry garments, tucking him beneath the blankets once they finished. He mumbled deliriously throughout the process.

"I will make some tea to warm him," Sarah announced, her voice wavering with anxiety, and she rushed to the kitchen to boil some water.

Meanwhile, Lazarus set about lighting a fire in the fireplace and then gathered up the blankets from his own bed to add to the pile. He sat next to Levi, keeping watch over him until Sarah returned with his tea. He dozed in and out of consciousness, murmuring incoherent snippets occasionally before falling back asleep.

Lazarus helped rouse him and prop the man up so he could get down some of the warm tea. It seemed to help bring him about and he offered them both a weak smile before reaching out to grasp Sarah's hand. Lazarus stood, wanting to give them some time alone, and returned to his own room, sinking down into his desk chair with a pained exhale.

He rested his head on top of his arms, folded one over the other atop the desk. His mind swirled with thoughts; his brother was clearly ill, they would be under even more scrutiny than ever, and he had promised the shadow demon that he would release him. Everything had escalated so quickly, and it seemed like problems were coming at him from every direction.

One thing at a time. Take care of Levi first, he thought, taking a few calming breaths. *A healing elixir may help.*

He searched through the grimoire, opening it to the section on healing potions with practiced ease. Though he had most of these simple recipes memorized, he didn't want to leave anything to chance in this situation. Carefully, he gathered the herbs needed for the concoction, grinding them with mortar and pestle until they were mixed in a fine powder. Adding the powdered herbs to a couple drams of saffron syrup, he left the mixture to steep while he saw to some of the more direly overdue chores about the farm.

Things were in better order than Lazarus had expected. It was clear that the Dodson boys had been by to help, and knowing that they were still willing to lend a hand was a small comfort. Perhaps they still had some friends in town after all. Throwing himself into physical labor gave his weary mind a break from ruminating for a precious few hours, surfacing finally in the late afternoon when exhaustion began to catch up with him.

It was time, anyway, to finish crafting the healing concoction and he could give Sarah a break from watching over Levi. Dissolving the herbal syrup in a small glass of peony water, he quickly ate an apple and some bread to stave off hunger and adjourned upstairs.

"How is he?" Lazarus asked, finding Sarah seated at his brother's bedside. She was delicately pressing a cloth to Levi's forehead while he slept.

"No longer shivering," she said, quietly, without looking up. "The chill, at least, seems to be gone. He is still confused when he wakes though."

Levi did look a bit better, some of the pallor had gone from his complexion, although a ruddiness replaced it that didn't seem entirely right either.

"I crafted a healing elixir for him," he offered, holding up the glass of light amber liquid. "Help me give it to him and then I can take over for a while, if you wish."

Together they roused the sleeping man to get him to drink the concoction. He seemed a bit more lucid than before, thanking Lazarus for the potion and sitting up with them for a few minutes.

"What happened?" Levi asked, propped up with pillows against the headboard. His limbs were still a bit too clumsy, so Lazarus held the glass of water to his parched lips while Sarah held the man's hands.

"You caught a chill in the rain last night," his twin explained, "we brought you straight back here to warm you, after Reverend Poole released us."

Levi nodded, appearing relieved to be back home with his family. He squeezed his wife's hand affectionately, his grip still unusually weak.

"And Elijah," he said, "where is our son?"

"With the Barnets," Sarah explained, softly. "Anne offered to look after him to help out. Now that Lazarus is here, I can go and fetch him." She rose, pressing a chaste kiss to Levi's lips and hurried off to retrieve their son.

As her footsteps echoed down the hallway, Levi spoke to his brother, "You look tired, Laz."

"Is that so?" Lazarus laughed, amused at the absurdity of the appraisal considering the ordeal they had been through. "Well, then we are twins in looks finally, because you do not appear so fresh yourself, brother. Get some sleep, I will watch over you until Sarah returns." He moved to sit in the rocking chair a few feet from the bed, but Levi stopped him.

"I know you, brother," his twin said, seriously, his eyes regaining a bit of the brightness they usually held. "And I know what goes on in that head of yours. This is not your fault. Do not waste your energy with blame. We have always known the danger in embracing our family's legacy."

As boys, their mother had instilled in them the need for secrecy with their practice. She and her sister had been their tutors, bringing them up with traditions passed down through generations stretching as far back as anyone had recorded, and probably further still. The grimoires they owned now had once belonged to the two women, tomes of the collective knowledge of their ancestors which each new generation added to before bequeathing to the next. It had always been dangerous to practice, but magic was in their blood and both brothers had felt its call, although Lazarus perhaps more intensely.

"I suppose you are right," Lazarus agreed, reluctantly, though the guilt of his part in recent events still gripped him tightly. "Rest now, we can speak of this later."

It was easy, distracted as the humans of the household were, for Tenebrae to lurk in the dark corners of the Graydon manor unnoticed. He observed them as they went about their evening, eating supper gathered around the ailing man's bedside so that he could enjoy the company of his family. While Lazarus and Sarah cleared away the dishes, Levi read little Elijah a bedtime story. And when they finished, Sarah and the boy were sent to bed at Lazarus's behest, insisting that he would keep watch over his brother so that she could get some much needed rest. She had, after all, been keeping the home afloat the entire time of their absence.

Though obviously worn out himself, the witch kept vigil over his weakened twin, fetching water when he needed and keeping the fire stoked so that his chill would not return. It was clear to the demon how devoted these humans were to one another. Their tenderness was a far cry from the fear and anger that had marked his experiences with their kind. Now that he stopped to think about it, Lazarus had not once treated him like the monster that he knew other humans saw him to be. Even when confronted with his wrath, the witch had tried to reason with him, person to person.

However angry he might be at what Lazarus had done, he could now understand his intention in committing the ritual that bound him. And though he was as eager as ever to be free of the tether to this place,

Tenebrae decided that he would not press the matter until the witch's kin had recovered.

Until then, he would keep watch. He had only promised not to do anything until they were freed from the stocks. Should those ignorant villagers come threatening his witch now, there were no oaths to keep him from harming them. For the time being, he settled into a corner of the room to bide his time, a mist-like black fog darkening the already deep shadows there.

Days passed and Levi's health seemed to ebb and flow like a fickle and inconstant tide. His mind would clear and his strength would return, seeing him up and about the house for a time, only for him to tire quickly from even mundane activities. He was inevitably rendered back to bed, weakened and feverish once again.

Tenebrae watched from the darkness as Lazarus and Sarah worked tirelessly to take care of the man while he languished in sickness. The steadfastness of their care never wavered, taking shifts at night so Levi was never alone. Lazarus brewed more healing potions, each one bolstering the man's constitution for a shorter time than the last.

Levi's body was at war with itself. And it was clear to see that he was losing the battle. The shadow demon could hear the growing irregularity of the sick man's heartbeat and the increasingly labored sound of his breathing.

It seemed incongruous to him, how fragile humans were; capable of wielding incredible power in some ways, yet at the same time, so vulnerable in comparison to his kind. There was nothing he could do to forestall the end that was swiftly coming for the man, and yet he almost found himself wishing there was. It confounded him, this alien urge to intervene and the helplessness of being unable to do so. It was frustrating.

Whether it was denial or their less keen senses, it took the humans longer to notice Levi's declining state, hindered by his own stalwart insistence that he would recover. It was Sarah, to the shadow's surprise, who first broached the subject, staying the witch's hand when he turned up at the bedroom door with the latest of his potions. Tenebrae watched from the dark staircase, as she pushed him back into the hallway and gently closed the door behind her.

"He is not getting better, Laz," she said, eyes brimming with tears and a grim strength set in her face. "We must focus on spending what time with him that we have." She clutched his sleeve tightly in her hand, imploring him to understand.

"No, I-… He will get better. He has to," Lazarus insisted weakly, his voice breaking under the weight of the lie. He had to be able to see, as she could, that Levi's condition was only worsening. He took a sharp breath, fighting back the tears that stung his eyes.

"I know," Sarah whispered, wrapping her arms around his stiff frame. He tucked his arms around her shoulders, woodenly at first, before sagging into the embrace and burying his face in her hair.

"I'm so sorry," Lazarus said, his voice barely audible as it muffled against her dark locks.

She merely shook her head in response and clutched him tighter, both of them shaking with quiet sobs. Tenebrae shifted uncomfortably in the dark, a reluctant spectator to their grief but unable to look away. After a few minutes, Sarah pulled away, wiping her tears on her apron and smoothing her hair.

"Fetch Elijah and keep him company," she instructed Lazarus, falling quickly into lady of the house mode to keep her composure. "I am going to make us a nice supper and we will all spend the evening together."

She squeezed both of his hands encouragingly and then set to work. The fog of the shadow demon's incorporeal form slid along the ceiling unnoticed, following Lazarus into the bedroom with the boy.

Settling on the bed at his father's side, Elijah babbled to him about a butterfly he had seen in the yard earlier that day, while his uncle and father listened as attentively as if it was the most fascinating speech. Levi smiled and smoothed down an unruly tuft of hair on the boy's head, sitting beside him on the bed. Lazarus sat a few feet away, watching his twin dote on the boy and occasionally interjecting with a question to keep Elijah talking. Tenebrae skulked in the deep shadows beside a tall wardrobe in the far side of the room.

When Sarah returned a short while later with what, by their standards, was practically a feast, the boys had just finished reading Elijah's new favorite fairy tale, *Aurore and Aimée.*

Despite Levi's fatigue, the meal was passed with lively conversation and laughter. With the four of them gathered around and the dishes all laid out on the bed, it seemed almost like a picnic. And even after they finished eating, they lounged around chatting and enjoying each other's company. Elijah appeared delighted at being allowed to stay up past his bedtime, but fell asleep in his father's arms not long after.

Eventually, the shadow demon watched them part with warm hugs and whispered 'I love you's', and the four human members of the Graydon household went to bed with hearts as full as their bellies. But when morning came and its golden light gently woke the manor's residents, it roused only three.

Lazarus was grateful for the local custom of entirely silent funerals; he was not certain that he could stand hearing what the people of the village had to say about his brother, especially Elbert Poole and the Reverend. Without their instigation and the Reverend's pompous need to make an example of them, Levi would be alive today. He felt his own share of guilt for the events that took his twin from them, but he felt blame rise in his throat like bile when he looked upon the people who had condemned the two of them to the stocks.

Standing beside Sarah in the small cemetery to the north of Graymourne, Lazarus felt eyes upon him. The townsfolk assembled all had their gazes demurely cast down towards the ground that would eagerly accept their fallen neighbor. The sensation of being watched buzzed at him from the shade of a small copse of trees nearby. He knew at once that it was Tenebrae, having felt the same odd sense of being observed frequently in the days since they brought Levi home to convalesce.

Though he knew the shadow demon was most likely just biding his time until Lazarus would fulfill his promise to free him, it still brought a sense of comfort. The demon's watchful presence was grounding amidst the tumult of tragedy, and he found himself dreading its absence once they would soon be unbound. Their conversation that night at the stocks had felt like a turning point. The brooding shadow had seemed curious and even a bit concerned for him.

It felt as if they had finally begun to understand one another, and Lazarus started to wonder if there could be more to his feelings towards the demon, beyond the physical attraction that would not seem to wane. He wanted a chance to find out. But, personal desires aside, he would not go back on his promise. When the demon came to collect, he would be honor bound to deliver.

For now though, he leaned into the protective feeling of the shadow's unseen presence and the comfort of Sarah and Elijah beside him. When the funeral was over, the three of them stayed as the rest of the townsfolk returned home, standing at the foot of Levi's fresh grave together to say their goodbyes. Tears ran silently down Sarah's face, and Lazarus squeezed her hand in support, willing his own emotions back to stay strong for her and Elijah. There was nothing that he could say to ease her suffering that had not already been said; only time and the strength of each other would lighten that burden.

Finally, when the three of them were ready to return home, Lazarus picked up the tired Elijah and offered Sarah his arm, guiding them home as he had seen Levi do many times. He knew that the best thing he could do to honor his brother's memory would be to take care of his family.

"Bye, Papa," Elijah called softly, over his shoulder as the sight of the cemetery receded in the distance.

Chapter 9

COMPROMISES

Tenebrae silently observed the witch, who was seated upon the edge of his bed with his head bowed, elbows leaned heavily against his knees. Occasionally, a small droplet would fall, adding to the tiny pool of tears gathering where he gazed emptily at the floor. His black mourning garb was stark against the contrast of his tanned skin, and his chestnut brown hair looked almost black in the dim light. Not for the first time, the shadow wondered if it was as soft as it looked.

"I can feel your eyes on me, you know," Lazarus whispered without bothering to raise his head.

His announcement took the shadow demon by surprise. The human had previously given no indication that he was aware of the other's presence.

Taking solid form, Tenebrae stepped across the short distance of the room to stand before him. Lazarus straightened then, craning his neck to look up at the tall demon from where he sat on the mattress. His eyes were red-rimmed and swollen, and his face was streaked with the lines of old tears. The demon could practically taste the man's grief and it left a bitter flavor in his mouth.

"I am sorry," Tenebrae rumbled, quietly, "for your loss."

They stared at each other in silence for a few moments, neither sure what else to say. He fought the urge to wipe a glistening tear from the man's cheek.

"Thank you," the witch breathed, eventually, looking away from the intense gaze of the shadow demon.

He rose, walking mechanically across the room to his desk, where he picked up a thick leather tome with an eclipse etched on the cover. Slowly, he turned the pages, and the demon caught on to his intentions.

"If you need some time before…" Tenebrae began, moving to stand behind him.

Now that the moment was here, it felt wrong somehow to expect the witch to perform the unbinding so fresh from the death of his twin.

"I will keep my word," Lazarus said curtly, cutting him off abruptly. He pointed to a familiar sigil on the page. "This is the binding spell, the unbinding will be after it."

He flipped past the details of the ritual to a pair of pages that laid out how to complete the reversal. Much of the text was in a language that Tenebrae could not read, but what he could make out seemed simple enough. It was nearly a mirror of the summoning, only the incantation seemed different. The witch dragged his finger along the lines of text, carefully reviewing the contents of the untranslated section. About a third of the way down the page, he stopped suddenly.

"Oh," Lazarus said, in a disquieted tone.

"What is it?" Tenebrae asked, frustrated at not being able to read the text on his own. The man's finger pointed to the phrase 'periculum mortis' in looping hand-written script. It was underlined in red.

"It would seem that the unbinding process is not without its dangers," the man clarified, speaking in a slow lifeless monotone. "Not to you, of course, but for the human counterpart there is a 'risk of death'."

He tapped the phrase again to indicate exactly where the text explained this. Hesitantly, he glanced over his shoulder towards the shadow demon standing just behind him, presumably trying to gauge his reaction to this new information.

Tenebrae closed his eyes, taking a steadying breath. He could not very well ask this man to undertake such a risk, and potentially leave the woman and her boy alone just after the loss of his brother. Well, he could, but it felt needlessly cruel, even for a demon. There would have to be another solution, at least for now.

Opening his eyes, he found the witch still watching him with a fearful look on his face. Tenebrae studied the man to whom he was currently bound, settling on his forest colored eyes when the idea struck him.

I am bound to him, not to this place, Tenebrae thought. *Perhaps it is possible to leave if I simply take him with me.*

So averse had he been to the idea of keeping company with a human, that the possibility had not even occurred to him before now. But, he had become sort of used to the witch's presence by this point. It was worth a try at least.

He reached out, wrapping an arm around the man's waist and pulling him back securely against his chest.

"What are you doing?" Lazarus hissed, flailing with panic and dropping the grimoire. It landed with a thud on his desk.

The demon lifted the six-foot-tall man off his feet easily, and began walking them towards a dark corner of the room at an alarmingly swift place.

"Testing a theory," Tenebrae said, cryptically, not slowing even slightly as they approached a solid expanse of wall bathed in deep charcoal shadows.

The witch braced his arms in front of his face protectively as they walked straight into what should have been a hard surface, but met no resistance. Instead, they continued to move forward into a near pitch darkness.

The shadow demon moved effortlessly through the vast nothingness, ignoring the quiet noises of confusion that his cargo was making. He walked with purpose towards the place he had in mind, swiftly locating it. It was always easiest navigating to somewhere he had been before, the pathways seeming to shorten with familiarity.

Pressing back through to terrestrial space, Tenebrae took a few steps forward and deposited the spluttering human onto the mossy ground. Lazarus stumbled, disoriented by the unsettling method of travel, and then whirled around to glare at him.

"What the fuck was that?" he demanded, irately, furtively looking around at their surroundings. Tall pine trees crowded thickly around them in all directions, the dense greenery blocking out much of the natural light. And where at home it had been night, here it appeared to be early morning judging by the color of the sunlight and the chirping of birds. "And where the hell are we?"

"Be at ease, Lazarus," the shadow demon chuckled, smirking at him in amusement. "I will return you to your home soon enough. A temporary change of scenery may do you some good. And I needed to prove my suspicion correct."

Tenebrae's relief was palpable, and it felt as if a weight was lifted from his shoulders. His changed demeanor seemed to soothe the rankled man somewhat, his posture relaxing though he retained an air of confusion.

"And what suspicion would that be?" Lazarus asked, this time in a much softer tone.

He smoothed his clothes, which were rumpled from the demon carrying him. A flutter of nerves broke through his melancholy, as he belatedly registered the way that Tenebrae's muscular body had felt against his back when he was clutched tight against it.

"That I may travel freely as I wish," the demon explained, stepping closer and reaching out to tap the man's chest with the point of one sharp claw. "So long as I have you with me."

The witch's eyes widened as he put the pieces together. They were bound to each other; wherever one was, the other must be.

"But I promised to free you," he mumbled nervously, and Tenebrae could see the guilt and confusion battling within him. Lazarus backed away from the demon, shaking his head. "I cannot leave Sarah and Elijah, not with Levi gone. You have to take me back."

Hot tears began to fall anew and he clenched his fists by his sides.

"And if you die trying to unbind us? You will leave them all the same," Tenebrae pointed out, crossing his arms over his chest.

Lazarus's shoulders sagged then, defeatedly, and he dropped his head with a hopeless sigh.

"Goddamnit. This is all my fault," he said quietly, as if only speaking to himself. "They will be all alone."

His heart was racing and his breath coming in shallow gasps, panic completely overtaking him as he began pacing anxiously. He was so consumed by his thoughts that he didn't seem aware of the shadow demon's approach, until Tenebrae gripped him firmly by the scruff of the neck and forced his head up.

"Look at me," the demon commanded, sternly, his thundering voice breaking through the noise of the witch's despair. Lazarus stared up at him with wild eyes, hiccuping softly as he caught his breath. Once he had his attention, Tenebrae continued in a more neutral tone, "I will not ask you to abandon them. What I propose is an agreement. You will care for your kin as needed, and the rest of the time you will travel with me."

"A-an agreement," Lazarus stammered, trying to nod his head without much success, thanks to the shadow demon's unshakeable grip. "Yes. I can, um, I can do that."

He blinked like a startled deer, staring warily into the demon's bottomless night eyes.

"Good, it is settled then," Tenebrae said with finality. He gave the witch's neck a gentle squeeze and then released him, shouldering past him dismissively toward a point deeper in the forest. "Now, while we are here, I wish to see something other than that forsaken town of yours and the same tiny swath of forest."

Lazarus stared after him, watching the way the dappled light penetrated the inky haze of the demon's skin to play along the dark skeleton beneath, while tendrils of shadow flared out from his body like smoke in the rays of morning sun. It took him a moment to realize that he should be following, and he shook himself alert, stumbling after the dark figure into the trees.

They walked for at least an hour, as far as Lazarus could tell. The hesitant blush of sunrise brightened to a warm morning glow that occasionally managed to break through the lush tree cover. Tall and straight, the trees were tightly packed around them like columns; as they moved, they wove in and out around the vertical sentinels littered across mossy ground.

The forest was beautiful.

Dramatic and seemingly endless, it looked to Lazarus like something out of a fairy tale. The shadow demon strode through it effortlessly and with purpose. Though tall among his own people, the witch had to hurry to keep up with his towering companion. Even still, Tenebrae paused periodically, looking back with a withering glance to allow the human to catch up.

Between the brisk pace and the bracing morning air, Lazarus found his mind blissfully empty of anything but the present. For a blessed hour, there was only the burn of his muscles, the scent of pine, and the lithe figure ahead that he followed like a dark guiding star.

Eventually, they came to a small creek, crossing at a narrow point and then following it as it wound through an increasingly narrow valley. On either side, tree-covered walls of rock rose sharply, leaving them at the base of a long incision cut through the landscape. A rush of water sounded, growing louder as they proceeded.

Stopping beside the now still demon, Lazarus saw they had come to a dead end of sorts. Here was where the creek began, flowing from a verdant pool fed by a cascade of water from a higher ledge. Over the din of the waterfall, he could hear another more distant noise; there were more falls above. The sound was soothing, combined with the babbling of the creek and the gentle rust of leaves. He breathed a deep sigh and felt some of the past weeks' tension melt from his body.

Lazarus looked up and found Tenebrae watching him.

"Have you been here before?" he asked, although he was already certain of the answer. It was clear from the intent path the shadow demon had lead them on that he knew where he was going.

"I have," Tenebrae said, and gestured ahead of them. "Come, there is more."

Lazarus looked dubiously in the direction he was pointing. The options were a wall of moss and plant covered rock or a rushing cascade of white water over vertical stone.

"You cannot seriously expect me to climb that," he told the shadow demon, giving him an incredulous look.

Tenebrae looked down at the human, studying his blunt clawless fingers, soft delicate skin, and smaller stature. He hummed thoughtfully, the man had a point.

"I will carry you," he announced with a sigh, after a moment of consideration. It seemed the most expedient solution, since Tenebrae was not willing to compromise his intended route to accommodate the human. Lowering into a crouch, he gestured impatiently for the witch to climb onto his back. Lazarus blinked at him in surprise, and then awkwardly clambered on using the slightly protruding charcoal bones of the demon's spine for leverage.

Once his arms were locked around Tenebrae's neck, Lazarus noticed thick tendrils of shadow rise up from the surface of his skin, weaving around his arms and securing them tightly in place. He gasped quietly as he felt more of them encircling his torso and his legs at either side of the demon's waist. They constricted with a firm but gentle pressure, and Lazarus blushed as he was locked flush against the muscular expanse of Tenebrae's back.

"Ready?" the demon asked, smirking at the way the man fidgeted against the grip of his shadows. He gave them a very intentional squeeze to see what reaction it would elicit, and Lazarus promptly froze, ceasing his embarrassed squirming.

"Mmhmm," the witch hummed, not entirely trusting himself to speak while they were in such close proximity.

He tried not to think about the fact that the last time they had been this close to each other, the shadow's tongue had been down his throat. Instead, Lazarus focused on what he could see over Tenebrae's right shoulder, watching as the shadow steered them towards the cliff to the left of the falls. With little effort, the shadow demon sunk his black-tipped claws into the rock and casually ascended the sheer wall as if going up a flight of stairs.

Atop the ledge they had seen from below lay another pool with a second falls streaming down from further up the narrow canyon. Tenebrae paused here, looking around to appreciate the scenery. A pensive rumble emitted from the demon's chest, almost too low to hear, but not to feel. The sound vibrated the places where their bodies pressed together, distractingly.

Lazarus did his best to admire the impressive tableau of landscape that stretched before them, while preoccupied by the sensation of shadows gripping tightly around his upper thighs. He was relieved when the demon began moving again, walking them towards the falls where Tenebrae made quick work of climbing to the next ledge.

They continued this way for some time, slowly ascending all seven of the connected cascades in a peaceful silence. This was by far the most time they had spent in each other's presence at all, but especially without an altercation of some sort. At the top of the waterfall, Tenebrae stepped to the side of the rushing water, unwinding the shadowy restraints that secured Lazarus to his back and then bent down to let him climb off. Getting his footing, the human wavered slightly before turning to look down at where they had come from.

"It's beautiful," he whispered reverently, gazing down the length of the valley where the water twisted and wound its way down amongst the trees and ferns. "Thank you, Tenebrae, for bringing me here."

It felt bittersweet, seeing this place and being reminded of the immense beauty that existed in the world outside their small town, but knowing that Levi would never see it. He felt the absence of his twin keenly, but a little spark of determination kindled within him and began to burn ever so slightly brighter.

I will keep them safe for you, brother, he vowed silently, picturing his sister-in-law and nephew at home, probably sound asleep in their beds at this moment.

Lazarus brushed a stray tear from his cheek and turned, finding the shadow demon looking at him with a strangely gentle expression. It morphed quickly back into Tenebrae's usual impassive demeanor, and the demon held out his hand.

"It is time I returned you to your home," he rumbled coolly, choosing to ignore the warmth that had bloomed in his chest as he watched the man's awestruck appreciation of the scenery. Seeing him react in such a way to one of his favorite places stirred feelings of connection that Tenebrae was not ready to entertain. This arrangement of theirs was merely supposed to be transactional, so he focused on keeping up his end of the deal.

Lazarus took the offered hand and allowed the demon to pull him into a nearby shadow, plunging them both back into the void.

The mood in the Graydon manor during the following weeks was expectedly somber, yet pragmatic. Time marched inexorably forward, and the tasks of living refused to pause for the dead. Farm work had to be done, animals needed tending, and household chores had to be conducted. The heavy business of grief was relegated to quiet moments of rest, when the noisiness of living subsided enough that the absence of Levi Graydon could be heard loud and clear.

Most evenings, when Elijah had been read his story and tucked into bed, Lazarus and Sarah would sit together by the fire. Silence hung around them like a shroud, while they allowed the toils of the day to fall away and make way for mourning. On good days, there would be memories of Levi recounted, little remembrances lighting between them like fireflies in the gloom of their loss. On others, the dam of their misery would give way to a torrent of anguished tears.

Inevitably, Sarah retired first, leaving Lazarus alone with his thoughts and the weary ache of his muscles. Not only were they bereft of Levi's loving presence and skilled hands around the farm, but the Dodson boys had been unable to spare more than one of them to help work the Graydon's lands lately. That left Lazarus with little choice but to work longer and harder days, and yet the to-do list seemed never to shrink.

He was grateful for the distraction, when every few nights Tenebrae would show up, eager to collect him and abscond to some strange new location. Their forays were never boring, thanks to the scenery and the fluctuating nature of the pair's still tenuous truce.

Most recently, they had been in a vast desert of rolling dunes, trudging about under an endless star-encrusted sky. Lazarus huffed as he stumbled again on the shifting sand, trying in vain to keep up with the shadow demon who seemed utterly unaffected by the instability of the ground beneath their feet.

He looked up, pausing to catch his breath, and saw Tenebrae observing him from near the top of the dune with a posture that Lazarus had become acutely familiar with. It was a rigid set to the shoulders coupled with an opposing tilt of the head that only seemed to occur when the demon was particularly annoyed with the limitations of his human travel partner.

Quickly, Lazarus resumed his climb, attempting to head off the intervention he could already sense coming his way. He nearly managed to half the distance before Tenebrae reached him, unceremoniously hauling the man over his shoulder like a protesting sack of potatoes.

"How you humans manage to thrive on this earth when you are so ill suited to its environments is a fucking mystery," the shadow demon grumbled to himself, ascending back to the top of the dune with effortless grace.

It was frequently easier to carry the human over difficult terrain, rather than wait for him to traverse it so slowly. Tenebrae had convinced himself that convenience was the sole reason that he had developed a habit of picking Lazarus up whenever he felt like it. It certainly wasn't an excuse to touch him or because he enjoyed it, and he definitely wasn't fighting the urge to slide his hand further up the witch's firm thigh right now.

"Oh, a thousand pardons for slowing down your journey with my inferior mortal body," Lazarus sniped, his tongue loosened by indignation and the sudden rush of blood to his head that came with hanging upside down.

It was difficult to tell if the scoff that his comment elicited was one of amusement or irritation, but the sting of claws digging deeper into his thigh made him think it was the latter. He made a valiant effort not to stare at the taut muscles of the shadow demon's ass, though his vantage point allowed the sight of little else.

"Your fragility is forgiven," Tenebrae declared, with an antagonistic smirk, dropping the incensed witch back onto the sand with a thud. "I suppose you cannot help that you were born so… soft."

"How magnanimous of you," Lazarus scoffed, hiding his blush with a quietly uttered insult under his breath. "Boorish bastard."

Studiously avoiding looking at Tenebrae, he clambered to his feet, wondering what the shadow meant calling him 'soft'. It didn't exactly sound like an insult with the way he had nearly purred the word. Coming from a human, he would have interpreted it as flirting. But at most, he assumed the shadow barely tolerated him, so that couldn't be it.

The entertained look on the demon's face deepened the longer the human refused to look at him, busying himself with brushing the sand from his breeches. The whispered slight hadn't been nearly quiet enough to escape Tenebrae's keen ears and the dark did little to hide the man's flustered expression.

"If you are finished cursing me, you may wish to enjoy the view," the shadow quipped, turning to face the horizon with a smug grin.

Still bristling, Lazarus swallowed the urge to refuse out of spite and followed the demon's instruction. He was glad he did.

Great waves of sand stretched out in a boundless sea before them, the soft starlight washing it in tones of the darkest blue. At the horizon, the desert merged seamlessly with the clear sky, which was encrusted with infinite tiny points of light. A hazy ribbon of light bisected the visible night sky, cutting a swath through the twinkling lights. He stood, captivated, feasting his eyes on the sight with childlike wonder.

"I stand by my estimation of your character, but I will admit that this was worth the trouble," Lazarus said, not taking his eyes off the glittering space above them, "company included."

"Agreed," Tenebrae rumbled, taking a seat on the cool sand to get comfortable while they appreciated the sights. He leaned on one large hand with his legs crossed, slowly scanning the landscape with his eyes. Lazarus had never seen him so at ease.

"Have you never been here before?" he asked, sitting down next to the relaxing shadow demon. Most of the places they had visited so far were ones that Tenebrae knew. It was curiously pleasant seeing the usually nonchalant demon visibly enjoy something for a change.

"No," Tenebrae said, quietly, "this place is new to me." He paused, looking down to run his fingers through the sand. "I like it."

"So do I," Lazarus replied, smiling at the unexpected softness in the shadow demon's voice. He turned back to the desert, settling in to the comfortable silence.

As he often did, Lazarus wished that Levi was there to see this remarkable place. Their whole lives, where one went, the other followed. New places were something to be experienced together. But now the air next to him felt empty, a sense of hollowness where the once constant presence of his twin should be. He wondered if the shadow demon had someone he missed.

"Tenebrae," he said, tentatively, "do you have a family? Is there anyone you wish to visit one of these nights?"

Guilt nipped at him, as he realized that he might have torn the demon away from someone who cared for him. Was there someone out there longing for Tenebrae's presence and wondering where he'd gone?

Slowly turning away from the landscape, Tenebrae looked at him quizzically. He could always tell when something he said shocked the demon; it never failed to smooth his almost permanent scowl into a blank mask of confusion.

"No," he eventually grunted. He stared at the witch intently for a long moment, as if he could discern the purpose of his question with his piercing gaze alone. It began to seem as if that was all he had to say on the subject, until Lazarus looked away and he surprised him by continuing. "My kind are rather solitary creatures. We are few to begin with and our home is vast. I have sensed others from afar, but they did not approach, so neither did I."

"That sounds lonesome," Lazarus murmured.

He had always been half of a duo and surrounded by acquaintances. Deep friendships were difficult due to the need for secrecy around their magic, but he was used to having many a person to talk to should he desire it. It was hard to imagine going long stretches without speaking to another person, only ever passing like ships in the night. The shadow demon's standoffish nature made a bit more sense to him now.

Tenebrae hummed noncommittally, and returned to quietly watching the stars twinkle. Lazarus decided not to push his luck further, content with having learned even a small morsel of information about the shadow.

Two days later, Lazarus was still picking sand out of the pockets and crevices of his clothes distractedly, while he sat on the narrow rigid pew beside his family at service. Though he would rather traverse a thousand sand dunes than be here in this church, he knew that it was necessary to keep up the appearance as a contrite, god-fearing citizen of the village in order to ensure their safety. Sarah patted his hand knowingly without averting her eyes from the droning clergyman at the head of the meeting house. He ceased his restless fidgeting and concentrated on a knot in the wood at the back wall, to give the appearance of listening attentively.

Finally, the interminable service ended and everyone rose to file out in orderly rows. With Sarah and Elijah in front of him, they followed the Barnets out into the cool morning air. Lazarus cringed when Elbert Poole stopped to speak with them before they could get far.

"Mistress Graydon, I pray this day finds you well," Elbert remarked, standing in front of the three of them with a manufactured smile on his face. He gave Lazarus a more simple greeting, nodding with a clipped, "Mr. Graydon."

"We are well, thank you for your concern, Mr. Poole," Sarah answered, politely, drawing Elijah closer to her side.

"I know what a difficult time this has been for you," he continued, his words slathered with saccharine sympathy that made Lazarus's skin crawl. "And I am glad to bring some good news. Thaddeus Gale has declared to the good Reverend and I his intent to ask for your hand in marriage."

He looked at her expectantly, as if she might accept on the spot. Sarah's eyes widened slightly, but otherwise she remained carefully composed.

"Well, I thank you for the news," she said, slowly enunciating the words in a way that Lazarus knew meant she was furious. "But, I am not yet ready to consider marrying again."

"Think on it, at least, my dear," Poole insisted, "A widow so young and lovely as yourself deserves a godly man to take care of her." His furtive side glance at Lazarus did not go unnoticed by either of them, and Sarah's jaw tensed despite her polite smile.

"I will think on it, good day to you," she said, quickly, giving him a short nod and then stepping around the man with Elijah in tow. Lazarus hurried after her, barely gritting out a goodbye to the presumptuous man, and caught up to her swift pace along the path back to the manor. He could see her seething, but she didn't say a word until they were alone in the safety of the Graydon household.

"Elijah," she said, softly, "Go up to your room, please, while I make us some lunch." Sarah watched as he trotted off up the stairs and then motioned for Lazarus to follow her to the kitchen.

"How dare he," she hissed, finally, when the boy was well out of earshot. "My husband has been in the ground for mere weeks and already these vultures begin their circling." Taking out her anger on some bread, she sliced aggressively while she spoke.

"It is callous and offensive, I agree," Lazarus said, portioning out some cheese onto a couple of plates. "However, I am not surprised. Thaddeus Gale's farm has been floundering these last years, and I wager he would jump at the chance to get his hands on ours."

By law, a third of Levi's estate automatically went to his widow. The remaining two-thirds were to be divided equally between his son and his brother, and since Elijah was just a boy, his inheritance fell to his mother until he came of age. This meant that Sarah now owned a sizable portion of the Graydon estate. Any single man in Graymourne would be eager to court her, with or without their family's questionable reputation.

It was the wealthiest property in the village.

"I will not marry that man," she said, slamming a tray of sliced bread and meat down on the table with enough force to shake the heavy wooden surface.

"You will not have to," Lazarus promised, knowing that she could fight her own battles but ready to stand beside her nonetheless. He would be damned before he let some greedy villager attempt to prey on her loss to further his own fortune. "Just say the word, and I will do whatever it takes to keep you and Elijah safe."

"I know, Laz," Sarah sighed, sitting beside him at the table. "Promise me something, please? No more magic. It's too dangerous, we cannot afford to lose you too."

Her eyes were tight with worry, brows drawn as she asked him to forsake the magical heritage that he and Levi had shared.

Whatever it takes, he thought, *I did say that. And really, what need do I have of it now?*

He looked at her pleading face, the grief for her husband and the fear for her child etched on it plain as day. The question hung over her like a cloud, as if he could ever refuse her now.

"You have my word, Sarah," he said, putting a gentle hand on her shoulder. "I will even hide my grimoire away somewhere safe. Levi would want Elijah to have his though, you will keep it for him until he is older?"

Her mouth flattened into a terse line, but she nodded, willing to compromise if it meant he would agree to her request.

Chapter 10

REALIZATIONS

That night, when Tenebrae stepped out of the darkness in his bedroom, Lazarus was still stewing over the audacity of the men of this town. The shadow demon could see the rigid tension running through his body as soon as he entered the room.

"Something has happened," he observed, lurking next to the desk where Lazarus sat. Unconsciously, a tendril of shadow curled out towards the man's shoulder, and when he noticed, he snapped it back before it could make contact.

"It is nothing you need worry about," the witch sighed, looking up from the journal he had been furiously scribbling in. "Just humans being… humans."

He sounded irritated, and the demon almost wanted to press for more information, but he was also restless and eager to get on with their travels for the night.

The days in between their jaunts were growing more tedious and the shadow found himself spending much of it contemplating where he would take Lazarus for their next expedition. It was simply boredom, of course, not because he looked forward to the man's company. Though he was, admittedly, a surprisingly tolerable travel companion in the demon's opinion.

"Hmm. Perhaps it is just as well that we are going somewhere there are no humans," Tenebrae mused, extending one clawed hand in invitation.

He noticed the immediate relief in the man's face, a smoothing of his furrowed brow and the tension dropping from his shoulders as a tentative smile brightened his expression. A warm feeling settled in the demon's chest and he felt a grin tug at the corner of his mouth unbidden.

What's this? he thought, frowning against the alien sensation. There was an unexpected satisfaction at being able to banish the human's downcast mood with only a few words. *Why do I care so much about how he feels all of a sudden?*

His eyes narrowed in suspicion, searching the contents strewn on the desk for evidence of a spell or some kind of charm. There was nothing but a well-worn journal, a quill, and a cup of tea. If not bewitchment, Tenebrae was lost as to the cause for his seemingly unfounded interest in the human's happiness.

Lazarus opened his mouth to ask where the demon was taking him, but was promptly silenced when Tenebrae seized him by the arm and hauled him out of his chair. Before the man could protest, he was already dragging him deep into shadowspace, focused on whatever destination he had in mind. Tenebrae deliberately ignored the human's stumbling along beside him, as Lazarus struggled to keep up with his long strides.

This witch has been occupying entirely too much of my thoughts lately. It is becoming a nuisance.

It was bad enough, he felt, this insidious sympathy that had wormed its way into his mind. Thinking back, it seemed to begin with that night he found the brothers in the stocks. And the more time he spent with the witch, the more he found himself drawn to him like a slow but inexorable tide.

His hands itched to touch that smooth, supple skin of his, and his shadow tendrils seemed to reach for him of their own accord. There was a craving growing in him, and it always seemed to lead Tenebrae back to that moment in the forest, the witch pinned beneath him and groaning into his mouth.

It made him feel feral.

"Watch the claws," Lazarus hissed beside him in the dark.

The shadow demon eased his hold, which had begun to dig into the meat of the human's bicep as his thoughts wandered. Fortuitously, they reached the end of the path, and Tenebrae pushed through the barrier, dumping them out into a dark stone archway.

The demon released him then, dropping his arm swiftly as if it had burnt him. He walked away without looking back, just missing the flash of hurt and confusion in the witch's eyes.

Lazarus turned to the surroundings, trying to distract himself from the shadow demon's confusingly mercurial moods. This had become a pattern over the course of their now regular expeditions, though he struggled to understand the cause.

Most times, the shadow was perfectly civil, if a bit aloof. At others, he could turn teasing and, if Lazarus didn't know better, almost flirtatious, seeming to delight in flustering and provoking him. And then suddenly, a biting coldness would slam down over the demon's demeanor, shutting him out like a heavy portcullis closing off a fortress.

Which was exactly where they appeared to be now, both figuratively and literally.

Lazarus stood in what looked like a medieval gatehouse, leading to a stout castle looming in the dark. There were no lights on in the structure and it appeared abandoned, judging from the state of disrepair and proliferation of plant growth along its walls. Tenebrae was right, there were no humans here. The shadow demon was many things, but deceptive was not one of them. With a sigh, Lazarus wandered in the direction the shadow had gone.

Beyond the archway, the space opened up to a wide courtyard before the stone fortress. The pathway took Lazarus past a low wall and through a second gatehouse that was set into the castle itself. He spotted movement ahead, finding the demon striding up a steeply sloped grass-covered ramp into the building at the far side of a large inner courtyard. After a moment of hesitation, he followed, retracing the footsteps of his moody companion.

Entering the building there was a pair of spiral stone staircases to his left, leading to a tower and the higher floors. He ignored these in favor of the great open hall to his right.

The ceiling was long since gone, open to the night sky which bore the faintest hint of growing light, telling Lazarus it must be close to dawn wherever they were. The floor was crumbling, fallen away in large chunks towards the center of the room, but the sides near the walls looked stable enough. It had, presumably, supported the shadow's considerably heavier weight, given that he was currently ducking through an archway set in the far wall.

"Really," Lazarus called, walking across the open space towards the retreating back of the shadow demon, "do not concern yourself, so, Tenebrae. I will catch up. It is not as if you need my presence for these explorations, after all."

The demon paused, turning slightly to throw a challenging look over his shoulder, and Lazarus could almost swear he saw the dark figure give a begrudging snicker at his sardonic tone.

"In fact," he continued, coming to a stop a few yards from the shadow demon as a wicked idea sparked in his head, "I wonder what would happen if I simply walked in the opposite direction? How far do you think you would get before the magic that binds us would have you following after me like an obedient puppy?"

His heart beat wildly in his chest, well aware that his bold taunting was the verbal equivalent of poking an angry bear with a sharpened stick. The barb would either amuse or provoke the demon, potentially both.

Tenebrae's eyes flashed dangerously as he turned back to face him.

"You would not dare," he growled, threateningly, the muscles in his lean figure tensing as if already preparing to pounce.

Provoke, it is, Lazarus thought, returning the demon's glare with a haughty grin.

Perhaps it was unwise, but he would take an angry shadow over one that was pointedly ignoring him for some unknown reason.

"Wouldn't I?" he asked, blinking at the demon with round-eyed faux innocence for a moment before flashing a defiant grin. "Let us find out, shall we?"

With that, he turned on the spot, briskly heading back the way he had come.

A snarl from behind him had the witch breaking into an ill-advised sprint across the precarious floor, as his instincts prioritized the danger of the advancing predator at his back over the environmental hazards. This, however, turned out to be a costly mistake. He took only a few bounding steps before there was a loud crack, and the floor beneath him gave way.

Lazarus scrambled to catch himself, only succeeding in slicing open his hands on the jagged edge of the floor. He flailed twelve feet in the air, suspended briefly in slow-motion as adrenaline kicked in, before time and the unforgiving stone ground below came rushing up to meet him. He hit the ground with a sickening thud, sprawling flat with one leg twisted beneath him at an awkward angle and his head cracked harshly against the rocky surface.

Too far to away intervene, Tenebrae could only watch him fall as he raced over, arriving to find the witch knocked unconscious with a disconcerting amount of blood leaking from a large wound in his head. He was seized with a visceral and irrational fear at the sight of his injuries, despite the knowledge that their bond would not allow the man to die. His earlier vexation dissipated like smoke, and now all that he desired was for Lazarus to be upright and irritating him again.

He jumped down and knelt on the floor, carefully gathering the human into his arms to get him off the cold, now bloody ground. Wispy black threads swiftly closed the cuts in the witch's hands, and the flow of blood from his head wound slowed and then stopped completely.

Minutes went by and still Lazarus didn't stir. Tenebrae could hear his pulse; it was weak but steady and the man appeared to be breathing at least. But the longer he stared at the limp and unresponsive human, the more anxious he felt. It was becoming painfully obvious to him that, whether the shadow demon wanted to or not, he cared for the witch.

Why isn't he waking up? Tenebrae worried, concern coiling around his bones like a snake. He wondered, then, how long it had taken Lazarus to heal that night after the ritual. It could have been minutes or hours, he had no idea.

He had never thought to ask.

Looking down at the smooth bared flesh of the man's throat, a hot flash of guilt washed over him, coupled with the vivid recollection of how easily his claws had cleaved it open. He lightly trailed the pads of his fingers over the warm skin there, and along the defined line of the witch's jaw. The burn of guilt gave way to a warmer feeling that simmered low in his gut, a sense of want that gnawed at him from within.

To distract himself, he looked Lazarus over, shifting him to drape more comfortably across his lap. His eyes fluttered as Tenebrae rearranged his position, and his heartbeat was beginning to sound stronger, almost normal. Tenebrae straightened the witch's still bent leg out, earning a pained groan from the now semi-conscious man.

"You are alright," Tenebrae reassured him, adjusting the witch so his head was supported against his own shoulder. He breathed a sigh of relief, the constricting feeling of unease beginning to loose its hold as the human showed signs of waking.

"Hurts," Lazarus wheezed, tensing against him as his body worked to finish putting itself back together. He could feel the bone in his shin knitting splintered pieces whole and the back of his skull stitching itself together again; the sensation was nauseating. He burrowed into the comforting warmth of the shadow demon, shamelessly clutching onto him as a wave of pain crashed over him.

"I know," Tenebrae rumbled softly, cradling him as gently as he was able. "Just be still and let your body heal. You stupid, fragile, infuriating man."

There was a tenderness mixed in with his acerbic tone, and it did not go unnoticed by Lazarus even in his impaired state.

"No, you're infuriating. You gargantuan, bitter inkblot," he slurred against the demon's skin, shuddering as the shadows in his blood finished up their work.

When the feeling passed, he looked up at Tenebrae, managing a strained grin. Despite the painful price he paid for it, he couldn't help but relish the inkling of fondness and care from the shadow. He was further rewarded with an exasperated eye-roll and a dry chuckle. Lazarus knew he had glimpsed something deeper beneath the demon's anger and practiced detachment just now, and he was more determined than ever to uncover more of it.

A coppery metallic taste made him lick his lips to rid himself of the flavor, noting that he must have bitten his tongue at some point during the fall. Lazarus was surprised to catch the shadow demon's eyes track the movement, lingering a little too long on his mouth before returning to his eyes. His face flushed at the attention, and he waited with bated breath to see what Tenebrae would do.

Why does he look like he wants to kiss me?

The demon's arm tightened around his waist and Lazarus's heart beat wildly as he leaned in close enough to feel his breath on his face.

"You should be more careful," Tenebrae chided, much to his disappointment. The shadow stood then, setting the witch back on his feet but keeping a steadying hand on his shoulder. "We will miss the sunrise if you fall again."

He led the way back upstairs, this time keeping Lazarus close by his side, crossing the treacherous floor of the great hall to the entryway at the far side. Tenebrae had to duck below the low stone opening, and he looked ridiculously outsized in the narrow spiral staircase they ascended.

"I can manage a staircase," Lazarus argued, when the demon ushered him ahead onto the twisting stone steps.

"We shall see," he countered, pushing the man forward insistently. He was apparently not willing to risk another accident in the dilapidated castle.

When they reached the battlement that crowned the tower, a sliver of pinkish-orange light was just beginning to crest on the horizon. Lazarus leaned against the stone perimeter, looking out of one of the square cutouts to admire the way the light sparkled on the river just to the North of the castle. The wind was chilling at this height and he was grateful for the radiating heat of the shadow demon beside him.

Sparing a sideward glance, he noticed that Tenebrae was not watching the sunrise, but rather observing the way the ever-increasing light illuminated the smoky flesh of his own hands. It made his appearance even more starkly inhuman, clashing against the brightness in equal measure to how effortlessly he blended in to the dark.

"Is it strange," Lazarus asked, curiously, "going around in daylight? I assume you couldn't do so before." He recalled the grimoire saying something about bound shadow demons gaining a resistance to sunlight.

"I could not," Tenebrae confirmed, distractedly, "it was uncomfortable at best and often completely impossible."

The warmth of the light felt rather pleasant now, he noted, where it had felt oppressive and disintegrating before the binding. He had not grown used to the feeling yet.

"That must have been quite limiting," the witch mused, seeing how the light swiftly crept in and systematically banished the shadows strewn across the landscape as it rose.

The shadow demon turned to him with interest; he had never really thought of it that way but he supposed it was true. He had only ever existed in the darkness of his natural element, but now the whole sunlit world was open to him.

"In a way, yes," he said, agreeing with the witch's oddly insightful observation. "Though I suppose that I have simply traded one limit to my freedom for another." It still rankled him, having been robbed of the choice, but it no longer seemed such a loathsome exchange. Were he given the choice right now, whether to accept a bond including the immunity and all of the conditions that came with it, he was no longer so certain that he would refuse.

"What, being burdened with a handsome and witty traveling companion?" Lazarus teased, "Indeed, how ever will you survive?"

He swooned with mock empathy, and then burst into laughter at his own joke. The orange glow of sunrise shined along the waves of his hair and his eyes glittered in the light. The joyous picture of his mirth was hard to resist and this time Tenebrae didn't fight the smile that broke out as he watched the witch sparkle with amusement.

"I suppose there are worse fates," the shadow demon conceded.

Chapter 11

AS ABOVE, SO BELOW

"**W**here is our destination, this evening?" Lazarus asked, eagerly, following closely behind the demon who tugged him into the unsettling void of shadowspace. He was becoming more used to the experience, and thankfully feeling less disoriented while traversing its dark pathways. Returning to Graymourne grew easier each time, and the witch noticed an almost magnetic pull that grew stronger the closer they got to home. He was not yet confident that he could find his way without the shadow demon's aid, but it did help him feel a little less unmoored.

"You will see," Tenebrae said, unhelpfully, as he dragged the man along behind him by the hand.

Lazarus rolled his eyes at the predictably laconic answer. The shadow had warmed a bit in the days since that morning at the castle, thawing into a somewhat cool demeanor that was a marked improvement over the dangerously arctic temperament he had exhibited at first.

Still, it had done little to loosen his tongue, which frustrated the more extroverted man to no end.

"You-will-see. Hmm, I believe I have heard of that," Lazarus drawled, sarcastically, "A quiet hamlet near Ipswich, is it not?"

He grinned, hearing the demon huff what might have been a laugh in response. It was invigorating whenever he was able to break through that stoic exterior and catch sight of what lay beneath. Each wry chuckle he managed to draw from the shadow only made him want more, and he was growing even bolder at joking with the demon.

"Not even close," Tenebrae said, a pleasantly amused tone mellowing the rough edges of his primordial voice. He pulled the witch to his side and then stopped.

Lazarus had felt the brief pressure of the void giving way to the more familiar earthly atmosphere, but they were still shrouded in near total darkness. Even with his supernaturally enhanced vision, he could only just make out a few light reflections dancing ahead. There was the occasional sound of dripping and gently moving water, but it was difficult to tell which direction it came from with the way it echoed in the space. If he had to guess, he would venture that they were in an underground cave of some sort.

"You are right, this is nothing like Ipswich," he remarked, dryly, keeping his grounding grip on the shadow demon's hand. "In fact, it rather looks like nothing at all. Are you certain we are not lost?"

This elicited the first genuine laugh that he had heard from Tenebrae. It sounded like volcanic rock shearing in two, as the rumbling sound bounced off of the unseen walls around them.

"Impatient little human," the demon admonished him, playfully, "we have a bit farther to go."

He resumed walking, shortening his usually long gait to keep the smaller man beside him.

"Yes, well, if you leave me alone in this gloomy cave, I will be quite cross," Lazarus grumbled, begrudgingly following the shadow's guidance in the near blind space.

"That, I could not do, even if I wished it," Tenebrae quipped, his tone still teasing.

The remark seemed off-hand and casual, simply a jest at their situation, but all that Lazarus could hear was the implication that the shadow demon didn't want to leave him here. That maybe he wanted to spend time with him, after all. His chest fluttered distractingly, robbing him of the witty retort he would usually have made.

They rounded a corner and his dark-attuned vision was suddenly suffused with bluish green light. As his eyes adjusted and he was able to more clearly see their surroundings, Lazarus gasped in delight. Craggy stone walls arched over them, stretching from the rocky earth on which they stood to a lazy underground river a couple meters away. The ceiling of the cave was dotted with innumerable tiny blue lights, some seeming to drip down from the surface in long tendrils. They covered the entire expanse, giving it the appearance of an eerie, star-packed night sky. It was breathtaking.

While the witch stood spellbound by the magical scene, Tenebrae wandered over to where the water gently lapped at the stone. Sitting down cross-legged on the cool surface, he leaned back onto his hands and gazed languidly into the lights above. When Lazarus eventually realized the demon was no longer beside him, he struggled for a moment to find the dark figure in the dim space. His almost perfect stillness made him even more difficult to spot amidst the dusky monochromatic backdrop.

Crossing the space with echoing footfalls, Lazarus sat down beside him on the ground. He looked up at the shadow, who hadn't moved, with his head tilted back to stare at the luminescent landscape above. Silhouetted against the bluish light, the sharp angles of his profile made him look like he was cut from a dark glacier; his deep set eyes half-hooded above an aquiline nose, lips shaped in a perpetually petulant frown, and a strong narrow chin. The illumination lent a soft glow to the demon's flesh, so that his pitch-black skull was just barely visible through the murky sea of his skin. Lost in the macabre beauty of his companion, Lazarus had no idea how long he had been staring when Tenebrae turned to look at him.

"How did you find this place?" he asked, quickly averting his gaze, embarrassed at being caught so blatantly ogling.

"Accidentally," the shadow demon admitted, chuckling softly. He sat up straighter, drawing one leg up to rest his arm against his knee. Even in a casual pose, he was a little menacing, draped in the confident air of an apex predator at rest. He lounged like a lion would. "I was wandering shadowspace, aimlessly searching for something interesting. I chose a random point and pushed through, ending up there."

He gestured to the water in front of them.

"Where? In the water?" Lazarus laughed, picturing the shadow demon emerging from the void into the bottom of a subterranean river. He could imagine the demon's irate facial expression perfectly, indignant as a wet cat and growling twice as loudly.

"It is deeper than it appears," Tenebrae offered, a hint of a smile playing at the corners of his mouth.

The witch grinned back at him, sitting in comfortable silence for a few moments. When it seemed the shadow was not going to elaborate further, Lazarus took a chance and spoke again.

"Is that all you used to do? Explore to pass the time?" he asked, always eager to keep the conversation going while the demon seemed amenable. "Before I so rudely interrupted by summoning you, of course?"

He kept his tone light, giving the shadow a cheeky wink and making fun of the less than cordial circumstances under which they met. Tenebrae raised an eyebrow at the mention of the ritual, but his amused expression didn't falter, to the human's relief.

"Yes, for the most part," he confirmed, humming thoughtfully before he continued. "Sometimes I would remain and observe the humans I came across. That is how I learned your language. Foolishly, I thought that perhaps if I could communicate with your kind they would be less hostile."

He laughed, but it was edged with a subtle bitterness, and his eyes grew distant as he became embroiled in the recollection.

"No, I suppose they wouldn't be," Lazarus agreed, with a cynical chuckle. He could only imagine the reception that the shadow demon received. It cast Tenebrae's contentious demeanor in somewhat of a different light. He would be guarded too if he was greeted with fear and loathing by everyone he met. "So, you did all your wandering alone. Did you never want a companion?"

"I did not consider that it was possible."

Tenebrae shifted his gaze out over the water and grew quiet. Lazarus opened his mouth to ask him another question, but thought better of it. The shadow demon appeared deep in thought, his brows knit in contemplation. Instead, he watched the gentle undulation of blue light reflecting on the dark water, the mesmerizing twinkle lulling him into an almost meditative state.

"I have a question to ask you," the shadow announced suddenly, breaking him out of his reverie.

"Oh, of course," he replied, apprehensive of what the shadow could possibly have been deliberating so intently for the past several silent minutes. "What do you wish to know?"

"That day in the forest when you put your lips on mine. Why did you do that?" Tenebrae asked bluntly, his eyes still trained on the opposite side of the cave.

The question had been eating at him since it happened. It was what had stopped him that day in the castle, when their lips had been inches from each other. He wanted to close that distance and taste the human's mouth again, but he needed to know why Lazarus had done it the first time. It felt even more pressing, since he had begun allowing himself to actually enjoy the witch's company.

Lazarus was rather easy to be with; he was unafraid to banter with him, volleying back his own quips and barbs. He was clever and though curious, he didn't pry for more information than Tenebrae was willing to give. He simply seemed to accept the demon as he was.

It also did not hurt that he was extremely nice to look at.

Tenebrae could fathom only two reasons for Lazarus's actions all those weeks ago; either it was a cunning manipulation of some kind that he still didn't understand, or the man was somehow genuinely attracted to him, a literal demon. As far fetched as the idea seemed to him, he ventured to hope that it was the second option.

Lazarus froze at the question, turning towards the demon and blinking owlishly at him while every thought in his head promptly ground to a screeching halt. This was not at all the type of question he had been expecting.

It was impossible for him to forget the aforementioned incident, but in the weeks since, he had come to assume that the shadow would prefer to ignore it. Sure, there were a few moments here and there where he thought he saw a spark of something in the way that the shadow looked at him, but he was quick to dismiss those lingering looks or unnecessary touches as wishful thinking. Now, he wasn't so sure. In his state of shock, it took a few moments before he was able to answer, and by then Tenebrae had turned to him with an opaque yet expectant look.

"Why did I kiss you, you mean?" he managed to sputter eventually.

Tenebrae nodded, and his whole body felt flushed. He could feel his pulse beating loudly in his ears like a drum. Lazarus searched the shadow's face, desperately trying to discern a clue about Tenebrae's feelings amidst his characteristically detached expression. It was like trying to determine the emotions of a mountain.

He began to sweat, and he blurted out the first answer that came to mind. "B-because I wanted to. I probably shouldn't have, but I was so frustrated and you were just so maddeningly handsome."

"And, now," the demon growled, emboldened by the human's confession. He shifted the hand at his knee down to the ground and leaned towards Lazarus. "Do you still want to kiss me?"

Lazarus's earlier impression of a lion returned. It was such a small movement, and yet, it instantly made him feel like prey. His senses lit up with the primal warning bells of danger, though the feeling was quickly subsumed by a recklessly blazing desire.

There was only one possible answer to the shadow's question.

"Yes," he whispered, breathlessly, feeling like he was in a dream. He didn't move a muscle, just in case. If this was a dream, then he definitely didn't want to wake up.

Throwing caution to the wind, he added, "I would do more than that if you will permit me."

Tenebrae flashed him a brief predatory smile, and then impulsively yanked the man into his lap. He wasted no time, immediately crashing their lips together. It was a little clumsy and every bit as ferocious as their first kiss.

"Wait," Lazarus gasped, pressing both hands against the shadow's chest to get him to slow down. The action got Tenebrae to pause, looking down at him with an expression of irritated confusion. He took the demon's face in his hands gently, and held him still while he angled their lips together again more slowly. "Like this."

He led the demon in a softer, more sensual kiss, while running his thumbs delicately across his jawline. Hesitantly at first, the shadow indulged him, but he soon mastered the unhurried pace and sensuous movements. His body, however, remained awkwardly stiff, as if he didn't know what to do with his hands. Lazarus stroked a hand down one of the demon's powerful arms, coaxing it around his waist. Tenebrae took the hint, tightening his arm around him and dropping his other hand to knead at the man's hip. The low sound he made when Lazarus's tongue licked softly into his mouth was almost infrasonic.

Lazarus trailed his lips down the demon's jaw to press open-mouthed kisses against the length of his throat. He grazed his teeth along the warm flesh, biting down when the shadow's breathing grew heavier. He sucked hard at a point just below the demon's jaw, wondering if it was even possible to leave a mark on him but putting in the effort nonetheless.

Tenebrae growled at the sensation and his hand found its way into the witch's hair, gripping the wavy locks tightly. He used the claws tangled in his hair to pull Lazarus away from his neck and tilt the man's head back. His mouth quickly descended on the exposed column of the witch's throat, having just enough presence of mind to temper the strength of his bite.

When his teeth grazed a particularly sensitive spot, Lazarus gave a soft moan and ground his hips down against the demon's lap, pressing the growing bulge in his breeches against Tenebrae's stomach in the process. The shadow rumbled, feeling his own arousal harden in response.

Lazarus felt something shift beneath him, and deftly slid an exploratory hand down the front of the demon's lean torso. Dipping his hand between them, his palm met the large tapered head of a thick cock covered in smooth ridges. When he ran his hand down the impressive length of it, Tenebrae drew a sharp breath and stilled.

"Do you want me to stop?" Lazarus asked quietly, pausing his ministrations immediately at the change in his companion's demeanor. He didn't remove his hand, but leaned back slightly so he was able to look Tenebrae in the face. Even seated in the demon's lap, he had to look up at him.

"No," the shadow ground out, decisively, his gravelly voice even rougher than usual.

The intensity of the look on his face was borderline murderous; in fact, it would have been frightening if Lazarus hadn't seen it before. Now, it simply amused him to realize that the shadow demon's facial expressions for lust and bloodlust were nearly identical.

A smirk curled at his lips, encouraged by the effect he was having on the shadow, and he shifted back slightly on the demon's lap so he could better see what he was doing. Tenebrae's claws tightened around his hip as if to prevent him from leaving.

"I assume you have never been with a human before?" he murmured, curious to know if his suspicions about the shadow demon's experience, or rather lack thereof, were true.

As he closed his fingers around the textured length, Tenebrae shook his head, his jaw clenched tightly in concentration. A strange sense of pride bloomed in Lazarus at being the first person to touch the shadow demon like this. They both looked down, watching as his hand stroked slowly downward to where the dark grey base connected inside a now splayed open seam between the shadow's legs.

Interesting.

Intrigued by the demon's unusual anatomy, Lazarus brought his other hand down to lightly rub the soft smoky skin inside the now exposed sheath, delighting in the way Tenebrae's abs rippled from the touch. He leaned up to place a light kiss on his lips, while he continued leisurely pumping the demon's cock.

"Does that feel good?" he asked, lips brushing against the shadow's as he whispered the question,

"Yes. Fuck," Tenebrae swore, canting his hips up into the human's touch.

He closed his eyes, leaning his forehead against Lazarus's while his mouth dropped open with heavy breaths. The feeling of the witch's skilled hands squeezing and sliding over his length was overwhelming; he didn't know how much of this he could stand but he also never wanted it to end.

A small sound of protest escaped him when Lazarus paused to climb off his lap after a few blissful minutes.

"Lie back for me," the human purred at him with a placating grin, pressing a hand against his chest to encourage him to lay down.

The shadow demon complied. He would have done nearly whatever the human asked, eager for him to continue his tantalizing touch. While he reclined against the stone floor, Lazarus settled on his knees straddling the demon's thighs.

Tenebrae sighed contentedly, closing his eyes as the man resumed stroking his aching cock. He had just relaxed into the sensation when he felt the warmth of Lazarus's lips close around the tip. His breath caught in his throat and his eyes shot back open. In heated fascination, he watched as the human's pink tongue swirled around the inky head and then flicked gently over the tip, startling a surprised moan out of the shadow.

The witch gave an appreciative hum, which vibrated against him deliciously, and then sank his mouth further down, enveloping his cock in a hot, wet sensation that had the demon straining to hold back from bucking his hips. Tenebrae hadn't been certain what the man meant when he said he wished to do more than kiss him, and his curiosity was being rewarded beyond any of his expectations. The exquisite feeling of the human's mouth around him was slowly driving him to madness as Lazarus flattened his tongue against the underside and began bobbing his head slowly, while using his hand to work the generous length that wouldn't fit in his mouth.

Lazarus was determined after hearing the first, to drag more moans from the shadow. So, when Tenebrae's cock hit the back of his throat, he swallowed around it purposefully. The demon keened loudly, the sound echoing in the subterranean cave, and Lazarus pulled off of his length with a loud pop.

"Let me hear that beautiful voice of yours. You're doing so well for me," Lazarus encouraged him in a sultry tone.

He smiled at the whine that Tenebrae tried to stifle and then took him back into his mouth. It seemed that the formidable shadow was not immune to the effects of praise, quite the opposite judging by the sound of it. In his many daydreams, he had never imagined the stoic demon submitting to his instructions like this, or making such intoxicatingly plaintive sounds. It was absolutely addicting.

The shadow combed his claws through Lazarus's hair, resting a heavy hand against the back of his head. The sharp points of his other hand dug into the stone below them as Tenebrae desperately tried to ground himself amid the onslaught of pleasure. He could feel himself losing what little control he had left, his hips now thrusting shallowly into the witch's mouth of their own accord, though he tried to hold back his strength.

The human's murmured praises only unraveled him more, and Tenebrae greedily drank in each honeyed word. His mind buzzed pleasantly from the man's approval, each beguiling word making him feel more eager to please him. Warmth was pooling low in his gut and his spine tingled in anticipation.

Sensing the shadow demon was getting close, Lazarus matched his pace to Tenebrae's thrusts, bent on making him come undone. The low sound of the demon's moans had his own cock twitching in his breeches and he groaned around the thick length, feeling the claws in his hair tighten as he did.

"Such a good boy, Tenebrae," he murmured in a velvety tone, relishing the choked whimper that sounded from the shadow's throat in reaction to the pet name. He would have to remember that little tidbit for later. "That's it, come for me."

He barely managed to get his mouth back around the textured girth, taking him as deeply as he could go, before the demon was spilling down his throat with a thundering cry. Lazarus swallowed what he could, some of the shadow's inky release leaking from the sides of his lips as he worked him through an intense climax.

When the shadow demon had stilled and was easing back down from the high, Lazarus sat up, soothing his hands over the still tense muscles of Tenebrae's thighs. The demon eyed him heatedly, tracking the movement of his tongue as Lazarus licked away the dark earthy-tasting remnants of liquid that stained his lips. He had a brief moment to enjoy the smug satisfaction of a blowjob truly well delivered, before Tenebrae seized him by the hips with a startling speed, and dragged him up his body to sit on his chest.

"My turn," he snarled, menacingly.

Chapter 12

HELPING HAND

Tenebrae's hands roamed over the witch's hips, claws hooking underneath the waistband of his soft woolen breeches. Lazarus seized the demon's wrists in a tight grasp with a panicked noise of protest, anticipating that yet another one of his garments was about to meet its demise by those razor-sharp appendages.

"If you wish these to remain intact, I suggest you remove them," the shadow demon advised, lowly.

It became abundantly clear that the balance of who was in charge here had just shifted, without Tenebrae ever having to budge from his position underneath the human.

Lazarus found himself sweating under the demon's scorching gaze, and let go of his wrists to rid himself of the offending piece of clothing. His hands shook lightly with excitement as he undid the buttons at the tented front of his trousers, while Tenebrae watched him with rapt attention. Raising up to his knees, he untucked his long linen shirt and pulled it over his head, and the demon helped him slide the pants down his hips far enough for his cock to spring free, already hard and leaking with arousal.

Mimicking what the witch had done to him, Tenebrae palmed the man's erection, gently smoothing a rough textured hand down the velvety skin and thumbing over the flushed head. Minding his claws, he wrapped his fingers around it firmly and begin stroking at a languid pace, enraptured by the way the human's eyes fluttered shut and his swollen lips parted in a quiet moan.

He watched Lazarus's expression carefully, honing in on the right pressure and speed to elicit increasingly loud sounds out of him. The demon's free hand roamed over the taut planes of his hips and torso while he worked, eventually settling with a firm grip on the muscular flesh of the witch's ass.

An opportunely timed squeeze that dug a few claws into a rounded asscheek had Lazarus bucking into the demon's hand with a familiar whimper. Tenebrae recognized the sound from one of their earliest encounters, when he'd gripped him by the throat. On a hunch, he snaked his right hand up to wrap around the witch's neck.

Lazarus's eyes snapped open with a gasp, and he locked a startled gaze onto the shadow who smirked below him, looking extremely pleased with himself. Tenebrae squeezed the sides of his throat just enough to make the sound of his breathing raspy and his head light, feeling the man's length twitch in his grasp while his whines grew louder.

"Do you like that?" the shadow demon purred, flexing the hold on his throat for emphasis. His left hand, steadily stroking the witch's cock, sped up incrementally while a few tendrils of shadow rose up from the demon's ribs to curl around Lazarus's wrists and bind them together behind his back. He squirmed helplessly against the shadows that ensnared him, while Tenebrae continued with a sharp grin, "You have always liked it when I am rough with you, haven't you, Lazarus? I didn't know what that pink color on your face or those pretty little noises you're making meant before, but I do now."

The witch's cheeks burned with a combination of embarrassment and arousal at the truth of Tenebrae's comment.

"Yes… oh, fuck… yes I like it. Please," Lazarus groaned, struggling to get the words out around the demon's constricting grip.

Distantly, he realized that he should have known better than to assume that the keenly observant demon hadn't noticed his reactions all this time. Now that the shadow had connected the dots, he was well and truly fucked. Or, at least, soon to be.

With a pleased hum, Tenebrae shifted the human forward, so that he was close enough to replace the hand on the witch's cock with his mouth. He took it down to the base in one motion, pressing his nose into the soft curls at his groin while Lazarus let out a beautifully wrecked moan.

The shadow demon's obscenely long tongue coiled around the shaft while he used one large hand on the human's hip to move his pelvis in slow, controlled thrusts, sliding his length in and out of the searing heat of his mouth. No matter how Lazarus struggled against the restraining hands and tendrils, Tenebrae refused to deviate from the steady, simmering pace. When the witch keened in frustration, the shadow indulged a cruel urge to deny him, slowing even further for a few moments to savor his torment until the man was begging incoherently. When he finally had his fill of the fervent pleading, the demon decided to take mercy on his prey.

"Bloody hell," Lazarus swore, catching himself with his hands as he fell, suddenly released from the tight hold on his wrists and neck all at once. He was pitched forward over the demon's face, knees still on either side of his chest and cock still buried in his mouth to the hilt.

Tenebrae stroked his palms up and down his waist and thighs, guiding his movements with a much lighter hold while his tongue worked over the witch's length. He gave an approving growl when Lazarus realized that he was going to allow him to control the pace and take what he needed.

He looked down, locking eyes with the shadow just as his dark tongue slithered down to stroke over the sensitive flesh of his balls. The sensation caused his hips to buck harshly into the face of the demon, who only smiled at him shamelessly and then hollowed his cheeks around the intrusion. Lazarus moaned, his eyes rolling back in his head as his thrusts picked up speed, fucking into the shadow's mouth with abandon.

When Tenebrae responded with a low rumble, it vibrated down his cock and spread warm pleasure across his entire pelvis. He came with a loud cry of the demon's name, losing himself to the wet choking sound of Tenebrae's throat taking everything he had to give.

Lazarus dropped to his elbows, unable to support himself any longer with the way his arms and the rest of his body were shaking. He breathed heavily, beginning to slowly return to coherence, when he felt the shadow demon's tongue move, cleaning up the last vestiges of his release. With an overstimulated cry, he rolled off of him and onto his back, lying next to the shadow and melting bonelessly into the ground.

Tenebrae prowled over him with a low chuckle, immensely pleased at the debauched state to which he had managed to reduce the human. He licked a burning stripe up Lazarus's front, and then stole his lips in a passionate kiss. His ridged length was already growing hard again where it was pressed against the human's thigh.

"I think I may have created a monster," the witch groaned, mostly to himself. The shadow demon's earlier pliancy had lulled him into a false sense of security, and Lazarus hadn't anticipated him returning the favor quite so voraciously. Although, considering the ferocious zeal with which Tenebrae did most things, perhaps he should have.

Tenebrae laughed and buried his face in his neck, sucking at the flesh tenderly before placing a firm bite over his pulse.

"No, but you did bind yourself to one, pretty little human," he purred, with a wicked smirk. "Perhaps you should have considered the consequences." The remark was punctuated with a sharp slap to the outside of his still naked thigh, causing the man to cry out in surprise.

If he had known that the consequences would be getting his soul sucked out of his dick by a gorgeous seven-foot-tall nightmare, Lazarus thought the only thing he would have done differently was perform the ritual sooner. At the moment, however, he was entirely too exhausted for the continuation of any carnal activities.

"I will happily consider further consequences. After a rest," Lazarus countered cheekily, putting emphasis on the 'after.'

He took the demon by the shoulders, and moved him to one side so he could right his clothing, tucking himself back into his breeches which were thankfully still in one piece. Once he was properly attired again, Tenebrae allowed him to arrange their positions so that the human was cuddled into his side and they could both look up at the illuminated ceiling of the cave. They lay in peaceful silence for a while.

Now that the raging squall of their lust was calming, Tenebrae struggled to make sense of what he was feeling. Desire was easy, it felt like hunger and rage and happiness all melted together in a viscous honey. But the gentle satisfaction that came after was unfamiliar. With the pliant warmth of the human pressed against his side, his claws resting on the small of his back, the shadow demon felt the insidious buzzing of uncertainty creeping in, unsure of what to do now. He didn't regret the amorous encounter, far from it. In fact, he very much wanted a repeat performance, or several. Still, he prickled restlessly beneath the contented warmth that settled over them like a blanket. The human seemed happy enough to simply lay in his arms and stare at the glowing stone, and eventually, the taciturn shadow realized that he would have to be the one to break the silence.

"They are tiny creatures, you know," the shadow demon commented, gesturing to the lights above, "innumerable minuscule life forms that each emit their own light."

Lazarus turned his head to look at him curiously, both surprised by the demon actually starting a conversation and at the awkwardness of his pillow talk. He smiled and slung an arm across the shadow's waist.

"Hmm, fascinating," he said, drowsily, still comfortable in the fuzzy warmth of their afterglow. "I thought perhaps it was a quality of the stone." He trailed his fingers lightly back and forth across the demon's torso as he spoke. Curiosity soon got the better of him and he paused his idle caressing to ask, "So, you really have never been with a human before? You were quite, um, adept."

"I learn swiftly, and you provided an excellent demonstration," Tenebrae replied with a sultry rumble. He sighed and continued in a more serious tone, "But no, I have known precisely two humans who did not flee from me in terror or attack on sight. And one of those is you."

Lazarus perked up at the admission, he had half expected the demon to deflect away from such a personal question. He was interested to see how much of his past he would share.

"Who was the other one?" he prompted.

The shadow demon eyed him dubiously, but found only genuine interest in his expression. Though it felt strange to divulge such information about himself, he was at least grateful for the distraction. As long as they were talking, he didn't have to think about what he was feeling, or why he was feeling it, or who he was feeling it for.

"Another witch," Tenebrae said. "He was the first one to summon me."

"And what happened to him?" Lazarus inquired, although he had his suspicions.

"He died," the demon growled.

Lazarus thought back to the night of the ritual; even now he was almost able to feel the sharp slice of Tenebrae's claws tearing through his flesh. It was not difficult to imagine the manner of the other summoner's demise, and he decided not to press the shadow for more details.

"When was this?" he asked, instead. The shadow demon appeared to consider his question for some time.

"Perhaps seventy years ago," Tenebrae ventured, "it is difficult to be certain. Demons do not measure time as strictly as humans. Much of the time, we simply exist."

He shrugged and Lazarus did some math in his head. There was a relatively small percentage of the world's population who were likely to even know how to summon a shadow demon in the first place, much less do it successfully. Still, for Tenebrae to only have been summoned once before, it made him curious.

"How old are you, then? Approximately, of course," Lazarus asked. It made no difference to him what age the demon was, but he craved every little bit of information he could learn about the creature beside him.

"I had only come into being a few decades before that," the shadow mused, mulling over the somewhat murky first years of his existence. "Somewhere around one-hundred and fifty, I suppose." He paused for a moment and then turned towards Lazarus. "And you?"

"Twenty-six," the witch answered, quickly, a bit surprised by the reciprocation of his question. He wanted to ask more about how shadow demons were made, but his eyes were growing heavy. He leaned further into Tenebrae's side and stifled a yawn. The siren call of sleep was getting louder. Distantly, he wondered how long they had been gone.

"We should return," the shadow demon mused, seeing the fatigue settling over his companion.

He gently untangled himself and stood up, holding out a hand to help Lazarus up. The human wobbled unsteadily on his feet, so Tenebrae swept him up into his arms in a bridal carry. The unexpected gesture made the witch giggle, and his belly fluttered at the ease with which the demon manhandled him.

A small genuine smile graced the shadow's face as he listened to the sound of his delight, but Lazarus only saw it for a moment before they were plunged into the encompassing darkness of shadowspace.

Leaning against the long stack of firewood a few days later, Lazarus let the axe fall to the ground, having just finished chopping another cord of logs. He wiped the sweat from his brow, sagging against the rough surface. A delicate hand settled on his bicep and he startled, bolting upright to find Sarah beside him looking equal parts concerned and annoyed.

"Come inside and rest," she said, sternly, in a voice usually reserved for the rare times when Elijah was being defiant. "You look like you could fall asleep on your feet at any moment."

"Just one more cord and we will be caught up," he countered, smoothing his hair back from his face. "I will be in after."

When he moved to pick up the axe once more, though, Sarah quickly stepped in front of him, blocking his way.

"Absolutely not," she declared, crossing her arms resolutely. She was furious, eyes flashing dangerously as she stared him down. "You cannot keep on like this, doing the chores of two men all day and then taking off to wherever it is that you go at night. I will not have you working yourself into an early grave, Laz." Her tone softened at the end, a plea amongst the chastising.

He sighed, she was right of course; with Levi gone, they needed him. He couldn't afford to exhaust himself this way for much longer, trying to keep up with the demands of running the farm and keeping his bargain with the shadow demon. He shouldn't have been surprised that Sarah had noticed his nocturnal absences, as sharply observant as she was.

"I'm sorry," he offered, contritely, shoulders slumping in defeat as he followed her into the manor. They entered the kitchen and she thrust a cup of water into his hand. "The work must be done though, and as for where I go at night. It is part of my bargain with the demon, I go with him where he wishes, and he refrains from sowing chaos."

Lazarus had hoped to keep his dealings with Tenebrae out of her mind, not wanting to burden her with more than she was already dealing with, but it seemed to be growing more difficult.

"Then, if he wants to monopolize your nights," Sarah stated, pragmatically, "you tell him that he can lend a hand around the farm during the day. It is only fair."

Lazarus barked out a laugh before he could stop himself, picturing a sullen Tenebrae dragging the plow through the fields. He fell silent when Sarah raised a disapproving eyebrow at him, and considered the idea more seriously. With the shadow demon's size and strength, he would be able to make quick work of the most strenuous chores.

He could have chopped that wood in at least half the time that it took me, he thought.

The question, though, was whether he would. As he pondered the thought, his eye caught a shift in the darkness of the hallway behind her and he began to notice the familiar prickle of being watched.

"I think you may have just told him yourself," he told Sarah, tilting his head curiously towards the loitering fog of shadow.

She turned, just in time to see the dusky haze assemble itself into an intimidating, statuesque figure. With a surprised yelp, she backed up, putting a few more feet between herself and the demon, who merely regarded her with mild amusement. When the shock of his appearance wore off, her face hardened into a determined frown.

"Well?" Sarah challenged, straightening her apron before putting her hands on her hips. "You heard me. If you want his nights, you help during the day. Understood?"

Neither of them moved, locked in a stand-off when both of them refused to look away.

Half of Lazarus was wildly entertained to see the diminutive woman fearlessly scold the towering shadow; the other half was terrified that the strength of the protection amulet she wore was about to be put to the test. For a tense few moments, he held his breath, poised to dart in front of her if necessary.

Finally, Tenebrae chuckled, the low rumble of his mirth breaking the thick tension in the room.

"I suppose I could do that," he mused, and both humans relaxed instantly. If the distinctly inhuman sound of the demon's speech disquieted Sarah, she did not show it.

"Thank you," she said, addressing him with a curt nod. "Now, if you will excuse me, I have tasks to attend to."

Tenebrae took one large step aside, clearing the way for her to exit the room. She passed by him, keeping a watchful side-eye on the demon as she moved. When the woman had disappeared down the hall, he grinned and sauntered over to where Lazarus stood.

"You agreed to that rather quickly," the witch said, eyeing the unusually agreeable shadow demon suspiciously.

He had fully expected him to refuse, or at the very least to demand something in return. Judging by the mischievous twinkle in his black eyes, there would be a price for his services one way or another.

"I have my reasons," Tenebrae hummed, running the tip of one claw down the man's neck. "Now, what assistance do you require?"

"Well," he replied, swallowing thickly as he tried to remain focused with the object of his desire looming enticingly, "there is still firewood to be split. And then the north field needs plowing." His muscles ached at the very thought of more work, and he was suddenly grateful for Sarah's intervention.

"Show me," the demon said simply, inviting him to lead the way.

He followed Lazarus out the back door to the line of stacked wood, where the witch picked up an axe and held it out to him. Tenebrae looked at the proffered object with disdain, choosing instead to pick up a log with his bare hands. He sunk the claws of both hands into the center of one end. It split easily with a bit of applied pressure, so he gripped both sides and pulled, ripping the chunk of wood neatly in half.

Lazarus stared, awestruck, as the shadow tore each of those pieces in half as well. He set the axe down and sat on the ground, leaning his back against a large birch tree. His eyes roved over the lean musculature of Tenebrae's arms and shoulders as the demon continued splitting logs into neat quarters with alarming ease. He was methodical in his work, and the repetitive motions were hypnotic to watch. With his already exhausted state, it did not take long to lull Lazarus into a deep sleep propped comfortably in the afternoon sun.

The next thing he knew, he was being gently shaken awake to find the shadow demon crouched before him. Looking past the blithely smirking figure, Lazarus could see the wood pile, stacked high with firewood and an empty space where the store of uncut logs had been. The sun was a bit lower in the sky now, but he couldn't have been out for very long. Still, he felt worlds better after the rather peaceful nap.

"Sleep well?" Tenebrae asked, plucking a stray leaf from the man's hair. When he sleepily murmured his assent, the demon said, "Good, you needed it."

"You finished already?" Lazarus asked, incredulously; the task would have easily taken him until dinner time. The shadow demon, however, didn't seem the slightest bit fatigued, and he realized that he had never seen him anything less than fully alert. "Do you not need rest? When do you sleep?"

"I do not," he replied, tilting his head in amusement at the bewildered stare the answer got him. "It is unnecessary. Take me to this field that must be plowed.

You can explain what plowing is on the way." He gripped the witch by the biceps and hoisted him to his feet.

"It's this way," Lazarus said, brushing the dirt from his clothes as he turned to lead the way.

He was still astonished that Tenebrae was being so helpful, and more than a little curious to see how this would go. Explaining the basics of the task as they walked, he eyed the hulking figure at his side.

"Usually, we would need horses for this, but I have a feeling that you will not require the assistance. Also, I am fairly certain that the animals would be terrified of you."

"As are most humans," Tenebrae pointed out, looking down at the witch with a teasing glint in his eye. He reached out a shadow tendril to coil around the human's waist and yank him closer to his side. Resting a large hand at the back of his neck, he gave a sharp-toothed grin at the way Lazarus's pulse jumped under his thumb. "You, however, have a much different reaction to me. So easy to fluster."

"Perhaps," Lazarus conceded, unable to repress the light shiver that went down his spine at the velvety tone of the demon's voice. "And yet, I recall you were the one whining for me like the good boy you are only three nights ago."

Now that he knew that the shadow desired him just as much, he couldn't help but poke the beast, so to speak, just to see what kind of reaction it would get out of him. And get a reaction, it did.

Swift as lightning, Tenebrae shoved him up against the nearest tree with a menacing growl. The shadow demon's claws sprawled across his collarbones, pinning him against the rough bark. Looking up into the demon's face, teeth bared and eyes sparking with intensity, Lazarus returned his licentious glare with a cunning smile.

Oh, he likes being called a good boy, he thought. *He likes it, and it makes him furious.*

There were not many ways he could gain the upper hand on the shadow demon, surpassed in strength, speed, and sheer size as he was; so this was a precious gift fallen into his lap. He intended to use the knowledge for good, mostly, but the temptation to bait him at least a little was too great.

"Careful now, Tenebrae," he purred suggestively, sliding his hands up the armored planes of his chest. "What am I to make of this, do you intend to plow the fields or me?"

The innuendo seemed to confuse the demon, a quizzical furrowing of his brows now tempering the fury of his gaze.

Right, he has never been with a human before, why should he understand such a euphemism, he thought, and it dawned on Lazarus that the tall, fearsome, incredibly beautiful creature caging him in right now was a virgin.

"What do you mean?" Tenebrae asked, warily.

He found the indirect way that humans communicated to be so confusing sometimes. He was able to infer a general sense from the flirtatious tone of the witch's voice, but the meaning eluded him. If it was anything like what the human had done the other night, though, he was very interested in plowing him.

"Be a good boy and help me with the fields, and I will show you," Lazarus promised, prying Tenebrae's hand from his chest and slipping out from between him and the tree. The demon let him go, curiosity overriding the riled state that the witch seemed to be so adept at stirring in him.

"Fine," Tenebrae grumbled, following him the rest of the short walk to the field in question.

He wasn't embarrassed, exactly, at the way the pet name made him feel; he was just surprised. It had blindsided him the first time the witch said it, sending a wave of satisfaction that quenched a need he hadn't even known was there. It was a vulnerable feeling, which was an entirely unfamiliar experience in itself. Nothing had ever made him feel vulnerable in the way this aggravating, enticing human did, and it unsettled him how badly he craved to feel that way again.

The plow was already in place at the field when they arrived, and Lazarus launched into a quick explanation of its operation. It all seemed simple enough to the shadow demon; furrow long lines in the soil in a regular pattern. The contraption was heavy, but easy enough for Tenebrae to move. Teasingly, Lazarus suggested that he would steer, while they hitched the plow to the shadow demon, in the horse's place. That idea was promptly shut down with a glare that didn't quite manage to quell the man's amused snickering. He filed that insolence away to deal with later.

"Go rest," an exasperated Tenebrae told Lazarus when the instructions concluded. He grabbed the man, winding shadow tendrils around him tightly and stealing a short but ravenous kiss. "I suspect you are going to need it. I will fetch you when I am finished here."

The witch looked a little dazed when he released him, lingering for a moment as if he was trying to figure out what to say, before heading off to the manor while the demon set to his task.

True to his estimation, Tenebrae made short work of the field. This part of the farm was far enough from any roads that it was unlikely he would be seen, but he still kept his guard up for anyone moving about nearby just in case. Other than a few deer grazing by the edge of the trees, there was no one to disturb his work. By the time the sun was setting, he had carved neat parallel lines in the entire field. The work was done and now it was time to collect his reward.

Slipping into a shadow at the tree line, he quickly emerged in Lazarus's bedroom on the second floor of the manor. The latter was curled up on his side, fast asleep and tucked haphazardly beneath a blanket. It looked like he was still in his day clothes, although he had removed his jacket and waistcoat. Tenebrae slid into the bed behind him, pulling him against his chest with one arm. As he nuzzled into the side of his neck, Lazarus began to stir, sleepily registering the demon's presence.

"Well, this is a most pleasant way to wake up," he hummed contentedly. He pressed back against the demon encouragingly, while the shadow's hand wandered over his front. It was only when the demon cupped him through his trousers that he blinked fully awake, realizing with alarm where they were.

"Wait. Tenebrae, not here," he hissed, gripping the demon's forearm tightly, despite his hips pressing further into the errant hand. He could see it was dark outside, so the rest of the family would surely be inside.

"Why not?" the shadow demon taunted in a low rumble. "Afraid you will not be able to stay quiet?"

His fingers gripped around Lazarus's hardening length, stroking him through the thick fabric of his breeches. The demon's other hand quickly snaked under him to clamp down over the witch's mouth.

"Mmhmm," he hummed from behind the large, rough palm that now covered half of his face. A muffled moan escaped as he writhed in the shadow's hold, and Tenebrae chuckled sinisterly.

"Very well," he relented, rolling them both off the bed and straight into the shadows at its side.

Chapter 13

COURTING DANGER

A light puff of dust arose and a soft whoosh sounded as Lazarus and Tenebrae landed, falling out of shadowspace onto a sumptuous, pillowy surface. The shadow demon released his hold, and Lazarus rolled to one side, settling next to him on the plush velvet blanket of what appeared to be an ornately carved four-post canopy bed. He looked around them in the dim light of the quarter moon, which streamed in through tall arched windows framed by heavy brocade curtains. Artwork in gilded frames adorned the dark walls, a mix of finely crafted baroque and Ottoman furniture filled the room, and a large empty stone fireplace was set in the wall to their right.

"Where are we?" Lazarus wondered aloud, getting up to explore the room; it was unlike any place he had ever been.

It was certainly far too rich to be a home in the colonies. The densely patterned textiles and painted furniture held distinctly Eastern influences. Metallic embroidery glinted in the moonlight. Wherever they were, it was a feast for the eyes, even in the dark.

"Somewhere we will not be disturbed," the demon answered, cryptically. He lay on his side, watching Lazarus intently.

"Does no one live here?" the witch asked, amazed that such a luxuriously decorated space would go unused. He brushed at the thin layer of dust that clung to the thick curtains draped around the bed. It was evident that no one had been in the room in quite some time.

"Some do," Tenebrae said, stretching out on the absurdly large mattress with his hands behind his head, "but this area of the property is unused. The humans here believe it is haunted."

Lazarus crawled onto the soft surface, sitting next to the demon lounging in the middle of it.

"Surely," he said, running a hand softly over the shadow's exoskeletal ribs, "that belief has nothing at all to do with your presence, does it?" He leaned down, lightly kissing the demon on the lips.

"Of course not," Tenebrae replied with a proud smirk, tangling his claws in the human's chestnut waves to pull him further into the kiss.

He took his time, savoring the witch's full lips and exploring his mouth with his tongue the way Lazarus had taught him. His instincts protested against the softness of it, urging him to devour the man voraciously, but he ignored them for now. There would be time enough for that later.

When they came up for air, he reminded him, "I believe you had something to show me?"

"Hmm, that I most certainly do," Lazarus murmured, excitedly, already beginning to kiss his way down the demon's body. "Humans often use words like 'plow' as a euphemism for sex. It is considered more polite, I suppose."

His hands roamed freely, groping and squeezing every inch of his long torso, taking note of which spots seemed the most sensitive and lavishing them with attention while he spoke. A contented rumble vibrated the shadow's chest as the human's blunt teeth scraped along his hipbone; it sounded the way a volcano would, if it could purr.

"The impolite version," Lazarus continued, "would be to say that I wish to fuck you. Do you know what that means?"

The shadow demon shook his head. He was familiar with the expletive of course, but not its meaning in their current context.

Lazarus eased Tenebrae's thighs apart, kneeling between them before pulling his shirt over his head and quickly shedding his breeches. The shadow growled lowly at the sight of him completely bared, his eyes lingering on the crescent moon shaped mark on the man's inner thigh. He was propped up on his elbows to better appreciate the view, and Lazarus watched in fascination as his smoke colored cock unfurled from its sheath and stood at attention. The size of it, even having seen it before, was mildly intimidating.

Fortunately, Lazarus adored a challenge.

"Do you want me to touch you?" he asked, huskily, massaging the thick muscles of the demon's thighs as he coaxed his legs up into a bent position. He worked his way higher to the apex of the shadow's legs, stopping just shy of his twitching length.

"Yes," Tenebrae said, roughly, growing impatient to see what the human had in store for him. At his sides, his claws sunk through the layers of fabric and feathers beneath them. The tendrils of shadow that usually flared lazily from his body now writhed restlessly around him like snakes about to strike.

"I want you to tell me if I do something you don't enjoy," Lazarus instructed, meeting Tenebrae's intense gaze with a soft look, and inching his hands closer to where the demon so desperately wanted them. "Do you trust me to make you feel good?"

When the shadow demon nodded in response, Lazarus took his cock in one hand, spreading the leaking arousal over its surface in slow strokes. Tenebrae laid back against the pillows with a satisfied groan. Smiling at the sound that the motion pulled from him, Lazarus kept a steady, massaging pace until he felt the demon's hips begin to move, chasing his hand. Tenebrae let out a discontented grumble when he paused to pull a small vial of oil from the pocket of his discarded breeches. Lazarus locked eyes with him as he coated his fingers with the slippery liquid.

"Stay still for me and relax," he instructed.

With his left hand returning to its place wrapped around Tenebrae's thick length, he slid his right hand between the demon's muscular asscheeks, circling his entrance experimentally. The shadow's eyebrow raised inquisitively, but he made no protest, so Lazarus began gently pressing a slick finger against it, encouraging the tight ring of muscle to relax. The shadow demon's eyes fell closed and his breath grew heavier.

"Is this alright?" Lazarus asked softly, as he worked the digit deeper inside, still stroking his cock with a firm hand. The shadow demon moaned as he started lightly moving the finger in and out of his tight channel.

"Yes, don't stop," Tenebrae gasped, softly. The sensation was strange and intense, but it somehow enhanced the pleasure he was already experiencing. He opened his eyes to see a gratified smile spread over the witch's face at his response, and the feeling intensified as he felt him press a second finger inside. He felt himself twitch in the human's practiced hand.

"Good. You're being so good for me, Tenebrae," Lazarus praised, leaning down to lick the onyx tip of his cock, swirling his tongue around it generously. He was rewarded with one of those needy whines that sounded so delicious coming from such a fearsome creature. He kept his pace slow, taking his time as he worked him open. When he was able to move two fingers with ease, he asked, "Do you want more?"

"More," the shadow demon gritted out, his claws shredding the material at his sides as he strained to keep still. He wanted more of everything. More of this feeling, more of Lazarus's praise, more of that hungry look in his eyes as the human watched him unravel under his touch.

The witch added a third finger, pressing deeper inside and rubbing a spot that had Tenebrae's eyes nearly unfocusing. He barely even registered the loud keen emitting from his own mouth.

"Perfect, darling, you're taking it so well," Lazarus cooed, feeling the muscles relax around his knuckles. He gave a few more thrusts of his fingers just to make sure that the shadow was ready. By now, he too was struggling to wait much longer with his own need throbbing insistently between his legs. Pulling his fingers out, he oiled his own length generously before lining it up with the shadow's waiting entrance. The blunt head of his cock just barely pressed in, temptingly, conveying his intent as he asked the demon in a sultry murmur, "Do you want it?"

"Yes. Please," Tenebrae whined, almost inaudibly, staring imploringly into his eyes.

He was surprised at the plaintive sound of his own voice. The simmering desire he felt for Lazarus's touch and approval was quickly morphing into a burning need. If the witch told him to beg right now, he would do so without hesitation or shame. But Lazarus just smiled benevolently at him, and began pushing inside him with shallow thrusts. This felt infinitely better than the human's fingers had, and it was only the man's firm grip at the base of the demon's cock that kept him from coming undone right then.

"Fuck," Lazarus swore, when he finally sunk in all the way, his hips pressed firmly against the demon's ass. He closed his eyes for a moment, stilling as the snug warmth enveloped him and pleasure coiled deep at the base of his spine. It was almost too much, the decadent sight of the shadow laid out before him combined with the feeling of being sheathed inside him. Taking a deep breath to collect himself, he drew his hips back, pulling almost all the way out before thrusting back in deeply.

"You feel so fucking good."

"Lazarus!"

Both of them moaned at the same time. Fueled by the wanton sound of Tenebrae crying his name, Lazarus picked up the pace, fucking the shadow demon almost feverishly. For a while, the room was filled with nothing but their pleasure-drunk voices, and the resounding slap of flesh upon shadowy flesh. He held on tightly to Tenebrae's hip, using it as leverage to thrust deeper and harder, spurred on by the shadow's moans and desperate whines.

Tendrils of shadow clung to the human, wandering and gripping aimlessly as if of their own volition. Tenebrae was far too overwhelmed with sensation to do anything but allow them to grab instinctually at the witch's body. One of his hands splayed open-palmed over the human's smaller one at his hip, needing to touch Lazarus but in a way where he wouldn't accidentally harm him with his claws in his delirium.

"Such a good boy, letting me fuck you like this," Lazarus purred, his voice thick and gravelly with lust. The demon's back arched while he let out a shuddering groan at the praise. The witch could feel Tenebrae's hips pushing back into him, instinctively seeking more friction as he got closer to his end. His palm squeezed tighter as he pumped the shadow's dick, watching his ethereal features contort with ecstasy. "Are you going to come for me? Go on, darling, let me feel it."

A shattered whimper was the only affirmation Tenebrae could get out before he clenched around him, his length pulsing as he shot ropes of molten black liquid over the front of them both. His eyes stayed locked on the human above him, sweat glistening on the man's toned body and his head thrown back as Lazarus continued fucking him straight through his orgasm. It was the most beautiful sight he'd ever seen.

"That's it, darling, so good," the human moaned, his hips stuttering as he chased his own impending release. It only took another single look down into the starstruck eyes of the shadow, who was gazing at him in unabashed adoration. His muscles seized and he was emptying himself into the demon's body, punctuating the final grinding thrusts with praise. "My. Good. Fucking. Boy."

Lazarus panted, collapsing against one of the shadow demon's raised knees, a hand splayed out on Tenebrae's stomach. For a moment, neither of them moved, catching their breath after the intensity of the encounter. When the witch gingerly pulled out, they both groaned; Lazarus at the sight of the mess they'd made of each other and Tenebrae at the sudden feeling of emptiness. He sat up, seizing the human's face in both hands and kissing him with a feral passion.

"That was incredible," he breathed, pressing their foreheads together and caressing the human's cheekbones with his thumbs. He could feel the unfettered grin that bloomed on Lazarus's face. His body felt warm all over and his thoughts sluggish, but pleasantly so. This must be what humans meant when they said 'intoxicated.'

"Yes, it was," Lazarus agreed, holding onto the demon's wrists to keep him close. He could hardly believe this was real; he had certainly dreamed of similar scenarios enough times, but the reality eclipsed any of them. Much as he wanted to curl up with Tenebrae right now, they were both sticky with their combined fluids. He pressed a tender kiss to the shadow's palm and got up from the bed. "Let me find something to clean us up."

He returned shortly with a simple throw blanket that had been draped over a chair. Even the most modest textile in this room seemed too fine to use for such a purpose, but there was no other option. Besides, if the residents truly thought this place haunted, then they would probably never miss it. He wiped them both down with the luxurious cloth and let it drop forgotten on the floor, as they lay entangled in the curtained bed.

Tenebrae combed his claws through the silky brown waves of the witch's hair, breathing a contented sigh. He allowed the warm haze to settle over him, less unsettled by the feeling this time than he had been that night in the cave. Watching the man slumber, he lightly ran his fingers across his back so as not to wake him while he enjoyed the tranquil silence. It was akin to the comforting nothingness of shadowspace; which had, until now, been the only place that felt like home to the demon.

The places he visited in his travels were fascinating enough, but the void was always where he belonged. Now, here in this forgotten room in a mouldering Transylvanian castle, Tenebrae looked at the human who had drifted off to sleep in his arms and found that for once he didn't wish to be anywhere else.

When Lazarus woke some time later, he was half sprawled across the demon's chest with his face turned towards him but his eyes still closed. He listened to the muffled drum of the shadow's heartbeat, loud against his ear in the otherwise silent space. The sound of it was much like his own, except for the eerie plodding slowness of its rhythm. It would have lulled him back to sleep, were it not for the whirlwind of his thoughts as the sights and sounds of their coupling returned to the forefront of his mind.

The way the shadow had moaned his name in supplication was sin incarnate to his ears, and heat curled in his stomach thinking about it now. Despite having just awoken, he was still a bit drunk with power from the way Tenebrae readily yielded to his desires, and a roguish energy thrummed in his veins. As much as he delighted in the shadow's unexpected softer side, he also craved to see what he would be like once unleashed with the new carnal knowledge that Lazarus had bestowed upon him. The urge to rile the momentarily mellow demon itched at him.

"What is it, my pretty little troublemaker?" the shadow demon asked, sensing that he was awake. He did not need to see the sparkle in his eyes to know what the human was thinking; the impish curl of his lips gave him away. "I can see you thinking."

An edge of warning crept into his tone, a sharpness that advised Lazarus to choose his words carefully. It was one that Tenebrae knew by now he was more than likely to ignore.

"I was simply dreaming about those lovely sounds you made for me," Lazarus said innocently, smiling up at the shadow demon from his place on his torso. "Such beautiful moans and whimpers."

His fingers idly drew circles along the shadow demon's skin as he mused, falling silent again though the mischievous glint didn't leave his gaze.

"Mmhmm," Tenebrae hummed, dubiously. He did not, for a second, believe that was all that was on the witch's mind.

"Only, it makes me wonder where all that angry growling went about being a good bo—, ah!"

He didn't even have a chance to finish the sentence. Instead, his gloating tone morphed into a yelp, as Tenebrae efficiently manhandled him. In mere seconds, he was face down on the mattress with the hefty weight of the demon pinning him against the plush surface.

"Brattish little thing, aren't you?" Tenebrae sneered lowly into his ear, claws raking lightly down the side of his torso. They raised pink welts in their wake, just hard enough to sting but not break the skin. Lazarus trembled beneath him, sucking in a harsh breath at the feeling.

"That sharp little tongue of yours is going to get you in trouble, Lazarus."

"You seem to enjoy my tongue well enough," the witch countered smugly, the arrogant grin on his face only adding fuel to the fire that he was willfully courting.

He tried to turn to look at the demon over his shoulder, but Tenebrae ducked his head and began mouthing toothily at the back of his neck. Lazarus jolted at a particularly sharp bite, a tiny voice in the back of his mind cautioning that it was perhaps foolish to taunt the supernatural apex predator in his bed.

This advice was promptly ignored.

"Hmm, I think trouble may be what you desire, though," the shadow demon purred against his skin, shifting his hips to press against the back of the human's thighs. He chuckled lowly at the little gasp that sounded when Lazarus realized the demon was already hard again. "Do you need me to fuck the mischief out of you, is that it?"

The human didn't have to say a word; his body answered for him, instinctively pushing back against the demon who hummed knowingly.

"I thought so."

"Think you can manage that, do you?" Lazarus teased, intentionally rubbing up against the ridged underside of the demon's erection. It was all the movement he could manage, crushed as he was beneath the shadow's bulk. "I must warn you, the amount of mischief I contain is considerable, or so I've been told."

"You are going to be so full of me, little human, that there won't be any room for mischief," the shadow demon growled, hiking the witch's hips up high so his face pressed further into the pillows and his ass was raised in the air. "I believe I will start with that vexing mouth."

Lazarus opened his lips to retort, and a couple of thick shadow tendrils quickly shoved their way inside, spreading his jaws wide and effectively gagging him. Wide-eyed, he drooled around the writhing dark mass, while Tenebrae lavished his shoulders with sharp-toothed kisses and slid a hand around him to palm his growing erection. The witch moaned, still slightly sensitive from their earlier activities.

When the shadow demon sat up, the tendrils finally ceased their assault on the witch's mouth. Lazarus had a brief moment of panic at the sensation of claws sliding over his backside, but a blunt slick feeling quelled his fears when one of the shadow tendrils teased his rim instead. Another coiled itself around his cock, leaving the demon's hands free to roam.

One of those rough hands smoothed heavily up the witch's spine, making his back arch further, before gripping the back of his neck assertively. His face heated at the way the gesture sent a bolt of pleasure through him. Taller than average with strong muscles built from hard work on the farm, he was not by any means small nor weak by human standards, so it was astounding how easily the shadow demon overpowered him. He loved it.

His next clever retort died on his tongue as an oiled tendril began working its way inside him. The one at his front constricted with a gentle pressure, not stroking, just squeezing tantalizingly. The lack of movement had him canting his hips with a disgruntled huff, seeking more stimulation. His breath caught as a set of claws sunk into his hip with an ironclad grip and promptly put a stop to his wiggling. When he stilled, the sharp points retracted slightly and the flesh tingled where he could feel it healing.

"Much better," Tenebrae hummed, pleased with the witch's acquiescence. He concentrated more shadows into the undulating tendril, thickening it gradually and watching attentively to where it plunged in and out of the human's body. Listening to his quickening breathing and soft moans, the demon couldn't help but smile.

"Out of clever quips for me already, Lazarus?" he asked, chuckling at the irate grumble his taunting garnered him.

"You wish," he answered, breathlessly, struggling unsuccessfully to move in the vulnerable position the demon had him trapped in. "It will take more than a few of your shadows to shut me up, darling."

He gasped suddenly, as the previously motionless tendril that was still wrapped tightly around his cock began to move. With the shadow's hands and tendrils all working in tandem, his mind short-circuited slightly at the feeling of so many appendages touching him at once.

"Is that so?" the shadow demon drawled darkly, sliding the now girthy shadow tendril out of him. If the man wanted more, he would gladly give it to him.

Pressing against the back of the witch's thighs, he allowed his cock to settle between the globes of his ass. Lazarus groaned as Tenebrae began leisurely rutting against him, smearing his leaking arousal over the human's oil-slick hole without entering.

"Yes, now stop teasing," he whined, while his hips restlessly tried to push back into the textured length or forward into the tight hold of the tendril; he didn't care which. Increasing desperation was starting to eclipse his urge to sass the shadow demon.

"Very well," Tenebrae growled, notching the flared head of his cock at his entrance. He pushed in slowly, feeling the human's body reluctantly give way to make room for the sizable intrusion. Lazarus shuddered beneath him, breathing hard as the first few textured ridges slid in one at a time.

"Oh, fuck," he gasped. Tenebrae's dick was not larger than the shadow tendril that had coaxed him open, but the smooth appendage had not quite prepared him for the ribbed topography of the demon's cock. The slight ridges that lined it felt so much more prominent this way than they had in his hand or his mouth. Each roll of the shadow demon's hips drove slightly deeper, working them in one after the other relentlessly. "Go slow, please."

The shadow demon draped over him, slowing his movements as his lean muscled torso pressed against the witch's back. Tenebrae's arms slid beneath his chest, crossing over his front to grip Lazarus's shoulders for leverage. The human was now completely surrounded, inside and out, not able to move an inch except to spread his knees wider. The stretch burned deliciously, and he groaned as he felt the thickest part of the demon's girth easing into him.

"Too much for you, little human?" Tenebrae cooed in a mocking tone that belied the sincerity of the question. He held the man tightly as he gradually slid in further. A quiet groan rumbled in his throat at the feel of the witch's snug channel gripping him. It felt incredible. The restraint it took not to just slam into him was immense, though the only evidence of his internal struggle was the slightly too hard grip of his claws.

"N-no," Lazarus breathed shakily, concentrating on relaxing in the demon's constricting clutches. "Keep going."

He felt the shadow's mouth twist into a grin where it pressed against his temple. His heart raced as another slow roll of the demon's hips drove him the rest of the way in with a wet squelch and then stilled. He could barely think, his ass stuffed impossibly full while a shadow tendril coiled tightly around his dick.

"Tenebrae, please. Move."

"Since you asked so nicely," the demon purred, his warmth leaving the witch's back as he rose up on his knees, grabbing Lazarus by the hips with both hands.

The first few slow and purposeful thrusts already had the human moaning wantonly and twisting the blankets mindlessly in his grip. Once Tenebrae began fucking him faster and stroking his cock with his shadows at the same time, he was insensible, drooling into the pillow beneath him.

The shadow demon growled, restraint leaving him as he listened to the man's muffled cries of his name. Wanting nothing more than to hear all those sweet, broken sounds, he looped an arm around the witch's torso and pulled him up against his chest. Tenebrae held him upright, tightly pressed against the demon's front while he continued mercilessly fucking him. With a hand around Lazarus's throat, he tilted his head back to look into his tear-filled eyes.

"T-tenebrae," he cried, with a loud moan, clutching tightly to the arm that held him aloft. A stray tear rolled down his cheek, and the demon's dark tongue darted out to lick it away.

"Mmm, cry for me, pretty thing," Tenebrae groaned, feeling a hot wave of pleasure shoot through him at the wrecked sight of his witch. Smoky tendrils slithered up from his wrist to coil into the man's open mouth. "Show me how loud you can cry with that insolent mouth full."

Lazarus keened loudly around the shadows, his eyes rolling back in his head as he surrendered fully to the onslaught of sensations. His mind went blank, registering nothing except for the overwhelming pleasure of the demon roughly taking him and the inevitable orgasm that was rapidly hurtling towards him. A vicious growl vibrated into him from the shadow demon's chest and suddenly he felt the sharp clamp of Tenebrae's teeth, as the demon seized his neck in a possessive bite. He cried out, a mixed sound of pain and ecstasy, and his climax ripped through him like a storm.

Tenebrae groaned around the flesh in his mouth, feeling Lazarus shudder in his arms. He bit down harder, satisfying something primal deep in his being. With the sharp tang of blood blooming on his tongue and the sight of the witch coming undone in his arms, he could hold back no longer. Hot liquid flooded the human's insides as the shadow demon came with a territorially growled, "*Mine.*"

He licked over the already-healing bite, gently lowering the pair of them onto their sides on the bed. Lazarus whimpered quietly when the shadow demon carefully slid out of him, and Tenebrae shushed him with a tender kiss to his temple. The shadow demon held him tightly to his front, caressing his side soothingly with one large hand until the man melted into him.

"Are you alright?" Tenebrae asked, softly.

Lazarus nodded weakly and mumbled an affirming but unintelligible sound.

"Did I hurt you?" he pressed, mildly concerned by how uncharacteristically quiet the witch was now.

Lazarus shook his head and squeezed the demon's arm across his front reassuringly. Satisfied for the moment, the shadow let him rest until he felt coherent enough to speak. After a few minutes, the man rolled over to face him.

"Not to worry, I enjoyed the consequences of my actions very much," he rasped with a breathy laugh, voice still hoarse from screaming. A crimson blush bloomed across his face as he admitted, "You didn't hurt me any more than I wanted you to. And I'm sorry for teasing you so, I quite adore when you're a good boy for me."

"And you also adore provoking me," Tenebrae chuckled. "There is nothing to apologize for, so long as you are prepared to reap the rewards of your efforts." He arched a brow at the witch suggestively, earning him a flirtatious giggle.

"I am… not particularly gentle by nature. You will tell me to stop if I go too far," he added more seriously.

"Always," Lazarus agreed, snuggling further into the demon's embrace. The giddy high was wearing off and his energy was rapidly waning.

"Sleep," the shadow told him, "I will take you back before dawn."

Chapter 14

LEGALLY BINDING

With the aid of the shadow demon, daily life on the Graydon property began to run smoother than ever. During the following weeks, he took over the bulk of the more laborious tasks, like constructing fences and stone walls, splitting firewood, and clearing land. This left Lazarus free to tend the animals and crops. On days when the Dodson brothers were available to work, the shadow typically made himself scarce, lurking incorporeally in the dark corners of the house or retreating to the peaceful gloom of shadowspace for some much needed respite.

Though he had very much come to appreciate Lazarus's company and the presence of the other two Graydons was proving tolerably amusing, he was unused to interacting with other sentient creatures so frequently, human or otherwise. The void was a welcome refuge from the cacophony of the farm. When Lazarus had told him there would be company this evening for dinner, he was not put out in the slightest.

The youngest Graydon, however, was miffed.

"Won't you stay for dinner, Mr. Ten'brae?" Elijah pouted, having overheard his uncle bidding the shadow demon goodbye in the living room.

The boy had taken to the gruff demon rather quickly, unquestioningly accepting of his monstrous appearance in the way that curious children can be. His uncle liked the demon and so, he did too. It was as simple as that.

"No, I must be elsewhere," Tenebrae answered briefly. He would leave it to the more eloquent human to explain why to the boy.

"Well, can you do that thing where you turn into mist, then, please?" Elijah bargained, his piping voice full of hopeful determination.

"Very well," the shadow demon acquiesced, promptly dissolving into a dark haze that wafted into the dark space behind a bookshelf and disappeared.

The boy clapped delightedly.

"Elijah, when cousin Alden is here, you mustn't mention Tenebrae," Lazarus said, crouching next to the boy to speak to him face to face. "It is important that you speak to no one about him. No one but your mother and I. Do you understand?"

The child pursed his lips, thinking over the information.

"Like with the magic?" he asked, thoughtfully.

The twin brothers had always intended to pass their knowledge down to Levi's son, provided that he wanted to learn. It had long been decided that they would wait until he was older to begin teaching him, but the importance of secrecy had been instilled in him early. One slip of a child's tongue could be enough to bring danger upon the whole family.

"Yes, exactly like that," Lazarus agreed, relieved that the boy seemed to understand so readily.

He looked up, seeing that Sarah had come into the room. She had a serious look about her, so he patted Elijah on the shoulder and stood.

"I need to speak with you," she said, an uncharacteristic tremor to her voice.

Gesturing for him to follow, Sarah led Lazarus into the kitchen, where she could still keep an eye on her son but not be heard. He patiently waited for her to continue as she wrung her hands nervously.

"I… I think I am with child," she said, taking a deep sighing breath and finally raising her eyes to look at him.

"Are you sure?" Lazarus asked, calculating the time in his head. It had been a little over two months since Levi's death.

"Yes," Sarah said, more resolutely. She paced as she spoke. "At first, I overlooked it. We were so busy keeping the farm afloat after Levi passed. But, I am certain. I have not bled these past two months."

Lazarus reached out to stop her restless movements, taking her hands in his.

"Then it is a gift," he said gently, squeezing her hands reassuringly. "Levi has left us a child to love in his absence. We will raise them together. You and Elijah, and soon this child, you are all the family I have. I would do anything for you. You know this."

Sarah shut her eyes tightly, tears of relief escaping as she did.

"Thank you, Laz," she said, gratefully, throwing her arms around him in a fierce hug. "You are a good man."

When she released him, Lazarus handed her his handkerchief to dry her tears. Just as he began to speak, there was a knock at the door.

Alden was here.

"We will speak more of this later," he assured her.

An easy smile graced Sarah's face throughout dinner as she conversed with her cousin; it was the brightest one Lazarus had seen on her in many weeks. Alden did most of the talking, catching her up on the news from his side of the family back in Manchester and chatting with Elijah, who was only too delighted to have a new person to pepper with enthusiastic questions.

"How many children do you have?" the boy asked, after Alden mentioned that his son Isaac enjoyed playing checkers as well.

Lazarus had recently taught the child to play, and it was his new favorite pastime. He had even managed to rope Tenebrae into a game one afternoon. The image of the shadow demon crammed into a too small wooden chair whilst moving the small pieces around the board in his deadly, oversized hands had nearly sent Lazarus into a fit of laughter.

"Well, there is Isaac, who is a year older than you," Alden began, holding up a finger to help the boy count along with him, "and the girls, Mary and Hester. They are seven and nine years of age. And my wife is soon to welcome our fourth into the family."

He smiled broadly, looking from the impressed Elijah to his mother, whose gentle smile wilted for just a moment at the news. Lazarus cleared his throat, the sound drawing the attention of the table.

"Alright, young man, I think we have questioned Cousin Alden quite thoroughly enough for one evening," he said, patting the boy on the shoulder. "Come, let's get you ready for bed."

With only a small amount of protesting, he was able to lure the boy off with the promise to read him a story, allowing the cousins some time to catch up on their own.

Their hushed voices could just be heard from the sitting room when Lazarus pulled the door to the boy's bedroom shut. Elijah was tucked in and finally fast asleep, after having cajoled his uncle into reading him three of his favorite fairy tales. He stepped quietly down the hallway and wooden stairs to rejoin the other adults in the cozy glow of the warm fireplace. As he entered the room, their conversation came to an awkward halt.

"Is everything alright?" Lazarus asked, directing his question to Sarah while eyeing the stiff posture of her cousin who was seated in Levi's chair.

Her mouth pressed into a tight line that indicated she was displeased about something. Alden, however, looked exasperated.

"It is the obvious solution, Sarah," he pleaded insistently, leaning forward as he gestured for her attention. "At least discuss it with him."

His hand waved in Lazarus's direction, though his attention remained on her. She sighed loudly, folding her hands in her lap as she considered whatever it was he had suggested. While the silence stretched on, Lazarus took a seat next to her on the small sofa. He waited patiently for her to look at him, which she avoided for several uncomfortable minutes. Eventually, she threw a withering glare at her cousin and then turned to the man next to her.

"I spoke to Alden of my news," she began, reluctantly, bringing a hand to her belly as she spoke. "Like us, he believes it a gift, but, he has some rather interesting... advice regarding its future."

He scoffed at her description of his words and sat back in the chair.

"I am merely being pragmatic," Alden insisted, as Lazarus looked back and forth between the two of them.

"Will one of you speak plainly? I am at a loss as to whatever this dispute may be," he said, growing weary of their dancing around the topic at hand.

When Alden seemed no more inclined to elaborate, Sarah rolled her eyes at him.

"For the security of the children and myself, my dear cousin has suggested that I marry," she explained, irritation bleeding into her tone. "Sooner, rather than later, considering my condition. And he suggests that I marry you."

Both of them stared at him, awaiting his reaction, while Lazarus tried to regain his senses over the sudden ringing in his ears.

Marry? Me?

His thoughts raced from one extreme to the other. It was not entirely unheard of for a man to care for his brother's widow and children in such a manner. And it could help to alleviate the town's suspicions towards his bachelor lifestyle, while avoiding the awkwardness of having a wife who might expect him to perform husbandly duties.

On the other hand, he would have a wife, and Lazarus was not certain how the shadow demon would take to that idea. And what of Sarah? Might she not wish someday to love again? She was young after all.

They were still staring, and he realized he had to say something.

"That is… quite the suggestion," he began slowly, trying to give his tumultuous thoughts time to catch up with his mouth. "I can see a certain logic to it, of course, but is that what you wish?"

He looked to Sarah, hesitant to dismiss the idea before understanding her feelings.

"I don't know what I wish," she sighed, appearing simultaneously relieved and deflated that he had not outright refused.

What they both wished, in their hearts, was for Levi to be here to raise his child by her side. But fate had decided otherwise, it seemed.

"This way yours and the children's futures would be secure," Alden offered, softening his tone as he plead the case. "And you would never need consider the proposal of Thaddeus Gale or any of the other village men. You know his will not be the last."

Both Sarah and Lazarus made a noise of indignation at the mention of Mr. Gale's offer. They shared a look as they considered Alden's words.

"Would you do this, Laz?" Sarah asked, hesitantly. She put her hand atop his as she spoke. "For convenience only, of course, to help me raise the children."

Her eyes brimmed with hope, and he could not bear to disappoint her.

"I said that I would do anything for you and the children, and I meant it," he reminded her, clasping her hand gently. "If it is what you want, I will be your lawful husband."

She nodded gratefully, and the decision was made.

"Shall we drink to it, then?" Alden asked, retrieving one of the bottles of wine he had brought back with him from his travels.

Lazarus fetched a couple of glasses while he uncorked the bottle. Together, they toasted the future of the Graydons and stayed a while by the fire talking. With the weight of uncertainty lifted from Sarah's shoulders, she laughed freely at her cousin's stories and it warmed Lazarus to see her happy.

"Will you stay with us another night?" he asked, taking Alden aside when the three of them decided to retire for the evening. "Your company lifts her spirits. It would do her good if you would stay."

"I was going to ask if I might," Alden chuckled, as Lazarus showed him to the guest room. "It is not often that I get the chance to spend time with my favorite cousin. And besides, I left my cart with William Mantle across town. He offered to re-shoe my horse as partial payment for his goods, and I know he does good work."

The man was a shrewd merchant with an eye for a good trade and a fair deal; it was a handy skill to have and he did well for himself.

"We will be glad to have you," Lazarus said, patting him on the shoulder affectionately as they said goodnight.

It wasn't until late in the evening, that the shadow demon returned. He found Lazarus cleaning up at the porcelain wash basin in his bedroom long after everyone had gone to bed, wiping away the toils of the day with a cloth soaked in rosemary water. His shoulder length brown locks were gathered neatly back with a black ribbon, and he had removed his waistcoat. Tenebrae admired him silently for a moment, how his features were illuminated by the silvery moonlight and the warmth of a single candle.

"Are you going to stare or say good evening," the witch smirked, sensing the demon's presence.

He had an uncanny ability to do so, and Tenebrae wasn't sure if that was a result of the bond or some innate talent that Lazarus had. Regardless, he found it unusually difficult to sneak up on the man, despite his stealthy nature.

"Neither," Tenebrae said, crossing the room in a few long strides.

Lazarus turned towards him, and the shadow demon grabbed him by the waist, pulling him in for a voracious kiss. The witch clung to his arms for balance, head spinning slightly as he devoured his mouth greedily. He relented after a moment when Lazarus breathlessly urged him to pause.

"Much as I enjoy this form of greeting, there is something I must tell you," he said, placing a chaste kiss at the side of the demon's lips.

Lazarus unwound the dark limbs encircling him and gently pushed the shadow to sit on the edge of his bed. Tenebrae heeded his non-verbal instructions and sat, waiting for him to explain with a slightly puzzled expression.

"Sarah is expecting another child," he said, uneasily. "It seems my brother left us a parting gift before he perished."

"This is good news, is it not?" the shadow demon asked, puzzled by the way Lazarus was absentmindedly wringing his hands as he spoke.

"Yes, but it is complicated," the witch explained, rubbing the back of his neck in discomfort. "To make sure they are safe and provided for, she asked me to marry her, and well, I have agreed."

"What does that mean, 'marry'?" Tenebrae asked, cautiously, judging by Lazarus's uncomfortable demeanor it was not something he expected would please the demon.

His brows furrowed and his already puzzled expression morphed into outright confusion. He'd had no cause before now to familiarize himself with the customs and terms of human familial relationships beyond the bare basics. He knew "merry" to mean happy, but this sounded like something different.

"Well, legally, it means that I would be her husband," Lazarus began, trying to sort out how to best explain the situation, "and thus, responsible for the welfare of her and the children, as Levi was before."

An audible growl stopped him from speaking further. He paused, looking to the shadow demon warily.

"You cannot marry her," Tenebrae rumbled dangerously, swiftly rising to his feet. His claws clenched and unclenched at his sides, as his posture stiffened in agitation.

Husband, he thought scornfully. He knew that word and what it meant. *He said he never wanted a wife. He lied to me?*

His teeth clenched and his blood boiled as he considered the time they had spent together, the intimacy between them. A bitter pit formed in his stomach as old fears surfaced.

What if it was all just a trick after all?

"Yes, I can. I have to," the witch stammered quietly, taken aback by the shadow demon's unexpectedly vehement reaction.

He had expected some resistance or confusion, but the tone of Tenebrae's body language was nothing short of rage.

"I owe it to Levi to take care of them," he insisted more firmly, intent on making the demon understand why he had to do this.

He couldn't let his twin brother's children be raised by one of the villagers who had betrayed them. Lazarus reached for the shadow demon, hoping to soothe whatever was causing his vigorous objection.

"No," Tenebrae roared, seizing him by the shoulders with both hands.

Before Lazarus could blink, the shadow demon had shoved him away. While the man stumbled, just managing to stay on his feet, Tenebrae stalked towards the deep shadows next to the armoire and shouldered through them into the void.

He seethed, vibrating with the force of his emotions, yet rooted to the spot. A cynical part of him wanted nothing more than to flee as far into the void as he could go, angry and hurt that Lazarus would cast him aside for this woman. But another part of him refused to believe that his witch would betray him in such a manner, not after everything.

"Tenebrae, wait!" Lazarus shouted, beating his hands against the wall where the demon had just disappeared. He could feel the shadows flex slightly under his palms, but he hesitated, not knowing how to move through them without the shadow demon's guidance.

He dropped his forehead against the plaster with a thunk, closing his eyes as he wracked his mind for an explanation to Tenebrae's volatile reaction. Before he had long to ponder, though, a claw-tipped limb materialized out of the darkness in front of him. His eyes flew open just in time to catch Tenebrae's furious eyes for a split second before he was forcefully thrown against the far wall.

"No," the shadow demon growled again, one muscled forearm pressed across his collarbones.

Tenebrae leaned his considerable weight against him so hard that it was difficult for the human to breathe. His bones strained under the pressure.

"What do you mean, no?" Lazarus gasped, struggling against the immovable force that crushed him.

His resistance only made the shadow demon press on him more harshly. Tenebrae's claws scraped against the plaster wall at his side threateningly.

"No, you will not marry her," the shadow demon snarled through clenched teeth, leaning down until he was suffocatingly close. "You. Are. Mine."

Realization struck him like a bolt of lightning, and Lazarus understood the demon's fury with sudden clarity.

He was jealous.

Relief coursed through him at identifying the source of their misunderstanding, and along with it a simmering heat at the possessiveness in Tenebrae's words. He dragged in a few ragged breaths, considering how to respond before the situation got even more out of hand.

"Yes, yours," he wheezed, futilely pulling at the shadow's heavy arm across his chest, trying to gain himself more room to breathe. "You misunderstand. It is simply a formality, for appearances. I would be her husband in name only."

The demon's growling intensified, further explanation did not seem to be placating him much, if at all. The nuance of the details was lost on him, and all he could hear was 'her husband'. Lazarus raised his voice to be heard above the angry noise.

"Tenebrae, listen to me! I do not love her. Not the way that I love you."

It was out of his mouth before Lazarus realized the full gravity of what he was saying, and his eyes widened as the words rang in the sudden silence like a death knell.

The shadow demon froze, gaping at him in shock. Tenebrae's skin felt hot all over, and all he could do was stare down at the witch, who was looking at him like a frightened animal. Eventually, he found his voice, although it was much smaller than usual.

"You love me?"

"Yes, you irascible bastard," Lazarus sighed, his gaze softening towards the befuddled demon. "Now stop crushing me. I am all yours."

Tenebrae removed the forearm that had been weighing his ribs down like an iron bar, and he took a grateful deep breath. Winding his arm around the demon's shoulders, he pulled him into a lingering kiss, which begrudgingly ended only when they had to come up for air.

"You will not fuck her," the shadow demon stated flatly, once their lips parted.

Lazarus nearly choked at the blunt phrasing.

"Of course not!" he asserted, immediately. "No one will come between us. I promise."

Tenebrae clutched him tightly, as if Sarah would appear to steal him away any moment. The warm glow of the man's confession had done much to soothe the shadow demon's raging jealousy. Though, he still did not like the thought of Lazarus marrying the woman. Not even if it was all for show.

An idea came to him suddenly.

"You will marry me first, then"

I suppose that is probably as close to an 'I love you too' as I am likely to get, Lazarus thought, grinning widely at the shadow demon.

"Such a romantic, darling," he said, "Of course I will marry you. I will bind myself to you in any way you desire, for as long as you wish."

"Careful what you wish for. You do not know the depths of my desires," Tenebrae rumbled, allowing a few stray shadow tendrils to weave tightly around the witch. "What does this marrying entail?"

"Well, under usual circumstances, we would go before the magistrate and declare our agreement to marry. It would be recorded in the town records, and there might be a small celebration with food and drink," Lazarus explained, trying to ignore the persistent shadows creeping around his limbs. "For rather obvious reasons, we cannot do that, however I suppose we could cast a circle for a simple joining rite and let the universe be our witness."

He almost expected Tenebrae to balk at the suggestion of another ritual, however minor, but the shadow demon merely hummed thoughtfully and then released him.

"Do you have what you will need?" he asked, gesturing to the witch's desk and its assorted contents.

Lazarus thought for a moment, before pawing through a few drawers to take inventory of the necessary items: salt for the circle, a few beeswax candles, some cones of incense, and an anointing oil that was already prepared. He turned to find Tenebrae holding open a satchel for him expectantly.

"Now?" Lazarus said, brows raised in surprise. "You want to marry me… right now?"

He paused, then, as Sarah's voice echoed in his mind. *No more magic.*

Recalling his promise, a pit formed in his stomach. But the shadow demon before him wore an expression of such hopeful expectation, that he would rather do almost anything than deny him.

It's only a minor rite, barely a spell at all. What harm could one tiny, last working do? After this, no more, I swear.

"Yes, now," Tenebrae answered simply, as if it were the most obvious thing in the world. "When else?"

He opened the satchel wider, encouraging the witch to place the items inside. Once Lazarus finished loading up the bag, he slung it over his shoulder. Seeing the shadow demon with such a mundane accessory hung about his person was truly odd, and Lazarus fought off a snicker.

Gods, I love this ridiculous creature, he thought.

"Now is perfect," the witch agreed, hastily grabbing his woolen overcoat and taking Tenebrae's outstretched hand. The shadow demon slipped into the void, pulling him in after. "Do you have somewhere in mind?"

"We will do this in the place where you first bound me," he said, without a hint of the malice that usually accompanied discussion of the night they met. He turned, and Lazarus could just make out his face in the teeming darkness; he looked down at the human with a scheming smile. "It seems fitting enough. And this time, I will bind you."

Chapter 15

TIL DEATH DO US PART

The frigid November air gave them an icy welcome when Lazarus and Tenebrae stepped out of shadowspace into Devil's Circle. Cold starlight did its best to illuminate the standing stones under the cloudless new moon sky, but at this hour when late night met early morning, it was nearly as dark as the void they had just come from. Lazarus shivered, his breath fogging in the air as his teeth chattered. Immune to the biting temperature, the shadow demon looked down at him, his features drawn in concern.

"I will fetch wood for a fire, while you prepare," he announced, quickly melting into the near black line of trees at the edge of the clearing.

Cracks and rustling sounded from the darkness as the demon broke dry branches from dead trees and collected fallen limbs. The noise broke the otherwise eerie silence of the place.

It felt strange to Lazarus to be back here at night; this was only the second time he had returned to the site since the summoning. The first was a couple of weeks ago, to hide his grimoire after the promise to Sarah. What better place to shield it from prying eyes than the last patch of land any of the people of Graymourne would dare set foot in? Wrapped in a bit of fabric and protected by an old lockbox, he had buried it near the base of a tree. He had no need of it tonight, this rite was a small working he could perform from memory.

Lazarus marked out a wide circle, using a branch to scratch the border into the frozen soil and then fill it with salt. He brought over a wide flat stone from outside the circle to set up a makeshift altar, on which he placed the three candles and incense. By then, the shadow demon had returned with great armfuls of dry wood.

He spread the branches and kindling around the exterior of the circle that the witch had created, intent on making the space as warm as possible for his human. Catching on to his purpose, Lazarus retrieved his flint and striker to light the carefully crafted wood border at several points along the circle. The winter had been unusually dry so far and the flames spread quickly, soon warming the area inside the standing stones.

"Very clever, darling, thank you," Lazarus said, smiling at the demon as he felt the shivering tension of his muscles melt in the warming air. He used the flames to light the cone of incense and the deep, musky smoke scented the air with hints of spice and amber. Beckoning

Tenebrae over to join him in front of the impromptu altar, Lazarus grinned up at him excitedly. With the anointing oil in hand, he drew a line down the front of each of their faces, from forehead to chin, and then took hold of both of the shadow demon's hands. "The rite is very simple; the intent is the heart of the magic. Joining hands, we recite a short incantation. I will lead, you need only repeat after me. And then we use two candles to light the third as one. Are you ready?"

"I am ready," the shadow demon intoned deeply. His intense gaze never wavered from the human during his explanation. He squeezed Lazarus's hands lightly and nodded for him to begin. It would not be difficult for him to focus on the intent of the spell; he could think of little else at the moment besides making the witch his, in more ways than one.

With a steadying breath, Lazarus began reciting the spell, with the deep rumble of the shadow demon's voice echoing each line as if carving the words in stone.

"By stars above and earth below,
By deepest sea and winds that blow,
I call upon these all to see,
Be witness as I bind to thee.

As fires burn and cold does bite,
I swear myself to thee this night,
My body, mind, and soul I give,
Thine to keep, long may we live.
Whither one, the other be found,
Heart to heart, so be us bound

Before new moon I make this vow,
O universe do hear us now,
To be my husband, I take thee,
As to thyself, Husband, take me."

When the final line had been spoken, Lazarus picked up the beeswax candles, handing one to Tenebrae. They each lit their respective candles and then pressed the flames of their own to the final candle to symbolize their union.

"What comes next, husband?" Tenebrae asked, taking the witch by the chin and tilting his face up with a sultry smirk. Lazarus's hazel eyes sparkled in the firelight and the flush of his cheeks reminded the demon of their first meeting here months ago. His veins pulsed with just as much fire as they had that night, but this time instead of anger he felt only desire.

"We seal our vows with a kiss," Lazarus suggested breathlessly, his pupils already dilating from the salacious lilt to the shadow demon's question. "And after that, we consummate the marriage, according to tradition, of course."

He didn't need to explain the meaning of the word, his rising pulse told Tenebrae exactly what he needed to know. Slowly, the demon drew him in, sliding an arm around his waist and leaning down until their lips were just barely touching. When Lazarus tried to bridge the final distance, Tenebrae's grip on his jaw tightened, preventing him from moving any further.

"Tell me again," the shadow demon demanded in a velvety purr.

"I love you," Lazarus whispered feverishly, each barely there brush of the demon's lips making him more desperate.

His fingers dug into the sides of Tenebrae's waist, where he gripped it tightly. When, finally, the shadow demon's warm lips slotted against his own, his head spun from how divine it felt. The demon's hands roamed, peeling Lazarus out of his clothes so skillfully that he hardly noticed until a frigid breeze danced across the skin of his back. Pressed against the warm figure while safely inside the circle of still burning wood, he now stood comfortably bare.

Tenebrae slid his hands down the man's thighs, hoisting him up and spreading them around his waist. He sat down with Lazarus straddling his lap, using his own body to shield the witch from the frozen ground. As they kissed, their fronts pressed closely together, trapping their hardened lengths between them. He reached down to wrap one surreptitiously oiled hand around both of their cocks and slowly stroked them.

"My pretty little human husband," the shadow demon murmured, kissing the sensitive spot just below the man's ear, "are you ready for me to make you mine?" He felt the witch's fluttering pulse beneath his lips and the vibration of his throat as he moaned softly.

"Yes," Lazarus breathed, too far gone already to muster a witty response. "Make me yours."

He obediently opened his mouth when a tendril of shadow pressed against his lips, swirling his tongue around it mindlessly. An amused hum from the demon prompted a flash of lucidity, and he grazed his teeth along the dark appendage, earning a warning growl for his trouble. It was soon replaced by the demon's tongue, and Lazarus rocked his hips into the hand still gripping him while the tendril moved to slick over his entrance.

Tenebrae's other hand smoothed up the witch's spine, anchoring with a heavy grip around the back of his neck. He nipped sharply at Lazarus's bottom lip when the human moaned at the feeling of the tendril beginning to work him open. It wasn't long before he felt the man's hips pressing eagerly back against the shadowy limb, in need of more. Tenebrae lifted the witch up with one arm and eased the tip of his aching cock inside him, groaning deeply as Lazarus rocked his hips to sink down further.

"Oh fuck, Tenebrae," Lazarus whimpered, as the demon finally bottomed out. His fingernails scraped down Tenebrae's back, raising dark welts for a brief moment before they healed just as quickly. The shadow demon's intense gaze held him fast, and he struggled to keep his eyes open as Tenebrae began moving inside him.

"Keep your eyes on me, Lazarus," the demon instructed, his grip tightening at the nape of the human's neck.

Lazarus nodded dazedly, and his rosy lips parted as little pants and moans fell from them. Tenebrae growled lightly at the sight of him; face flushed, mouth open, and eyes glittering in the firelight. He grazed his claws over the witch's chest, contemplatively.

"So soft," he mused, darkly, as deep possessive desire coursed through his veins. "It makes me want to carve my name in your pretty flesh. It will heal, but I will know that it's there. And you will always know that you are mine."

Lazarus whined, his cock twitching against the shadow demon's stomach at the suggestion. Despite knowing that it should have frightened him, the savage nature of the shadow's desire only made him feel more wanted, more treasured in a twisted way. He rocked back in Tenebrae's lap, meeting each of the demon's thrusts ardently.

"Do it," he gasped, surprising both himself and the shadow demon. "Mark me, husband."

Tenebrae kissed him hard, and then pressed the razor tip of one claw to the witch's sternum. He traded the feverish thrusts for slow rolls of his hips to keep from jostling Lazarus while he worked. Grinding his cock deeply inside him, the demon cut the letter T in the skin of Lazarus's chest with two quick swipes of his finger. His eyes flicked back to the human's face, examining his reaction before he went any further.

"Go on, darling," Lazarus urged, biting his lip as he ground down against the demon's lap. "I can take it." Goosebumps rose all over his body as he anticipated the next sharp touch of the demon's claws, and his short nails dug deeply into his ribs.

Tenebrae's blood burned at his partner's encouragement, and a deep sense of pride settled in his bones at the blatant trust Lazarus placed in him. With an approving growl, he continued zealously, pausing to let each letter heal before carving the next. Lazily thrusting his cock into the witch's tight channel all the while, he had the man moaning and trembling under his ministrations, eyes rolled back in his head by the fourth letter. The demon's arm that curled around his back was the only thing holding him upright now.

"Almost finished, pretty thing," Tenebrae purred, completing the letter R with a flourish. His length throbbed at the strained whimper that sounded from the human's throat. "Tell me, Lazarus, who do you belong to?"

"You," he moaned, shaking as pain and pleasure wracked his body, twisting together into a singular white hot sensation. He could feel little rivulets of blood running down his front and the tingle of shadows healing the cuts as the demon clawed his name across his skin. He tried not to squirm as his senses overloaded, no longer entirely in control of his muscles. "Oh, gods. Y-you… I belong to you."

"That's right," the shadow demon said, dragging a horizontal line to complete the final letter. He slid his hand softly down the witch's front, admiring the sculpted planes of his body as it shook in his grasp. As his fingers moved to encircle the man's dick firmly, his lips quirked up into a satisfied smirk, seeing the way Lazarus jolted at the touch. Leaning in closely to growl into his ear, Tenebrae's hand worked over the man's length in time with the rhythm of his hips as his pace grew faster. "You are mine."

Lazarus threw shaky arms around the demon's wide shoulders, wrenching him down into a needy kiss. He moaned into the shadow demon's mouth, holding tightly to the last shreds of his sanity as his climax came rushing at him like a bolt of lightning. Every inch of his skin buzzed at the precipice of devastating pleasure. The wave rose and rose, seeming to last forever, until it finally broke with a barely audible whisper, as Tenebrae breathed three short words.

"I love you."

He cried out as his cock throbbed and spilled over in Tenebrae's hand, causing the shadow demon's thrusts to stutter. The hot, wet sensation of his husband's release on his skin had him driving his length deeply into Lazarus, muscles tensing as he painted his insides as dark as the moonless night. Their combined cries ripped through the crisp winter air like a supernova, leaving the silence that followed charged with energy. The fire that surrounded them burned low on the ground, and their heaving breaths wafted clouds of rapidly crystallizing steam into the atmosphere.

"Here," Tenebrae said gently, plucking the overcoat from the ground to drape it around Lazarus's shivering shoulders. "This will keep you warm until you are ready for me to warm you again."

"How consider- ah… considerate of you," he replied, wincing as the shadow demon shifted and eased his still semi-hard cock out of him. His hands trembled slightly, the muscles spent and weak, reaching into the pocket of his coat for a handkerchief to clean up the mess he'd made of Tenebrae. Embers of lust flared brighter momentarily, as he looked down at the moon-white liquid splattered across the sharply cut, onyx musculature of Tenebrae's midsection. His desire must have read on his face, and the shadow demon chuckled as he dragged the cloth across his abdomen.

"Keep looking at me like that, Lazarus, and we will be consummating this marriage until the sun comes up," Tenebrae warned, idly winding a few wisps of shadow around the man's thighs. They pulled Lazarus tight against the demon's front, the ends curling about his hips and caressing him lightly.

"Darling husband, that sounds less like a threat," the human said, arching into the touch of the wandering shadows, "and more like a promise."

He knew by the vicious grin that bloomed across the demon's face that he would be getting no rest this night. Not, of course, that he minded in the slightest.

Despite the bitterly cold temperature, the second time Lazarus awoke in Devil's Circle was much more pleasant than the first. Encased in the warm cage of the shadow demon's limbs and the cozy glow of happiness, the chill barely touched him when the brightening sky roused him from a deep and dreamless sleep. He vaguely recalled Tenebrae helping him dress a scant hour or two ago, for which he was grateful. The embers of the fire had long since burnt out, and a light breeze whistled through the leafless trees.

Casting his eyes upwards, he caught the rare view of a relaxed Tenebrae leaning against one of the standing stones while Lazarus lay in his lap. His seemingly perpetually furrowed brows were smooth, and the peaceful expression lent an unusual softness to his angular features. He admired his freshly wedded partner in silence for a few moments before the shadow demon realized he was awake.

"I think you may be even prettier when you are not awfully vexed at something," Lazarus said, in lieu of a good morning. He grinned drunkenly at the shadow demon, feeling giddy from the hours of amorous exertions and the lack of sleep.

Tenebrae huffed, rolling his eyes.

"That something is most often you," he commented, dryly, the slight upturn of his lips betraying his amusement. He returned to looking at the scenery, feigning disinterest while twirling a few strands of the man's hair with his claws.

"Nevertheless, you married me. Insisted on it, actually," Lazarus teased, pushing himself up to a seated position. He leaned over to kiss the shadow demon quickly on the cheek, and then stood, stretching his stiff limbs.

"You may be an aggravating human," Tenebrae said, moving to stand beside him, "but you are my aggravating human." He brushed his knuckles along the side of the witch's face, affectionately, and then turned to survey the forest. The sun shone through hazy white winter clouds, casting the landscape in an even grayish light. The skeletal trees with their barren limbs threw thin slashes of shadow on the ground. Tenebrae frowned, Lazarus would never fit through those. "There are too few shadows, we must go further into the forest before I can take us home."

"The manor is not terribly far, come, let us go on foot," Lazarus said with an unbothered shrug. His joyous mood would not be soured by a bit of walking this morning. "Besides, of all the places we have been together, we have yet to explore these lands beyond the fields of the farm." He took Tenebrae's hand, pulling him towards the familiar trail home with an easy smile.

Begrudgingly, the shadow demon followed. He had traversed these woods often enough in the days after Lazarus first summoned him, but it was, admittedly, more pleasant with the witch's hand clasped tightly in his own and the sound of his voice enthusiastically prattling on while they walked. He hardly heard what the man was saying as they went, too bewitched by his animated expressions and the way his hair shone in the morning light. It was difficult to imagine now, how intensely he had detested this man only a few short months ago.

How did he do it? Tenebrae wondered, bewildered at how Lazarus had managed to work his way into the depths of his black heart.

"You have not heard a word I said, have you?" Lazarus asked him suddenly, peering up at him with a coy smile. "Barely married a day, and already you tire of my voice. You wound me, Tenebrae." His faux outrage could not hide the playfulness that lurked beneath it, crinkling the corners of his eyes and lending a coquettish curve to his lips.

"Certainly, it is for your own safety," the shadow demon said, looming ominously over the shorter man.

"That tongue is liable to get you bent over a fallen tree if I listen to it for very long, and I imagine your chores today will be more difficult when you can hardly walk." He chuckled at the crimson blush that his threats sparked on the witch's handsome face.

"Well, perhaps it should be you on your hands and knees then," he quipped right back, not to be outdone by the demon's lascivious taunting. "You do seem to listen far better with my cock inside you."

The path towards the manor came into view as they spoke. Too embroiled in bantering back and forth with increasingly filthy remarks, neither of them noticed the drab, lone figure just visible on the East side of the riverbank. They continued on, unaware of the eyes that followed their every move.

As Lazarus and the shadow demon disappeared into the tall trees that surrounded the Graydon manor, the rigid form of Clarity Poole stood staring wide-eyed and frozen.

The Devil, she thought, *Lazarus Graydon walks with the Devil.*

She knew she should run back to town, but she was too frightened to move, clutching her husband's favorite wool jacket in her hands. She shouldn't even have been here, this early on a cold winter's morning. Clarity would have been warm at home, had it not been for James and Amity Cresswell's infant son spitting up on her husband at dinner last night.

Elbert Poole was a vain man, a fact that was unbecoming of a man of his station as a church elder and one that his wife would never voice out loud. Yet, she knew that losing the prized garment to a baby's bile was something he simply would not stand, so here she was at the crack of day on a frigid morning, scrubbing the stains in the icy, clear river water because boiled well water would just not do for Elbert Poole's precious vestments. No, his wardrobe must be washed in water fresh from God's green earth.

Clarity's fingers cramped from her tight grip on the fabric, and she roused from a state of shock. Emptying the wooden washtub back onto the riverbank, she tucked the jacket into the empty vessel and scurried back towards the village, her lungs already burning with the need to proclaim her news.

Clarity Poole had seen Lazarus with the Devil and soon every soul in Graymourne would know.

Lazarus was washing up, having just come in from the field, when he heard the first faint sounds of commotion. He paused, listening closer to the distant clamor of voices. There were a lot of them, and they seemed to be getting closer.

He dried his hands and hurried down the stairs, where he found Sarah and Alden looking through the curtains in the sitting room. Elijah clung to her skirt, trying to get a peek over the windowsill that was just too high for his short stature. The din grew louder and Sarah looked to him with a mixture of concern and irritation written across her face.

"What is going on?" Lazarus asked, joining them at the window. Across the front garden and down the path, he could just make out a clump of figures headed their way. It was far too many and too boisterous to be mistaken for a friendly visit. His heart sank and he swallowed thickly, watching his worst fear striding towards them.

"Tell me you have kept to your word, Laz," Sarah implored him, her worried eyes searching his face for answers.

He ran nervous fingers through his hair, trying to discern a reason for the villagers to be descending upon the manor like this. All had been peaceful of late, the weather had been fortunate, nothing had gone awry. Last night's magical working, a small rite deep in the woods and away from prying eyes, should not have drawn any notice.

Unless someone saw us this morning, he realized. His eyes widened and a cold fear washed over him. If that were the case, this might be a lot worse than five days in the stocks. Sarah watched the thoughts and emotions flit through him, from confusion to realization to terror.

"You promised," she hissed, inferring his answer from the look of abject horror that fell over him. Grabbing Elijah's hand, she backed away from the windows as she glared at him. Alden looked between the two of them, only more confused as to what was going on.

"It was only once," he blurted, the icy knife of turmoil twisting deeper in his guts at her disappointment.

And once was all it took.

He breathed deeply, trying to shove away his cloying guilt so he could think. He needed to get them out of here before the mob arrived.

"It doesn't matter," he said, deciding that it was more important to get them to safety than quarrel over things that could not be undone. "Quickly, pack your things, only what you need. And take Levi's grimoire with you. Go!" His urgent tone spurred her to action, and Sarah hurried upstairs to gather their essentials.

"Lazarus, what is happening?" Alden asked, as the two men gazed out at the approaching horde.

"A witch-hunt," he sighed, unhappily, a desperate plan forming in his head. "And this time, I fear they will catch their quarry." He turned to Alden and took him firmly by the shoulders. "I realize that I will be asking a lot of you in this, but I need you to trust me and do exactly as I say. Your cousin's safety depends on it. Do not be afraid."

"O-okay," Alden stammered, hesitantly. He seemed to take stock of Lazarus's deadly serious demeanor and nodded more firmly.

"Tenebrae!" Lazarus shouted, as loudly as his voice would allow. He turned away from the man beside him and cast his eyes about the house, looking for movement. He hoped against hope that the shadow demon would hear him, that he was nearby merely lurking in the shadows as he was wont to do.

Please be here, he begged silently. If the demon was not here, he would have to send them on foot and he did not like their odds of outrunning an incensed mob with a small child in tow.

"I am here, husband," the low volcanic rumble of the shadow demon's voice rang out from the hallway. He stepped into view and Alden let out an audible gasp. "There are humans coming. Let me deal with them."

Tenebrae ignored the man quaking by his side and moved to stand by Lazarus.

"No, I need something else of you, my love," the witch insisted gently with a sorrowful shake of his head. "If you massacre the whole town, there will be nowhere we may go where word of it will not follow. I need you to take my family to safety." As he spoke, a tumble of footsteps sounded down the stairs, as Sarah and Elijah hurried back into the room.

"I will not leave you to their hands," Tenebrae growled, clutching his arm tightly as he crowded into his space.

"You must," Lazarus declared, firmly, returning the shadow demon's unwavering stare. He would not be swayed in this. "Get them to safety and I will buy us time. They will want to have a trial, Reverend Poole would never forego the opportunity for such a spectacle. While he bloviates, you will take these three to Alden's cart in the village, so they can flee to Manchester." He looked pointedly at Sarah's cousin to make sure he understood his role in all this. The man nodded feverishly before returning his wary gaze to the hulking demon.

"And what of you?" Tenebrae prompted, entertaining the witch's plan but still somewhat unconvinced. He did not trust these humans of the village.

"I will stall them as long as I can," Lazarus explained, attempting to imbue his words with a confidence he did not entirely possess. "The most they will do is hang me. I have recovered from worse. And if they think me dead, then perhaps their need for blood will have been sated and they will not seek to follow Sarah and Elijah." The shadow demon listened with a grim countenance, seeing the logic in his thinking but abhorring the plan all the same. "Please, do this for me, Tenebrae. There is no time to argue."

The shouts of the crowd were closer now, identifiable words and phrases rising out of the din. The frenzied crowd was livid, from the sound of it.

"I do not like it, but I will do as you ask," Tenebrae acquiesced, resigning himself to carrying out Lazarus's wishes despite his trepidation. He grabbed the witch, cupping his face with both massive hands and capturing his lips in a surprisingly chaste kiss.

"Thank you," Lazarus whispered against his lips, reluctantly breaking the embrace to speak to his family. "Elijah, I need you to go with Mr. Tenebrae, alright? He is going to take you and your mama and Cousin Alden away from here." He crouched down in front of the boy, taking his small hands in his own. "Behave for them, understand? I love you."

Lazarus stood and Sarah fixed him with a tearful look, shock written plainly on her face as she looked from him to the demon and back again. She had noticed, of course, that their relationship had improved since its contentious beginnings, but until now Sarah had not known the extent of their connection.

"Laz, I- ," she started, but cut off with a yelp as something thudded against the door. The crowd jostled restlessly, some calling for the Graydons to come out and others lobbing rotten vegetables at the manor.

"It's alright, Sarah," Lazarus soothed, herding her and Elijah next to Alden. "Go. Everything will be alright."

He watched as Tenebrae took Sarah and Alden by the arm, the latter carrying Elijah, and guided them into the deep shadows in the hallway. They disappeared from view with a lingering look back from Tenebrae, and Lazarus put a hand on the doorknob, steeling himself to meet his fate.

Chapter 16

TRIALS AND IMMOLATIONS

Wrenching open the door before he could lose his nerve, the first thing that Lazarus noticed was the wall of sound that hit him. It seemed the entire town was here. Their individual shouts and murmurs blended together into a singular incomprehensible voice. Elbert Poole stood at the head of the rabble, smugly silent from his place at the foot of the manor's porch stairs.

The Reverend was suspiciously absent.

"Good day, Mr. Poole," Lazarus offered conversationally, ignoring the incensed crowd for the moment. "To what do we owe the pleasure of your visit? It is not often the whole of Graymourne comes to pay a social call." He gripped the door jamb until his knuckles were white, to stop his hand from shaking.

All I have to do is stall them long enough for the others to get away, he reminded himself.

The crowd hushed when Poole raised a hand high into the air, signaling for them to listen. He lowered it slowly, steepling his fingers in front of him as he regarded Lazarus with a sly grin.

"We are here today as God's instrument, Mr. Graydon," Elbert said, cryptically, his grin widening when confusion flitted over Lazarus's face.

"Then why is the Reverend not with you?" Lazarus asked, nervously. It was not often if ever that he wished for Hezekiah's presence, but he was the more reasonable of the two Poole men and the fact that Elbert was here leading the crowd did not bode well.

"The good Reverend was unfortunately called away," he said, the smirk twisting his thin-lipped mouth revealing just how unfortunate he considered the circumstances to be. "In his stead, I will take responsibility for meting out justice."

"I must admit, I am still confused as to the purpose of your visit," Lazarus said, speaking carefully as he attempted to stall for time. "I would offer you to come in and sit for a cup of tea, but there are so many of you, I fear you all would drink me out of house and home. Perhaps you would allow these good people to return to their own homes whilst you and I discuss whatever it is you require. Justice for Graymourne is, of course, as dear to my heart as no doubt it is to yours."

"Clever words and lies will do you no good this day, Lazarus," Elbert announced, dramatically. His eyes crinkled with hateful mirth; he was enjoying this entirely too much to be swayed by any reasonable appeals. "God sees you for what you are, and so too do we. A witch!"

The shouting resumed upon hearing the proclamation, even more enthusiastically than before. A few stray rocks and vegetables rained down on the porch, hurled from somewhere near the back of the crowd.

"Wait a moment now, that is quite the heavy accusation, Elbert, what reason could you possibly— ," he began, steadying his voice despite the fear that gripped his bones.

"Silence!" Poole shouted, cutting off Lazarus as well as the grumbling throng of villagers. "The witness will speak."

The crowd parted behind Elbert Poole on his left, and out came the meek figure of his wife, Clarity. She glanced in Lazarus's direction, furtively, as if she was afraid he would bewitch her if she looked him in the eye for too long. Shakily, she raised a stick straight arm to point in his direction.

"I saw Lazarus Graydon walking with the Devil!" Clarity proclaimed, with a volume and venom that he had never heard from the mousy woman. The mass of people at her back erupted again into jeers and shouts, crowing loudly at the assumption of the witch's guilt.

So much for a trial, Lazarus thought, wearily. Of all the people to catch a glimpse of him with Tenebrae, it just had to be her, the fucking Reverend's sister-in-law. An accusation like this would be bad enough no matter who the accuser was, but coming from the nigh unimpeachable source of Elbert Poole's wife, he knew he didn't stand a chance of refuting it.

He moved quickly to shut the door, ignoring the outraged shouts of his neighbors. Lazarus ran to the back of the house, only to see the back door opening as someone made their way inside. Turning on his heel, he bolted for the stairs to the cellar. There was another exit to the backyard there.

His feet thundered down the stairs and thudded against the dirt floor as he raced across the dark space. The wood protested creakily as he flung open the angled cellar doors. He was momentarily blinded by the influx of daylight, but not too much to see the stout silhouette of Amos Dinsmore before him.

"Fuck," Lazarus swore, backing away as two more silhouettes joined the hunter. Behind him, he could hear slow plodding steps descending the interior stairs.

He was surrounded.

"We will accept your fleeing as a confession of your guilt, Mr. Graydon," Elbert Poole drawled, crossing to the middle of the cellar. More figures fanned out behind him as they filed down the stairs from above. Beside him stood Bazel Cresswell, his sour countenance and Elbert's smug face illuminated by a single torch.

"I will confess nothing to you," Lazarus spat, edging away from the villagers who had begun to crowd around him on all sides.

"We searched the whole house, but the woman and child are not here. They must have fled with Mr. Taylor," James Cresswell said, pushing through the crowd. "We didn't find his witch book, but I did find this though."

A loud thud sounded as something heavy was dropped on the floor, and then he shoved the object into the small clearing. It was the wooden chest he kept beneath his bed. The lid was open, revealing a damning assortment of herbs, crystals, and other magical ingredients.

"There is no need, Mr. Graydon," Poole gloated, "the good people of this village can see your wickedness plain as day. You have been found guilty of witchcraft and consorting with the Devil, and you shall be punished accordingly."

He nodded and two men suddenly seized hold of his arms. Lazarus struggled, kicking and flailing against their grip. It looked like Amos Dinsmore and another man whose name he couldn't remember just then. The pair dragged him deeper into the cellar before shoving his back against one of the wide support beams.

"Amos, you know me, do not do this," Lazarus pleaded, trying to reason with the neighbor he had known for years. The hunter grunted and averted his eyes, holding him in place while a couple other villagers looped thick ropes around him, securely tying him to the post. His heart sank further with each passing moment as he realized that they were not planning to hang him at all. "Damn you all, think about this! What have I ever done to harm any of you? How can you be so cruel?"

A few of the dim figures shuffled uncomfortably, grumbling at his words. Still, others brought wood in from the yard, piling it around the beam at his feet. His chest constricted with panic. He had mentally prepared to be beaten or hung, but this was going to hurt a lot worse.

Amos returned, crouching down to pour something over the pile of wood and kindling. Lazarus craned his neck to see what it was and caught a glimpse of black powder.

"Be quicker this way," the man said gruffly, giving Lazarus a curt nod before blending back into the crowd. It was apparent that this was all the mercy he would get from the lot of them.

"Repent and God may have mercy on your soul," Poole said, his condescending tone betraying his doubt that Lazarus would do so.

"Fuck you," the witch cursed, furiously, struggling in vain against the ties that bound him.

Elbert only smiled at him and waved James Cresswell forward with the torch.

He closed his eyes, unable to bear seeing the faces of his neighbors as they condemned him to burn.

Tenebrae trudged through shadowspace, dragging the three humans along with him. He frowned deeply; this was already taking far too long for his liking. Both of the adult humans had been disoriented by the vast nothingness that surrounded them. Sarah had adjusted quicker than the man, who was still distractingly terrified of the shadow demon, judging by his racing heartbeat and the sharp smell of his fear.

Once Alden had calmed enough to actually hear Tenebrae's insistent questions, the demon had pried as much information about their destination as he could out of him. Traveling in shadowspace was not like traveling in the terrestrial realm; distance here had less to do with space and more to do with familiarity. Tenebrae had never been to the village aside from that time he found Lazarus in the stocks, so navigating to the blacksmith's shop on the south side of town where Alden's cart sat was not as simple as he would have liked.

Sure, he could bring them to the square where the stocks sat, but it was large and bathed in sunlight this time of day, leaving few shadows from which they could exit. And if there were any villagers about, they would easily be seen. He knew Lazarus would not want him to have to kill any witnesses.

So, he impatiently listened as Alden described the shop and its location in detail. Then using the village square as a reference point to orient them, he set out for their destination. The magnetic pull on his shadows towards the location was weak, and he had to concentrate to keep them on target.

"Do not speak," he growled, sensing it as the man drew in a preparatory breath. They were growing nearer and he didn't want any distractions. Finally, he felt the pressure before them increase and shouldered his way heavily through into terrestrial space, yanking the humans out with him.

They were in a cramped space littered on all sides with tools and equipment, all of which had a cared for but well used appearance. The singular small window was dingy and smudged, letting little light into the shop.

A large stone fireplace dominated the interior; there were still smoldering coals in its gaping maw.

"Th-the cart should be through here," Alden stammered, avoiding the shadow demon's impatient and unforgiving stare. He led them out the front door and around to the side where a covered stall sat, open to the elements on two sides. The merchant's cart was parked in the center of the space, where it would be most sheltered from the open air.

Alden rushed over to it, grabbing the breeching to pull it out into the lane in front of the blacksmith's shop. It rolled a few feet before lurching to a stop with a sickening crack. The merchant paled at the sound.

"What was that noise?" Elijah asked, from the safety of his mother's arms. Sarah hushed him, to keep his curiosity from distracting Alden as he looked over the cart for damage. He sighed in frustration when he identified the source of the problem.

"One of the felloes on this wheel is broken," he said, dourly. The splintered wood came away easily in his hands, neatly split at three points along the piece. The cuts were clean, too clean to be anything but deliberate. "Someone sabotaged it. We won't get far with it like this."

Tenebrae growled, loudly. He itched to get back to Lazarus, but he could not leave until his charges were safely on their way.

"What must be done to fix it?" he demanded, tersely, as Alden rushed to check the other wheel. Fortunately, the second was unscathed.

"Well, uh, I will have to craft a new felloe," Alden explained, already scurrying around the space to search for supplies. "There should be wood around somewhere and I can use the tools that William has in the shop to shape it. The rim is intact, luckily."

"Will this do?" Tenebrae asked, presenting a sizable log to the man.

"It needs to be half that size, let me find an axe," the merchant replied. Before he could turn, the shadow demon dug his claws into the wood and ripped the piece cleanly in half. Alden's eyes rounded and his mouth dropped open. "Or that works as well, I suppose."

Tenebrae snorted, derisively, and handed him one half of the log. He followed Alden into the blacksmith's shop, waving Sarah and the boy ahead of him. It would be easier to keep an eye on all of them indoors. Elijah was kept busy as Sarah took him around the shop, quietly getting him interested in the various tools and items so her cousin could work.

Alden quickly measured and marked out the shape of what he needed on the wood, then sawed off the extra material. The roughly hewn curve needed to be shaved down and smoothed. He began shaping the wood, but his hands shook with the urgency of the situation and it kept slipping.

"Let me do it," the demon insisted, seeing what the man was struggling to accomplish. The merchant moved aside, and Tenebrae dragged a single razor-like claw along the edge of the felloe. The pale wood peeled away in thinly curled sheets, the outer curve becoming smoother and smoother until it was a perfect arc. When he was finished, the shadow turned back to the merchant once more. "What else?"

"We need to drill holes for the spokes," Alden answered quickly, grabbing a small auger he had placed to the side. Hesitantly taking the felloe from Tenebrae, he marked the placement for the spoke holes and the shadow demon held the wood in place while he drilled out the necessary spaces.

Alden's nerves calmed as they worked together, and though he was still as anxious for them to be on their way as Tenebrae was, he at least felt slightly more at ease with the unsettling demon. The shadow's stoic and methodical nature helped as they advanced through the rest of the steps in making the wheel repair. Even with both of them working efficiently, it took time to craft the new part and then still more to install it correctly.

Breathing a sigh of relief, Alden stepped back from the freshly repaired wheel and wiped the sweat from his brow. He did not rest long though, already feeling the demon's unflinching gaze boring into him.

"Right, I need to retrieve my horse," he said, nervously. Taking the impassive silence for permission, he jogged the small distance to the barn where he usually housed his horse.

"You will not see me, but I will still be here," Tenebrae said, turning to Sarah where she stood in the doorway of the shop. "It is better if I do not frighten the horse." He started to go incorporeal, backing into the shadowy corner of the stall.

"Tenebrae, wait," she said, reaching towards him. "Thank you for helping us. Take care of Lazarus, will you? He deserves to be happy. I can see that he loves you, and you him."

The shadow demon allowed her to take his hand, and he squeezed hers gently as she gave him a sad smile.

"Try as I might, I cannot do otherwise," he said, wryly, a smile tugging at his lips even as his eyes rolled in feigned annoyance. "Be safe. My infuriating little human will be cross with me if any harm befalls you." With that, he melted into the darkness, an invisible guard to watch over them.

He did not say goodbye when Alden returned and hitched the horse to the merchant's cart. Tenebrae kept vigil, ensuring there was no danger, until Sarah and Elijah had been loaded into the cart with their few belongings and Alden drove the cart down the lane.

When finally they were out of sight and there was no sign of anyone to pursue them, Tenebrae eagerly leapt back into shadowspace and hurried back to the manor.

All that Tenebrae could see when he exited the familiar black void was red. The hot orangey red of the flames that were swiftly engulfing the Graydon manor and the deep crimson that tinged his sight as all his worries melted into a blinding rage. A fearful gasp tore his attention away from the inferno and his vision snapped to the side with a snarl, locking eyes with a stocky, bearded human whose eyes bulged at the sight of the demon emerging from the tree line.

The unfortunate man babbled incoherently as he tried to run but refused to take his eyes off of the terrifying being in front of him. Tenebrae grabbed him by the arm, his claws swallowing up the man's entire forearm, and yanked him forward. He delivered a powerful swipe with his other hand, striking his claws across the human's front with such force that it ripped the arm he held clean off.

The narrow vision of his fury expanded and he took notice of the rest of the crowd; screaming humans fled in all directions. The man nearest him foolishly brandished a pitchfork at him, as if it could do any substantial damage at all. He plucked it from the human's shaking hands, and hoisted him up by the front of his coat.

"Where is he?!" Tenebrae shouted, directly into the paling face of the hapless villager, whose feet kicked in wild panic several feet off the ground.

"I-inside," the man managed to wheeze from between chattering teeth, as his eyes darted toward the blazing building.

A trickle of cold fear ran down the shadow demon's spine upon hearing the answer he had dreaded. It was quickly subsumed by the pit of wrath that gripped him, and for the next few moments instinct took over completely. The whirling tornado of black claws and tendrils cut through the few unlucky souls who had the misfortune of finding themselves in the rampaging demon's path.

The only thing that stopped him from systematically hunting down every last human in the immediate vicinity was the impossible sound of a familiar voice calling his name.

The first thing that Lazarus had noticed when he returned to awareness was the acute lack of pain. He was grateful for the human mind's efficient capacity to dull the sharp edges of memory when it came to physical pain. What he did remember of burning had been excruciating. Mercifully, he had passed out from either shock or smoke inhalation within a few moments.

He opened his eyes to see the fire still raging all around him in the cellar. The space was vacant of other humans, and the fire had spread out, latching onto any flammable surfaces. Lazarus could hear the roaring of flames and the cracking of wood even on the floors above; it seemed the entire manor had been engulfed. He could feel the heat from it, but the sensation was oddly dull.

Looking down at his hands, he found them partially translucent, a pale and eerily desaturated look to his body. He moved away from the charred and broken beam where he had been tied, and his stomach turned with nausea when he made the mistake of glancing down to its base. There, in the still raging gunpowder-fueled flames, he could see charred bones sticking up from amongst the pile of burning wood and debris.

That is my body. Holy shit, those are my fucking bones. Am I dead?

He shook bodily, from head to toe, wracked with disbelief and yet unable to deny the obvious truth of what lay before him. For several minutes, all that Lazarus could do was stare at the flames dancing over blackened bits of his own skeleton as if in a trance. Just as it occurred to him with a strangely detached calm, that they reminded him of the shadow demon's charcoal bones, a deafening sound came from outside.

"Where is he?!" an unmistakeable voice roared, its deep, stony cadence raw with rage. A chorus of higher pitched shrieks rang out, shocking Lazarus into motion.

He ran for the stone stairs that lead to the backyard. The voices sounded from the front of the house, but the stairs that lead from the cellar to the first floor had already burned away. Rounding the house, he could see people fleeing down the path and through the woods in any direction their feet could take them away from the manor. A growl, accompanied by a sickening gurgle, propelled his phantom feet to move faster.

"Tenebrae!" he shouted, sprinting past the side of the burning manor and into the front yard. He skidded to a halt as the shadow demon turned to look in his direction. The limp body of a man dangled from one upraised arm, appearing miniature in comparison to the demon, who now towered at least three feet taller than usual. Spiny plates of bone covered his shoulders, ribs, and lower legs like shard-encrusted armor, while spear-like spikes jutted back from his elbows. His already sharp canines had grown more pronounced and fang-like, while behind him, long ribbons of shadow flared out, waving in agitation like shredded black wings. He was magnificent, and he was also drenched in blood.

"Lazarus?" Tenebrae whispered in disbelief, dropping the body to the ground where it landed with a wet thud. He stalked towards the witch, as Lazarus approached, both of them meeting in the middle. "Why are you so small? And transparent?" The shadow demon reached down for him, grabbing his shoulders with sinewy taloned hands. The touch felt strangely muted to both of them.

"Firstly, I am not small. You, husband, have grown much larger and sharper than usual," the witch corrected, his almost colorless cheeks darkening as he looked over the titan-like figure before him. It seemed not even death could quell his lust for his monstrous paramour. His eyes sobered at the thought and he frowned. "As for the second, I fear I may have perished."

"Ghosts do not have form that can be touched," Tenebrae countered, running his hands along the man's arms. He took one of Lazarus's hands and sunk a claw into the palm, both of them watching in wonder as black droplets floated upwards from the cut before it wove itself back together. "This is shadow."

"The ritual must have bound your shadows to my spirit," Lazarus mused, morbidly fascinated and somewhat relieved, "allowing me to still live, more or less, even though my corporeal form was burned away." It was not ideal, but presumably better than being dead. He grew quiet, contemplating the implications of this revelation and what possibilities it might open to them.

At the mention of his burnt body, a growl burst from Tenebrae, who glared out over the carnage as if hoping for a stray survivor on whom to take out his rekindled wrath. From what Lazarus could see, a handful of villagers had fallen to the shadow demon's fury before he had intervened.

He recognized a couple of farmers, Linus Gibson and Jedidiah Stalsworth, among the dead, but he was unsure who the others may be. After what they had done to him, though, he found it hard to mourn their losses. And in a grisly sort of way, it was a touching testament of the shadow's devotion to him.

"I will eviscerate each of them slowly," the demon threatened, his teeth grinding audibly as his jaw clenched in anger. Lazarus reached up as high as he could, gently placing his hands on his husband's chest, ignoring the slightly wet sensation of gore beneath his fingertips.

"Tenebrae," he said, softly, calling the furious shadow's attention back. He fixed him with a firm but loving look. "You will do no such thing. If we are to have hope of restoring my body, I require them alive."

"What do you mean?"

"I know of a resurrection spell," Lazarus explained, idly running his fingers over the spiky textured ribs lining the shadow demon's torso. "There is a ritual which can reconstitute my form and allow my spirit to merge with it again."

Next to the summoning ritual, it was one of the oldest spells in the grimoire. He had been fascinated by it as a boy, because it was the only necromantic magic the book contained, making it forbidden and rare. Despite the unlikeliness of ever performing it, he had read it many times and memorized much of it.

"What are we waiting for then? How do we begin?" Tenebrae asked, bewildered by the human's lack of urgency. If there was something they could do to resurrect his body, he didn't want to waste a moment more.

"It is not so simple, my love," the witch sighed, his eyes full of soft forbearance. "The rite is not complicated, save for the preciseness of the conditions it requires. The stars must align, quite literally, for a resurrection of this magnitude to succeed."

Lazarus assumed that's why none of the witches in his family had ever removed the spell from the book. Why bother hiding a spell that couldn't even be performed except once every five hundred years or so? There was little danger of it being used and it would be a shame to destroy the knowledge unnecessarily.

"And when will that be?" the shadow demon asked, dubiously.

"Without charting out the celestial paths properly," Lazarus said, humming as he quickly made some general calculations in his head, "approximately two-hundred and fifty years from now."

"Two-hundred and fifty fucking years?!" Tenebrae growled, his shadow tendrils writhing agitatedly. He glared down at the witch. "You are lucky that I love you, otherwise I would kill you all over again right now."

"Not technically dead," he countered, cheekily, at which the shadow demon rolled his eyes dramatically before wrapping his arms and several tendrils around him.

Lazarus had not lost his sense of humor in the flames, at least, which was a good thing because it was the only thing keeping him from collapsing in a heap of despair at the moment. That, and the sliver of hope that the resurrection spell provided.

It would be a very long wait, but at least, in the meantime, they had each other.

Chapter 17

257 YEARS LATER

The early light of dawn sparkled along the blanket of snow that covered the clearing around the ruined manor. Icicles dripped down along the stones and hung from the lattice of ivy branches that clung to the walls of the formerly grand house. A flash of red stood out among the stillness, as a cardinal flitted between the bare branches of a nearby tree.

Lazarus exhaled a breath into the frigid air. It was still strange, after all this time, to not see the crystalline cloud it should have left behind. The chill of the day was distant to him, like a half-remembered dream. The shadows that animated his spirit were unaffected by the extreme temperature, unlike his human body had been. It was convenient when it came to the weather, but less so for other more intimate sensations. But, thankfully, this was the last year that would pass this way.

"It is time we begin preparing in earnest," he said, turning towards the eyes he felt upon him from the dark cavern of the cellar doorway. Tenebrae stepped out into the bright, snow-reflected light to join him.

"You are certain of the timing?" the shadow demon asked, hopefully. He did not doubt the witch's calculations, but it was almost hard to believe that the day would finally come after two and a half centuries in this limbo of theirs.

"The stars are right," Lazarus said, nodding. Late into the night, the sky had given him a clear view of the twinkling stars. The pattern of their light matched his prediction and as the new year dawned, so did his excitement for the prospect it offered. "In six fortnights from now, the golden conjunction will take place. It is in confluence with a solar eclipse, though, which will be even more powerful than the conjunction alone. We will have only three and a half minutes to complete the ritual."

"If we do not complete it in time, then what?"

"Then it is another five hundred years until the next conjunction," Lazarus said with an air of anxiety, "and longer before it will coincide with an eclipse again."

"We will not fail," Tenebrae growled. There was nothing he would not do to ensure that the resurrection spell succeeded. He spun the man around to face him, gripping him by the jaw and slotting his lips against the Shade's slightly incorporeal ones. "I will not wait another five hundred years to taste you properly."

Lazarus groaned, melting into the shadow demon's embrace. He slid his hands up Tenebrae's chest, anchoring onto his shoulders to pull himself more firmly against the demon, as if that would intensify the limited range of feeling his current state allowed. Frustration built swiftly, and he bit down hard on Tenebrae's lower lip, barely tasting the inky blood that leaked from the cut even as it healed.

"Fuck… sorry, darling," he winced, pulling away quickly. He glanced up to his husband, finding the same ferocity of longing that he felt echoed in his fathomless black eyes. Tenebrae tenderly ran a thumb across his lips.

"I will go and check on the ingredients."

With a final kiss to the Shade's forehead, he disappeared back into the shadows, leaving Lazarus alone with his thoughts once more.

Focus, I need to focus, he thought, returning to the remnants of what used to be his kitchen. He moved a loose stone at the side of the hearth, retrieving the small metal lockbox from the concealed hollow. It was just large enough to fit his grimoire, which Zori had graciously returned, as well as an old notebook and writing implements that Tenebrae had pilfered for him from somewhere in town.

The small notebook's lined pages were covered in his scribbled calculations and notes. Charts of star positions and dates sat next to lists of names and locations over many years. Sitting down in one of the garden chairs, he began transcribing last night's celestial observations, making adjustments to the ritual layout according to the new information.

It appears we will need to demolish part of the floor in order to access a clear view of the eclipse, Lazarus contemplated, walking along the layout of the ruins. He was crouched down poking at the leaf strewn floor, when he heard voices coming from in front of the manor.

"I can't believe that asshole is making us come out here on New Year's Day," a disgruntled and unfamiliar male voice complained.

"Well, he's payin' us double, so quit your complaining, Lewis," another man said, impatiently shutting down the first man's griping.

Lazarus crept towards the front of the ruin, keeping low and to the shadows. It was easy enough to blend in with them as a Shade, and if he really needed to, he could disperse himself enough to be virtually invisible. He hated doing that though, it made him feel more dead than alive and it was a stark reminder that his appearance, clothes and all, were merely a shadow construct created by his mental image of himself rather than a real body.

"I don't see why the hell anybody would wanna buy this moldy old place, anyhow," the first man, Lewis, grunted. "Even if it wasn't a pile of rubble, it would still give me the creeps."

From where Lazarus peered out of a hole in the front wall, he could see the speaker, a stout balding man in navy blue work coveralls and a flannel coat, setting up some kind of device on three metal legs.

"Don't care why," the other man argued. He wore a matching outfit, though he was slightly shorter and skinny as a rail. "All I care about is whether his check cashes. If he wants to pay us to survey every inch of stone in this place, that's fine by me."

"Let's just get this over with," Lewis complained, fiddling with the equipment.

Buy the manor? Oh, no, no, no. That will not do at all, Lazarus thought, reeling in panic.

They were so close to being able to perform the ritual, they could not afford to have humans crawling all over the manor now. If they dug up the cellar, who knows what would become of his crumbled bones and ashes that still lay embedded in the soil there? Without these remnants of his form, the ritual wouldn't work, no matter how perfectly the cosmos aligned.

The shadow demon had been keeping tabs on the three founding families of Graymourne over the centuries. Their blood would be the key to reviving the witch's mortal body, so it was essential that they survive. Their happiness, however, was not essential to the spell, so Tenebrae had taken it upon himself to make the lives of the Pooles and Cresswells a living hell for the first few decades after Lazarus's corporeal death. He doled out just enough mischief, mayhem, and the occasional light maiming to mollify his need for vengeance, but not enough to permanently harm them or drive them to leave.

Once that first generation passed, he eased up on his torment. Their progeny were not responsible for the actions of their forefathers, and so did not warrant the same level of enmity. That's not to say that he didn't enjoy surprising them with the odd jump scare here and there. One had to stave off boredom somehow.

Branches of the three families had come and gone as years went by, and their numbers dwindled, but fortunately at least one member of each line remained in the village. Dylan Cresswell and his daughter Kelsey lived on the south side of town. John and Lily Graydon moved further than the radius of where Tenebrae could travel, but their child Skye owned a business in town. And eighty-seven-year-old Annabell Poole was the last of her family in Graymourne. She still lived in the family home. The house had been modified with additions and modern amenities over the years, but the core of the original house from the 1700s was still there.

By now, he knew the layout by heart, emerging from the shadows in a seldom used corner of the second floor. He listened for the warbly voice of the elderly woman. Even when younger, Annabell had a habit of chattering to either herself or a succession of scruffy orange cats as she puttered around the house. The quiet that blanketed the house was unusually thick, today, though.

Tenebrae skulked through the house, moving along the shadows stealthily while he searched it from top to bottom.

There was no one here.

Disconcertingly, there were half packed boxes in some of the rooms, and an unfamiliar suitcase sat open in the main bedroom. None of these were here the last time he visited, several weeks earlier.

As he rifled through the contents of the suitcase, noting the obviously masculine clothing, the front door opened and shut. Footsteps, much heavier than the soft, shuffling sound of Annabell's feet, sounded on the old wooden floorboards below. There was a loud sigh, followed by the sharp clink of a set of keys dropped on a table.

Stepping through a patch of shadow, Tenebrae emerged in a narrow coat closet near the front door. Melting into a misty haze, he slid out of the small space and up to the ceiling where he could get a better view of the intruder. The man's back was turned towards him.

He wore a tailored dark gray suit that was far too fancy to be something one of the villagers would wear. His leather shoes shone in the dim light, completely unsuitable for the weather. As he turned, Tenebrae studied his short dark hair peppered with silvery strands; it was carefully brushed and swept to one side so that not a single strand was out of place. His rounded features were pulled taut with an arrogant expression that suggested he was about to or had just yelled at someone.

Tenebrae instantly disliked him.

The man pulled out a small black cellphone and dialed a number, the line ringing loudly through the tinny speaker.

"Douglas Realty," a feminine voice answered.

"Susie, I'm going to need you to set all my meetings to remote for this week," he said, barely giving her time to speak before he was talking over her. "Freddie can handle anything that needs to be a face meeting."

"Of course, Mr. Douglas," Susie agreed, the clicking sound of computer keys clattered in the background. "Everything going ok?"

"Yeah, yeah, the old lady's estate is almost wrapped up," he replied, pacing across the living room with the phone in one hand, "but an opportunity has presented itself. This place has potential, I could make it the next Salem. Really put this town on the map."

"And put another couple zeros on your bank account?" Susie asked, teasingly.

"Obviously," Douglas chuckled, checking his hair in the reflection of the parlor window. "I've got to be compensated for my work. And maybe I'll take you to that new restaurant uptown."

"I'm holding you to that," Susie said with a giggle, still clicking away at her keyboard. Another line rang in the background.

"Sounds like you better get that, doll," Douglas said, hanging up in the middle of her goodbye.

Tenebrae glared at the man, his claws itching to tear the self-satisfied grin off of his tanned face. He didn't need Lazarus to explain what was going on here. The shadow demon knew as much by her fading scent as by the new presence of this unpleasant human that Annabell was dead. And that could pose a very large problem for their future. Not to mention, whatever plan this Douglas guy was hatching.

Fucking humans, Tenebrae thought, vanishing into shadowspace with a snarl.

"We have a problem," they both said at the same time.

Lazarus gestured for the shadow demon to go first, aware of just how limited Tenebrae's patience could be.

"Annabell is dead," he said, flatly.

Lazarus took a deep breath, closing his eyes tightly to contain the frustrated outburst that threatened to overtake him. Things had been so quiet for so long, and now that the opportunity for his resurrection was finally here, suddenly complications arose.

It felt as if fate was mocking him.

"Alright," he said, slowly, his carefully even tone at odds with the buzzing anxiety he felt. "We will find another member of the Poole family. She must have kin."

Tenebrae nodded; it was sound logic, even though he had no idea how to go about tracking down the woman's relatives. Lazarus certainly could not do it, being confined to the manor property.

"What is the problem you spoke of?" the shadow demon asked.

Lazarus stopped pacing and looked up at him.

"While you were gone, two men came to the manor," Lazarus explained, gesturing towards the front. "They had equipment and seemed to be taking measurements of some sort. I overheard them speak of someone buying the manor and surrounding lands. That cannot happen, not until after the ritual."

His form wavered with stress, as if his mind was too fractured to hold the shadows together properly. Tenebrae took his face in both hands and looked intently into his eyes until the witch met his gaze.

"I would kill them before I allowed that to happen," he said, darkly.

"I fear it isn't as simple as that, darling," Lazarus said, placing a light kiss on one of the demon's palms before taking his hands. "We need help and we need someone familiar with this modern world who can travel where we cannot."

"You want me to ask the others."

"Yes."

Chapter 18

THAT'S WHAT FRIENDS ARE FOR

Tenebrae strolled along the bank of the Lucent River under cover of darkness. This time of year the days were short and it was much easier to get around unnoticed. Eventually, he left the water's side for the cover of trees when it veered west. His destination was further south. He would have preferred not to make this journey alone, but he didn't have much choice. In his current state, Lazarus was confined to the small area around the ruined manor, barely a half-mile in diameter.

It was fortunate that the Dew Lane house wasn't any further, or the shadow demon might not have been able to reach it either. Certainly, it would have been faster to get there through shadowspace, but after spending more than two centuries in their small sliver of Graymourne, Tenebrae preferred to walk. He was feeling more restless than usual, and hoped the change of scenery might alleviate some of the turmoil.

He stepped out of the tree line and past the dense shrubbery that bordered the backyard of the quaint two-story home. Though the architecture was old-fashioned by modern standards, it had been built at least a hundred years after Tenebrae was summoned to this place. He shuddered to think that Myrkrið had been trapped inside its walls for four decades. It was a cage even smaller than his own, and without the comfort of a companion for most of it.

Dim colored lights shone from the windows on the first floor. Zori almost never kept bright lights on in the house, both for her own preference and her shadow demon partner's comfort. It was small gestures like this that had softened Tenebrae's sharpness towards the diminutive human over the last few weeks.

He listened carefully, keen not to disturb the couple in an intimate moment. But, hearing only soft laughter and the sound of music, he stepped through a shadow and emerged in the living room. Zori was giggling as Myrkrið twirled her around in place, her long golden waves fanning around her as she spun. She stumbled as she caught a glimpse of the other shadow standing nearby and Myrkrið had to grab her around the waist to keep her upright.

"Tenebrae!" she shouted, managing to sound surprised, delighted, and annoyed all at once. "You have got to learn to knock. You can't just come into people's houses unannounced!" She put her hands on her hips for dramatic effect and glared at him with a defiance in her green eyes that reminded him of Lazarus.

"You did not knock when you came to the manor," Tenebrae challenged, referencing their first meeting when she had come to the ruins in search of Lazarus's grimoire. Myrkrið chuckled behind her, and she shot him a sharp look.

"That's different!" Zori insisted, throwing her hands up in exasperation at the two shadow demons. "I didn't know anyone lived there. It's literally a ruin, okay. What if we'd been doing something… private?" She blushed slightly, knowing that the odds of Tenebrae catching them in a compromising situation were not exactly low.

"I would have heard and waited to enter," he answered honestly, which only made her grow redder.

"Oh my god, you're impossible!" she exclaimed, shaking her head with an exasperated laugh. "Well, you're here now, so come on in I guess." Zori waved for him to follow and led the group to the kitchen, where she started making tea.

Myrkrið leaned against the counter nearby, subtly positioning himself between her and Tenebrae.

While they were on good terms, shadow demons were rather territorial. So few of them existed that they had become largely solitary creatures by default, crossing paths with each other perhaps once every few centuries in both shadow and terrestrial spaces. The budding friendship that had developed between the two demons was unusual to say the least, and certainly not enough to override Myrkrið's protective instincts towards his human.

"What brings you so far south?" Myrkrið asked, regarding the other demon with a casual curiosity.

Usually, he and Zori went to the manor to visit Lazarus and Tenebrae; he was surprised to see him here alone.

"Lazarus and I need your help," Tenebrae said, with a sigh of resignation. His angular shoulders drooped, betraying just how uncomfortable he felt asking for assistance.

He and Lazarus were quite similar in that regard; both fiercely proud and independent. But as the conjunction drew near and complications arose, it had become evident that they could not complete all the necessary preparations alone.

"Of course we'll help, whatever you need," Zori replied, setting a steaming cup of tea on the kitchen island in front of him.

The shadow demon looked at it apprehensively, and raised a brow when she handed one to Myrkrið as well. The other demon only shrugged at him, raising the mug to his lips and taking a small sip. Clutched in his substantial hand, it looked like a cup from a child's tea set.

"We do not need to eat or drink, you know," Tenebrae said to the smiling human, as she breathed in the fragrant steam from her own mug. Her oversized sweater was pulled down over her hands to protect them where she held the warm ceramic.

"Yeah, I know," Zori laughed, glancing at the taller demon next to her. "But it won't hurt you and chamomile is good for relaxation. You look like you could use some of that, buddy."

She grinned brightly at him, and Tenebrae blinked at her awkwardly, still unused to her casually affectionate teasing. It was different from both Lazarus's flirtatious banter and the absolute terror he was used to inciting in most humans. Zori just treated him like a friend, which was decidedly not his area of expertise.

"Should we go to the manor to discuss the help you require?" Myrkrið suggested, as Tenebrae took a tentative sip of his beverage. It was surprisingly pleasant and he downed the rest of it in one large gulp.

"Yes, Lazarus can better explain the specifics than I can," he agreed, setting the ceramic mug back down on the wooden surface. He would also be glad to have the social buffer of his gregarious husband for this. He waited, expecting the other demon to take hold of Zori so they could travel through shadowspace. Instead, she tensed and beamed wildly at both of them.

"Race you there!" she shouted gleefully, and bolted for the dark hallway, disappearing into the shadows.

It took Tenebrae by surprise; he had forgotten that she could do that, having only seen it once before. He snapped out of his momentary shock when Myrkrið quickly stalked after her with a low growl. Following them into the void, the shadow demon wondered if he would be able to teach Lazarus to travel on his own as she did once his body was restored.

A high-pitched squeal announced the arrival of visitors, and Lazarus turned to see Myrkrið emerge from the thick vegetation at the edge of the property with a flailing human woman tossed over his shoulder. He smiled, watching them with amusement through the broken window frame as they approached.

"Ugh, no fair! It's not racing if you tackle me," Zori complained, her annoyance undercut by the smiling lilt to her voice. She wiggled in the shadow demon's grip, but instead of putting her down, he merely shifted her into a bridal carry.

"You know the consequences of running from me, little sunbeam," he admonished, smirking down at her as he walked. "You are lucky I do not wish our friends to see what usually happens when I catch you." He laughed at her scandalized gasp and looked up to see Tenebrae materialize behind the waiting Shade inside the dilapidated structure ahead of them.

Seeing their playful physical interaction sent a pang of longing through Lazarus. He leaned back against the familiar warmth of his demon husband, who slid an arm around his waist. It was but a dim echo of how he remembered Tenebrae's touch, and he soothed himself with the knowledge that he would feel the real thing again soon. As long as everything went according to plan, that is.

"Hi, Lazarus!" Zori said, grinning apologetically at him as Myrkrið carried her into the ruins. He parked himself in one of the garden chairs, settling her on his lap while the painted iron creaked in protest beneath their combined weight. An arm around her waist forestalled any attempts to move from her current position, and she looked at the shadow demon exasperatedly. "You can put me down now."

"You are not wearing shoes," he said, with an air of finality, making no move to release her.

Zori looked down at her feet, still clad in her fluffy house socks with the grip pattern on the bottom.

"Ah, oops."

Lazarus laughed as he took a seat across from them, the pair's antics temporarily chasing away the stress of the day.

"Thank you for coming so quickly," he said, "but you needn't have rushed over without proper footwear. I, well, we wish to ask for your assistance. Some unexpected variables have arisen that may affect our preparations for my resurrection." Lazarus paused, to collect himself and to gauge their reactions.

Zori looked concerned, while her demon appeared calmly attentive.

"Well, tell us what the problem is and we'll figure out a solution," she asserted, confidently optimistic that the four of them could solve whatever hurdles presented themselves.

"I adore your enthusiasm, my dear," Lazarus said, grateful for her hopeful determination. They might come to need it. "This morning, men came here to take measurements around the property. They spoke of someone who has the intention to purchase the manor, but they did not say a name. If people were to tamper with or, gods forbid, dig up what is left of the manor… it could render our task impossible."

The dread he felt reflected in Zori's face as she considered the ramifications. She looked to Myrkrið who hummed disapprovingly.

"Then we must stop the sale," he offered, "by whatever means necessary."

"Why don't we start by finding out who the current owner is and who wants to buy it?" Zori countered, patting him on one of his thick forearms. She shook her head with an amused snort and looked at Lazarus. "Shadow demons, always thinking with their claws first."

"Again, the zeal is appreciated, but I agree with Zori. We might consider non-violent options first," Lazarus agreed. Both shadows huffed in offense, but deferred to the humans' judgement.

"It may relate to our second problem," Tenebrae drawled, recalling the phone conversation he overheard earlier in the day. "The man I encountered at the Poole house this morning, he spoke of turning Graymourne into 'the next Salem'. Does this mean something to you?"

"Oooh, Margie's not gonna like that," Zori said, stiffening at the new information. Her next-door neighbor, and many of the town's longtime residents, prided themselves on Graymourne's quiet atmosphere and would be quite happy for it to continue flying under the radar of public attention. "Salem is a popular tourist spot in Massachusetts, known for its spooky history. That would make sense if he was the potential buyer."

"Who is this man?" Myrkrið interjected.

Tenebrae shook his head.

"I do not know," he said, "but I believe he is living in Annabell Poole's house. This is the second problem. She is dead."

Myrkrið and Zori shared a confused look, unsure how the elderly recluse might fit into the grand scheme of things.

"I don't understand," she said, plainly. Zori had heard of the woman's passing recently, but as far as she knew she had died of natural causes. Her death was, by all accounts, unremarkable. "Why is that a problem? Did you know her?"

Lazarus sighed, knowing he would have to explain the workings of the ritual now. He only hoped they would still be willing to help once he did.

"In order to restore my body, the ritual involves blood magic," he explained, reluctantly, "specifically, the blood of one of my descendants and the descendants of those who, for lack of a better term, killed me. A Graydon, a Poole, and a Cresswell, to be precise." He looked up to see an intense look of contemplation on Zori's face.

She was quiet for a few moments before speaking.

"How much do you need, exactly?" she asked, hesitantly.

"A non-fatal amount," Lazarus reassured her, venturing a guess as to the source of her hesitation. Desperate as he was to be returned to his former self, he didn't want it to be at the cost of his descendant's life either. "However, I do not expect they will part with it willingly, which poses its own challenge."

"Not if you leave it to me," Tenebrae murmured, ominously. Both the human and Shade's heads snapped towards him sharply.

"No," they shouted in unison.

Tenebrae merely shrugged, leaning back in his chair while they continued.

Myrkrið chuckled to himself; the capricious other shadow reminded him of himself in younger, more volatile days. Time, captivity, and an unexpected certain ball of human sunshine had done much to temper his reactions to a more measured ferocity. That is not to say he didn't empathize with the younger demon's sentiments.

"So, assuming we have a non-fatal way to collect enough blood from each descendant, with their permission," Zori mused, drumming her fingers on her chin, "we need to locate another member of the Poole family and keep mystery guy from trying to buy the manor. You know who the other two descendants are?" She looked back and forth between the witch and his demon, shivering slightly in the cold air. Myrkrið tightened his arms around her, wrapping her in shadows to keep her warm.

"Yes," Tenebrae confirmed, "there are two Cresswells: a man called Dylan and his child Kelsey. The only Graydon still in the range where I can reach is called Skye."

"We know them!" Zori exclaimed excitedly, her eyes lighting up. "Skye is a good friend. I'm sure I can convince them to help somehow. And I think Dylan Cresswell owns Tales and Tails, it's a bookstore and animal rescue."

Myrkrið nodded in agreement, he did not know this Dylan person, but Skye was one of the very small number of humans he approved of. They were a good friend to Zori.

"We will begin with searching for the new descendant and identifying the current owner of this land," he offered. Zori would know where to look for this information, or at least how to find out, and together they could travel outside of Graymourne if necessary to track someone down.

"Tenebrae can ward off any further surveyors that may come trespassing," Lazarus said with a sly wink at his husband, who was more than happy to take on the responsibility.

"They will not likely come at night, so I may also visit the Poole house to keep an eye on 'mystery guy,' as you call him," the shadow demon agreed, a little too enthusiastically.

Lazarus narrowed his eyes at his handsome partner. Something about the way he said 'keep an eye on' sounded suspiciously like 'menace from every dark corner.' something he had been on the receiving end of many years ago.

"To observe only, husband," the witch insisted, firmly. "Keep those claws and tendrils to yourself. I know well what your 'keeping an eye on' can be like."

Tenebrae smirked at him, unapologetically. He didn't need to touch the human to terrify him.

"He will not be harmed by my hand, husband."

Satisfied, Lazarus turned back to their two guests, contemplating his role in the plans. There was little he could do from the manor grounds, aside from continue to prepare himself to perform the ritual. But perhaps it would be a good idea to set up some defenses against further unwanted visitors.

"And I will create some protection wards around the manor," he said, pondering how to do this without access to the arsenal of ingredients he once possessed. "Zori, would you be able to procure some items for me? I believe I can gather some from the forest, but not all."

"Of course, whatever you need. That's what we're here for," she smiled at him reassuringly and took out her phone to jot down a list.

Myrkrið stepped out of the shadows into the warmth of their bedroom, depositing the shivering human in the center of the queen-sized bed. She immediately burrowed into the nest of blankets, while he went to retrieve her laptop. He knew she would want to begin investigating immediately; she was difficult to distract from a task once she was focused on one.

Handing her the computer, he settled behind her, curled around her to fit his long limbs on the bed. They needed a larger one, this one was never made to support a seven-and-a-half-foot demon. It was a miracle he hadn't broken it yet.

Zori hummed as she typed and clicked through websites and Google searches, while the shadow demon idly combed his fingers through the ends of her long hair. She scrunched her nose in an expression of distaste.

"What is it?" he asked, peering over her shoulder at the screen she was currently glaring at.

"I can't get the property records online," she grumbled. "It isn't on any of the real estate records, probably because it was never sold. So, I have to go to the town clerk's office and talk to a person to find out who the owner is."

"I am certain you will survive," the shadow demon teased her. His introverted human was not fond of other people, strangers especially, but he knew her desire to help their friends would override her social anxiety. Still, he didn't like to see her uncomfortable. "It is kind of you to do this for Lazarus."

"And Tenebrae," she added, snuggling back against her shadow. "He might be kind of surly, but he loves Lazarus a lot. And I think he could learn a thing or two from you about coexisting with humans."

"He seems to coexist with his human just fine."

Zori rolled her eyes at him, unamused.

"You know what I mean," she said, returning to her computer and typing in a new search. "Now, let's see if I have more luck with genealogy records."

Myrkrið watched as she clicked through branching names on a family tree, sorting through humans named Poole until she located the correct lineage. At the bottom left of the tree was a small square with a photo of a woman and the name "Annabell Poole" under it. There were no descendants listed.

"Hmm, it doesn't look like she had any kids," Zori mumbled clicking on another box to the right, "but maybe her brother did."

A profile for Michael Poole opened up in a new tab, with a black and white photo of a serious faced man at the top and a timeline of information below. Michael himself had passed away several years ago, but it appeared he had two living children: Ryan and Emily.

"Okay, we've got names and birthdates, but no pictures," Zori noted, settling in to do more digging. "Let's hope that's enough to track down at least one of them."

Chapter 19

DEAD AND BREAKFAST

The first week of the new year was quiet. There were no surprise visitors to the Graydon manor grounds. The pristine white blanket of snow that lay over it was unmarred by human footsteps; only dainty little tracks of bird feet and the occasional fox tracks disrupting the smooth glittering surface.

In contrast to the peaceful stillness of the winter landscape, the inhabitants of the snowbound ruins buzzed with restless energy. Lazarus rifled through the large plastic tote that Myrkrið had dropped off on Wednesday. It was packed with herbs, spices, candles, a few crystals, and some tools. It was a less elegant container than his heirloom chest had been, but just as comforting to have familiar instruments of magic at his fingertips. Zori had also included some books, a mix of literature and history to help him begin to catch up on some of what he had missed in the last two and a half centuries.

He was immeasurably grateful for the distraction. One could only check the astronomical calculations for the ritual so many times before it began to feel like a compulsion. Creating the wards was a simple process. Without the fear of discovery that had so restricted him in his time, Lazarus felt free to paint a protective sigil on trees in the four corners of the property with a mixture of oil and ash. These would have been too easily identified as 'witch marks' by the people of his day to be useful.

Around the manor itself, Lazarus drew a large circle, sprinkling the perimeter with a mixture of grave dirt, powdered bear bones, and field garlic. It was, admittedly, a bit more aggressive than he would normally use for a protective spell, but he really could not afford to allow strangers to come treading upon the grounds, not when the day of the ritual was so close at hand. Any unwelcome humans crossing this line would sorely regret it.

Once the wards were in place, Lazarus embroiled himself in learning about art history from the nineteenth century and onwards from one of Zori's college textbooks. It was rather fascinating, he had always appreciated beautiful things and it gave him a glimpse into modern life in ways that he had previously only learned of secondhand, from Tenebrae's forays into the village. He would often return and tell Lazarus of the strange new things he had observed in the humans' homes. The shadow demon's descriptions frequently left a little to be desired in context and detail, so it was helpful to fill in the gaps with the images and information in the books.

Tenebrae lacked his husband's studious temperament and preferred to keep himself occupied in a more active manner. He alternated between patrolling the property line during the day, keeping tabs on the Cresswell and Graydon descendants, and haunting the man who was staying in Annabell Poole's house. He made sure to keep his promise not to harm him, but putting a little fear into the human wouldn't hurt. And the former mystery man now had a name, thanks to the shadow demon's diligent stalking.

Spencer Douglas.

Currently, Spencer was on a phone call. He seemed to be on the phone more often than not, when he was awake. It was helpful for eavesdropping purposes that he always insisted on having his conversations loudly and with the speaker on, but Tenebrae found it incredibly irritating nonetheless, especially when he was out in public. The shadow demon could tell, based on the facial expressions of the people around Spencer, that this was considered rude even by human standards. But, if the man was aware of the looks it garnered him, he didn't show it.

"I'm telling you, Freddie, this place is a goldmine," Spencer enthused, holding up his phone to center himself in the camera. The face of a disinterested looking blonde man peered back at him from its screen. "The original part of the house was built in seventeen-whatever, and then built onto after that. Think Winchester Mystery House, but less manic. Plenty of ghost story potential to get tourists hooked, and it's big enough that with decent guest turnover, we can rake in a pretty penny."

He walked as he talked, giving the other man a half-assed tour of the old house. Tenebrae followed, glaring at him from the shadows.

Ugh, more humans, the shadow demon lamented. The more he heard of Spencer's schemes, the more his abhorrence deepened.

"It sounds solid," Freddie interjected. He spoke only occasionally, either content with or used to Spencer's monologuing. "What about the other place? The one in the photos you sent. It looks like, uh, quite the project."

Spencer set the phone down, propping it up on a desk in the study while he poured himself a drink from an antique decanter set.

"Yeah, that one has potential," he said, plopping down in the tufted leather chair and putting his feet up on the antique desk. He paused, swirling the amber liquid around in his glass before taking a sip. "So, it's about fifty acres of land, unmaintained but previously cleared for farming. River adjacent and extends into the local 'haunted' forest. It's even got the ruins of a burnt down colonial manor on it."

Tenebrae unconsciously moved closer as the man started talking about the Graydon ruins. The study was illuminated only dimly by a green shaded bankers lamp and the light of Spencer's phone. The shadow demon's eyes remained locked on the back of Spencer's perfectly coiffed head, while he crept towards him in the gloomy room.

"Is someone there with you?" Freddie asked suddenly, leaning towards the camera on his end of the call.

"What? No. Pay attention."

"It's just… I saw something move behind you," Freddie insisted, his previous vaguely detached expression now keenly interested.

"Ha ha, very funny," Spencer jeered sarcastically, taking another sip of his bourbon. "Save the haunting schtick for the tourists, yeah?"

Tenebrae held perfectly still, dissipating his shadows further in case either of them made an actual effort to search the space. Fortunately, the skeptical Spencer was too focused on business at the moment to care.

"Anyway, where was I?" he began again. "Right, so here's what I'm thinking. This place is a done deal, with a little remodeling we turn it into a bed and breakfast. I'm working on an offer for the other place. Once the sale goes through, we build a series of trendy little cabins on it, maybe even some of those yurts for the glamping crowd. Then we get some influencers out here to build hype, and tourists will be crawling all over this place by fall."

"You really think this place could be the next Salem?" Freddie asked with a touch of skepticism. "It's got spooky Americana vibes, I'll give you that, but Salem's got the whole witch trials thing."

Spencer grinned arrogantly, holding his glass up as if to toast the other man.

"Yeah, well, they might have the trials," he gloated, "but according to local legend, Graymourne actually burned a witch back in the day. Right in those ruins I'm about to buy."

An ear-splitting growl cut off the rest of what he was about to say, and the glass tumbler slipped out of Spencer's grasp, shattering on the floor. His feet came off the desk and he teetered back precariously in his chair, before righting himself at the last second and slamming his hands down against the leather desk mat.

"What the hell was that?" Freddie's panicked voice shouted from the cell phone as it tipped over.

Spencer snatched up the fallen device and whirled around, searching frantically for the source of the noise. He saw nothing. Tenebrae had already absconded back into the shadows after his momentary lapse in control.

"Nothing," Spencer finally replied, smoothing a tousled lock of hair back in place. "Probably just a bear or something outside. The woods aren't that far away."

"Yeah, Cocaine Bear, maybe," Freddie joked, laughing uneasily to cover his shaky nerves. "Well, keep me posted. Just try not to piss off the ghosts or whatever, Spence. I don't want to have to explain why we're taking a tax write-off for an exorcism."

Tenebrae ducked through shadowspace into the main bedroom while the two men finished up their conversation. He didn't need to hear any more to know that he wanted Spencer Douglas out of this town one way or the other. He seethed in the dark space for a few moments, trying to calm the storm that raged inside him. His claws itched to slice into something, so for the moment he decided to sate his destructive anger on the man's belongings.

First he cut every one of the bristles off of his hairbrush, leaving the bare wooden handle lying out on top of the chest of drawers where he found it. Next, he shredded through all of the laces on his shoes, without untying or unlacing them. And finally, when he was able to focus a bit more, he deftly sliced open each of the seams on Spencer's favorite gray suit. Tenebrae made sure to leave small sections of the stitching intact in strategic places, so the garments looked normal enough hanging there in the closet. But as soon as the man tried to put it on, the suit would disintegrate around his body.

The shadow demon decided this would be a good time to leave, not trusting himself not to lash out if he saw Spencer again tonight. He would have to be content knowing that the vain man would be beside himself at the unexplained destruction of his things, rather than stick around to see it firsthand. Besides, he needed to get back and tell Lazarus what he had learned.

It was the weekend before Zori and Myrkrið came to visit again, which was timely because Lazarus had stress-read more than half of the books she had lent him. She looked sheepish when she knocked at the crumbling stone doorframe and called out to them.

"Hello?"

"What a welcome sight you both make," Lazarus greeted, materializing out of the shady interior. He beckoned her and her shadow demon inside.

"Sorry it took us so long," she apologized, following him into the ruins. "I was hoping to have more news to share, but we hit a roadblock. I've been trying to find out who the current owner of the manor is, but the town clerk wasn't returning my calls or emails. So, I stopped by the office today and there was a sign on the door that said they're out of town on vacation until the fifteenth. The inconvenience of small towns strikes again." Zori gave an exasperated sigh and flopped down into a chair.

"Hmm, that is a bit dispiriting," the Shade murmured, thoughtfully, "but I suppose another week will not make too grave a difference. And what of the Poole descendants, did you have any luck there?" He looked at her with a mix of hope and trepidation. If they couldn't find another member of the family line, it wouldn't matter much whether the manor was sold or not.

"Yes," Myrkrið supplied quickly. "We have located one called Ryan Poole."

"I'm still looking for an address for his sister, Emily," Zori explained, shooting the shadow demon a terse look that Lazarus didn't quite understand. "Ryan lives in England in a care home. I'm hoping that Emily is a bit closer."

"We should still visit him, he is a viable option for the bloodline," Myrkrið insisted. As the most expedient and, in his opinion, practical option he didn't understand why she was so adamantly against this.

"For the last time, I am not going to another country to steal blood from an old man in a nursing home!" Zori exclaimed, throwing her hands up dramatically.

Lazarus could see clearly that the pair had been over this argument many times already. It was validating in a strange way, to see that her shadow partner could be just as hard-headed as Tenebrae. Perhaps that was simply something all shadow demons shared.

"I did not say we would steal it," Myrkrið said, a cheeky smirk playing at his lips as if he knew the comment would goad her.

"What are you going to do, just ask him?" she questioned, incredulously, before she continued, dropping her voice as low as it would go to imitate the shadow's deep rumble. "'Hello, I'm a demon. Can I have some of your blood'?"

The Shade couldn't help but laugh at her impression of her hulking paramour. Even while arguing, they managed to be playful with each other and he could see Zori's eyes sparkle with amusement despite their opposing opinions. Logistical considerations aside, they had found someone and that was what really mattered. The ritual was still possible. He decided to let their argument play out, if only for the entertainment of it.

"Perhaps," Myrkrið agreed, "I do not think it would take much for me to persuade him. And none of the humans there would believe him even if he were to speak of it later."

Zori sighed, knowing he was right. Most people were far too skeptical to believe in the supernatural, sometimes even when it was right in front of their faces.

She should know, she'd swathed the tall demon in black robes and marched him straight into town last Halloween, introducing him as her boyfriend 'Mark' and not a single villager had been any wiser for it.

"Fine, but only as a last resort, ok?" she conceded, before turning her attention back to Lazarus. If it came down to freeing her friends or not, Zori would ask the elderly Poole herself. "I'm certain I can find Emily with a little more time, but, either way we have options."

"That is excellent news, my dear," Lazarus said, smiling genuinely at her. After what Tenebrae had told him of Spencer's plans for the Graydon property, he was in dire need of more encouraging information.

"What news?" a low voice rumbled, as the shadow demon in question finally joined them. Tenebrae melted out of a dark alcove and moved to sit at his husband's side.

"Zori and Myrkrið have located two members of the Poole line," Lazarus explained, sliding his hand down the demon's forearm where it was quickly wrapped in dark tendrils.

"Hmm," Tenebrae rumbled, nodding. He looked at the pair of them pensively. "What is a 'bed and breakfast?'"

"Uhh, well, it's like a cozier version of an inn. Why?" Zori stammered, caught off guard by the abrupt change in subject.

Tenebrae explained what he had overheard while observing Spencer Douglas the other day, as he had already explained to Lazarus. He detailed the plans that the man and his business partner had discussed for both properties, turning one into a bed and breakfast and the other into a luxury cabin campground. But, he intentionally left out the part where he had growled at the two humans and then sabotaged the man's wardrobe.

"Oh, absolutely fucking not," Zori seethed venomously, when the shadow demon finished describing Spencer's schemes. "If that jerk thinks he can just waltz into this town and turn it into some Instagram tourist nightmare, he's got another thing coming."

Myrkrið seemed unfazed by the vehemence of her reaction to the news, simply gazing at her fondly, but it took Tenebrae by surprise. For someone so fragile looking, she could be astonishingly intense. She reminded him a bit of Sarah Graydon. Looking at his husband, he could see by the wistful expression on his face that he was thinking the same.

"Indeed," Lazarus said, agreeing with her. "I fear it will take more than some light haunting to dissuade him from the cause, though." He was loathe to suggest more extreme measures, but he was having a difficult time coming up with practical solutions.

The two shadow demons shared a look, a silent understanding passing between them.

"I have some experience in haunting troublesome humans," Myrkrið rumbled ominously, giving a curt nod to the other demon. "Tenebrae and I will work together to discourage this Spencer from his ambitions here."

Lazarus looked at the pair of them, catching a hint of mischief brewing in the way their black eyes sparkled. Having been on the receiving end of one shadow demon's ire once upon a time, he could only imagine the havoc that Myrkrið and Tenebrae could wreak together. He would not wish to be the unlucky soul who managed to draw the attention of two pissed off shadow demons at once.

"I'll tell my neighbor what our newcomer is up to," Zori offered, "if anyone can stir up some drama in the village, it's Margie. If we can turn the public against him, it'll make Spencer's plans a lot harder."

Margie Caldwell lived in the house next to Zori. She was a sweet lady, an excellent baker, and a prolific gossip. It wouldn't take long for the whole town to know all of Spencer Douglas's business once she had heard about it.

The idea of provoking public sentiment stirred feelings of apprehension and unpleasant memories in Lazarus. He would not be the focus of the mob's ire this time though, and, he hoped, much had changed in Graymourne since his time.

"We can use all the assistance we can get," he conceded, putting aside his visceral reaction to the idea. "If you believe you can rally the people of Graymourne to our cause, I trust you."

Chapter 20

FRIENDS THAT HAUNT TOGETHER

Myrkrið bellowed a deep, volcanic laugh, traversing the void beside Tenebrae. The younger shadow demon was recounting the methods he had employed so far in haunting Spencer Douglas.

"That is quite creative," Myrkrið said, commending the other shadow on his inventive approach. "I would have enjoyed seeing his reaction when the garments fell apart. I will have to remember this idea."

Tenebrae preened at the compliment, gaining approval from one of his own kind was unexpectedly satisfying. He had not anticipated caring so much what the other demon thought of him, but he had come to respect the other's opinions. There was a sense of kinship growing between them, entirely different to the closeness he felt towards his human husband.

Is this what Lazarus felt like with his family? he wondered, the thought tinged with sadness for what the man had lost. Motley crew though they were, this was the closest thing to a family that Tenebrae had ever experienced.

"Do you have a favored method of frightening humans?" Tenebrae asked, curious after the other demon had mentioned running off several owners of the Dew Lane house before Zori came along.

Myrkrið considered the question for a moment; there were so many to choose from.

"I suppose it depends on what you wish to achieve," he said after a while. "Coming at them with claws and teeth will terrify them, for certain, but there is something much more satisfying about building a quiet sense of creeping dread. Most humans will frighten themselves if you provide the correct atmosphere."

Tenebrae pushed through the invisible barrier back into terrestrial space, leading them into a darkened spare bedroom in the Poole house. Their mist-like incorporeal forms melded into the gloom of the space naturally.

"Disembodied sounds and appearing behind them in reflections or in their periphery are quite useful for this," Myrkrið added. Both demons paused to listen for movement in the large house. A steady heartbeat sounded in the downstairs parlor, along with occasional clicking sounds.

Spencer must be on his computer.

"This did not work on your human, though?" Tenebrae asked, unconcerned that the occupant would hear them from the floor below as they glided out into the hallway, clinging to the shadows.

"Not at all," the shadow demon huffed in affectionate annoyance. "I clawed ominous words into a kitchen implement and she responded by purchasing a notebook and asking me to write her more messages in it. She was delighted by my attempts to scare her. It was maddening."

Myrkrið dragged his claws along the spine of an antique radiator as they moved down the hall. The screeching sound of sharp edges on metal echoed loudly through the silent space. Tenebrae pushed at the heavy wooden door that led to another one of the many bedrooms, allowing it to creak open loudly on its antique hinges. The sound of typing that had been coming from the floor below ceased.

"I know the feeling," Tenebrae said with a dry chuckle. "I tormented Lazarus for weeks and somehow he became so cross that he kissed me. It was confusing."

He shifted into his more corporeal form, allowing his slow, heavy footsteps to reverberate through the wooden floors with a foreboding thud. Muttered curses sounded from the parlor, followed by the hurried patter of feet. They had Spencer's attention. Tenebrae melted back into an inky haze, easily camouflaged in the dim space.

"I will go further down the hall," Myrkrið suggested, passing the landing at the top of the staircase. "If you remain here, we will flank him."

The two demons moved into position, lying in wait for the human while Spencer began to ascend the stairs. He grumbled to himself irritably as he made his way.

"Alright, who the hell is up here?" Spencer demanded as he rounded the top of the stairway. His head whipped left and right, and he paused, listening for any trace of what he had heard. There had to be someone up here, he clearly heard footsteps, right?

The house was still as a tomb, with the exception of his labored breathing.

Spencer spotted the spare bedroom door that was now ajar and started towards it. Just as he approached the threshold, Tenebrae reached through shadowspace and slammed the door shut in his face. The human jumped back with a shout.

He stood frozen for a moment, his adrenaline spiking. Spencer got ahold of himself, glaring at the door and then wrenching it open. The room beyond was dark and empty.

"There better not be anyone hiding in here. So help me, I will have you arrested and then I will sue you into oblivion," he threatened, cautiously entering the space to search for intruders. Spencer searched the closets and even looked under the bed, but found nothing. He exited the room, shutting the door firmly behind him, already rationalizing the odd noises in his head.

It's just an old, creaky house, a draft must have blown the door shut, Spencer thought, trying to shake off the lingering nerves. He turned back towards the staircase, and just then a low snarl sounded from behind him. He broke into a run, overshooting the stairs and finding himself in front of the door to the main bedroom when he finally came to a stop.

Tenebrae chuckled, slinking closer while the man stood catching his breath. When Spencer ducked into the bedroom, the shadow demon slipped in behind him unseen. He could sense Myrkrið's presence already inside the room as well, his silhouette barely identifiable next to the tall curtains along the west wall.

Unaware of the hidden entities in the room with him, Spencer walked over to the chest of drawers, leaning his hands on it to look at himself in the mirror. He nervously smoothed the graying flyaways at his temples and smacked himself lightly on the cheek.

"Get it together. You don't believe in ghosts," Spencer chastised his reflected self.

"You should," a deeply inhuman voice murmured. It sounded more like an earthquake rumbling through a catacomb than a person.

The sound made a chill run down his spine.

Spencer's eyes widened as he shook, rounding further when something impossibly tall and dark moved next to the curtains in the reflection of the mirror. He whirled around, hands supporting himself on the polished wood furniture as he scanned frantically for the source of the voice. The large shadow he had seen next to the window was noticeably absent and it made dread twist in his guts.

"He will," another harsh monstrous voice chuckled from somewhere to his right. A responding laugh echoed from his left, closer than before and that was enough for Spencer.

"Fuck this," he breathed, racing out of the room while more dark laughter sounded behind him. He snatched his phone and keys from the parlor and slammed the front door shut on his way out. A drive would clear his head, and maybe a drink. This town had to have a bar somewhere.

Inside the house, the two shadow demons congratulated each other on a job well done.

"This was a good start," Tenebrae said, pleased that they managed to make the man flee on their first venture together. They made a good team.

"Agreed," Myrkrið said, "we should allow him to get comfortable again before we make a further appearance. It will be more effective if we return when he believes that he is safe."

This seemed like solid logic to Tenebrae, who admittedly had far less experience at this sort of thing than the older demon.

"I would still like to keep an eye on him in the meantime," he said, "in case he makes any changes in his plans." Tenebrae didn't want to be caught off guard again. With only weeks to go until the date of the ritual, they could not afford any more surprise obstacles.

"We will take turns watching over him," Myrkrið offered, again surprising the younger demon with his generosity.

If this is what friends are, then I am glad to have them, Tenebrae thought.

Nine o' clock in the morning was not a time of day that Zori was in the habit of leaving the house. She was firmly not a morning person and never had been. But, it was the fifteenth, which meant that the clerk's office would finally be open today, so here she was, coffee in hand driving into the center of town.

Fortunately, weekday morning traffic in Graymourne was a far cry from the busy California grind she was accustomed to before moving here last fall. It was easy enough to find street parking on the main thoroughfare that was a short walk to the small office. An unnecessarily loud chime rang as she entered the front door. The inside of the clerk's office was so compact that she wasn't sure a chime was even necessary. You could see the door easily from anywhere in the office.

At the sound, a person's head popped up from behind the counter like a startled meerkat. It belonged to a reedy middle-aged man with short ash blond hair, glasses, and an outfit that screamed 'nerd.' Zori briefly wondered if this person had seen Rick Moranis's character in *Ghostbusters* and thought, 'that's the look for me.' The resemblance was uncanny.

"Oh, uh, hello," he said nervously, pulling at the hem of his sweater vest. "Come in."

"Thanks, hi," Zori smiled, approaching the counter slowly. The guy looked like he might spook at any sudden movements. "Are you the clerk?"

"Yes! Yes," he replied, with a little too much enthusiasm before correcting to a more moderate tone. "Cameron Hess, Town Clerk. How can I help you?"

Cameron reached out a hand and shook hers stiffly. Zori stifled the urge to laugh. She usually felt awkward meeting people, but somehow he managed to out-awkward her and actually make her feel at ease at the same time.

"Zori Quinn, I own a house over on Dew Lane," she explained, noticing his startled expression. It was one she got frequently at the mention of her house, thanks to its sinister reputation. "I was hoping you could help me find out the current owner of a property in town?"

'Yes, of course," he said, waking up an ancient looking computer monitor that sat yellowing on the counter. "What's the address?"

"Oh, uh, I don't know if it actually has an address," she mused, "but it's the Graydon Manor ruins and surrounding land."

Cameron gave her a curious look and she thought for a moment that maybe he didn't know the place.

"You know, off the trail into Whitmack Forest on the other side of the river?" Zori said, hoping that more description would help.

"I know the place," Cameron said, shaking his head and typing something on the clunky keyboard. "It's just strange. You're the second person today to come around asking about that old place. Are you thinking of buying it too?"

Zori's heart dropped. Spencer must have been in here right when they opened for her to have missed him.

"Really? That's so odd," she lied poorly, ignoring his question for the moment. "Who was the other person, if you don't mind me asking?"

"Some out of towner," Cameron shrugged. "Expensive suit, impractical shoes. Not a Graymourner." He looked at her conspiratorially, obviously counting Zori amongst the locals. It was oddly flattering to be included.

"Anyway," he continued, tapping away at the keys as he spoke, "I'll tell you the same thing I told him. It's still owned by the Graydons. Been passed down via inheritance, so technically, it's owned by John Graydon, the guy who runs Pizza Paradise. But I don't think the family has ever planned to do anything with it."

Skye's dad owns the manor? Maybe they can help us convince him not to sell it, Zori thought, accidentally staring at Cameron for a little too long while she was lost in thought.

"Sorry, thanks!" she said quickly, nodding nervously. "That's actually really helpful, I appreciate it."

She took out her phone, sending a quick text to Skye. It was about time for them to catch up over coffee anyway.

Now she just had to see if Margie was home to put her gossip plan into motion.

Chapter 21

SKYE WATCHING

"**W**here's Tenebrae?" Zori asked, finding Lazarus in the back garden behind the manor ruins. He was sitting with his back against a wide tree, one of her books propped open on his lap. He looked up from the novel at the sound of her voice.

"Probably haunting our dear nemesis, Mr. Douglas, at the moment," Lazarus said, closing the book with a bright smile. He was glad to see his husband staying occupied with something he enjoyed.

"Ah, yes," she said, nodding knowingly, "I don't know which one is having more fun with it, him or Myrkrið. At least they're getting along, it's actually pretty cute." Zori laughed as she sat down on a stone beside the Shade, recalling the slightly rocky start they had at introducing the shadow demons. But once they got past their initial standoffishness, she wasn't surprised that they found themselves to have quite a bit in common.

"Do you not get cold?" Zori asked, looking down at where the Shade sat in the snow. He was still attired in his usual woolen frock coat and breeches, and it now occurred to her that she had never seen him in anything different.

"Ah, no, not as such," Lazarus admitted, searching for the right way to explain. "I can feel the cold of the snow and air, but it is distant or muffled, if you will. It is the same for most sensations. I am missing half of my form and so it seems my senses are halved as well."

"That must make things difficult," she said, empathetically, "for you and Tenebrae, I mean."

"That it does," he sighed wearily. Being bound together for more than two centuries, while only ever able to feel a pale echo of each other's touch had been a special kind of torture. One he hoped they would be free from soon.

"Well, I have good news," Zori said, hoping to lift the melancholy that she seemed to have inadvertently caused with her curiosity. "I found out who owns the manor property and I think it will work in our favor. Looks like it never left your family. The deed was passed down to John Graydon."

Lazarus brightened at the news. It was touching to know that Sarah had passed the family land down to her children, and they to theirs. He wondered how much the Graydon descendants knew about what had happened here. Surely, they must know something if they had held onto the property for so long without making any attempts to refurbish it.

"And you think he will be unwilling to sell it, then?" he asked, hopefully. It did seem less likely, given how long the land had stayed in the family.

"I hope so, but he's also my friend Skye's dad," Zori explained. "They own an antique shop in town, and they have a soft spot for spooky, historic things. Should be pretty easy to get them on our side and then hopefully they can help convince John that selling is a bad idea."

"Certainly, it sounds like a mark in our favor," Lazarus agreed, heartened by the development. His brows furrowed as he considered her wording more precisely. "I must ask, why do you say 'they' when you speak of Skye?"

Sometimes her modern colloquialisms caused him confusion, and this was one such occasion. He never heard her refer to another singular person in such a way, so it stuck out to him.

"Oh, Skye is non-binary," she replied simply, and then quickly realized this would require a more in depth explanation. So much had changed for queer people since Lazarus was last among the living. "That means they aren't a man or a woman. Their gender doesn't fit in the binary categories. So, for non-binary people, we use they/them pronouns."

His confused expression morphed to delight as understanding sank in. It took him a moment to speak, stunned as he was with how casually she spoke of something that would have been incredibly taboo in his time.

"I see, that's marvelous. And this is just accepted?" he asked, incredulously. Perhaps more had changed than he ever considered. For so long, his focus had been on getting his body back, his life in a sort of permanently paused state. Once he fully rejoined the land of the corporeal, he would be entering an entirely different world from the one he left behind.

"Well, not everyone is totally accepting of queer people, but things have come a long way for us," Zori said. When she noticed the inquisitive look he gave at her inclusion of herself, she realized the subject of sexuality had never come up between them before. It was so normal to her that he had a husband, that it hadn't dawned on her that sharing her own orientation might make a difference to him. "I'm bisexual, which means I'm attracted to people, and demons, of more than one gender. Some people say pansexual instead, but I like the colors of the bi flag better, so I stick with that."

"There are flags??"

Zori's eyes crinkled with happiness at his awestruck words. It wasn't every day that she got to introduce a friend from a foreign time to the brave new world of openly queer living.

"Yeah, we have parades too, in June for Pride. Pretty much every major city has one," she said, grinning widely at him. "I'll take you sometime once we get your body back." The shadow demons might not be able to join them, at least not corporeally, but the idea of bringing Lazarus to his first Pride made her buzz with excitement. Graymourne would probably have something small, but she would love for him to experience one of the bigger celebrations in the area, like Boston or Providence.

While Lazarus sat quietly digesting this new information, she scrolled through the photo app on her phone. She pulled up a photo and turned the screen so that he could see it.

"Here, this is me at Pride a few years ago in San Diego," she explained, handing him the device. He was used to it by now, but the first time she had showed him a photograph on her smart phone, he'd been adorably fascinated.

The image showed a grinning Zori in the middle, dressed in a cropped tank top and leggings with rainbow sunglasses and accessories. On either side of her were three other young women in colorful attire, all smiling in the bright sunshine. Behind them, there was a crowd of people, some holding up handwritten signs or colorful flags while others embraced each other in casual displays of affection. The clear blue sky was framed by tall palm trees. The picture radiated joy and for a moment, Lazarus felt completely overwhelmed by it.

"Who… who are the people with you?" he asked eventually, his voice shaking with the power of his emotions. His eyes prickled with tears and he wiped at his face when he felt one fall, fingers coming away damp with black liquid.

"They were my best friends back home. That's Beth," she said, leaning over his shoulder to point at a dark-haired woman at the right side of the photo. "And these two are Devin and Emma. They got married like a month before this, I think."

"Were?" Lazarus asked with a tinge of concern, handing the device back to her. "Did something happen to them?"

"I kind of lost touch with them for a while," Zori explained, chewing at her lip as she paused. "There was an ex-boyfriend, a bad one, that drove us apart. But we reconciled a few months ago. I'm trying to be better about keeping in contact with them now."

"And this ex-boyfriend?" he prompted, worried by the way her eyes darkened when she spoke of him.

"Definitely not a problem anymore," she said, emphatically shaking her head. The hard look in her eyes softened with gratitude. "Myrkrið took care of him."

Lazarus didn't need to ask what she meant by that. He was familiar enough with having an overprotective shadow demon for a partner to know what their problem solving skills looked like. He simply nodded sagely and was glad for her to be free of whatever had happened. The idea of anyone mistreating her did not sit well with him.

"Well," he said, patting her on the arm affectionately, "I am glad for your reconciliation, and I would be indescribably delighted to see this Pride with you, my dear."

It was not often that the gregarious Lazarus found himself at a loss for words, but he truly could not begin to describe the swirl of feelings that this new knowledge had given rise to. Anger, for himself and all the others like him, who had lived their lives in fear and hiding simply because they were born who they were in a time and place that reviled them. Grief, for all the lives lost to the treacherous cruelty that masqueraded as morality. Joy, that this was a world where people lived and loved proudly, and yet sadness that even still there were those who didn't accept them.

Lazarus chose to cling to the joy, and the hope that accompanied it, vigorously. His resurrection was coming, and perhaps the world he would return to was a better place than the one he came from.

The sign on the front door of the Grace Street antique shop, Salvage Garden, was turned to the side that said 'Closed'. Inside, music filled the space as upbeat yet macabre sounds spilled out of a bluetooth speaker near the register. Skye Graydon swayed along to the beat of their favorite horror synth playlist, scribbling checkmarks and tallies on a clipboard.

It was Wednesday, so that meant it was inventory day.

After holiday and New Year's sales, Skye was looking forward to getting out of the shop and visiting some estate sales to replenish the store's goods soon. Graymourne might be a well-kept secret for physical visitors, but the online sales were more than enough to make up for any lack in foot traffic. Skye had a natural talent for finding the strange and unusual as well as the internet savvy to carve out a nice little niche on the web.

They were running a bit low on taxidermy, by the look of things. The shop owner twirled a pen restlessly in one hand, looking over the list again. They squinted at their own messy handwriting on the page.

Did it just get darker in here? Skye thought, scrunching their nose as they looked around the shop.

The lights seemed dimmer for some reason, soft shadows pooling in the narrow aisles between vintage furniture piled high with curiosities. Wandering over to the counter, they set the inventory list down next to the register and flipped the light switch on and off. All of the lights seemed to be on, but maybe one of the bulbs was starting to burn out.

With a sigh, Skye headed back to the store room to fetch a replacement just in case.

Reaching up to grab the box of spare lightbulbs, they paused, the hair on the back of their neck rising suddenly. Skye's back tingled, feeling like they were being watched. They spun around, eyes darting around the space hawkishly but there was no movement. Straightening up with a disconcerted frown, they turned back to the shelf and grabbed the box.

I must've picked up a cursed object in that last batch, they thought, climbing on top of a footstool to replace a flickering bulb in the wall sconce. *Wonder which one it is?*

From murky edges of the shop's right aisle, Tenebrae observed them curiously.

Skye's hair had changed again.

This time it was shorter and spikier, in a royal blue asymmetrical cut with vibrant green highlights. It was strange to think of them as Lazarus's kin, but now and then he caught a mischievous twinkle or a determined frown that made a certain resemblance shine through.

As they hopped down from their perch, they gave another furtive glance around. More so than the other humans he kept an eye on, Skye seemed able to sense when he was watching them, another trait they shared with his husband. Still, they had never managed to spot the stealthy presence that occasionally haunted their shop.

Tenebrae shifted from shadow to shadow, following them as they made their way back to the front of the space. He took up a post in a dark patch between a tall ornate armoire and a bookcase, while they resumed their previous task. It was oddly entertaining to the shadow demon, watching them dance around to the strange music they favored while they worked.

Like a colorful bird, Tenebrae thought, observing as they flitted about.

A rhythmic knock at the front door interrupted the steady, driving beat of the music, and Skye bounced over to answer it. They peered through the curtains that lined the glass door and then quickly straightened to unlock it.

"Oh my god, you're the best!" Skye exclaimed, throwing open the door to reveal a smiling Zori on the other side with two cups in her hands. One of those was promptly snatched up by the excited shop owner, who was already taking a large sip while their visitor stepped inside. They locked the door again before throwing their arms around her in an enthusiastic hug.

"When I told the barista it was for you, he insisted on making your gingerbread latte an extra large," Zori laughed.

Skye was practically an honorary resident at Brewed Awakening, Graymourne's best and only coffee shop.

"Robin, right?" Skye asked, leading them both back to the register. "He knows I do inventory on Wednesdays. It's a more is more kind of coffee day. Take a seat, I've still got some lists to check, but I can multitask."

Zori hung up her coat and took a seat in an antique rocking chair near across from where Tenebrae lurked. Skye turned down the music and began sorting through a box of smaller items, tallying their numbers on a printed chart as they went.

"So, I've also got some tea for you, too," she began, sipping her coffee as she settled into her seat. Skye looked up from their list with an expectant expression. "Did you hear that some out of town guy is trying to buy the ruins in Whitmack Forest?"

"No! What the hell?" they said, indignantly. "Where did you hear that?"

The clipboard was set down immediately and now Skye's full attention was now on this juicy tidbit of news. They loved small town drama almost as much as they loved finding rare curiosities.

"I talked to Margie the other day," Zori said, leaving out the detail that she had been the one to inform her lovable busybody of a neighbor about the potential sale. With that seed planted, it didn't take long for the rumor to sprout and it was quick to spread around town. She was surprised that it hadn't made its way to Skye already.

"Ugh, the one week I don't have time to get down to the coffee shop and I miss the best gossip," they bemoaned, throwing their hands up dramatically. "What does he want with it?"

"Sounds like he wants to turn it into a tourist attraction," she said. Her distaste for the idea was evident in the way the corners of her mouth turned down in a disgruntled expression. "Put cabins on the property for people to rent out."

Tenebrae's formless shape shifted with annoyance in the narrow space he occupied, rattling the contents of the armoire lightly. Zori's eyes shot to the dim alcove and then narrowed for a moment as if to indicate she had caught a glimpse of him there. It was only a brief acknowledgement and then her attention returned to Skye.

"Oh man, the townsfolk are not gonna love that!" they said with a grimace. Sipping their coffee, they pondered for a minute, the wheels of their thoughts spinning almost visibly in the space above their head. "I don't love it either. That would royally suck."

"Doesn't your family own the property?" Zori asked, tilting her head curiously at her friend. She wasn't sure if Skye knew or not; it seemed unlikely given their reaction.

"Oh, uh… I dunno," they replied, clearly taken aback by the question.

"I figured you knew," Zori said, honestly. She didn't want to lie to her friend any more than was necessary, so she decided to come clean about her visit to the clerk. "I was curious so I asked over at the clerk's office. He said that it was passed down in the family, to your dad." She paused, gauging Skye's reaction, but they looked unbothered by her snooping. "You don't think he'd really sell it, do you?"

He will not if he knows what is good for him, the shadow demon thought, darkly.

Tenebrae watched Skye's face closely as they pushed the box of products to one side and hopped up to sit on the counter. Their mouth quirked to one side as they thought it over, quietly, swinging one foot side to side as they contemplated the question. The fingers of their left hand tapped at the edge of the counter restlessly. It was not comforting to the shadow that they had to think for this long about the answer to Zori's question.

"I don't think so," Skye said eventually. "I mean, he's never mentioned it one way or the other, so I can't be sure. But it would be such a shame to sell a historic site like that, especially with the family history it has."

"Yeah, I heard about what happened there," Zori said, sympathetically, her eyes flitting to where Tenebrae was hiding briefly. "Seems disrespectful to develop it for tourism. It should be protected, like a historic landmark or something."

She could see the gears turning already in Skye's mind; the excitement and curiosity about the history-steeped ruins, and the determination to throw up a roadblock to their development. It was the perfect trifecta to grab their attention: old stuff, good gossip, and a challenge.

"Yeah. No way," Skye agreed, nodding vigorously. They jumped down from their seat next to the register and snatched up their phone in one hand. "I'm gonna call my dad right now. I'm not letting some random dude buy up our family history and turn it into an AirBnB. Hang on a sec."

Zori gave them a thumbs up and they practically darted back towards the storeroom to make the phone call. The sound of ringing receded as they made their way back to the other room. When she was certain that they were out of earshot, Zori stood and crossed the small space to where Tenebrae was coiled into the shadows.

"What are you doing here?" she hissed, glancing back towards where her friend had gone as she spoke into the dark alcove.

"Keeping an eye on our young Graydon," he rumbled, coalescing just enough that she could make out his face. "I visit this human and the other descendants regularly, you know this."

She frowned at him. Zori was aware that Tenebrae checked up on members of the three founding families, keeping tabs on them until the time for the ritual came. She hadn't exactly pictured him sticking around to observe them though. It made her want to know why.

"You're not haunting them, right?" she demanded, suspiciously, crossing her arms as she leaned back to glare at the shadow. "You better not have been scaring Skye."

Tenebrae chuckled, amused by the diminutive human's irate posturing and protective nature. She posed little to no threat to him and yet did not hesitate to challenge him. He wondered what she would do if he said that he had been frightening them. It wasn't worth lying to her, though.

"No," he assured her, his usually flat tone lightened by his obvious entertainment, "I do not frighten your friend. Only observe. They are… curious."

She looked at him skeptically for a moment, but he seemed genuine. Besides, she knew he would have no qualms admitting to haunting Skye if he had done so. It was one of the things she liked about both shadow demons, they were blunt and honest almost to a fault.

"Yeah, they're pretty great," Zori whispered back, more at ease now that they knew he was merely intrigued by Skye."Myrkrið likes them too."

Tenebrae did not have time to respond, melting back into a dim haze as soon as he heard footsteps begin to approach.

"Who are you talking to?" Skye asked, returning to the front of the store, phone still in hand.

Zori took a step back from the armoire, turning to look at Skye with wide eyes. Unlike the shadow demon, she didn't hear them coming until they spoke, already only several feet away.

"Uh, no one, just talking to myself, I guess," she said, nervously. Stealing a glance at the bookshelf standing next to where Tenebrae was concealed, she quickly glanced the titles, pointing at one that caught her interest. "I was just browsing. What'd your dad say?"

"Well," Skye said, grabbing their coffee and leaning against the counter, "he definitely owns it. I asked him why he never told me that the family owns a freaking haunted ruin right outside town, and he said he didn't want me traipsing all over it and getting hurt. Which… I mean, fair enough, I guess. But still!"

That was exactly what they would have done, had Skye known about the family-owned land. The only reason they'd never explored it was out of respect for their dead relative. Of course, they knew all about how the town kids dared each other to go into the ruins; there were plenty of stories of them getting spooked and chased out by something. It served them right, as far as Skye was concerned, trespassing like that. But knowing it was technically their family's land, they would have been extremely tempted.

"How does he feel about selling it?" Zori asked, hesitantly. She really hoped John Graydon would be on their side, it would make things so much easier if he just refused to sell.

"This Spencer Douglas guy did make him an offer, like, out of nowhere," Skye admitted, apologetically. "Apparently, nobody's ever been interested in the land before, so the family just hung onto it. Dad didn't sound super into the idea, but the money Spencer's offering isn't exactly pocket change. I think he's considering it."

Not for long, Tenebrae thought furiously.

The room darkened as the incorporeal shadow's anger grew and his mist spread out over more of the space. The armoire rattled with a low almost inaudible growl, and Zori shot the mostly invisible demon a chastising look.

"Man, I really need to figure out which of these new acquisitions is cursed," Skye said, shaking their head. "It's been weird in here all afternoon." They ran a hand through their tousled hair, casting an appraising eye around the space. Nothing stuck out to them at first glance.

"My guess would be that doll," Zori offered, pointing at a porcelain doll with chipping paint and eyes that looked like they'd seen some things that cannot be unseen. "Do you think you could talk some sense into him? I know people in the village would have a fit to see a bunch of tourists camping out there. It's bad enough he's planning to turn the oldest house in town into a bed and breakfast."

"Not the Elbert Poole house?" Skye gasped. The original building went all the way back to when the town was founded; it was more of a relic than a house in their opinion. "Who the hell does this guy think he is? Ugh, I already don't like him. Don't worry, my dad agreed to have dinner later this week and I'll do my best to talk him out of it."

The room lightened again as Tenebrae relaxed slightly with Skye's agreement. They seemed ready to fight for him and Lazarus, despite not really knowing what they were fighting for exactly.

"Thanks, Skye, I know you can do it," Zori said, smiling gratefully at her friend. She wished she could explain the real reason the sale had to be stopped. If Skye knew, she was sure they would be even more determined, but it wasn't exactly her secret to tell. She watched as a glint of scheming chaos entered their expression. "What's that look, I can see you thinking."

"Margie goes to the town hall meetings, right?" Skye asked, waiting for their friend's confused nod before continuing. "What if somebody petitioned the town council to grant the ruins and the Elbert Poole house historic landmark status? The zoning bylaws would prevent any modifications to the property or its structures without approval by a review board, which would make it a massive pain in the ass for Spencer to get either place ready for visitors."

"Holy shit, that's brilliant!" Zori exclaimed. "I'll talk to her about it, I bet she'd love to petition the council. How do you know all that?"

Skye smiled and picked up the haunted looking doll, using its arm to wave at her.

"I didn't go to school for historic preservation for nothing," they explained, gesturing at the antique-packed shop with the doll, whose eyes blinked lazily and out of sync. "It takes more than just a love of old weird shit to keep this place running."

Clever, like their ancestor, Tenebrae thought, melting back into shadowspace.

He was eager to get back to Lazarus and update him on this news. It felt good to have the youngest Graydon on their side, whether or not they knew whose side that was.

Chapter 22

SUPPLICATION IN SHADOWS

Lazarus paced the overgrown garden restlessly. Though thick snow and leaves covered the short layer of stones that was all that was left of the garden beds, his footsteps still followed the paths that had been there two centuries before. It was a habit, leftover from before he had lost his corporeal form to the flames. When he was stressed and feeling out of sorts, he would walk the rows of plants until his mind was soothed.

As the long-awaited day drew nearer, his patience for idleness dwindled further and further. He and Tenebrae both had learned to bide their time out of pure necessity; neither was predisposed to patience. Discipline waned these days though, and at present there was nothing to keep him occupied.

Young Skye had been conscripted into convincing their father not to sell the manor. Zori and Myrkrið were chasing down a lead on another possible descendant of the Poole line. And Tenebrae was out gently encouraging the troublesome Mr. Douglas to abandon town altogether by virtue of his oh-so-welcoming supernatural presence.

Being left alone with his thoughts these days was less than ideal, but that is precisely where he found himself now. There were still more variables than he would like threatening to affect the success of the ritual. Lazarus was too consumed with his thoughts to notice the dark figure approaching until a clawed hand stopped him in his tracks.

He turned, startled, following the line of the arm that gripped his shoulder up to the stunningly handsome face of his husband. Tenebrae's brows were pinched with worry, and Lazarus couldn't help but smile softly at him. He would never tire of the way the shadow looked at him as if he were the only person in the universe.

"You are pacing again," the shadow demon observed in a concerned tone. He slid his hand down to the Shade's slightly transparent wrist and tugged him closer.

"A bit restless is all," Lazarus assured him, "it is nothing that need worry you." He stepped closer to the shadow until they were chest to chest and wrapped an arm around his waist. A faint warmth greeted him where his specter-like limb touched the demon's skin.

Tenebrae rumbled thoughtfully, and released his wrist to trace his claws lightly along his cheek. He handled the Shade delicately like a frozen cloud, a solid form that would swiftly turn to vapor under too great of pressure.

"Perhaps you need a distraction," he purred, leaning down to place the ghost of a kiss atop the witch's lips.

As soon as Lazarus began agree, the shadow demon wrapped several dark tendrils around him and corralled him into the gloom of the manor's cellar. The human felt the space give way and suddenly a familiar void surrounded them.

It felt more natural to Lazarus to be in this once foreign space now. He had spent nearly as much time in shadowspace as he had in the manor over the past two and a half centuries. It was a bit easier to maintain his form without the solidity of the world all around to mock him with a substantiality that he couldn't have. Here, there was only the warm rough body of the demon beside him, ready and willing to remind him that he was still alive and desired, no matter what his shape was made of at the moment.

"Astute as ever, husband," Lazarus said, smoothing his hands up the shadow demon's chest. He sighed contentedly as Tenebrae leaned forward into his phantom touch. "How could I refuse such a handsome distraction?"

"You cannot," Tenebrae said with a cocky smirk, leaning down to capture the man's lips in a lingering kiss. His movements were slow and gentle, leashed to the very limits of his restraint. He pulled back, pointedly looking his husband up and down with a demanding stare that Lazarus knew all too well by now.

One of the advantages of being a Shade was that getting undressed was as simple as imagining himself naked. He tilted his chin up and held contact with the hungry eyes of his husband, while the immaterial clothing melted away to reveal his bare body. He stood still to allow the shadow demon a moment to devour him with his gaze, until he felt a tendril of shadow curl around his calf and begin to slide up his leg.

Tenebrae started to reach for him, but Lazarus stopped him with a firm look. They hardly needed words to communicate at this point, knowing each other's expressions and body language by heart. The slightly raised eyebrow and flinty look in the witch's hazel eyes told him to be on his best behavior. The rewards would be well worth it.

"Get on your knees for me, darling," the Shade commanded, pressing down gently on the demon's wide shoulders. Even after countless years, it still managed to send a thrill through him to see the fearsome Tenebrae eagerly comply with his demands, sinking down to kneel before him with his thighs spread on either side of the witch's feet. "Good boy."

The shadow demon huffed happily at the praise and pressed his face against the Shade's waist, gripping his hips as tightly as he dared while trailing his lips across the insubstantial flesh.

Lazarus caressed his shoulders, feeling the muscles flex under his light touch. He scratched his short nails up the back of Tenebrae's neck, satisfied at the shiver that he felt run down the shadow's spine. Soft shades of gray gave the demon's flesh an almost velvet sheen, nearly blending into the seamless void around them. Lazarus felt his length stiffen at the sight of the shadow below him, as his arousal instinctively altered the Shade's physical appearance to match his state of mind.

The change in him did not escape Tenebrae's notice and his black tongue eagerly traced along its underside, base to tip, while he gazed up at Lazarus with eyes already half-lidded with lust. He practically purred when the Shade lovingly traced ghostly fingertips along the sides of his face.

"You are so beautiful like this," Lazarus said, sliding a transparent hand around the back of the shadow's head. With his other hand, he hooked a thumb in his mouth, coaxing it open further to drag his cock across Tenebrae's tongue in a teasingly slow manner. The motion drew a whine from the shadow, but he remained obediently still. "My ferocious shadow demon, so pliant and needy. All for me."

"Mmhmm," Tenebrae hummed his assent, eyes glazing over as he sank deeper into the submissive headspace that only Lazarus had ever had the privilege of seeing him in. Dark tendrils wound themselves affectionately around the witch's legs, tethering him to the kneeling demon. As soon as the Shade removed his thumb, the shadow carefully wrapped his lips around the tip and began to work his way down the length of it.

Lazarus guided his movements into a languid pace, pressing the shadow demon's mouth further onto him with every pass until he bottomed out. The pleasure felt different as a Shade, much less intense but it echoed through his shadow-constructed form until it suffused his whole being. He moaned at the feeling, dropping his head back with eyes closed for a moment.

The desperate sound that Tenebrae made in response snapped his attention back to the shadow demon, whose claws dug slightly into his thighs as he picked up the pace. Lazarus looked down into his husband's eyes, ablaze with desire. He didn't need to see it to know that the shadow's cock was extruded from its sheath, thick and hard between his spread knees.

"Touch yourself for me, darling," Lazarus demanded, smiling down at the demon who happily obliged.

Tenebrae's claws retracted from his leg and reached down to wrap a large hand around his aching length. He moaned around Lazarus's cock as he began to stroke himself, eyes glued to the Shade's face.

The vibrations of his mouth sent a fresh wave of pleasure careening through him, and his form shuddered, disintegrating around the edges as Lazarus momentarily lost control of his shape. The grasping tendrils that were greedily groping his lower half helped ground him and he regained his senses quickly. He gripped the back of Tenebrae's head with both hands, holding him in place while he thrust himself deeply into the shadow's eager mouth.

A pleading whimper echoed in the vast darkness, as the shadow demon's hand worked faster, jerking himself in time with movement of the Shade's hips. The sound had Lazarus's nails digging into the back of Tenebrae's neck as hard as he was able, drawing more muffled needy cries from the demon.

"Feels so good," the Shade moaned, mouth open and head tipped forward so he could watch the where the shadow's lips were wrapped around him. His eyes caught onto the faltering rhythm of the demon's movements, the tempo of his hand growing uneven as he became distracted by the mounting pleasure.

A jumble of murmured praises washed over Tenebrae, his mind too deep in bliss to recognize anything more specific than the occasional "good boy." The warm haze of surrender clouded his thoughts, a tight coil of pleasure winding around his bones as he looked up into the adoring eyes of his husband. His hips jerked as he fisted his cock as the witch instructed, eyes slamming shut in rapture while his climax overtook him.

Lazarus slowed his pace, savoring the sight of the shadow demon coming undone until the last drops of his release had been wrung from him. He stroked Tenebrae's cheek, gently calling his name to bring him back to himself. The shadow's eyes blinked open and he whined low, a plea for the Shade to keep going. He would not be truly satisfied until his husband was.

It had taken time, at first, to discover how to pleasure his human in this form, but Tenebrae was nothing if not determined. They had little but time in the long years they spent awaiting the proper alignment for the ritual, and he took the opportunity to diligently experiment until he knew just how to touch the Shade and with how much pressure. It was a delicate game, working within their new physical limitations and relying heavily on stimulating the man's pleasure mentally.

He found that the gentleness required of him to handle the Shade's partially incorporeal body paired especially well with handing over control to Lazarus. Taking charge of their pleasure allowed the witch to focus less on his own physicality and more on enjoying having the shadow demon succumb to his whims. If it took an eternity on his knees to make his husband feel good, he would spend his days there happily.

Tenebrae clung to his legs, grasping shadows creeping up nearly every inch of the witch's form, while his talented tongue worked over his cock. Consumed with the shadow demon's touch and painfully turned on by his submission, it didn't take much longer for the pleasure reverberating through Lazarus to reach a crescendo, his body flickering between mist and solid forms as the height of it broke him apart. The Shade disintegrated and reformed, sinking down into the shadow demon's warm embrace where they leaned into each other, sated.

"Better?" Tenebrae asked, when the pair had enjoyed a few minutes of blissful rest in the still nothingness of shadowspace.

"Mmm, yes," Lazarus replied, softly. His earlier stress and restlessness had entirely melted away now. "Much better. Thank you, husband, I needed that."

"As did I," the shadow demon agreed, drawing the Shade down with him as he moved to lay on his back. There was still much to do before the ritual, but nothing that could be accomplished this minute. In the meantime, they could afford to indulge in each other's company and some much needed relaxation.

Breaking and entering was not the way Zori expected to spend her first visit to Boston, or its suburbs.

Well, just entering I guess, no breaking, she thought as she followed Myrkrið out of the void and into a fenced yard. It was immaculately gardened with carefully trimmed shrubs and an arched trellis leading out into the street. The streetlamp on the corner of the sidewalk cast a pool of yellow light that didn't reach where the pair stood in the recesses of the yard.

To their left stood a two story red brick home with deep espresso brown painted trim and fresh white siding. The windows were all dark, same as the other houses on the street at this hour. At two o'clock in the morning, the quiet suburban street in Belmont just outside the city was near silent. It was so quiet that she worried the anxious pounding of her heart would be audible to anyone who cared to listen.

Myrkrið squeezed her hand reassuringly and ducked through a shadow, tugging her back into the void behind him. A few short steps later, they found themselves in a dark, formal dining room. It looked more decorative than functional with fine dishes in glass cabinets and pristine white linens adorning the table. The shadow demon crept soundlessly around the furniture, heading deeper into the house.

He was impressively stealthy even when fully corporeal, moving with a silent grace that seemed at odds with his forbidding size. Zori tiptoed slowly behind him, trying to keep her steps as hushed as possible. Fortunately, the home was carpeted in a thick, beige plush that dampened any stray sounds.

They passed through another room that looked like it didn't see much use, a parlor with pastel upholstered sofas and a small upright piano. The frames on the walls held the sort of art that reminded Zori of a dentist's office waiting room, but disappointingly no family photos.

Continuing on, she stopped at a table in the front entry hall, pawing through a small pile of mail to confirm that the subject of their search lived here. Most of it was addressed to Emily Poole.

Jackpot, Zori thought, excited that her internet sleuthing had finally paid off. And that they wouldn't have to trek all the way to the UK to try and convince an elderly man to give them his blood. *We just have to convince a more local slightly younger woman to donate to the cause, somehow.*

She was frowning at the junk mail in her hand when a noise from the second floor caught her attention. Zori's head whipped to the side, where she locked eyes with Myrkrið. Shuffling footsteps pattered overhead and her eyes widened comically in panic.

The shadow demon appeared as calm as ever, but moved quickly, grabbing Zori and shoving her through a nearby patch of darkness into the void of shadowspace. He wordlessly motioned for her to stay and then promptly disappeared.

Zori fidgeted in the endless permanent night that stretched out around her. Compared to this place, the quiet of sleepy Belmont seemed positively cacophonous.

Deep rumbles that were inaudible to her human hearing rolled through the space occasionally, as the atmosphere shifted and moved. Gentle waves of pressure passed by like gusts of wind. And as her eyes adjusted further, she could just make out shades and variations in the colors of the black world around her. If she squinted, faint details of what looked like terrain began to emerge, elusive as if glimpsed out of the corner of her eye.

It was difficult to gauge the passage of time here, but Zori was at least certain that this was by far the longest she had ever spent in shadowspace alone. She knew Myrkrið would not leave her there unless it was safe, but she also couldn't help wondering what would happen if another shadow demon happened to come upon a human like her alone in the void, however massively unlikely that might be. Before her anxiety could get the better of her, a familiar claw-tipped hand reached out from the blank space before her.

Myrkrið pulled her back into the unlit house, this time into a more lived-in-looking common room. A cozy couch and overstuffed recliner were draped with matching quilts. Chunky rustic oak side and coffee tables coordinated with a sturdy looking entertainment center at the end of the room flanked by large houseplants. The walls were littered with photos in mismatched frames.

"There is something you must see," Myrkrið whispered quietly beside her ear, beckoning her to follow.

The shadow led her to a cluster of photos. At the center, a medium sized family portrait showed a smiling woman who she recognized as a younger Emily, with a man sporting a dated brown suit and mustache, and a young brunette boy in a striped polo shirt. The surrounding photos included the three of them, along with a variety of presumably other family members. The boy was most frequently the subject, appearing at various ages throughout the collection.

"Her son?" Zori questioned, as quietly as possible.

Myrkrið nodded, pointing her to a lone frame slightly further along the wall.

The framed newspaper article was dominated by a color photo of a man with the same rounded features and dark brown hair, now clearly grown up by the time it was taken. He wore a gray suit and a cocky smile, standing in front of a realtor's sign with new construction in the background. The caption identified him as Spencer Poole-Douglas.

"Douglas? As in 'dude who wants to buy the manor' Spencer Douglas?" Zori hissed, nearly grinding her teeth at the prospect that the same man who was causing them one problem might also be the solution to another.

"The same," Myrkrið confirmed.

"I'm not sure if this makes things more or less complicated," she mused, looking up at the shadow demon inquisitively. "We need to talk to Lazarus."

Chapter 23

POLTERGEISTS AND PROPOSITIONS

Freddie Harper wondered for the thirty-seventh time how he had managed to let Spencer talk him into one of these situations again, as he drove west through the center of Graymourne. He should be spending this bright Sunday morning in bed with his partner and then enjoying a leisurely brunch, but instead, he'd been on the road from Boston for two hours already.

Two days. He made Spencer promise him that the walkthroughs wouldn't take any longer than that. Sidney would be livid if he didn't make it home in time for Valentine's Day. His business partner had the next couple of days to show and tell all the spooky properties he wanted and then Freddie would be on his merry way. That was what he told himself, at least.

Quaint, he thought, easing the luxury SUV through the old covered bridge as he crossed onto South West Highway. There was no parking lot, but the GPS cheerily beeped at him to let him know he had arrived at his destination.

I guess I'm just supposed to park on the side of the road and walk from here.

He pulled off to the side of the one lane highway, the tires crunching through undisturbed snow as he put the vehicle into park. Stepping out into the brisk air, Freddie could hear the rush of the nearby river just a few yards south of where he stood. He scrolled through his text chat with Spencer to find the directions he'd sent yesterday.

"Follow the Lucent River Trail about one hundred feet and make a right at the tree with a weird symbol on it."

Great, that's not ominous at all, Freddie thought, rolling his eyes. He had half a mind to call Spencer and tell the man to come fetch him, but his phone had almost no service out here. It taunted him with a singular bar, but the device refused to make use of it.

Tromping down to the trailhead, he was glad he'd had the foresight to wear his waterproof hiking boots. The thick white ground cover had one fresh set of footprints that helpfully pointed the way. He followed them, his mood beginning to calm as he walked. It really was beautiful here. He could see why his business partner had been captivated by it.

The footprints veered right, guiding him away from the soothing sound of the river and farther into the woods. On his left, he spied a tall birch tree with an angular symbol painted on it in some kind of gray paste. He shivered, not entirely from the cold, and a sense of foreboding roiled in his stomach as he stepped through an off-kilter iron gate and into an overgrown clearing.

Spencer stood near the center of the space with his cell phone in hand, camera pointed at the snow-covered ruins while trying to get the best angle. He turned when a branch snapped under the weight of Freddie's boot.

"Finally!" Spencer said, pocketing his phone and turning towards the other man. "It took you long enough."

"I'm fifteen minutes early, Spence," Freddie replied, giving him a one-armed hug with an exasperated sigh. "Why don't you show me around so we can get somewhere warm and go over the details?"

"This is the first I'm seeing it in person too, actually," Spencer conceded, leading them towards what was left of the manor. "The surveyors I sent out here took plenty of photos of the grounds, but they refused to go inside. Superstitious lot."

He walked them around the perimeter first, filling Freddie in on the history of the place. Most of the information was correct, with a few inaccuracies here and there where the local tales had been distorted over the years of retelling.

Their presence did not go unnoticed by the manor's occupants, who watched their movements from the shade inside the ruins with sharp eyes. A displeased rumble carried on the wind as the pair of humans made their way towards the front entrance, having circled around the stone dwelling.

"Remember, no bloodshed, husband," Lazarus reminded his seething partner. He trailed a hand down the tense muscles of his arm. "He may be a troublesome pest, but he is also a Poole. We need his health sound, at least until the ritual."

"Very well," Tenebrae acquiesced, bitterly. He bristled at the presence of these unwelcome visitors in their home. His partner said nothing of driving them off though. "Hide yourself and I will keep our guests entertained."

Lazarus shook his head, melting into the shadows and leaving the demon to his amusement. He wouldn't go far though. To be honest, he was looking forward to seeing how this would go. He could already feel the effects of his wards working on the intruders, twisting an anxious sense of unease into their minds. It was not quite enough to make them leave yet, but perhaps Tenebrae could give them the push required.

If they didn't leave soon enough, they would find themselves quite ill courtesy of the aggressive wards he had put in place.

Spencer crossed the threshold into the manor itself, with Freddie following a few feet behind him. He peeked into the parlor on his left with its collapsed and ruined floor, but then continued down the hall towards the back of the house. The staircase to his right, which once led up to the Graydons' living spaces, was now piled high with rubble and downed branches. It was all but impassible, pointless to attempt to climb even if the second floor had been intact.

As the man passed by, a spectral black hand slowly crept out from a dark hollow beneath a thick branch, reaching for the back of Spencer's collar. A couple of claws snagged on the coat, but just as they were about to pull, a frightened yelp caused him to spin around.

"Watch out!" Freddie cried, pointing frantically at the rubble along the staircase.

"For what?" Spencer asked, looking skeptically at the piled up debris. There was a small dark opening where the other man's shaky finger still indicated. "There's nothing in there."

He leaned down closely, peering into the tiny space. It was hardly big enough to fit any animals. To prove it, he reached out, intending to put his hand inside and show Freddie that there was nothing there. But as his fingers approached the shadowy opening, a sense of dread seized him and he hesitated. His body simply wouldn't allow him to move any closer.

"Don't," Freddie said, grabbing his sleeve a little too forcefully. "You're right, it's nothing. Let's go."

He didn't look like he believed that it was nothing, but Spencer didn't argue. Instead, he turned to lead them farther into the ruin. They came to a room that was mostly intact, the former kitchen, and both men looked confusedly at the set of garden chairs that sat in a circle in the center of the room.

"Must be kids coming up here in the warmer months," Spencer theorized. The furniture was much more contemporary than the house itself.

The two men turned around, just starting for the next room when the sound of scraping metal stopped them. Both of their heads whipped around, looking over their shoulders towards the source of the noise. One of the wrought iron garden chairs that had been pointed away was now turned one hundred and eighty degrees so that it faced in their direction.

"Yeah, kids, uh huh," Freddie said slowly, not taking his eyes off of the chair as if he expected it to leap at him.

"Oh, come on," Spencer taunted him, walking backwards towards the doorway behind him. "You're not going to get spooked out of this deal are you? Think of all the money, Freddie."

Reluctantly, Freddie tore his gaze away from the now perfectly still chair and looked at his business partner. Spencer had a look of mocking superiority on his face, but the scorn wasn't what made him pale. In the dim space behind his friend, Freddie swore he could make out the shape of a man. It was slight at first and fuzzy around the edges, like a shadow cast on the air.

He tried telling himself that it was just a trick of the light, even though, logically, he knew that was impossible. But as Spencer continued backing towards it, he could see that the shape was growing darker and more defined. It was much too large to be Spencer's shadow, and Freddie very much did not want to stick around to find out who or what it belonged to.

"You know, Spence, you're totally right," he said hurriedly, grabbing the other man by the lapel and forcefully dragging him back towards the front doorway. "I don't need to see any more. I'm convinced. Let's go take a look at the other property and I'll get started on the math."

He practically shoved the other man out of the ruin, power walking back towards their cars as soon as they were out of the manor. Spencer's ego wouldn't allow him to argue with someone who was already telling him he was right, so he followed along, slightly bewildered by Freddie's sudden agreeability.

"That was rather subtle for you," Lazarus remarked, materializing next to the shadow demon where he watched his quarry scurry away.

"I was testing some of Myrkrið's methods," Tenebrae explained, his posture relaxing as the humans finally moved out of sight. "It was surprisingly effective."

Lazarus smiled, imagining the two gruff demons comparing notes on how to most efficiently frighten humans. It was oddly heartwarming.

"I am positively thrilled to see you making friends, darling," he said, leaning contentedly into the shadow's side.

Leaning against a painted white column, Zori fidgeted in the morning sun. Anxiety, about the possible outcome of this adventure, as well as the unfamiliar social situation, had made her earlier than intended. She waited out front of the red brick town hall building, standing up straighter as people began to arrive for the council meeting.

"There she is!"

The bright, enthusiastic voice of Margie Caldwell drew her attention to her right, seeing her loquacious neighbor approach from the parking lot. She was dressed smartly in a navy blue peacoat with a paisley scarf and her short brown hair was carefully curled. Margie exuded a soft, warm aura that tended to put people at ease; it was like a perpetual feeling of enjoying a nice cup of tea with an old friend at a worn kitchen table.

The woman beside her could not have been more opposite. Her gray hair was scraped back into a tight bun, shrewd eyes stared out from behind wire-rimmed spectacles, and her tan tweed blazer was buttoned up tightly. Despite her strict appearance, Zori knew the librarian to be friendly in her own austere way.

"Hi, Margie," she said, waving at the pair as they came closer. "Nice to see you, Patience."

The librarian gave her a tight-lipped smile, while the bubbly woman beside her pulled Zori in for a generous hug.

"Wasn't expecting you to be so early," Margie exclaimed, ushering her along as they entered the building. She leaned in to whisper conspiratorially to her. "We've got a person on the inside, I already told Patience about the petition and she's on board."

Of course she is, Zori thought with amusement. It was no surprise to her that Patience Donnell, head of a library which still ran on the Dewey Decimal System, was opposed to change. Cresswell Library felt like a time capsule.

They took their seats in the front row, while Patience continued on ahead to sit at the long conference table with the other council members. The rows of chairs facing the council were dotted with townsfolk, chatting amongst themselves. The low murmur of conversation was amplified with the acoustics of the room, creating a blanket of noise as the assembly waited for the meeting to start.

After a few minutes, the council member at the center of the table, a woman with long white hair and former hippie vibes, cleared her throat loudly and called the meeting to order. The placard in front of her read, 'Hannah Carroll.' Zori didn't recognize her, but she was still getting to know the residents of Graymourne after moving here a few months ago.

As she began speaking, someone flopped down in the seat beside Zori, leaning into her space. She looked to the side, preparing to be annoyed, but was met with Skye's smiling face and a travel cup of coffee.

"Sorry I'm late," Skye whispered, handing her the cup and settling into their seat.

She smiled at them, grateful to have another friend here among the throng of mostly strangers. They listened to the council go through several points of order and upcoming calendar events. Next month in March, Graymourne would host its annual Spring Festival, which entailed a craft market, food vendors, children's games, and live music. The council listed out several volunteer positions that needed filling, and Zori surprised herself by offering to help with designing the flyer graphics. It was an easy task that she could fit in with her other freelance design work, and maybe her participation would engender some goodwill towards her proposition.

Finally, after all of the agenda items had been covered, the council opened the floor to questions from the crowd. Margie promptly stood up and waited for the five council members to acknowledge her. Hannah nodded in her direction and asked what she had for the council.

"By now, I'm sure you've all heard the news," Margie started, as if she hadn't personally been responsible for spreading the news in question to seventy-five percent of the people in this room. "We've got an out-of-towner looking to buy the old Graydon land in Whitmack Forest. He's already got his hands on Annabell Poole's house, God rest her, and is planning to turn both places into tourist attractions!"

Murmurs and grumbling broke out among the crowd as she paused, allowing her words to stir up sentiment in the people around her.

"Now, I know folks around here like their peace and quiet, as much as I do," she continued, "so, I would like to propose that the council declare both properties as historical sites. The Elbert Poole house was one of the very first built here in 1761. And we all know the history of the Graydon Manor. Those places ought to be preserved, not rented out to visitors."

Zori could see several members of the audience nodding in agreement as Margie spoke. She looked to her right at Skye, who abruptly stood up.

"I'd like to second Margie's proposal," Skye said, addressing the council. "As a member of the Graydon family and business owner in this community, any efforts towards conservation of Graymourne's historic places have my full support. I took the liberty of putting together some information on landmark status and historic preservation for the council to review."

They produced five folders from their bag, handing one out to each of the seated council members and then returning to their seat. Zori looked at them, impressed. She hadn't expected Skye to come so prepared.

"I third their proposal," she said, standing up between her neighbor and friend. "I know I'm a new resident, but I love this town. And I don't want to see its history get trampled on by some rich guy's real estate schemes."

A couple of folks in the back loudly agreed with her, and two of the council motioned for everyone to be quiet again. The two men and three women spoke quietly amongst themselves for a couple of minutes before addressing the room again.

"Thank you all," said the council member to Hannah's left, a balding man whose placard indicated his name as Anthony Wise. "We will take your proposal under advisement and render our decision at the next council meeting in two weeks."

His tone gave little indication of where he stood on the issue, and Zori looked to Margie for her reaction. She was smiling broadly, looking as pleased with herself as she did when she had a particularly juicy bit of gossip to share. Zori decided to take that as a good sign.

Now all that was left to do was wait.

With the status of both sites up in the air until the town council made their decision, there was little to stop Spencer from forging ahead with his plans for the Poole house. To Freddie's utter dismay, his business partner had, in fact, managed to cajole him into staying the rest of the week so they could bring in some potential contractors for estimates. Someone had to walk them through the property, and Freddie was just so much better at numbers, so it only made sense that he should show the workers around while Spencer continued attempting to wine and dine John Graydon into selling his land.

There was little to stop them, that is, except for two cunning shadow demons who enthusiastically dedicated themselves to making the process as difficult as possible. Myrkrið and Tenebrae took shifts stalking the two men, sabotaging them with minor inconveniences as frequently as possible. The mundane nature of these annoyances would have seemed like just a run of bad luck, except for the unrelenting frequency of them. It was a constant barrage of misplaced objects, sudden power outages, inexplicably flat tires, frightening noises, and mysteriously damp socks that had Spencer and Freddie irritable and on edge.

The shadows reserved any properly menacing behavior for when the contractors showed up, determined to make every construction company in the region too afraid to set foot in the Poole house let alone work on it. Today's unsuspecting target would be the third consultant this week alone. Judging by Spencer's increasingly irate mood, neither of the previous ones were returning his calls. Somehow both companies' calendars had mysteriously filled up just after their visits. How strange.

"Come in. You must be Mr. Morris," Freddie said, greeting the man who knocked at the front door. He was tall, middle-aged, and sturdy looking, clearly a person who spent as much time doing the work as booking the jobs. Morris Refurbishment was a small family-owned company from two towns over.

"Nice to meet you, Mr. Harper. Freddie, was it?" Morris asked, wiping his feet on the doormat before entering the front hall. He scanned the interior, keen eyes roaming over the structure and already beginning to assess it. Focused on the bones of the building, he failed to notice the ominously thick darkness watching him from the stairway.

"Yes, right this way, I'll give you a tour of the property and then we can go over the improvements we're looking to make," Freddie said, feigning enthusiasm in an effort to cover his nerves. They needed this consultation to go well. He said a silent prayer that nothing weird would happen this time. He wasn't sure he could handle much more of this.

Freddie led the man through the parlor and dining room, both illuminated brightly by west-facing windows. This part of the tour was calm as usual, and they circled through the kitchen, half bathroom, mud room, and den before returning to the front hall. It was eerily still. The fact that nothing odd had happened so far did nothing to prevent the foreboding sense of dread that gripped Freddie as he regarded the staircase with well-earned trepidation.

"Alright then, after you," he insisted, waving Mr. Morris ahead of him towards the stairs. He was not too proud to make the consultant go first, like a sacrificial lamb to whatever supernatural menace awaited them above. When he stepped foot onto the creaking wood floor of the second story and yet nothing creepy had disturbed their passage, Freddie began to think that perhaps today would be different. His shoulders lost some of their tension and he smiled tentatively at Mr. Morris.

"This way," Freddie said, pleasantly, leading the man left down a hall with doors branching off both sides. He made the mistake of glancing into a large gilt frame mirror as they passed it, and his voice died out mid-sentence when he spotted an amorphous dark shape following closely behind them. His heart rate spiked and he heard a low, mean chuckle from the bedroom to his left.

"You got guests already?" Morris asked, raising an eyebrow at the way Freddie purposefully skipped the room where the sound had come from, assuming that it was occupied.

"No, no, you know these old houses, they just make weird noises, right?" Freddie said hurriedly. His nervous laughter didn't make the lie any more convincing, but Morris didn't press him on it.

He opened the door to the next room, a small bedroom decorated entirely in pink. Annabell had been fond of a theme, and consequently each of the bedrooms had their own color scheme. Freddie began going over the improvements list with a bit of relief, beginning to feel more grounded as he rattled off the mundane assortment of upgrades. Logistics was his comfort zone.

As the men turned to leave the room, a loud creak sounded from behind them and they looked back to see the heavy wooden rocking chair in the corner now rocking back and forth as if occupied.

"Drafts," Freddie shrugged, half-heartedly, despite the fact that both men knew damn well that the chair was far too heavy to be moved by a simple gust of air.

He hurried Morris out of the room and into the next.

The bathroom was long and narrow, with vintage black and white hexagonal tile covering the floor. On the right side was a white porcelain pedestal sink with dual brass taps and a vintage medicine cabinet. On the left sat a freestanding clawfoot tub. Both men stilled as they noticed the large, person-shaped dark silhouette that was visible through the transparent white shower curtain.

Morris boldly stepped around the other man, who was rooted to the spot. He moved cautiously towards the tub, with one hand outstretched before him. Gripping the thin fabric of the shower curtain, he wrenched it aside suddenly, drawing a startled squeak from Freddie.

There was nothing there.

He stared at the worn porcelain, taking a deep breath and trying to rationalize what he had seen. Morris had heard stories from the other construction crews in the area, they all knew each other. He'd scoffed when two of the most salt of the earth guys he knew swore they'd never step foot in this house again, saying it was cursed. Both insisted they'd seen something they couldn't explain. Now that he was here, he was beginning to think there might be something to their claims.

Or maybe it was just Freddie's obvious anxiety that was getting to him. The man was strung tighter than a bow and looked like he could faint from too stiff of a breeze.

"Let's finish the tour, yeah?" Morris sighed, shooing the frightened man back out into the hallway.

If either of them heard the footsteps that seemed to follow along with them from the attic floor above, they pretended not to notice it.

They hurried out of the next bedroom when vicious growls began to emanate from beneath the bed, a green floral monstrosity with far too many ruffle-edged pillows. After briskly walking towards the office at the end of the hall, Morris then pulled up short, narrowly avoiding being hit in the face by the door as it suddenly slammed shut. Barely a second later, the main bedroom door, which was clear at the other end of the long hallway, closed with a loud bang.

"We can skip that one," Freddie offered, visibly shaking as he coaxed the contractor away from the unwelcoming office door.

Room by room, they found each of the doors stuck fast as they made their way back towards the staircase. Finally, they came to one that stood open; it was the navy blue bedroom.

It felt like bait, like they were being herded somewhere.

"Listen, Freddie, maybe we should pick this up another day," Morris offered, hesitating near the top of the staircase. He wasn't a man to put much stock in superstitions, but he couldn't deny there was something strange at work here. An urge to flee pulled at him, some primal part of his brain sensing the danger that he couldn't see.

Freddie turned to face him, putting his back now towards the open doorway. Morris could barely see into the darkened room behind him. The curtains were drawn tightly shut and the deep blue decor melded into a shadowy mass.

What he could see, though, was that something in the room was moving. His eyes widened as he helplessly watched the indistinct shape come closer and closer.

Seeing the fresh terror that bloomed in the other man's eyes, Freddie's heart dropped. His back tingled with the sudden hyperawareness of a presence there and he fought the urge to look behind him. He opened his mouth to agree, to say 'yeah, let's get the fuck out of here', but no sound came out.

In his peripheral vision, Freddie saw long sharp fingers move slowly into his field of sight. The image only lasted a second before the huge hand clamped over his face, while three others grasped onto his limbs.

"Leave while you can," rasped a voice that sounded like it came directly from the depths of the underworld.

Morris took off like a shot down the stairs, leaving the other man to his fate, whatever that might be.

The hands dragged Freddie back into the darkness and he promptly passed out.

Chapter 24

Lazarus shook his head, unable to keep a straight face as the two shadow demons proudly recounted their escapades from the past couple of weeks. They had been busy making it their personal missions to give Spencer Douglas and Freddie Harper no rest while the interlopers attempted to bring their real estate schemes to fruition. He wasn't sure which was more entertaining, the stories they told or watching them bond over a shared love of scaring the hell out of hapless humans.

This was the most talkative that he could remember seeing either of them, with Tenebrae and Myrkrið carrying the conversation while he and Zori mostly listened. They explained with pride and in great detail all of the supernatural havoc they had wrought upon the two men and their parade of unsuspecting contractors. It was a litany of minute yet menacing machinations punctuated by a more otherworldly outburst here and there. The two could teach a masterclass in effective poltergeisting at this point. Occasionally, Zori interjected with a question or a laugh, but Lazarus was content to simply observe.

"Oh my god, you did not make that poor man faint by dragging him through shadowspace!" Zori cackled, doubling over in her seat as she succumbed to another fit of laughter. "That's so mean, you guys!"

"He was perfectly safe," Tenebrae insisted, trying to assuage her concerns. With the dissonance between her outraged words and her enthusiastic laughter, he truly wasn't sure whether she was upset or entertained by the anecdote. "We placed him in one of the bedrooms and he awoke unharmed."

Myrkrið chuckled, watching her catch her breath and wipe a few stray tears of mirth from her eyes. He knew her well enough to know that as long as the man was not truly harmed, she would find it funny. She loved a good horror movie, particularly ones involving haunted houses, and the more creative the scares, the better. He had even picked up a few ideas from the films she introduced him to.

"You did not think it was mean when I did the same to you, sunbeam," he said, unable to resist teasing her, and laughed when she gasped in feigned shock. He forged ahead before she could protest, prompted to elaborate by the curious looks from their companions. "This brave little human requested, quite persistently, to be chased around the house and dragged through shadowspace when I caught her."

"We were bored! And Myrkrið was still trapped in the house. I had to think of something," Zori said, defensively, crossing her arms dramatically. She squinted at him in a valiant attempt at a glare, although it was undermined by the smile that tugged at the corners of her lips.

"And how did that work out for you, my dear?" Lazarus asked facetiously, laughing at the way the couple bantered.

"It was, uh, fun… ," she answered vaguely, a slight blush rising to her cheeks as she studiously avoided eye contact. What had begun initially as an innocuous game of tag had eventually morphed into a rather spicier activity, and she very much did not want to get into the details of that right now. Zori wracked her mind for a way out of this topic and finally, her sheepish look brightened as an idea popped into her head. "Anyway! New subject. I have something that might be good news."

The offer of a new development was enough to pry the group's attention away from any further potentially embarrassing anecdotes. The mood of the conversation shifted immediately from friendly ribbing to an air of keen anticipation.

"Oh? Do tell," Lazarus said, eagerly.

He was feeling optimistic. For the moment, it seemed that the looming obstacles were largely dealt with. The possible sale of the manor had been staved off and the three necessary descendants had been located. All in all, things were going well. So, he was very curious to learn what news she might have.

"So, remember I told you about the town council meeting?" Zori started, while she fished around in her bag to retrieve her tablet. "Well, there's a community celebration next month called the Spring Festival. I volunteered to design the flyers for it, and this morning they sent me the details for all the events."

She held out the tablet so that Lazarus and Tenebrae could see the screen. It showed a pretty poster design decorated with a floral folk art motif and elegant typography. He wasn't sure how this related to them or the ritual, but the art was quite lovely. She was obviously very talented.

"Your work is beautiful," he complimented, honestly. Lazarus could see the influences in her design from a few of the art styles that he learned about in her history books. It was fascinating to see the way she combined them with more modern elements to make something new.

"Oh, thank you," she said, gesturing with her fingers on the screen to zoom in closer to some of the smaller words. "That's not the news though, this is. The town is hosting a blood drive."

There was a moment of quiet as Lazarus and Tenebrae looked from the tablet to each other and then to her.

"What is a blood drive?" The shadow demon asked, voicing the question that Lazarus had also been thinking. The combination of words made little sense to either of them.

"It's when people donate blood, and then the donations are given to hospitals to help treat sick people,"

Zori explained, trying to simplify as much as possible with her admittedly limited medical knowledge. "They take small amounts of blood from healthy people and store it for when it's needed. It has to be kept cold, but it stays good for a while."

Lazarus vaguely recalled some anecdotes he had heard about blood transfusions involving animals that were conducted in the 1600s. What she was describing sounded closer to witchcraft than medicine by the standards of his era, but if it would allow them to collect what they needed, who was he to question it.

"And you believe that we can gather what we need for the ritual during this blood drive?" Lazarus asked, beginning to see where she might be going with this line of thinking.

"Exactly," she agreed, nodding enthusiastically. "If we can get one of the descendants from each family to donate blood, then Myrkrið or Tenebrae can sneak in afterwards and take the samples from the refrigerated storage. No awkward conversations necessary, and no one will suspect a thing!"

Lazarus and Tenebrae shared a hopeful look. It was a subtle approach, and one that would hopefully avoid any unnecessary confrontations. Her plan could work. And, the bloodthirsty sparkle in the shadow demon's eyes told him that if it didn't, he had a backup plan. The Shade hoped it would not come to that, but he knew that Tenebrae would do whatever it took to ensure the ritual went correctly.

"Marvelous idea, my dear," he agreed, giving his husband's hand a knowing squeeze. They could discuss whatever was on his mind later, in private. "Now, we only need convince the necessary individuals to participate. Do you think that will be difficult?"

Zori frowned, she was confident that she could convince Skye, but honestly, she didn't know the others very well. Spencer, at least, was a wild card.

"I'm not sure, I can talk to them and make sure to post some of the flyers where the descendants will see them," she offered, with an apologetic shrug.

Tenebrae's eyes narrowed in a calculating way that she didn't find particularly reassuring, but whatever he was thinking, he clearly didn't plan to share. At least Lazarus seemed to think her plan had potential.

It would have to be enough.

The front door slammed loudly, rattling the walls as Spencer stormed into the silent house. He sighed angrily, tossing keys haphazardly onto the entryway table and stomping noisily across the hardwood floors.

Tenebrae smirked in the darkness.

Whatever had the human in such a foul mood was undoubtedly a mark in their favor. He slunk through the shadows to get closer to Spencer, who poured himself a drink and flung himself into a leather armchair in the parlor. The amber liquid nearly sloshed out of the glass because of his careless movements, but the man hardly noticed, already fishing his phone out of a trouser pocket and tapping forcefully on the screen.

The shadow demon settled unnoticed in the depths of the fireplace, an amorphous dark cloud that was indistinguishable from the charred black surface of the bricks. From here, he could see the vein pulsing angrily at Spencer's temple and the way his teeth ground in agitation. The tinny sound of the line ringing several times before being picked up only seemed to increase his unpleasant mood.

"Hello, Spencer," Freddie's now familiar voice answered, eventually. He did not sound enthused to be speaking to his business partner.

"This fucking town, I swear," Spencer cursed, skipping the pleasantries of a normal greeting in favor of venting his frustrations. "The people that live here have no vision! They can't see a sure thing when it's right in front of them."

He paused his rant to take a swig of his drink, slouching in the well worn chair with the put upon air of a misunderstood tyrant.

"What happened now?" Freddie asked, almost hesitantly.

Spencer haphazardly placed his glass on a side table, not bothering with a coaster, and sprung up to pace around the room as he spoke.

"I got a notice in the mailbox," he said, pausing to look out the front window for a second, "inviting me to their town council meeting. I figured it was a welcoming thing or something. You know, appreciation for trying to build up their stupid little village, or some shit. But no, the ungrateful bastards have decided they want to make both of the properties that we want into historic landmarks."

Tenebrae stifled an amused chuckle. He had to admit, Zori and Skye's scheme seemed to be working so far. He was glad that Myrkrið's clever human and her friend were on their side; they were proving to be quite vexing enemies to have.

Freddie attempted to interject during a slight pause, but Spencer just barreled on, talking right over him.

"Now, Graydon is saying he won't even talk about selling until the status is sorted out," Spencer complained, pacing past the fireplace close enough that the shadow demon was able to trip him with a stray tendril. He recovered his footing quickly, and looked around in confusion without bothering to stop his outraged rambling. "As if that wasn't irritating enough, we can't start any of the improvements on this place until after the landmark status is finished. And then, the council wants to approve the plans first. How the hell am I supposed to work like this?"

He finally stopped talking long enough for the man on the other end of the phone to get a word in edgewise. After a rather surprised pause, Freddie realized that Spencer was done ranting for the moment and seized his chance to jump in.

"Listen, Spence," he said, speaking slowly and choosing his words carefully. He didn't want to make his friend's mood any worse than it already was, but some things had to be said. "Maybe this is a sign. I know you don't want to talk about it, but there is something very wrong in that town. Even if the council wasn't getting in the way, there's not a single contractor within four states that will set foot in that house of yours. It's fucking cursed."

Spencer scoffed, loudly, rolling his eyes as he flopped down in his chair again.

"No, don't you dare dismiss it, Spence," Freddie seethed, his unusually vehement tone forestalling whatever snide comment the other man had been prepared to say. "You didn't have to do the walkthroughs with all of them. Big, no nonsense, working men who ran out of there pale and sweating. Something in that house doesn't want us there. And I don't want to find out what it is. Not any more than I already have."

He trailed off, his voice shaking with both fear and anger. Spencer's brows knitted, confused by Freddie's statement. Sure, they'd both seen some weird shit since coming to Graymourne, but nothing he couldn't justify as his mind playing tricks on him in the dark. For better or worse, Spencer was willing to rationalize away quite a bit in exchange for a tidy profit. He had never heard his friend sound quite so genuinely terrified, though.

"What do you mean?" Spencer asked, suspiciously.

Tenebrae smirked, knowing exactly what the frightened man was talking about. He was surprised to learn that he hadn't already told Spencer about the haunting he'd endured at the shadow demons' hands.

"It doesn't matter," Freddie sighed, as if he knew that the other man wouldn't believe him even if he told him. "Just think about it, will you? Sell the house, you'll still make money on it. And please… get the hell out of there."

Spencer looked genuinely shocked. Tenebrae could tell from the human's presumptuous attitude that he wasn't used to being told no very often.

"I can't believe you're just giving up, Freddie," he complained.

It was the other man's turn to scoff, laughing bitterly at his business partner's disbelief.

"Believe it, Spence, I'm out," he said, firmly. Freddie was prepared for the man to attempt to convince him like he always did, but this time he wasn't going to fold. "I'm not getting anywhere near that town ever again. If you still want to do this after everything, you're on your own."

Tenebrae's satisfied smile sliced through the dark recesses of the hearth, and Spencer's eyes widened as he caught a momentary glimpse of dark, sharp teeth in the black space. It was gone in a flash, as was the shadow who was already making his way through the void and back to his husband's side.

With four short weeks until the date of the eclipse, the only thing standing between him and touching his beloved husband in the flesh once again was a little bit of blood. And that could be obtained one way or the other.

Chapter 25

DREAM DRAMA

With the shortage of event volunteers, it was almost too easy for Zori to get herself put in charge of scheduling appointments for the blood drive. Few people were interested in helping out with the boring logistics needed for the Spring Festival, with most folks opting to volunteer for something fun like running games or making decorations. Certainly, working the face painting booth would have been more interesting, but that wouldn't get them any closer to obtaining what Lazarus needed for the resurrection spell.

So far, both Kelsey and Dylan Cresswell were signed up for appointments. She hadn't expected the younger Cresswell to volunteer, but Kelsey was a senior in high school and old enough to donate. It definitely couldn't hurt to have a back up, so she wasn't about to turn the young woman away.

She was still brainstorming the best way to convince Spencer Douglas to take part in Graymourne's donation drive. He was probably going to be the most difficult to wrangle of the descendants. But, with any luck, she'd be able to check the Graydons off her list today, after lunch with Skye.

Checking the time on her phone, she noticed that her sprightly friend was running a bit late as usual. The coffeeshop was quiet this time of the afternoon though, so Zori didn't mind enjoying her latte while she waited. She knew it probably wouldn't be long before Skye came careening in through the front door, with a wild story to share. Hanging out with them was never boring.

"Hey!" a familiar voice exclaimed, sure enough, not even five minutes later. Like a colorful tornado, Skye whirled in and perched on the chair across from her. "Oh my god, sorry I'm late, it's been a day."

"No worries," Zori laughed, already sliding the extra latte she'd ordered across the table and into their waiting hands. "Robin said they're not doing gingerbread anymore because they're switching to the spring menu, so I got you lavender. Drink up and then you can tell me all about it."

"You're a life saver, Zori, seriously," they said, breathlessly, taking a large sip of the fragrant drink. Skye let out a grateful sigh and melted further into their seat. "I haven't even had coffee yet today, that's how my day's been."

This was truly shocking.

Zori couldn't hide her stunned facial expression. Things must have been especially dire for Skye to make it all the way to one o'clock in the afternoon uncaffeinated. It was unheard of.

"What? How? Why?" she asked, incredulously.

Skye laughed, dragging a hand through their unkempt blue locks and tucking a foot up underneath them on their seat. They got comfortable, preparing to dive into storytelling mode.

"I know, right?" they said, grinning widely at the utter ridiculousness that they were about to share. "So, first, I'm sorry to tell you that you were wrong about that creepy doll. It's definitely not the cursed object, because it sold a couple weeks ago and I've still got something weird hanging around."

Zori frowned, knowing exactly who and what that something was. Tenebrae had assured her that he wasn't doing any haunting shenanigans around Skye, so there was no reason that they should have noticed his presence. It made her wonder what the shadow demon had been up to in the shop.

"No way," she said, not having to feign her shocked concern, although it was not quite for the reason it appeared. "What happened?"

"Well, the lights have been all weird, sometimes it gets dark in the shop for no reason," Skye explained, gesturing animatedly while they spoke. "I've been replacing lightbulbs left and right, but it doesn't make a difference. No big deal, though. That's happened since I opened the shop, it's just more frequent recently."

Okay, that makes sense, Zori thought, nodding as her friend continued, *Tenebrae has been keeping a closer eye on them since the ritual is coming up.*

That was not particularly concerning in itself. Maybe Skye was just sensitive to supernatural presences or something.

"But then I started having these weird ass dreams last week," they said, "It's always the same, like somebody's talking to me in this scary deep voice, but I can't see who it is."

Oh no.

"What do they say?" Zori asked, unsure she really wanted to know the answer but compelled to ask nonetheless.

"Okay, this is gonna sound nuts, and for the record, I am acutely aware of that," Skye prefaced, putting both hands up for emphasis. "I kept waking up and not remembering what they said in the dream, but then last night I woke up while it was still happening."

I really hope that doesn't mean what I think it means, Zori thought with a grimace.

"So, it's like two in the morning and I'm dead asleep in my apartment above the shop, right?" Skye continued, dramatically setting the scene for what they were about to share. "The dream starts. Scary Voice is talking, but this time I wake up. And when I open my eyes, there is a fuck off huge person crouched next to my bed. But not, like, a regular human person. No. Nope. This one's eyes and teeth were black, like pitch black. And they had these big claws and super dark grey skin that I could kinda see through. Definitely not a human."

Goddamn it, Tenebrae, Zori swore internally, trying very hard to appear appropriately shocked and not fiercely annoyed.

"Wow, that's so crazy," she said, channelling her frustration into a reasonable approximation of concern. "What did you do?"

"I screamed my freaking head off and threw a pillow at them," Skye laughed, shrugging exaggeratedly. There wasn't much else they could have done, honestly. "I don't think they liked that, though, because as soon as I started screaming they stood up and just vanished into thin air."

Zori hummed noncommittally, taking a sip of her latte to give her a moment to think about what to say. She hated lying to her friend, but it wasn't like she could just say 'Oh don't worry, I know that guy.'

"Are you sure you weren't still dreaming?" she asked, feeling guilty about invalidating her friend's experience the very moment the words left her mouth.

Skye fixed her with a withering look and she cringed visibly.

"Really?" they asked, dryly. "You don't believe me, Miss 'I live in the most haunted house in town?'"

"No, I know!" Zori said, backpedaling furiously as she searched for a reasonable explanation for her skepticism. Both of them well knew that she believed in the supernatural. It would have been weirder to live in the Dew Lane house and not be a believer. "I believe you. It's just, it sounds like all those internet descriptions of sleep paralysis demons or whatever."

Skye snorted. She actually had a point there.

"I'll give you that," they said, "but I'm pretty sure sleep paralysis demons aren't supposed to work for the Red Cross. For some reason, Scary Voice is super concerned about me donating blood at the Spring Festival."

Zori choked on her latte, and the hot liquid nearly came out her nose.

"He what??" she spluttered, coughing to clear her windpipe of the coffee that had attempted to go down the wrong way. She grabbed a napkin, wiping up some of her drink that had spilled on the table and her pants leg in the process.

When she looked up, Skye was staring at her, head tilted and eyes narrowed suspiciously.

Shit.

"How did you know Scary Voice is a he?" they asked, leaning forward with their elbows on the table as they interrogated her.

"Well, you, uh, you said they had a deep voice," Zori stammered, trying to cover her mistake. She could feel her face flush. This was why she hated lying; she was terrible at it. Anyone who knew her as well as Skye did could read her like an open book.

"Zoriya Eloise Quinn! J'accuse!" Skye burst out, pointing at her emphatically. "Don't you dare lie to me, you know something!"

"That's not even my middle name," she laughed, relaxing slightly at her friend's ridiculous tone. They didn't sound genuinely mad and she would prefer to keep it that way.

"I don't actually know your middle name, so I made one up," Skye shrugged, casually. "That is not the point. You are hiding something. Spill it."

Zori rubbed a hand over her face frustratedly, and gave a resigned sigh. She had to tell Skye something.

They weren't going to let this go without a fight or a confession.

"Okay," she finally acquiesced, leaning in to speak quietly, suddenly keenly aware that they were having this conversation in a public place. Maybe she could stall and actually make this work in their favor. "I'll make you a deal. I promise that I will tell you what you want to know, but only after the Spring Festival. And! On the condition that you donate at the blood drive."

Skye's mouth dropped open in a cartoonishly shocked expression when she added the final stipulation.

"Holy shit," they breathed, incredulously. "You're in league with my sleep paralysis demon. You know him?"

"Ask your questions after the festival. Deal?" Zori insisted, dodging the question. She did want to reassure them however she could in the meantime. "I can tell you, though, that you're not in danger and it's not because of any cursed items in your shop."

Skye nodded, relieved. Inventory would go a lot quicker without having to meticulously re-inspect every item for potential curses or hexes. It didn't assuage their now burning curiosity, but it was reassuring to know that whatever their nocturnal visitor was, he didn't mean them any harm. It was still fucking weird though.

"Okay, deal," Skye agreed, "but I'm gonna need you to tell me what Scary Voice wants with my blood, like, immediately after the festival."

Finding out whatever mysteries their friend was hiding was well worth a pint of blood, even though Skye wasn't exactly fond of needles. Their curiosity was too strong to deny. It was going to be a long week until the festival, wondering what, exactly, their friend had gotten herself involved in.

The light of the nearly full moon bathed the Graydon manor ruins in a cold light, now that the clouds were finally clearing. It seemed improbable that the Spring Festival was tomorrow, given that the snow hadn't entirely melted and the past few days had been drenched with freezing rain. Lazarus had spent most of the time in shadowspace, primarily because spending extended periods of time outdoors in rain that would be bone-chilling, if he still had bones, dredged up unpleasant memories of the time he and Levi spent in the stocks.

The equinox came early this year, and with it the change of seasons, although the weather seemed not to have received the memo quite yet. But it did look like the precipitation would abate in time for the festival to go on as planned. He hoped it did; their plans for gathering the final ingredients for the ritual depended on it.

He picked up the sound of footsteps coming from the side of the house and murmurs of faint conversation. Lazarus could identify his husband's ominous tone easily, along with Zori's higher voice, and a low chuckle that must have been Myrkrið. He let the sounds lead him to where they stood.

"Well, you get to be the one to explain it to your husband," Zori insisted, crossing her arms sternly as she glared at the unremorseful shadow demon. It would have looked more intimidating had it not been for her fuzzy coat and pom pom beanie.

"Explain what to me?" Lazarus said with an amused lilt as he rounded the corner to join them.

Myrkrið appeared positively entertained, smirking openly where he stood behind his incensed paramour. She was still looking pointedly at Tenebrae, determined to wait for him to start talking. And the latter looked utterly indifferent to her outrage.

"She wishes to tell your descendant Skye of our existence," he said, eventually, turning towards Lazarus and speaking in an almost bored tone. "And she asserts that this is my fault."

"That's because it is your fault!" Zori exclaimed, throwing her hands in the air in exasperation. "I wouldn't have to explain anything to them if you hadn't jump-scared them in the middle of the night like an asshole."

"Perhaps if you could lie more convincingly, it would not matter," Tenebrae countered, taking a menacing step toward the small, seething human.

"I don't want to be better at lying. It's shitty," she sneered, defiantly, stepping forward to meet his challenge with her hands on her hips.

Lazarus had to concentrate to keep from laughing. They looked and sounded like bickering siblings in this moment, and he found it difficult to be mad when the scene stirred such warm familial feelings in him. He had enjoyed similar showdowns with his twin many times when they were young.

"Alright, that is enough, both of you," Myrkrið announced, his patience for their antics run out, and he looped an arm around Zori's waist to pull her away from her confrontation with the other demon. Though his words still held a tinge of amusement, he threw Tenebrae a warning look anyway.

"Come inside where it is marginally less wet," Lazarus beckoned the three of them, "and someone can explain to me what a jump-scare is."

He led them to the section of the basement that was still mostly dry, thanks to the intact section of flooring above it. The garden chairs had been moved here temporarily so they would have a place to sit out of the rain. He took a seat in one gracefully, folded his hands in his lap, and turned to them with keen interest.

"Husband, what have you done?" Lazarus asked, face alight with curiosity. He was not all that worried about his descendant learning of his existence, based on what he knew of them from Zori, they might even be delighted by the news. And he had to admit that he was intrigued to meet them someday, preferably when he had a more corporeal form.

"I merely encouraged some of the descendants to ensure they participate in the blood drive," Tenebrae said, simply.

"Yeah, if by 'encouraged' you mean whispered ominously at them in their sleep like a creeper," Zori scoffed, rolling her eyes.

Lazarus barked out a laugh at the mental image of the grim figure softly chanting to sleeping humans about giving their blood. It was entirely ridiculous.

"Whatever possessed you to do such a thing?" he asked, incredulously. It was a much softer approach than what he had grown to expect from the shadow demon. Perhaps spending so much time with Myrkrið and Zori was having some effect on him.

"When I was observing Spencer at one point, he fell asleep with the television on," Tenebrae explained, "it spoke of experiments where humans were influenced by hearing information in their sleep. I assumed you would prefer this over my other ideas for ensuring that we have access to the blood that we need."

"That is rather resourceful of you, darling," Lazarus said, though he was still confused on a point or two. "But why would Zori wish to tell Skye about us because of this?"

Tenebrae had the decency to look mildly guilty for the first time, his almost perpetual scowl deepening. Zori didn't say a word, keeping to her insistence that the shadow demon should be the one to explain what happened.

"This last time, Skye awoke during my visit," he sighed, his features darkening slightly in embarrassment. "They saw me."

Oh dear, Lazarus thought. *That must have given them a fright.*

As he observed the others, Myrkrið looked largely unfazed. Zori still looked agitated, but not as concerned as he would expect if Tenebrae had truly managed to frighten her friend.

"And what happened then?" he pressed.

"Nothing," Tenebrae said, shaking his head. "They screamed and hurled a pillow at me. I left."

Lazarus looked at Zori expectantly, waiting for her to fill in the gaps.

"They're fine," she acknowledged wearily. "A little weirded out, maybe, but mostly just curious. Skye is like me, they like spooky stuff. But they wouldn't drop the subject until I promised to explain. I did manage to get them to agree to donate at the festival though."

Well, that is something.

Lazarus felt strangely optimistic about his descendant learning of their existence. It wasn't ideal, no, but with modern attitudes much more lenient, almost to the point of denial, towards magic and the supernatural, there was little threat of consequences. It might actually give him, and Tenebrae, the opportunity to get to know one of his living relatives. That was something he never expected to have.

"If they are well, then I suppose no harm has been done," he concluded eventually, noticing the minute easing of tension in his husband's shoulders at his words.

"What about Spencer?" Myrkrið asked, directing his question to the other shadow demon.

"He did not see me," Tenebrae declared, before continuing with a razor sharp smile, "but I was perhaps a bit more forceful with my encouragement."

Chapter 26

Golden sunshine warmed the winter chill still clinging to Graymourne, casting its cheerful glow over the festivities that morning. It seemed the whole village was in attendance on this lovely Saturday in March, the center of town bustling with activity as festival goers enjoyed music, food, and games. Craft vendors had taken over the bank parking lot, and the square at the center of town even had a few small carnival rides set up.

The sounds of celebration wafted into the room where Zori sat, checking the sign-up list again. She was pleased to see that sure enough, each and every descendant had an appointment on the schedule for the blood drive, including Spencer Douglas. She wasn't sure what Tenebrae had been whispering to the man in the dead of night in order to convince him to take part, and she didn't particularly want to know. Whatever it was, it worked.

The Red Cross team had set up in the community center attached to Immaculate Harvest. The building had been a newer addition, built onto the old timber-frame church in the 1950s. It still sported rather dated decor inside, but at least the heating and air-conditioning system had been updated. As a result, it was actually quite cozy inside.

Fortunately for her, someone else had volunteered to arrive early that morning to meet the team for setup, so all that Zori had to do now was check in donors and make sure that they got their juice and cookies after their appointment.

No one was going to faint on her watch, not if she could help it.

The open space had been divided into a few private curtained-off booths, with a small waiting area of chairs set up, and the volunteer desk with refreshments placed near the front. The space was lit by large fluorescent ceiling lights which hung from the rafters. Above their glow, the vaulted ceiling was obscured by a curiously dense darkness. Zori didn't have to look up to know that both shadow demons lurked in the dim space, keeping watch over her and waiting for their marks to arrive.

"Hi, thanks for coming, let's get you checked in," she said, smiling at a young woman and middle-aged gentlemen as they approached the table. She gave them their paperwork to fill out and checked off their names on the list, reading them out loud for good measure. "Kelsey and Dylan Cresswell, you're right on time."

Though she spoke at a normal volume, the shadow demons above would easily be able to hear her from their vantage point. Since she wasn't sure how exactly the samples would be labeled, they had decided it was best for them to observe and then pilfer one of the vials as soon as the phlebotomist put it on ice. This would save them having to steal and then sort through a bunch of the unneeded ones later, less wasteful in terms of both time and resources. Zori didn't want them to take any more than they needed, even though it was technically going to a good cause either way.

She handed out stickers and snacks to the Cresswells once their appointment was finished, and then spent some time scrolling through social media on her phone. In between checking townsfolk in for their appointments, she left a few comments on photos of her old friends back in California and caught up on what was going on in their lives. Embroiled in reading a post about Beth's latest workplace nemesis, she wasn't sure how long it had been when she was distracted by the sound of someone impatiently clearing their throat.

A rather put out looking Spencer Douglas stood in front of the check in table. Judging by the dark circles under his eyes, he wasn't getting quite enough beauty rest these days. One of his loafer clad feet tapped restlessly against the floor, and his weight shifted to one side. His posture oozed annoyance.

"Oh, hello," Zori said, brightly, putting down her phone and handing him a clipboard with paperwork to fill out. "What's your name? I'll go ahead and check you in."

"Spencer Douglas," he grumbled, begrudgingly accepting the clipboard from her hands. Her chipper greeting seemed to ruffle his feathers a bit further, but he kept his responses clipped and minimal. As far as he knew, she didn't have anything to do with his misfortunes of late.

"Excellent, thanks for coming by Mr. Douglas," she said, cheerfully, putting a check mark next to his name on the schedule and then pointing him towards the waiting area. "Please have a seat over there and someone will be right with you."

"Not like I have much of a choice," he muttered under his breath, shuffling over to sit in one of the metal folding chairs.

Zori only just managed to catch his griping, and stifled a snicker at his harried tone. Tenebrae must have done a number on the guy. She almost felt sorry for him, but it was a little hard to empathize completely considering that all she'd ever seen him do since he arrived was be rude to the locals and try to mine his inherited family home for profit. Even Tenebrae had commented on the man's abysmal manners, which was impressive considering the shadow demon wasn't exactly known for his social graces either.

She looked up, noticing that the dark cloud that obscured the ceiling looked thicker now. Her companions had certainly noticed Spencer's entrance.

"What are we looking at?" Skye's voice came suddenly, startling her back to attention. They peered up at the ceiling where she'd been looking a moment ago. It was dark up there. Almost too dark.

"Oh, nothing!" Zori covered quickly, glancing at the time on her phone. "Wow, you're early."

Skye was never early. They were notorious for being fashionably late, in fact.

"Uh huh," they said, skeptically, raising a judgmental eyebrow before handing her a coffee and scone. They took a seat in the chair next to her behind the volunteer desk. "Figured you could use a little bribe, I mean, boost for your shift."

They grinned impishly at her, clearly impatient for her to share what she knew.

"Thank you, but no bribes necessary," she laughed, accepting the offering anyway. Zori wasn't one to refuse a free snack just because it was a bribe, she had already committed to telling Skye the truth anyway. "You'll get your questions answered soon."

"Fine, fine," they agreed, settling into an awkward looking position in the chair. Skye was virtually incapable of using a seat in its intended manner, or at least Zori had never seen them sit in one properly. "Can't blame me for trying! Anyway, what's the out-of-towner doing here?"

They lowered their voice, leaning in to whisper conspiratorially while casting a furtive glance at Spencer. He was sullenly walking back to a donation booth beside a person from the blood drive team, so he didn't notice their less than subtle observation.

"Looks like he's donating blood," Zori said, nonchalantly, tucking in to her scone. This was not technically a lie, so she managed to keep a straight face.

"Hmmph," Skye grunted, dropping the subject in favor of sharing some other gossip that they had picked up from a shop customer this week. The mayor's daughter, Jennifer, had been in to buy a piece of furniture, apparently, and told them all about her cousin's step-sister's best friend's hairdresser who just eloped with her secret boyfriend of three years.

Zori gratefully engaged with the change of topic, expressing appropriate shock and awe at this latest rumor that had their small town abuzz. They briefly paused mid-story while Spencer collected his sticker and snack with a tersely gritted thanks. But as soon as he was gone, Skye resumed their tale.

"So, anyway, that's why Samara's working at the salon now," they finished.

"Wait, who is Samara, again?"

"Jennifer's cousin's step-sister," Skye clarified.

"Oh, right," Zori said, checking the time on her phone, "Okay, looks like you're up! You gotta fill this out and then they'll take you back."

Skye did a tiny victory dance in their seat. Finally, it was actually time for their appointment.

"And then we're getting out of here so I can interrogate you about weird shit," they said, grabbing the clipboard with a look of determination.

It was about time, they were ready to get some answers.

For the sake of easing them into the potentially terrifying concepts of shadow demons and somewhat undead ancestors, it was decided in advance that Zori would explain things to Skye in the comfort of the Dew Lane house. They had been in the space before and there wouldn't be anyone else around to overhear things they shouldn't. Provided it all went well, Myrkrið would be her first real introduction to the supernatural. Despite being eager to make their acquaintance, Lazarus was unsure whether he wanted his young relative to see him in his current state, or wait until after the ritual when he'd be human again, more or less. And Tenebrae was off of the invite list for letting Skye catch him in the first place.

"I guess your haunted ass house is as good a place as any to find out whatever you're hiding," Skye breathed, excitedly.

Most of the time when the pair got together, they hung out at the coffee shop or the antique shop, but Skye had visited the Dew Lane house a few times. Myrkrið had always made himself scarce, but couldn't resist pulling a few minor haunting tricks for their benefit. The house was supposed to be home to something spooky, after all.

"Yeah, about that," Zori said, sheepishly, leading them to the living room. "It's not technically haunted. Well, at least not the way everyone thinks."

Skye sat down on the overstuffed green velvet couch, already giving her a look of disbelief. They'd heard way too many stories about this place for that to be true. Not to mention having a few experiences of their own.

"That's impossible, but let's put a pin in that for a sec," they said. Much as they were dying to find out what she could possibly mean by that, there were more pressing matters to clear up. "First, I wanna know what the hell I saw in my apartment."

Zori took a deep breath, preparing to dive into the explanation. Skye wanted answers and she promised to give them. There wasn't really a way to sugarcoat it, so she figured the best way was to just rip the Band-Aid off and then deal with any resulting questions.

"Okay, don't freak out, but your visitor from the other night is a shadow demon," Zori said, maintaining a calm matter-of-fact tone. "They're actually more like elementals, I guess, because they're literally made of shadows. So, they can be kind of a shapeless dark cloud or a more solid person shape, which is what you saw."

She elected not to mention the third form the shadows could assume, for now. The information that they could become twelve feet tall and covered in bone armor when enraged seemed like it might be more hindrance than help at this point in the conversation. Maybe later, once they got past the basics, Zori would explain what she affectionately referred to as the shadow demons' 'kaiju mode.'

Meanwhile, Skye blinked at her, waiting for the punchline. They half expected her to break out in laughter and admit she was messing with them, but she just continued to look at them like she'd just told them the sky was blue.

Oh, she's serious!

They were still absorbing the information while Zori paused to gauge how her friend was taking the news. Their blank expression wasn't giving her much to go on, and she was beginning to get a bit worried. Did they not believe her? Were they freaked out? Skye was rarely silent for this long and it was unnerving.

"Right, okay, and how exactly do you know that?" they asked, chewing their lip nervously while trying to connect what seemed like wildly unrelated dots. As far as they knew, their friend was a graphic designer and despite her penchant for all things spooky, wasn't super well-versed in actual occult knowledge. So, how did she know so much about these creatures?

"Because my house isn't haunted," Zori said slowly, choosing her words carefully to be as simple and non-alarming as possible, "it had one of them trapped in it."

"Had? As in, you let it out?" Skye questioned, eyes widening as Zori nodded. "Why? What do they want? Why the hell was a shadow demon trying to brainwash me into being a blood donor in my sleep?"

They stopped rapidly blurting out questions when Zori held up a hand, motioning for them to pause. Maybe a few answers would quell their increasingly frantic energy.

"They don't usually want much of anything from humans, to be honest," Zori explained nonchalantly, while her friend listened, and they slowly beganto calm down as she continued to speak. "But the one who visited you needed a sample of your blood for a spell to help one of your ancestors."

Seeing how utterly blasé she spoke about them did help keep Skye from freaking out. Though she'd been doing significantly better since she moved to Graymourne, they knew Zori suffered from PTSD and anxiety. As they grew closer, she'd confided in them about her struggles. So, if she wasn't worried about this whole shadow demon business, then Skye knew it was likely not something they had to fear. That didn't make it any less confusing or bizarre to learn about.

"What the hell does that mean?" Skye asked, fascinated but bewildered. If they hadn't seen the demon with their own eyes, it would be extremely hard to believe any of this. But they knew what they saw, and they also knew Zori to be an absolutely terrible liar, so she had to be telling the truth.

"It's complicated," she sighed, trying to think of how to succinctly describe the situation. She had Lazarus's full permission to tell them his story, but it was a lot to explain in one afternoon. "You know your ancestor Lazarus Graydon, the one who was burned as a witch?"

Skye nodded.

Of course they did, everyone in Graymourne knew the legend.

"Well, he was," Zori said, "A witch, that is. And he was, um, is married to the demon who visited you. The short version of the story is: the fire didn't completely kill him. And in order to get his body back, they have to do this whole ritual thing that requires the blood of one of his descendants for it to work."

They gawked at her, open mouthed and motionless. It was going to take a minute for that much shockingly strange information to sink in. She decided to give them some time to process their thoughts.

"It's a lot. I'm going to make you some tea and then you can ask me more questions," Zori suggested, patting her friend on the shoulder before she padded off to the kitchen.

When she returned a few minutes later with a fresh cup of chamomile tea, Skye had at least moved. They were now sitting cross legged on the couch with their hands folded calmly in their lap and a more open and alert expression on their face.

She set the cup on the table in front of them and took a seat, letting them decide when to begin.

"So, would I be correct to assume that you know my undead Great-whatever-Uncle Lazarus and his shadow demon husband?" Skye asked, nearly breaking into a laugh at how ridiculous the question sounded. This was, by far, the weirdest conversation they had ever had.

"Yes. His name is Tenebrae, by the way."

"Okay, cool, that's totally fine and normal," they said, chuckling nervously. "Was Tenebrae the one trapped in the house?"

Skye looked around the room furtively, as if he might appear suddenly. There hadn't been any weird, unexplained sounds or anything this visit, but they were no longer sure that meant that they were alone in the house.

"No, I met Tenebrae and your great uncle when I was trying to free him," Zori explained, simply. The story of how she met Myrkrið could wait for another time; for now she wanted to focus on helping Skye understand why Tenebrae had visited them. "They helped me get him out."

Skye nodded sagely, as if this all made perfect sense. Their closest friend was acquainted with two shadow demons and a hundreds-of-years-old witch. No big deal. Perfectly normal. They reminded themself that Zori had already said they weren't in any danger. And creepy tactics aside, Tenebrae hadn't threatened them, not really.

"Do I wanna know where the other one is?" they asked hesitantly. The realization was just sinking in that the eerie sounds they'd heard on previous visits to the Dew Lane house were most likely the work of one of the two shadow demons.

"Probably upstairs."

Despite knowing, logically, that it was a possibility, 'upstairs' was not the answer they were expecting.

Not by a long shot.

"I thought you freed him, why is he still in your house?" Skye squeaked loudly. They weren't sure what was more unsettling, the fact that there was currently a demon in the house with them or how casual their friend was being about the whole situation.

"Well, um, you remember my boyfriend 'Mark' that you met at the Halloween Fright Fest?" Zori asked, a furious blush spreading across her face as she looked away from Skye's intense stare. "His real name is Myrkrið and that wasn't a costume. Well, the robes were, but not the rest."

"Oh my god!"

Skye stood up, pacing a couple of laps around the room and then sat back down. They picked up the tea, chugging the liquid despite it still being quite hot. They hardly noticed the scorching heat of it, too focused on thinking back to last October when they'd apparently met another shadow demon and had no idea.

How many of them are there in this town? Skye wondered.

Zori gave them a few minutes to compose themselves, watching the wheels turn in her friend's mind as they digested everything she'd told them. She could practically see the lightbulb go on above Skye's head when they finally stopped to ask the question she'd been expecting.

"Wait," they said, suddenly, eyes snapping back up to her face, "was the 'boyfriend' part accurate?"

"Yeah. Do you want to meet him?" she asked, chuckling softly. Their look of shock was starting to transform into one of amusement and curiosity. She knew that eventually, after the initial surprise wore off, Skye would be delighted by the situation. It was a combination of their three favorite things: history, the supernatural, and gossip.

"Why the fuck not, let's do it," Skye laughed, settling back against the pillows as they prepared to be formally introduced to a shadow demon for the first time.

What a way to spend a Saturday!

Zori made a waving gesture towards the open doorway that led to the dining room. Skye followed the movement, immediately noticing the very tall dark figure that seemed to melt out of the shadows and solidify as he entered the room. He was even bigger than they remembered their visitor being, having to duck through the doorway, but he approached slowly and carefully, giving them a wide birth as he moved to Zori's side.

Myrkrið sat on the floor next to her chair, resting one massive arm over the armrest and draping it across her lap. He leaned there casually, his night black eyes regarding them with a relaxed interest.

"Hello Skye," he said, softening his booming voice as much as possible.

The sound of it was familiar. It was strangely inhuman in a way that was difficult to forget, even though the first time they had spoken, Skye had assumed it was a voice modulator. He had been dressed as the grim reaper at the Halloween celebration. It was very similar to Tenebrae's deep rasp, and they kicked themselves for not picking up on the resemblance sooner.

"Uh, hi," they greeted, unusually bashful as they waved at him from their spot on the couch. "So, not a human, huh?"

"No," Myrkrið said, chuckling gently, "Clearly not."

A small but genuine smile adorned his face. After the initial oddity of his appearance passed, Skye could see that he was actually quite handsome and seemed much friendlier than their visitor. They also couldn't help but notice the way that he and Zori leaned into each other, unconsciously seeking more of the other's touch. It was sweet, and seeing how obviously enamored he was with their friend helped make him a tiny bit less intimidating.

"You were right, you guys are pretty good at terrifying humans," they joked, referencing the short conversation they had with him during the Halloween festival. The exchange made a lot more sense now. "You seem nicer than the other one though."

"Tenebrae is young," he said, acknowledging the accuracy of their assessment, "and a bit impulsive. Though, I was perhaps more volatile at his age. Do not worry, you have nothing to fear from him."

Young? Skye thought. He had to be close to three hundred years old if he'd been married to Lazarus in the seventeen hundreds. They gave Zori an incredulous look, but she only shrugged. *Okay, then.*

"So, you're gonna help bring my great uncle back from the not-quite-dead, then?" they asked, curiosity coming back around to what had sparked this whole introduction in the first place.

"Yes, if he and Tenebrae require further assistance," Myrkrið confirmed. Now that the blood had been collected, he was not sure there was much more he and Zori could do. He trusted Lazarus to ask if he needed them, though.

"Cool, I'd like to meet him once he gets his body back, if he's up for it," Skye mused. Aside from getting to meet a real live ancestor, the idea of talking to someone who'd been around when Graymourne was still barely a town was remarkable. They had so many questions, for him and the shadow demons. Skye decided to start with the latter for the moment. "So, can I ask you a bunch of probably awkward questions about what you are?"

Myrkrið laughed loudly. The sound was mildly terrifying, but the feeling was tempered by how amused he looked. Zori grinned beside him, happy to see her shadow demon and her friend getting along. She was also relieved, Skye was her closest friend in town and it hadn't exactly been easy keeping the nature of her relationship a secret from them. It would be nice to finally be able to be open about it.

"What do you wish to know?"

Chapter 27

TOTAL ECLIPSE OF THE HEART

A fortnight had never felt so long as this one, the final stretch of days leading up to the day of the eclipse. Lazarus feared it would never end. Each day seemed to linger longer than the last, until finally the taut stretch of time snapped back to the present and he found himself watching the sun steadily climb to its zenith on what he hoped would be his final day as a Shade.

The preparations were all in place; ingredients procured and prepared, the obstructions cleared away for a prime view of the sky, and the site already painstakingly inscribed with the necessary markings. Once the totality began, he would need to be swift, and Lazarus was not willing to leave anything to chance. Tenebrae, Zori, and Myrkrið had all been tutored on the procedure for the ritual, tasked with standing by in case Lazarus became unable to continue for any reason. If that should happen, one of the others could step in to complete the rites and incantation.

His backup plans had backup plans.

Still, the exacting preparations did not completely assuage his nerves. The cost of failure was almost too great to contemplate, so the Shade tried his best to put it out of mind completely.

"The others will be here soon," Tenebrae rumbled softly, curling his long arms around Lazarus's waist and resting his chin atop the smaller man's head. "Ease your mind, husband, we will succeed."

Of course, the shadow demon could sense his apprehension. By now, he knew every slight quirk of expression and adjustment in posture, so that Lazarus hardly had to speak for Tenebrae to know what he was thinking. He too had wrestled with doubts, but ultimately he was confident the ritual would go as planned.

"I know," he replied, squeezing the demon's forearms that banded across his front reassuringly.

They remained like this for some time, quietly watching the sky shift as the stars and planets ever so slowly finished aligning themselves. The moment they had waited two hundred and fifty-seven years for was approaching at long last, and soon it would arrive with little fanfare. It was a brief blip in time, wholly indifferent to the monumental effect it would have on the fate of these two beings.

The soft crunch of leaves under booted feet eventually broke their silent reverie, and they looked up to see Zori and Myrkrið weaving their way through the still bare trees. Green buds had just begun to sprout along their branches in the newly warming season, sprinkling the skeletal forest with dots of color.

Lazarus thought how fitting it was to be resurrected amidst the spark of new growth. He took it as a favorable sign.

The ritual would work.

It had to.

Sunlight shone upon the hard-packed dirt floor of the ruined cellar for the first time. The floor above had been removed, clawed away by the industrious Tenebrae, so that the light would warm the blackened soil.

Permanently scorched, the ground was marred with angry ash, which stubbornly refused to erode. The burnt surface was now scored with intricately drawn characters, curling loops and geometric angles that formed an esoteric pattern across the ground. Though its intricacies were an incomprehensible foreign language to most of those gathered around it, the design still exuded an aura of power that even the uninitiated could sense.

Lazarus and Tenebrae stood in the epicenter of it, where the scorch marks were thickest. The witch directed the other two to a couple of chairs off to one side. If everything went correctly, they would merely observe and bear witness, but it was reassuring to have them nearby just in case. Of all those present, Myrkrið had the most experience with magic after the Shade.

"Once we begin, the ritual must be completed, quickly and precisely," he advised them all in a strong, confident voice. "No matter what happens, do not stop before all the steps have been performed."

Tenebrae frowned at the foreboding sensation that crept into his chest. Was this dread? He felt agitated, eager for this to be over and yet fearful of what the process would be like for his husband. The witch seemed to think he might be unable to recite the incantation alone once the spell began to work its magic on him, which worried him.

"We will ensure it is done," Myrkrið agreed, speaking up from the sidelines. He gave Tenebrae a nod, sensing his apprehension. It eased his fears somewhat.

The incantation portion of the spell was written in a form of Old English, translated from the original Mycenaean Greek. Neither of these were languages that Tenebrae spoke. He could recite it phonetically of course, and had practiced at length with Lazarus over the last two weeks. But the older shadow demon was practically fluent in the Anglo-Saxon language, if a bit rusty from disuse.

"I will take the vials now, if you please, Zori," Lazarus said, as he finished arranging the makeshift altar he had constructed from a few stray stones.

She opened up a small cooler and passed him three tubes of red liquid, each one neatly labeled in her small looping handwriting. Leaning as far as she could without losing balance and accidentally stepping on the intricate ground markings, she was just able to reach his outstretched hand.

The shadows cast into the cellar by the trees above had begun to shimmer, small crescent shapes dancing in the space as the moon began to cross in front of the sun. Zori's eyes lit up as she caught the movement of the light along her raised hand, and Lazarus smiled at her.

"It has begun," he said, sounding almost relieved. Looking up, but careful not to peer directly at the sun itself, he could tell by the quality of light that they still had perhaps half an hour until the totality.

It would be quite noticeable when it arrived.

"This is so weird," Zori commented, holding both hands out to watch the glittering shadows dance on her skin.

As the minutes ticked by, the light grew gradually grayer and grayer. It was almost like the air before a summer thunderstorm, thick and dim and buzzing with energy. While the sky steadily darkened, the temperature began to plummet in concert with the disappearing light. The crisp spring afternoon atmosphere plunged back into the icy depths of winter as the sun's warming rays were swallowed by an all-consuming moon.

Twilight fell upon the town of Graymourne, for the first of two times today. The orange and purple glow of a false sunset bloomed on the horizon while the sky took on a temporary night. Starlight flickered into existence, and constellations revealed themselves in the dimming firmament. A blinding spark flared at the edge of the ring that burned around the black moon, signaling the start of the totality.

Wasting no time, Lazarus picked up the first vial, beginning to recite the incantation from memory.

Tenebrae held the open grimoire in one large hand, ready in case the Shade needed it for reference.

"Under geblinded Sunne and wæccendlicre
Mōnan, þā tīd standeð stille wē āwierpen þis rīt,
Hwæt þā heofonas ne magon gesēon, lǣtað hīe
beon unmihtige tō forstōpan,
On þystrum gedōn, and mōnan bletsode,
Wē ceorfan tīd eft and ēacnian hit,
Hwæt ānfealde, þēah gerǣflod aweg,
Ġebrōht nīwe tō his rihtan stōwe."

His words seemed to vibrate against the pressurized gray air, a gathering energy rippling through the open cellar. A faint yet growing purple light began to pulse along the inscriptions that covered the ground.

"An lāc of blōde wē dōð, ūre blōd for hwæt wē nimað
Blōd clypað tō blōde, swā swā sīrenes sang
Ġeġeond tō hwǣr hit sceolde beon,
Gehȳrað þis clypian and tōsāmne hēr
Ġeġeond ūs, ēalā ūre blōd."

Opening the vial, Lazarus poured the viscous red liquid onto the ground at his feet, where the charred earth drank it greedily. The glowing sigils brightened, and the light pulsed like the breathing of a massive creature. Vines of dark ash began to coalesce on the cellar floor in a large ring around where the witch stood, still barreling forth through his recitation in a commanding voice.

"Þis lāc of blōde wē dōð, þæs blōdes þe ūs
tōscēawode
Falslīce ācweden and wranglīce genemned
Hīe ēaðelīce ūs ārǣfdon þæt wē ārǣrdon
Spillað þis blōd, tō drincan þīnne tungan
Unsprecað þā word, þæt ānes condēmnode."

He spilled the second vial onto the eager earth, where the vines of black soot had started to snake their way around his feet and ankles, swiftly climbing higher up his legs. Zori darted concerned looks towards Myrkrið and Tenebrae. They seemed similarly unsettled, but Lazarus had said the ritual should not be stopped for any reason.

"Se endebyrd of blōde wē dōð, þæs blōdes þe ūs
belēogan
Unrihtlīce āworpene fram līfe tō dēaðe
Hīe ēastodon ūs hwæt Wyrd ġesett
Underfōn þis cost, tō ġesettan þæt scyld
Rihtian þis wrang, and libban ǣft."

Lazarus's voice grew rough and labored, grimacing through the words as he emptied the final vial onto the ground with shaking hands. The quickening vines had wormed their way inside his shadowy form, burrowing into the center of his limbs where they twisted and branched as they rose higher into his chest and torso.

A mass of black formed, slightly off-center at his chest, and with horrified fascination, Zori realized that his circulatory system was rebuilding itself before their eyes.

"Under geblinded Sunne…," Lazarus gasped, his words choked off suddenly as the tarry veins grew up his throat and spread throughout where his skull should be. The Shade's eyes closed tightly, and he shook with what had to be intense pain.

Myrkrið shifted quickly through shadowspace, appearing next to Tenebrae without disturbing the now brightly blazing symbols. He grabbed the grimoire from the other demon's hands and immediately picked up where the witch had left off.

"Under geblinded Sunne and wæccendlicre
Mōnan, wē clypiað tō ūs hwæt ūre be bi rihte
On blōde and flæsce, on hæran and bān, wē
clawiað ūre weg eft in ūre hām,
On þystrum gedōn, and mōnan bletsode,
Wē ceorfan tīd eft and ēacnian hit,
Wē libbað æft, swā swā mennisce menn
Cum forma ūre, tō mē ġeġeond."

The air rippled and sparks crackled near the blinding violet fissures in the ground. Dirt rumbled as more dark ash forcibly dragged itself towards the mass at the center of the cellar, where it reassembled itself into the structure of bones. Tenebrae did his best to hold the Shade, whose form shuddered and bucked under the weight of the rapidly-forming skeleton inside it.

Zori glanced at the time, and then up at the eclipse. Two minutes and forty-five seconds had passed. They had less than a minute left before the totality would be over.

"Is there more?" she asked anxiously, looking to Myrkrið who had ceased speaking and was now watching the Shade with an alarmingly concerned expression.

"No, it is done," he said, closing the grimoire in one hand. "Now we can only wait for the magic to run its course."

Tenebrae gritted his teeth, wishing there were something he could do for his beloved husband, other than hold onto him desperately. If he could take every last scrap of pain in his stead, he would do so gladly.

When the scorch marks had all disappeared from the earth beneath their feet, the light from the inscriptions began to move. Amaranthine flames licked along the lines, streaming towards the pained figure at their center.

Lazarus was only dimly aware of his husband's hands leaving the surface of his form, consumed as he was by agony. He had thought nothing could be more painful than feeling his skeleton regrow itself from within. When the searing purple heat began to spread over the surface of his new body, he realized that he could not have been more wrong.

It felt as if he were being burned in reverse. The molten violet light spread along the outside of his form, melting his flesh back into place bit by bit. When he had been burned the first time, his body had done him the service of allowing him to pass out from smoke inhalation. This time, he would have no such luxury. He felt every scorching second, each one agonizingly long. It seemed to stretch on infinitely and he began to fear that he would lose his mind to the almost unimaginable level of pain, one that no human was ever meant to bear.

Around him, the other three stood helplessly. Tenebrae had been pushed back by the force of the flames, unwillingly releasing his love to endure the process alone. Myrkrið placed a steadying hand on his shoulder, anchoring the other shadow demon amid the tumult of his emotions. Zori blinked back tears that threatened to blind her, unable to look away from her friend's torment.

A light sparked at the anterior edge of the eclipse in the sky above them, flaring brightly for a second as the totality released its smothering grip on the sun. As the moon began to take its leave, the ravenous flames suddenly blinked out of existence, leaving the pale and naked but unmarked body of Lazarus Graydon behind.

Tenebrae dove forward, catching him as the man's weak form collapsed beneath his own weight. He was warm and solid and breathing.

He was alive.

"Lazarus?" he said, cautiously, attempting to rouse the unconscious man. The shadow demon shook his face gently, desperately willing him to wake.

His eyelids fluttered, but he remained otherwise unresponsive.

"Lazarus, my love. I need you to wake up. Please."

Tenebrae's volcanic voice cracked, heartbreakingly, as he begged his beloved husband to come back to him. He buried his face in the soft chestnut hair he had so longed to touch again for two centuries and felt warm tears run down his face.

A small, delicate hand rested gently at his back.

"Let's take him to my house," Zori offered, softly. "You can both stay there until he wakes up, okay?"

He turned, instinctively ready to refuse, but when he saw the shining trail of tears on her cheeks, his heart clenched. The warmth in her eyes had him nodding despite himself, rising to his feet with Lazarus cradled in his arms.

"Come on," Myrkrið urged, holding out a hand to guide him home with them.

Tenebrae stepped into the void, trusting in them to take him where he needed to be.

Chapter 28

COME BACK TO ME

For the first few hours, Tenebrae paced restlessly, certain there must be something that he could do to wake his sleeping husband. Lazarus lay in the spare bedroom of the Dew Lane house, alive yet unresponsive.

The shadow demon was at a loss for what to do.

He was accustomed to solving problems with action and intimidation. He would gladly raze this world and everything in it down to the ground if it would bring Lazarus back to him. But there was no foe to fight, nothing to sink his teeth into aside from diligent and painfully boring research.

Myrkrið was better at that, admittedly. His grasp of several languages, including a few dead ones, combined with the internet navigating skills he had learned from his human meant that he was far better equipped to seek out answers to the witch's condition. He also had the luxury of a detachment from the situation that Tenebrae did not.

So, while the older shadow demon searched for information, Tenebrae bided his time, either roaming the house like a caged shark or curled protectively around his human, like a dragon with its hoard.

A fragile peace reigned over the house until the third day after the ritual, when Tenebrae's emotions finally got the best of him.

"Why don't you take a break?" Zori offered, noticing how jittery the shadow demon was becoming, despite refusing to venture more than a few feet from Lazarus. "I can watch over him for a bit."

"I do not need a break, human," Tenebrae snapped, the edge of a vicious growl bleeding into his tone.

She flinched only slightly at the sharpness of his response, but it was enough that Myrkrið did not hesitate to intervene. Before Tenebrae could topple over the precipice into a further outburst, he dragged the younger demon from the witch's bedside and hurled him into the emptiness of shadowspace.

"What the fuck are you doing?" Tenebrae snarled, stumbling backwards as he regained his footing. A feral anger gnashed in his chest.

Without a word, Myrkrið launched at him, leveling swift strikes at the other demon. He moved with surprising speed and agility, catching Tenebrae off guard. Confused and sparking with pent up anger, he dodged the swiping claws before lashing out with an attack of his own.

Immediately, it was plain to see that his opponent had more experience in physical combat, but what the younger of the two lacked in technique, he made up for in ferocity. Despite their differences, they were fairly evenly matched. As they clashed, the two shadow demons shifted form, growing taller while jagged armor took shape on their bodies like a dark exoskeleton; two titans battling in the deep lightless space.

The void echoed with the sound of their snarls and growls, punctuated by dull thuds and wrenching slices. Tenebrae had no idea how long they fought; the focus of his thoughts had tunneled down to only the immediacy of combat. Everything outside that was forgotten for the moment. Neither of them pulled their punches. Claws slashed, dark blood flew, and teeth snapped.

When finally the flame of frenzy in him was exhausted, Tenebrae's awareness resurfaced. He was crouched with one knee on the ground, panting from the exertion. He could still feel some deep cuts along his ribs knitting themselves back together, drawing strength from the darkness around them.

He looked up to see the other shadow approaching him calmly.

"Better?" Myrkrið asked, offering his hand to help the shadow demon to his feet.

Tenebrae stared at him blankly for a moment, only now digesting the fact that Myrkrið had intentionally goaded him into indulging his more destructive tendencies to make him feel better.

And it had worked.

"Yes," he growled, still catching his breath. He grasped the other demon's outstretched hand. "I feel more calm."

"Good. When you require an outlet for your rage, I will give it to you," Myrkrið said, his tone brooking no room for argument as he pulled the shadow up to stand, "but you will not lose control in front of Zori again."

Tenebrae nodded, looking at him with newfound gratitude and respect. He would have fully understood if Myrkrið had attacked him simply out of concern for his human. But, in his own way, he had acted out of care for the other shadow demon as well.

When he was convinced that Tenebrae's ire had abated to a more manageable level, he led them both back into the light of the Dew Lane house.

Zori raised an eyebrow at the state of them when they returned, crowded together in the dim hallway and slightly stooped to fit their currently colossal forms despite the high ceiling. Her shadow demon generally avoided assuming this shape unless there was danger or she asked very nicely, so she studied their expressions warily. The encouraging look Myrkrið gave her seemed to assuage her concerns, though, and she smiled at Tenebrae then offered him a snack.

"Do you want to try a cookie?" she asked, holding out a bright blue plastic container. "Myrkrið doesn't like these, so we don't have to share."

He took one of the small, sandwich-like confections and tossed it in his mouth. For the time being, he no longer felt as if the weight of his anguish would crush him. And now Tenebrae knew that if it returned, he could always seek out the other shadow demon to spar.

Perhaps he would even pick up some improved techniques, as if he needed them to be more deadly.

The first thing that Lazarus noticed was light. A dazzling brilliance melted his surroundings into a sea of soft, indistinct shapes. He tried to blink, hoping to clear his vision, but nothing happened. Straining to listen for a clue as to his whereabouts, he heard almost nothing, not even the soft wind of his own breath. A distant, undulating hum, like the vibration of a single harpsichord string, played backdrop to the otherwise heavy silence.

Am I dead? he thought, for the second time in his already abnormally long life.

He no longer felt the gut-wrenching pain that had marked his experience during the ritual. His relief was fleeting though, as Lazarus concluded that he could not feel any other sensations either.

What could have possibly gone wrong? he wondered, going over the events again in his mind. His preparations had been exact; every detail was planned and carried out to the smallest minutiae. *I do not understand.*

You always did think you had all the answers, Laz, a familiar voice said, as if speaking from inside his own head.

The blurry landscape swayed as he attempted to turn in search of the source. What once was merely a blend of pastel color began to come into focus gradually. The ground, if one could call it that, was a rippling reflection that warped and glittered like liquid. It held a mirror image of the wispy, nebulous shapes that made up the terrain, clumped together like rock formations made of vaporous clouds. Like the sky above, they were cloaked in the soft pink, warm orange, and gentle lilac hues of a perpetual dawn. The heavens, however, were freckled with millions of twinkling black dots, as if someone had flipped the night sky inside out.

Over here, the voice chuckled.

The universe spun, briefly, and Lazarus set his eyes on the figure now directly before him. Or rather, the volumetric white void that occupied the space where a person ought to be. Pink highlights shone on the surface of the human-shaped emptiness from the ambient candy-colored light catching the surface of its form. Though it was like looking at the person in reverse, he would recognize those achingly familiar features anywhere.

Levi?

The void smiled at him, and Lazarus was filled with a sudden joy. Then, just as quickly, a hollowing sadness followed.

I'm so sorry, he lamented, reaching for his long dead twin. Centuries of old guilt arose, and the feeling of responsibility for his brother's demise became fresh again. He vaguely noticed that his own arm held the same void-like appearance as the other man, only his was dark instead of light.

I never blamed you, brother, Levi said, shaking his head gently. He stepped forward, clasping Lazarus's outstretched hand and pulling him into a hug.

It lacked the warmth of a human body, but the physical pressure was comforting nonetheless. Lazarus held him tightly for a few moments, basking in the familiar embrace.

You are too forgiving, he insisted, drawing back to look at his twin. As he observed longer, he became more and more used to the strangely inverted appearance, until his mind only registered that it was his Levi. *If I had done things differently, you could have lived to raise your family.*

The idea that his choices had robbed his twin of his chance at life was a thought that had plagued him for over two hundred years. It was one that he had never voiced, merely an unspoken shard of guilt festering in his soul in silence. Confessing it felt like ripping a sharp object out of his guts.

If the storm had come a week earlier or later, I might have lived, Levi said, patiently, setting a hand on his brother's slumped shoulder. *Or if we had moved to Manchester instead of Graymourne. And if you had not summoned Tenebrae, perhaps we would both have perished from exposure. Do not carry burdens that were never yours alone, brother.*

Lazarus sighed breathlessly, trying to make room in his mind for the forgiveness his twin so freely offered. Levi was right, of course, there were a million things that could have changed their fates along the way.

You always were the sensible twin, of the two of us, he said, wryly and with a tentative smile.

The musical sound of Levi's laughter echoed in his mind like brightly ringing bells. Hearing it again brought a wave of elation, and he could not help but join in.

And you, the brave one, Levi said warmly. *What you did for Sarah and the children, you are the reason the Graydon line lives on. Whatever ills you believe you committed, Lazarus, you have paid for them ten times over.*

How do you know that? Lazarus asked, bewildered by how much his deceased twin seemed to know of their lives after his death.

I have had a long time to get to know the generations of our descendants, he explained, *and when the veils are thin, I am able to get glimpses back into your realm.*

Lazarus looked around them then, wondering why he and Levi appeared to be the only two people in this place. If this was the afterlife, where were all the other spirits? It should be teeming with them according to what his brother claimed. But as far as he could see, there was only the glittering sea with its diaphanous stone formations and the sky of black stars above.

Where is everyone?

Levi looked at him quizzically, an expression he remembered well.

They would not be here, he said, *this is… an in between place.*

Lazarus frowned in consternation, wondering where exactly they were and glaring down at the fluid ground. The distant vibration thrummed again, slightly louder than before, and for the first time he noticed movement in the depths beneath the shining surface they stood on. Slowly and smoothly, something mind-bogglingly massive was moving below them, mountainous flexible limbs flowing in constant motion as they slid and coiled over one another. A deep, instinctual fear seized him and he tore his eyes away from it, looking back to the safety of his kin.

Why are you here, then? he asked, hoping that Levi would be able to help him understand how they were both here, if not where here was, exactly.

Your pain drew me to you, Levi answered, his brow knitting with concern. *The eclipse and the conjunction all but obliterated the barriers, so it was easy to find you. Then, I simply followed you here.*

That made sense, but it still didn't explain why Lazarus had apparently brought them to this strange, pastel limbo. Were he not a formless void at the moment, he would be grinding his teeth in frustration.

Am I dead, then? Why are we here?

Levi shook his head gently.

I do not know why we are here, Levi admitted, somewhat apologetically, *but, you are not dead. I believe your spirit simply became unmoored during the ritual. What you experienced must have been excruciating beyond what the mind is capable of enduring. I admit, that I was loath to waylay you without knowing where you were going or if you would recognize me in your daze.*

If he could breathe, he would have exhaled a massive sigh of relief. He wasn't dead, he just had to figure out how to get back to his body from wherever they were now.

You belong with Tenebrae, Levi said, taking one of his spectral hands in his own. *The veil is growing thicker again, but I will take you as far as I can. Let's get you back to your husband, brother.*

Tenebrae shifted, the bed frame creaking in protest under his weight. The antique canopy bed in Zori's spare bedroom was twin size, appropriate to their situation only in that the unconscious human that occupied it was himself a twin. It was, however, wholly unsuited to the task of supporting an adult man and the two-hundred and seventy-five pounds of sentient shadow that adamantly refused to leave his side.

Tucked beneath the floral quilt in a borrowed t-shirt and lounge pants, Lazarus lay perfectly still. His features were serene and his shiny, cognac-colored hair fanned out delicately on the lacy pillow. He looked like a slumbering prince from a fairy tale. With the lush color restored to his warm skin, he was even more beautiful than the shadow demon remembered.

Without bothering to uncoil from the snakelike hold he had on his husband's body, Tenebrae lifted his head when he heard a hesitant knock at the door. It swung open after a slight pause, and Zori peeked her head inside.

"I brought you some tea," she said, stepping quietly into the room and placing a steaming mug of spiced, orange tea on the bedside table.

Over the long, repetitive days of the last week, she had cycled through an array of tea flavors until she found one that Tenebrae seemed to like best. He didn't tell her that the reason he preferred this one was because the smell of the spices reminded him of Lazarus. The shadow had missed his husband's scent; it had been noticeably absent since that fateful day that made him a Shade. Now, with the cruel gift of having his body restored but his consciousness mysteriously missing, it was one of the only things keeping Tenebrae sane.

"Thank you," he grunted, as she picked up the empty water pitcher from the table and left to go refill it. The riot of emotions inside him raged for an outlet and his claws tensed, digging into the blankets, but Tenebrae did his best not to lash out at the human who had opened her home to them. She and Myrkrið had been more than patient with him even as he struggled to accept their help.

At the moment, he was beginning to think it was perhaps time to let off some steam again. Though he was hesitant to leave Lazarus's side more than necessary, he could feel the anxious twitch of his muscles picking up as his agitation increased. He moved the arm that was slung across the witch's torso, intending to get up, when the movement spurred a small sound of drowsy irritation from the human.

Tenebrae froze, eyes snapping to his husband's still form. He would know that sound anywhere; it was a grumble he had heard many times when the brunette was beginning to wake but did not wish to. He waited with bated breath to see if he would make another noise, not entirely certain whether he had imagined the first or not.

It felt like a small eternity, watching like a hawk for the slightest change, but finally his forehead creased, brows twitching almost in confusion.

"Lazarus?" he whispered, his gravelly voice unusually small and filled with tentative hope.

The human's head turned to the side, reacting to his voice. His eyelids tensed and then slowly blinked open to reveal hazel eyes, unfocused and searching. He hummed in confusion, and it took a few seconds before his sight found purchase on the shadow demon. When it did, a breath of heavy relief sighed from his lungs. His limbs twitched, trapped beneath the demon's bulk.

"Darling, I cannot move," the witch said, in a rough creaky voice. His face scrunched in concern, as he tried in vain to budge beneath the weight of both the blankets and the shadow.

Tenebrae moved quickly, snatching the quilt away and rolling them so that Lazarus was on top of him instead. The sudden motion disoriented him, but the witch quickly recovered, brightening as he realized that he could now move freely.

He hooked a hand around the demon's neck, pulling himself up his body to plant a desperate kiss on his lips.

The shadow demon returned it eagerly, while his hands found purchase on Lazarus's waist, sliding beneath the fabric of his shirt to press against his bare skin. The sensation of warm, velvety flesh under his fingertips made him sigh gratefully into the human's mouth.

"Never," Tenebrae demanded, breaking the kiss finally, "never leave me like that again. I could not bear it."

He pressed their foreheads together, tightening his hold on Lazarus as if he would slip through his fingers any second.

"Nor can I, darling," the witch said, sliding his hands around the demon's shoulders. He almost hesitated to ask, but he had to know. "How long was I gone?"

"Too long," his husband grumbled, irritably, before clarifying, "seven days."

"I am so sorry, love," Lazarus said, squeezing him tightly. He could see in Tenebrae's expression how much it had weighed on him, the days he spent in fear that Lazarus might never return. "That must have been terrifying. I will admit, I did not expect the ritual to be quite so excruciating."

He paused, closing his eyes tightly as the memory of searing purple flames flashed into his mind. With a shaky exhale, he willed it from his thoughts.

"But, it is done. I am here now and I will go nowhere without you, husband, I swear."

Tenebrae kissed him again, tenderly at first and then with increasing need. It was almost electric, the intensity of fully feeling the shadow demon's lips pressed against his own after becoming so used to the dim echoes he had felt as a Shade. His nerves lit up everywhere the shadow touched, his newly reformed body hypersensitive to the contact, as if he was experiencing it all for the first time.

He swiped his tongue into the demon's mouth, and Tenebrae groaned deeply, sliding a heavy palm up his spine. Lazarus arched under the touch, shivering at the feel of the rough flesh gliding over his own. He had waited so long to feel those coarse hands on his skin again, and it was nearly overwhelming. The movement caused his hips to tilt, unintentionally grinding against the shadow's lower stomach.

Moving his other hand to splay across the witch's lower back, Tenebrae eagerly flexed his own hips up in response. He caught the human's plush bottom lip between his sharp teeth, biting down just hard enough to break the skin before returning to kissing him deeply. The familiar coppery taste of the human's blood rolled across his tongue briefly before the small cut sealed itself again in a wisp of black smoke. A possessive purr rumbled at the back of his throat at the reminder of their unbreakable bond.

The firm touch of the human's hands roaming greedily across his body had warmth pooling at the base of his spine. Tenebrae wanted nothing more in this moment than to lose himself in Lazarus's touch, but the man had only just awoken and he needed to be certain that he was okay before fully giving in to his instincts.

"Are you alright?" he asked, hurriedly, pulling away reluctantly for a second to make sure. Tearing his eyes away from the man's face, he craned his neck to look him over, checking for any signs of lingering pain or weakness.

"Never better, darling," Lazarus assured him, smiling sweetly at the shadow demon's concern. It was the truth.

Mentally, he felt elated to be back in Tenebrae's arms and in a body that his husband could properly touch. Physically, he felt strong and healthy, with each one of his senses tuned acutely in a way he could not remember feeling before. The wild and untamed forest scent of the demon's skin made his head swim with desire.

"Good," Tenebrae growled, sliding his claws up the back of his neck and drawing the shirt up his body. He dragged the garment all the way off and tossed it aside. "Because I need you, Lazarus. The ghost of your touch has plagued me for two hundred years, and I may go mad if it is kept from me a second longer."

Careful not to rip them in his haste, he stripped the soft lounge pants from the witch's legs, quickly closing the space between them again so that their bare bodies pressed together as they lay on their sides. Tenebrae rumbled a deep satisfied sound, when Lazarus smoothed his hands over the demon's chest and down his front, exploring the body he had missed being able to feel like this for so long.

"We cannot have you going mad, my love," Lazarus purred, softly kissing along the shadow's throat over his binding mark. He traced the golden lines with his tongue. "I suppose I will simply have to touch every inch of this beautiful body to be sure."

He made good on his promise, mapping out the dark topology of Tenebrae's skin with thorough strokes of his hands and soft presses of his lips. Anytime the shadow attempted to rush or grab him, Lazarus simply paused and gently pushed the demon's hands back down on the bed where he wanted them. By the time he was finished with his explorations, the shadow demon was shivering with desperation, his seam splayed open with his cock aching for attention.

"What do you need, darling?" Lazarus asked, crawling overtop of him to grind his erection against the demon's needy flesh. He swiped a thumb across Tenebrae's pouty lips, smiling deviously when he sucked it into his mouth eagerly. "Hmm? Do you need me to fuck you, my sweet boy? Remind your body who it belongs to?"

"Please," Tenebrae groaned around his thumb, nodding.

He followed readily when Lazarus guided him to turn on his front, making a soft noise of content as the human trailed kisses down his back. Weight settled on the back of his thighs, as his husband straddled them and massaged his hips. The witch's deft hands parted his muscular cheeks and Tenebrae startled slightly at the wet slide of a warm tongue between them. He relaxed as the soft muscle explored him, melting further into the mattress. It felt good, but he needed more and soon he was pressing back wantonly into the human's mouth.

"Lazarus, please," he growled, impatiently.

"I have always loved how beautifully you beg for me, darling," Lazarus mused as he sat up, happily acquiescing to the demon's needy plea.

He pressed the head of his cock to the shadow demon's slick entrance, and it slid in with little resistance. They groaned in unison at the feeling of their bodies finally joining. Lazarus eased out slowly, pushing in a little deeper each time he drove his hips forward. His slow pace had the shadow whimpering for more, and he leaned down, laying his full weight on him as he pressed his chest to the demon's back. Their height difference meant that he could not quite reach the shadow demon's neck in this position, so he placed a tender kiss on his shoulder blade instead.

Grabbing one of Tenebrae's hands in his own, he laced their fingers together, both of them in need of the grounding touch. His other hand gripped the demon's hip tightly, holding him in place as he snapped his hips into him harder. The force of it ground the shadow's cock into the fabric beneath him, and he moaned at the added friction.

"Fuck, feels so good," Tenebrae groaned, lifting his hips to meet the witch's thrusts. He could not bring himself to stifle the wanton noises that spilled forth from him, uncaring if there was anyone else in the house to hear his shameless moans. The only thing he cared about right now was the weight of his human on top of him and the ecstasy rapidly building inside them both.

Hot pleasure zipped up Lazarus's spine, this new angle allowing him to sink even deeper inside the shadow.

"Good boy," he panted, open mouth pressed against Tenebrae's well muscled back. The soft slap of his hips against the demon's firm ass echoed loudly in the small room. "Gods, you take me so fucking well."

The shadow whimpered loudly at his praise, a pleasant fuzziness clouding his mind and warmth spreading in his belly from the combined physical and mental stimulation. It had been so long since he last felt his husband's touch while under the spell of his hypnotic words. His memories of it paled in comparison to the bliss he was feeling now.

Enraptured by the shadow's submissive sounds, Lazarus rewarded him by sliding a hand around his hip to palm Tenebrae's ridged cock. It twitched in his firm grip, sliding smoothly through his hand as his thrusts rocked the demon's body forward again and again. His eyes closed as he relished the thick weight of it in his hand, imagining how the textured length would feel when the shadow demon took him instead. He loved that they could switch roles so easily, each just as eager to dominate or be dominated by the other.

Right now, though, he enjoyed the heady feeling of power that came with having this stunning, ferocious creature underneath him, unraveling from the pleasure that he alone got to give him.

Tenebrae's moans grew even more desperate, the sound making Lazarus's groin tighten in a way that told him he wouldn't last much longer. But judging by the wrecked tone of the shadow demon's voice, neither would he. The witch groaned, sinking his teeth deeply into the hard flesh of the shadow's shoulder.

The bite drew a sharp gasp from the demon, whose hips bucked into Lazarus's hand, the thick member pulsing in his hold. A deep, rumbling groan rolled through him, partially muffled by the bed, as Lazarus stroked him through his peak.

Slowing to allow him a moment to recover, the witch rolled his hips gently as the shadow demon caught his breath. Tenebrae, however, wanted something different.

"Lazarus," he panted, shakily, gripping his hand tighter and pressing back into the human on top of him. "Please, I need to feel you come." A primal urge to have the man claim him gripped Tenebrae, and he would not be satisfied without it.

Make me yours again, husband, he thought, desperately.

His vision sparkled, slight overstimulation setting in as Lazarus's cock resumed pounding into him. His still semi-hard cock throbbed, and his body flushed with pleasure so intense it was almost painful. He basked in it, gratefully. Tenebrae had dreamt of their physical reunion many times over the centuries, and now that it was here, he was determined to savor every second of it.

"So. Good. Darling," Lazarus rasped, struggling to hold onto any semblance of coherent thought as he lost himself in the tight warm grip of his husband's body.

The witch wrapped an arm tightly around the demon's ribs, using his hold as leverage for a few final stuttering thrusts before grinding his cock deeply inside Tenebrae as he came. His eyes shut tightly, colors bursting on the back of his eyelids, and he let out a shuddering moan as intense waves of euphoria washed over him.

Collapsing onto the demon, he nuzzled his face into the warmth of Tenebrae's back, feeling the deep, satisfied rumble that vibrated in his chest.

"I love you," he murmured into the dark flesh that his face was pressed against.

He shifted back as he felt the shadow demon begin to turn over to face him. Tenebrae took his face in both of his large hands, kissing him reverently.

"I would claw the stars from the sky and lay them at your feet if I could. I would tear this world to its core and let it bleed fire if you desired it. There are no words to properly express the fierceness of my love for you."

Lazarus leaned into his touch, heart aflame from the sincerity of the shadow demon's confession. Perhaps, the intensity of his adoration would have frightened a lesser man, but he had been twice forged in fire and his strength tempered all the way to hell and back. There was no amount of ferocity that could scare him, not when the flames of his love for the shadow burned just as brightly.

"My fearsome, beloved husband," he said, running his hands over one of the shadow tendrils that was greedily curling around him, "I will not ask all that of you. I have all I need right here. However, I do have a question for you."

"Anything," Tenebrae agreed, without reservation.

The man twisted in his grip, taking in the room they were occupying for the first time since he awoke. He eyed the unfamiliar furniture; a wooden vanity crowded with computer equipment, the pink floral draped canopy bed that was too small for their combined bulk, and the velvet armchair in the corner.

He looked into the eyes of his paramour and asked, "Where are we?"

Epilogue

TWO WEEKS LATER

Rolling up the cuffs of the deep blue silk button-up shirt, Lazarus entered the kitchen. He grabbed an apron from a hook near the pantry and tied it around his waist to protect his new slacks from any cooking mishaps. It was a black cotton cloth with cartoon ghosts printed along the bottom edge of it.

The owner of the whimsical garment breezed back into the room just as a timer sounded.

"Oh good," Zori said, smiling brightly when she noticed him standing near the kitchen island. "Lazarus, can you help me with the cheese plate?"

She handed him a large wooden cutting board and set an array of cheeses, fruits, and meat in front of him. He turned the board over in his hands, looking at her inquisitively when he noticed that the reverse side had the words "NOT POISON" crudely clawed into its surface.

"It was Myrkrið's first note to me," she laughed, shrugging at his unasked question. "I can't get rid of it. Just use the other side, please."

He shook his head and laughed, setting to work on assembling the cheese plate under her instruction. Since he and Tenebrae had begun staying at the Dew Lane house, he had enjoyed falling back into some familiar domestic habits. He helped Zori with the cooking and household chores, much like he had with Sarah in his time, although modern conveniences had vastly simplified many of the processes he was used to, and he had no complaints about that. Lazarus was still adjusting to life in this strange new world; it would take some time to become accustomed to the place Graymourne had grown into in two and a half centuries.

"They are here," Myrkrið announced, appearing suddenly in the connecting hallway.

Lazarus fought a sudden bout of nerves. He was excited, and a little anxious, to meet his descendant tonight. They knew the truth of his existence, and he hoped they would want to get to know him as well, despite the rather frightening accidental introduction they had been treated to with Tenebrae. It would be nice to have a family member, and another human, who he could spend time with without having to pretend that he wasn't a witch from the 1700s with a seven-foot-tall demon for a husband.

"Don't worry," Zori said, patting him gently on the shoulder, "they're gonna love you. I know you'll get along great."

She gave him a reassuring smile and hurried off to get the door, opening it before Skye could even knock. There was an excited cacophony of greetings and then the bright blur of a figure swept into the kitchen like a whirlwind. They were a little taller than Zori, dressed in a color-blocked loosely buttoned shirt over a black tank top, high-waisted loose pants, and bright blue combat boots that matched their hair. Skye's amber eyes immediately sought out Lazarus and their face lit up with excitement.

"Not dead great uncle, hi!" they greeted, enthusiastically, as they practically skipped over to him. "Do you do hugs?"

"Yes?" he said, mildly confused by their phrasing until they pulled him into a brief but affectionate embrace.

"It's so nice to finally meet you," Skye enthused, releasing him to lean against the kitchen island and help themself to some cheese. "Where's your scary husband? I have a bone to pick with him."

As if summoned, Tenebrae materialized out of the dark space of the dining room. Skye did not immediately notice him with the way their back faced his direction, but Lazarus gave him a pointed look over their shoulder.

"Where is it?" the shadow demon asked, his ominous voice slightly startling their blue-haired guest. His curious gaze roved over their person in search of something.

"Where is what?" Skye asked, whirling around and regarding him with wide eyes. They paused, still as a statue with a piece of cheese halfway to their mouth.

"The bone you wish to pick," Tenebrae clarified, holding out one large hand like he expected them to place an actual bone in it.

Skye blinked at him for a moment and then burst into laughter. Tenebrae frowned at them and they waved a hand apologetically at him while they struggled to recover from a fit of giggles.

"No, it's just an expression. It means I'm mad at you," they chuckled, wiping a tear from the corner of their eye.

The shadow demon cocked his head, regarding them with confusion. Their words said one thing, but their demeanor and expression said another.

"Then why are you laughing?" he asked.

"Because apparently all of you shadow demons are unintentionally hilarious," they said, smirking at him. "Also, I'm only, like, a little mad. From when you scared the shit out of me in the middle of the night, remember?" They returned to snacking on cheese and looked at him expectantly.

"Yes, you were not supposed to be awake for that," he acknowledged, not exactly apologizing.

"Obviously," they snorted, smiling as they clocked the disapproving expression that Lazarus was giving the shadow, who did not appear chastened by it in the slightest. "No worries, though, it only took a year or two off my life expectancy. No big deal. If you wanna visit the shop, that's cool, just no more invisible creeping, okay?"

"Okay," he agreed, mildly bewildered. Talking to Skye was far different from simply observing them. The way they spoke was rapid-fire and energetically expressive, which seemed normal enough when he watched them interact with other humans. But being on the receiving end of it was quite a different experience.

"Cool, crisis averted," they declared, grinning at him widely before they turned their attention back to the rest of the room. "Oh, that reminds me! Did you guys hear about the Elbert Poole house going up for sale?"

"No, when did that happen?" Zori asked, pausing in the middle of slicing a pear.

"Just today, apparently," Skye said, "everyone was talking about it at the coffee shop. Rumor is, that guy Spencer's been having a real time of it living there. Came into the Graymourne Gazette office last week to put in a listing in the paper, looking like he hadn't slept in days. When the office assistant, Abby, asked him why he wanted to sell, he said he just 'didn't want to deal with it anymore' and 'this stupid haunted town could keep it for all he cares.'"

Myrkrið's low chuckle rumbled through the kitchen, and Tenebrae's satisfied smirk wasn't exactly subtle. Skye looked back and forth between the two shadow demons, suspiciously.

"You guys wouldn't know anything about that though, would you?" they asked in an amused tone.

Tenebrae merely raised a brow at them as if to say, *What do you think?*

"Of course not," Lazarus laughed, handing them a glass of wine to pair with the cheese before taking a sip of his own, "these fine gentlemen would do no such thing."

His eyes sparkled with proud exasperation. It was a relief to know that the town was rid of the man who had caused them so much stress over the past few months.

Despite Spencer's unwitting interference, though, the ritual had gone as planned and now the rest of Graymourne was free of his schemes as well. He smiled at Skye, who was looking at him curiously.

"So, Uncle Lazarus," they began, "I have about a million and twelve questions for you. Should I start now, or do you want to wait for dinner?"

"Whenever you wish. And please, call me Lazarus," he said, chuckling at their enthusiasm. "Perhaps afterwards, you can help enlighten me on some of the finer points of my new temporal home."

Zori was right, they were going to get along just fine. Skye was a curious, delightful force of nature, and he could not be more proud to see what the youngest generation of Graydons had grown into. He knew that Levi would be equally fascinated by them, and he hoped that somewhere his brother could see them now.

A few months later, Lazarus sat on a rocky outcropping, listening to the waves crash against the stones at the edge of a brilliant blue ocean. It stretched out for miles in every direction under a clear blue sky dotted with the occasional wisp of white clouds. The sun warmed him, while the salty breeze kept him cool.

It was a perfect day.

Feeling familiar dark eyes on him, he turned to see Tenebrae striding out of the lush rainforest vegetation and across the expanse of rock that led to where he now sat. In the brilliant island light, he looked like death incarnate, a smoking omen sauntering down the stony shore with the grace of a hunting panther. A few of the isle's primary residents, highly venomous golden snakes, shied away from him as he passed where they rested, sunning themselves in the warm afternoon light. They never bothered Lazarus either, seemingly able to sense the shadows in his blood, but they didn't cower from him in quite the same way.

Because of their deadliness and incredible number, this place was almost entirely deserted by humanity. There was a small, cozy lighthouse atop one of the higher points, which he and Tenebrae now sometimes used as a vacation home. Long ago it had housed keepers, but even those had finally given up their vigil decades before when the structure was automated. Save for the occasional intrepid research group who managed to garner permission from the nearby mainland, no one set foot on this island anymore. Until, that is, the shadow demon and his resurrected husband happened upon it during their travels.

Lazarus smiled, reaching for the shadow as he neared.

"Come sit, my love," he said, pulling Tenebrae down to the ground with him. "Did you have a nice wander?"

Tenebrae rumbled a sound of confirmation, settling onto the rocky ground before pulling the human into his lap. His arms bracketed tightly around the witch's middle and his chin hooked over his shoulder, placing a light kiss on the side of his neck.

"I did," the shadow demon purred, nosing against his pulse point affectionately as he breathed in the man's scent. "I found something for you."

He opened one of his hands to reveal a large flower carefully cradled in his palm. The bloom was entirely white except for the brilliant bluish-purple center. It was an orchid, but of a variety that Lazarus had never seen before. He picked it up delicately, examining its stark coloration.

"It is called laelia purpurata," Tenebrae said, returning his hand to its former place at the human's waist. "I overheard one of the scientists discussing it when we were here before. They call it 'the witch's jewel.' It seemed appropriate that you should have it."

The shadow demon could not have known that, magically, orchids were best suited to love spells, but that only made the gesture all the more sweet to Lazarus. He turned, kissing the shadow on the cheek and murmuring his thanks against his skin. This specimen would make a perfect addition to the new arsenal of magical ingredients that he was building.

One of the many benefits of Tenebrae's wanderlust and their newly regained freedom was that it allowed him to gather all manner of interesting and elusive plants, stones, and other sundry trinkets. Skye had gifted him with a beautiful wooden chest to store his growing collection. It amused him to think that he was older than the 'antique', and in fact most of the things they sold.

He enjoyed helping them around their shop when he and Tenebrae were in Graymourne, getting to spend time with them as well as learning all sorts of interesting things by studying the artifacts they procured. Occasionally, he even found something to bring back for them on his travels; the odd relic from an undiscovered ruin or a strange artifact from some far away marketplace. These ended up in Skye's personal collection most of the time.

Though much of their time these days was spent outside of its cozy atmosphere, Graymourne still very much felt like home. Lazarus attributed this largely to the motley little found family he and Tenebrae had acquired in Zori, Myrkrið, and Skye. Though he would always miss his twin, Levi, it helped knowing that they were each surrounded by people who loved them. And someday, when the veils thinned enough, perhaps they would meet again in that strange pastel limbo.

For now, though, he was content to lean against the warm figure wrapped tightly around him, basking in the peaceful silence of this beautiful place with his beloved monster. This was not the future that Lazarus had envisioned when he summoned Tenebrae all those many years ago, but he would not have it any other way.

About the Author

Sylvie Helstaff (she/they) is an American author who grew up forever crushing on the monster in their favorite books and movies. She loves mythology as much as spice and enjoys crafting rich worlds with engaging lore where her readers can embark on monstrously smutty adventures alongside captivating characters.

When they're not writing or creating art, they can be found enjoying a nice stroll through a cemetery, picking up bones on hikes, or relaxing with their huge dog.

Someday, she aspires to become the reason no one goes into that part of the forest anymore.